WC　　　ſ

The Hybrid Wol　eries: Book One

Ciara Delahunt

ALSO BY

Ciara Delahunt

The Hybrid Wolf Series
Killer Instinct (Prequel)
Wolf Bait

CIARA DELAHUNT

WOLF BAIT

THE HYBRID WOLF SERIES: BOOK ONE

Wolf Bait The Hybrid Wolf Series: Book © 2022 by Ciara Delahunt

Cover art by ***Original Book Cover Designs***

Contact information:
www.ciaradelahunt.com
ciara@ciaradelahunt.com

ISBN: 978-1-7391785-0-5

First Edition: October 2022

Before you Read

The Hybrid Wolf Series is aimed at adults and includes scenes of violence typical of the urban fantasy genre. Some of the content in this book may be triggering for some readers. To learn more about content, tropes, and triggers in my books, please visit my website:

https://www.ciaradelahunt.com/content-warnings

DEDICATION

To the readers that never grew out of their obsession with were-wolves, vampires, witches, and the paranormal.

CHAPTER 1

I woke in the dead of night. The ground was cool against my skin and my body trembled, yet all I could feel was the hammering of my heart in my chest and the adrenaline pumping through my veins. I was covered in a sheen of sweat. Slowly, I blinked my eyes open, disorientated and dizzy. My sight adjusted to the darkness at once, and I could immediately make out the clear outline of a park bench and large oak trees stretching into the night sky. Silence hung in the air and frost coated grass glistened under the light of the full moon. It was rather beautiful but something felt off. Even beyond the touch of the moonlight, what should have been shrouded in shadows was muted in colour and I could make out distinct shapes.

Why can I see in the dark?

Though my heart was beating rapidly, everything else felt heavy and numb. My limbs were stiff and refused to cooperate. The sound of car horns and distant voices bounced around to the point where I thought my head might burst. I could sense consciousness slipping away from me. As I drifted in and out of dream—dreams of running—I heard a man's voice.

"Are you okay?"

Warmth pressing against my side jolted me awake. I opened my mouth to scream but only a hoarse rasp came out. My body reeled at the sudden movement.

A man knelt next to me on the damp ground. "Are you all right?" he repeated, his words foggy and distant. He threw something warm and soft around me before I could muster the energy to protest.

It was in that moment I realised I was naked. I snatched what turned out to be a hoodie from him, frantically trying to cover my modesty despite my sluggish movements.

Where are my clothes? More to the point, where the hell am I?

I looked around, wild eyes searching my surroundings as I desperately tried to find my bearings. At first, I thought I was in a forest. We were surrounded by tall trees and damp undergrowth, but then I spotted an open area through the branches. Well-worn paths winding through the clearing, lined in parts by well-kept flower beds. Not a forest, I realised, but a park. The faint glow of streetlights was visible in the distance if I concentrated. *Was I still in the city?*

The stranger watched me in silence, his brow furrowed with concern. He was clearly trying to find the fine line between not staring at a naked girl and helping. I tugged the hoodie tighter against my chest.

"Where are we?" I croaked, finally finding my voice.

As soon as I asked the question, I wished I had asked several other far more pressing ones.

"You're in the park," he said, elaborating at the sight of my blank expression. "Stephen's Green."

Smack bang in the centre of the city?

I nodded slowly, struggling to process even the most basic of facts. A dazed, distant part of me wanted to bolt. My brain screamed danger, but my body wasn't listening.

"You've been out for a while by the looks of things." His voice was soft and husky, the kind that belongs in country music.

Reality began to sink in, and my heart skipped a beat. I attempted to stand, but my legs were limp. "What am I doing here?"

As shock finally registered and a tremor began, he raised his hands and shuffled back slightly.

"Hey, I found you like this. I'm just trying to help." He glanced around as if keeping sketch, but we were completely alone.

I'd watched too many serial killer documentaries to fall for this shit.

"Why haven't you called someone? An ambulance, maybe? Instead of standing over a naked chick in the park?"

He shook his head, confusion washing over his features. "An ambulance? That's not a good idea, the last thing you want is a blood test."

My anxiety soared and adrenaline flushed through my body. "What have you done to me?!"

"Okay, that was probably the wrong thing to say. I promise, I just found you like this and woke you straight away." He raised his hands to placate me, taking a slow step back as if he was dealing with a startled deer. Despite the situation, his voice remained remarkably calm. "I swear I'm not some kind of weirdo."

Isn't that what they always say?

I studied him, struggling to gather my thoughts with the incessant thumping in my head. If he was going to hurt me, he would have done it already. Plus, the only thing between me and the early morning summer frost was his hoodie covering my modesty. I could tell by the way he was avoiding looking below my neck that he likely wasn't a creep, which was good. I hoped.

"What's the last thing you remember?" He asked, keeping his distance.

The last thing I could remember was being at my apartment. Yes. That was right. I had a row with my boyfriend, Ryan, decided to spend the night slumped in front of the television, eventually fell asleep watching sparkly vampires and then... Nothing. I had no idea how I had ended up in the park or where my clothes had gone.

I frowned. "I remember falling asleep in bed and that's it."

"Has this happened before?"

"No... I don't really make a habit of ending up naked in parks," I said dryly. "What happened?"

I propped myself up on my elbows, keeping the hoodie draped around my body to cover as much as possible.

"I saw you running through the streets and when you—" He began, stopping short as my features scrunched in confusion. His eyes widened. "You really have no idea..."

"Running?"

Why was I running? Since when is sleep running a thing?

"This isn't the place. I can explain when we get out of here. What's your name?" The stranger interrupted my thoughts, dragging me back to the present. He crouched by my side, hands clasped, eyebrows knit together.

I hesitated, willing the pins and needles in my legs to go away so I could listen to the side of my brain begging me to run. He waited patiently, disarmingly relaxed despite the situation.

"Tell me yours first," I said finally, studying his face.

His steady gaze met mine. "I'm Luke."

"Luke," I repeated, tasting his name on my lips.

Luke nodded, a smile twitching the corner of his lips upward. Amusement danced in his eyes, their warm hazelnut reflecting the moonlight.

As the dazed mist began to lift, I looked at him properly, noting the fine stubble along his jawline that was darker than his sandy blonde hair, cropped at the sides and longer on the top. He looked as if he had stepped out of one of the many band posters that had papered my bedroom walls when I was a teenager.

"I'm Eve."

"Well, Eve. How about we get you out of here? I can call an ambulance if you want, but I don't know how we'd explain this."

A hysterical giggle bubbled in my throat at how absurd trying to explain me half-naked in his clothes would sound. It died as the sounds of drunk yelling and laughter pierced through the night, yet I couldn't see any figures approaching. Luke looked up at the noise and began unbuttoning his shirt.

"Woah, mate. I have a boyfriend..." I snapped, pulling the hem of the hoodie down as far as it would stretch and shuffling back. I wanted to stand but my legs weren't in agreement and I wasn't quite sure I could manage it without flashing him.

He laughed, a gorgeous timbre that sounded so out of place in this awkward situation. I must have hit my head hard. "It's for you, so we can get you to my car."

"It's okay, I can ring my boyfriend—Ryan—he can come pick me up, I know he'll be worried."

As soon as the words left my mouth, I realised that if I had no clothes, I definitely had no phone.

Luke stiffened, a muscle ticking in his jaw. "Ryan?"

"Yeah, he can pick me up no problem, if I could borrow your phone?"

"I knew I recognised that smell," he muttered, kicking a clump of grass and sending it skittering away from us.

I arched a brow and wiggled my toes, starting to feel more like myself. "What?"

"Nothing, we need to get you out of here before someone finds you in this state and I get arrested."

His attempt at a joke fell flat. The more the fog in my brain cleared, the more panic began to set in.

"I know that, but I have no clothes... I don't know how I got here. I need Ryan, please." I was rambling now, tears pricking behind my eyes. My voice rose higher, any sense of bravado was rapidly disappearing. I'd had some pretty crazy drunk experiences in college so far, but this was on a different level. I was ready to go home already.

I squinted to see further in the distance as I heard more laughter. They were closer this time but still out of sight. Luke cocked his head toward the noise. The sky was pitch black beyond the moonlight and I shouldn't have been able to see my outstretched hand so clearly. But the trees and the path, things that should have been faint shapes and shadows, were distinct objects. Even Luke was clear as day. Though colours were still dull, the sharpness of my surroundings was unnatural which only made my chest constrict further. I struggled to take even shallow breaths.

"Look, I'll explain when we get you out of here." Luke promised, offering a hand to help me up. He was full of nervous energy now, like a dancing horse ready to bolt.

Something about the panic in his eyes made me struggle to my feet, clasping his hand to pull myself upright. Luke quickly took off his shirt, offering it to me. He didn't seem the slightest bit perturbed about having his chiselled chest on show, perfectly comfortable standing there in nothing but a pair of jeans. My mind wandered to places it shouldn't.

He turned away, giving me a moment to wrap the shirt around my waist in a make-shift skirt and shrugged his hoodie on. I zipped it up to my neck with fumbling fingers, welcoming the snug warmth.

"You can turn around now."

Luke chuckled, somehow making the situation far less awkward than it should be. My cheeks were still flushed.

I jumped as a raucous cackle rang out too close for comfort.

"We better go," he said, starting towards the nearest path.

Looking like Bambi on ice, I wobbled forward a few paces. My legs weren't cooperating, and I was going nowhere fast. Luke wrapped an arm around my waist instinctively, pausing for a moment to give me the chance to shove him away. I didn't, too exhausted and unsteady on my feet to refuse his help.

"Thanks," I mumbled, glad that I was still too dazed to feel the level of embarrassment I should.

The entire situation was mortifying, but I was in shock and thoroughly confused. I had no choice but to trust him.

My bare feet slipped on the damp grass, but Luke kept me upright. He offered to give me a piggyback to the car when I tripped over one of many tree roots. I was polite when refusing the first time. The second time he offered was the last.

It was easier once we were on the even paths. As we neared the edge of the park, I could hear more late-night revellers roaming the streets. An even mix of laughter, yelling and boozy conversation drifted through the night. The distant sounds felt much closer than normal. Voices that should have been a distant buzz of drunken slurs were clear as if they were only metres away.

When we stepped out of the park and onto the dimly lit streets, the noise became overwhelming. The cacophony slowly building in my head exploded into stars. I could hear too much. The noise of several conversations, screeching breaks, and the excessive rumble of car engines in the distance assaulting my senses made it impossible to function. The city was too loud.

I froze and squeezed my eyes shut. "I can't."

My stomach lurched and I clung onto Luke, struggling to stay on my feet as the noise assaulted my senses. I'd experienced panic attacks before, but this was something entirely different. I felt as if the world was closing in and that I was lost in a wide, never-ending expanse all at once. Hundreds of distinct threads of conversation swirled in my mind, weaving into one jumbled mess as my focus careered from one to the next. Amidst the noise, my heartbeat pounded in my ears. Tears streamed down my cheeks, but the sensation felt foreign, detached.

Luke tightened his grip around my waist, the warmth of his hand on my side a small comfort as he guided me down the path. "It's not far now, Eve."

The certainty in his voice served to sooth my frayed nerves a little. I looked up, feeling his breath on my cheek, noticing the worry lines etched into his forehead. There was a smart response somewhere, but my usual sense of sarcasm or wit, along with the earlier adrenaline, had vanished.

I nodded numbly, stars dancing in my vision as I struggled to block out the constant onslaught to my senses. His gaze lingered on mine. I shut my eyes again, willing the world to quiet so I could think straight.

He gave me a reassuring squeeze. It felt so surreal having a stranger practically carry me to his car in the middle of the night, not to mention I would have been in the nip if it wasn't for his oversized jacket. I didn't even want to think about the fact that he must have seen me stark naked to begin with.

I flinched as the beep of a car unlocking pierced my ears. Luke had a bunch of keys in his free hand and directed me towards a black hatchback parked at the end of the road under the nearest streetlight. He gently helped me to the passenger side, and as I couldn't trust my legs, he lowered me into the seat. My chest heaved with each shallow breath. Once I was in safely, Luke swung the door shut. The sudden noise amongst the general din in my brain made me jump.

Before I could gather my thoughts, Luke was in the driver's seat beside me. I shook my head as if it would drown out the noise, but it just made my surroundings spin.

"Eve?" Luke's husky tone rang through the continuous hum in my ears. He repeated my name, and I followed his voice, drawing myself into the present.

I nodded, rocking back and forth as I struggled to steady my thoughts. My nails scraped my thighs as I gripped the hem of the hoodie, balling my hands into fists.

"Focus on my voice," he urged, his warm hand closing around mine as he loosened my death grip on the material. "You're going to be fine; this feeling will pass."

My chest constricted, but I focused on Luke's voice and fought to keep my eyes open, taking in large gulps of air. The countless noises of the city night swirled in my mind, all-consuming.

"You can do this. I know you can. I promise the noises will fade once you can bring your focus around to the present, but you need to listen. Follow my voice, pick it apart in the sea of noise and focus on taking slow, deep breaths."

I followed his instructions, dropping my gaze to our entwined hands. Every inch of my body was fighting this. It took time to pick his voice apart without another noise or distant conversation piercing my thoughts. Eventually, I managed to push the distant noises away, ignoring the calls of ambulance sirens, car horns, and drunken antics. I blinked slowly, released a shaky breath, followed by another. As minutes passed, the pressure in my chest began to lighten.

"Good, well done."

I looked up at Luke, struggling to bite back tears. "What's happening to me?"

My heart was still beating erratically as adrenaline pumped through my body. It was overwhelming. Not just the strange situation I had landed in, but the world itself still felt too close. Too big. Everything was so vivid and loud, it was claustrophobic.

"Has Ryan ever spoken to you about this?" He asked, his eyes searching my face.

I scowled and my temper surged. Frustrated and confused, I was swinging from one emotion to the next without warning or sense.

"Talk to me about what? Waking up naked in parks?" I snapped, snatching my hand away. "I've told you already, I don't know what's going on!"

I swallowed, struggling to suppress the urge to burst into tears.

"I'm sorry, I just don't understand..." Luke trailed off, running his hand through his hair. His eyes searched mine in confusion. "I've never had to explain this to someone. What about your parents?"

I was getting more questions than answers.

My tone hardened. "I never knew them. I was a one-night stand put up for adoption."

"Oh." He nodded to himself, as if a penny had dropped in his head.

If he could share that penny it would be great.

"Oh?"

"How long has this sleepwalking been happening?" Luke asked, twisting towards me in the seat. He was still topless, which was distracting and annoying in equal measures.

I paused. "A few weeks—a month maybe—but never like... this." I gestured to my state of undress.

"Since the blue moon," Luke mused, drumming his thumb against the steering wheel, only to stop when he saw me wince. "I don't know how to tell you this, and I'm probably not the right person but—"

The roar of an engine followed by the screech of metal on metal stung my ears. I lurched forward in the seat, smashing my head into the dashboard as the car lurched. Luke slammed into the steering wheel, his ribs taking the brunt of the impact. The airbags deployed a minute too late.

Everything went black.

CHAPTER 2

The noises came flooding back first and were followed by the sting of the streetlights in my eyes and a sharp twinge in my temple. I lifted my head, which was now throbbing for an entirely different reason.

"What the fuck?" Luke growled to my right.

I held my head in my hands, doubling over and groaning as the pain surged. "Ow..."

Luke slammed his fists on the steering wheel in frustration. He turned to me, and for the briefest moment I could swear I saw his eyes flash silver. A thin stream of blood trickled from a gash on his temple. His expression softened to one of concern as he reached up to examine my head. "You're bleeding."

I reached up to touch my forehead, wincing as the movement caused the car interior to spin. My fingers came away sticky. For a brief moment, there were two blurry versions of Luke in front of me. I was pretty certain I had a concussion.

A familiar voice called my name.

"Eve!" Ryan appeared, thumping the window with his fist.

I jumped and stared at Ryan's face pressed against the glass, my mouth gaping. *What was he doing here?*

He ripped the car door open, and I heard the handle ricochet across the road. Before I could get a word out, Ryan grabbed me by the shoulders and hauled me out of the vehicle. He pulled me into his arms, crushing me against his chest. I yelped. Everything hurt. The embrace felt far from comforting; there was a desperation in his touch.

"Now that's what you call a stalker," Luke said, bursting out of the driver's side, a deep growl rumbling in his throat.

Ryan looked me over, his expression cooling as he noticed that the only thing covering my modesty was Luke's hoodie. His loose black curls were dishevelled, those high cheekbones I normally marvelled at making him look gaunt. Without so much as a word, he pushed me behind him, his arm braced across my chest to keep me back from Luke.

"No! Ryan, wait! You don't understand." I rushed to explain, realising just how bad the situation looked. Me, half naked with another guy. "It's not what it looks like. He found me passed out and tried to help. There's something weird happening."

There was a hardness in Ryan's gaze when he turned to me that made my stomach lurch. Those gorgeous blue eyes that normally made my heart flutter were empty. *Oh god, he doesn't believe me.*

"Ryan please," I pleaded, tugging at his arm. "You don't understand, I was sleepwalking or something and—"

"Don't. I know, I was trying to find you." Ryan grit his teeth, his words disjointed. If he was trying to reassure me, the harsh tone of his voice was doing nothing of the sort.

I took a small piece of solace from the way he seemed to be trying to protect me from danger. But Luke wasn't a threat. If it hadn't been for him, I would still be out cold in the park.

Luke stood in the middle of the road, his fists clenched by his side. Ryan took a step in his direction, another guttural snarl ripping from his throat. Where Luke was sun-kissed blonde and muscle, Ryan was lean and dark fury with a dangerous edge.

"Ryan!"

He ignored my pleas, squaring up to Luke. They were ready to tear each other apart.

Luke watched Ryan's every movement with an intense hatred I couldn't quite fathom. But when Ryan turned his head towards me, I felt a lump grow in my throat. His eyes flashed, but there was no warmth in his gaze. The handsome features I had grown to love were contorted into a mask of fury. I could feel anger radiating from him.

"Get away from her," Ryan hissed, his narrowed gaze turning to Luke.

Luke looked between us and something clicked. "Why haven't you told her?"

"She wasn't ready," Ryan said, keeping himself angled between me and Luke, my back up against Ryan's car.

I watched in silent confusion, nursing the cut and inevitable bruise blooming on my temple.

Luke flashed a steely grin, taking another step towards Ryan. "*Clearly,* she is. You should have known. I would have thought hybrids were your area of expertise at this point."

"It's not that simple."

"What isn't?" I snapped.

Luke sneered at Ryan and chuckled, the sound at odds with the simmering rage between them. "You never were the brightest spark growing up." He shifted his weight from one foot to the other, every muscle tensed and ready to spring into action. "You should have known. Daddy won't be pleased..."

Ryan tensed. "Shut up."

"Make me."

Ryan snarled, or at least that's what it sounded like. I had never heard that kind of noise come out of a man's mouth before. He took another step towards Luke.

"Oi!" I interjected, becoming increasingly sick of being spoken about like some child. The rising testosterone levels weren't helping either. "What's going on? Do you guys know each other?"

Before Luke could answer me, Ryan cut across him. "He is... He knows my family."

"More lies." Luke shook his head, tutting at Ryan like he was a disobedient brat.

Ryan rose to the bait, his hand balling into a tight fist as he advanced on Luke. "You need to shut the hell up."

"Mate, I don't have to do a damn thing you tell me to. That's why I'm not in your filthy pack."

Pack? What?

Luke took a step forward, his shoulders set. They completely ignored my presence. The two men glared at each other, both itching to make the first move. I wasn't quite sure what was holding them back.

"Oi! Someone tell me the truth, right fucking now!"

Luke's gaze darted to me and Ryan seized his opportunity, lunging at Luke and tackling him to the ground. I wanted to beg them to stop, but my voice caught in my throat. My legs were rooted to the spot. Frozen, I watched them hit the tarmac, snarling like feral animals as they thrashed at each other. A glimpse of silver glinted in the dim light of the streetlamp. My stomach lurched.

I placed a hand on the car bonnet, the world still spinning. Ryan always had a bit of a temper, but this was not the man I knew—this was a stranger. I had no idea how to talk this version of him down.

"Someone tell me what the hell this is about?"

They didn't so much as look at me, too busy wrestling on the ground. I was a volatile mix of terror and fury all at once.

"Tell her," Luke urged Ryan with a smirk, pulling him into a headlock, "or I will."

Ryan's body went rigid at the threat. I didn't need to see his face to know that his eyes were blazing along with his temper.

"Tell me," I raised my voice and it shook. I sounded pathetic.

"You piece of shit! Look what you have done!" Ryan said, throwing Luke off him.

Luke snorted and backed out of reach. "What *I've* done? She deserves to know. You should have told her long before now."

"It's not your place. This isn't any of your business, or your pack's," Ryan spat, moving towards Luke again.

"It is when you refuse to tell her the truth and I find her naked in the damn park!"

I slammed my hand on the bonnet, flinching. "Tell me what?" My voice wavered, but I didn't care. I wanted answers, and I was sick of the two trading insults and punches like teenagers.

"No, Eve." Ryan shook his head, never taking his eyes off Luke.

I took a shaky step towards them. "Tell me."

I was running on empty and my temper was at boiling point. I caught Luke's eye, noting how his brow creased. He was on the edge of spilling whatever truth they were withholding. Ryan remained silent.

"Now." My voice was steadier this time as I stared them down, my hands trembling as I propped myself against the car.

Ryan turned to me, keeping his body tactically placed to block Luke's path to me. His expression was unreadable, an unwavering anger mingled with something else. Regret? Pity?

He didn't speak fast enough.

"Tell me now or I'm gone!" I demanded, taking another wobbly step towards them.

Luke stepped back, nursing his shoulder. It was then I noticed an open gash across his chiselled chest.

Ryan lowered his voice, whispering to me like you would to sooth a trapped deer. He reached out to me, faltering as I snatched my hand away from his bloody fingers. "Eve, we will talk about this later."

"You're a werewolf," Luke said, his revelation echoing in the empty street.

I'm a what?

My mouth went dry. I stared at Luke in disbelief. I didn't know whether to laugh or cry. This was ridiculous.

The sound of movement from Ryan's direction dissolved the moment of silence.

"Stay out of this," Ryan roared as he surged towards Luke, and they descended into chaos once more, their fleeting truce abolished.

Their carnal growls drowned out the sirens and screaming in neighbouring streets. Another flash of silver was closely followed by a piercing howl and a splash of red. I froze.

A *knife*? *Why would Ryan have a knife?*

It took several beats for my mind to catch up with reality. Not a knife. Luke reached up and swung his arm down, five silver claws glinting in the moonlight. Ryan shrieked, the heart-breaking sound making my stomach twist.

Time slowed.

"Ryan!" I darted in their direction, the sudden movement causing the world to flip upside down and me with it.

Before I hit the ground, strong arms wrapped around me, gently lowering me to the ground. My head lolled back against something soft. I smelled a familiar mix of musk and sweat. Voices became distant, only the erratic thrum of a heartbeat was audible.

Slowly, the road swung back into focus and the ringing in my ears subsided. Ryan held me to his chest, cradling me in his arms. His sleeve was ripped and streaked with blood, a fresh trail of crimson flowing from his bicep.

"Eve." He kissed my forehead, holding me so tightly I feared a rib might crack. His voice was barely a whisper. "I am so sorry you had to find out like this."

I nodded, not quite trusting myself to speak.

This couldn't be real. Werewolves aren't real.

I wanted so much to believe that, but Ryan was covered in blood and I could feel remnants of his claws gently brushing against my side.

Behind Ryan, Luke was bent over by his car, his jeans stained red and scratches streaking his bare chest. No doubt his shirt would have been destroyed like Ryan's if it wasn't wrapped around my waist.

I held his jacket tighter around me, beginning to feel the cool summer night creeping into my bones. A police siren sounded in the distance, the street wouldn't be empty for much longer. Luke hovered by the open door and for a fleeting moment his gaze locked with mine. With a solemn smile and a grimace, he ducked into his car and slammed the door shut before taking off into the night. The fear in Luke's eyes would haunt me more than the truth that night.

CHAPTER 3

I woke up on a warm bed I instinctively knew wasn't my own. My eyes burned as they adjusted to the morning sun peeking through drawn curtains across the room. I raised my arm to block the sting of the light, but my limbs were heavy, and I groaned at the smallest movement. My body was still exhausted from the night before, and there was the bonus of a dull throbbing headache that I had become far too accustomed to.

Although it wasn't my bed, I knew my surroundings like the back of my hand. Ryan's room was huge compared to mine and abnormally neat for a guy, plainly but tastefully decorated, with an enviable amount of wardrobe space and a bay window leading out onto a balcony. It was a bachelor's pad without the sleaze. His apartment had always been my haven. Now, the whitewashed minimalism made it feel more like a hospital ward.

After giving myself a few minutes to adjust, I slowly sat upright and swung my legs over the edge of the bed. I dug my toes into the wool rug and waited for the room to stop spinning. My body was stiff and tired as if I had run a marathon with zero training. Part of me knew I should stay in bed, my body was screaming for rest, but my throat was dry, and I had questions.

The events of last night kept looping on repeat in my head. It felt like a dream, fuzzy around the edges and disjointed at parts. But this wasn't a dream. The blood-stained shirt in the corner of Ryan's room and my stiff limbs served as a constant reminder. I wasn't crazy; this was real. The image of Ryan, the inhuman sounds. Those claws. It might have been the stuff from nightmares, but the memory was crystal clear in my mind. I knew what I had seen.

It took me a few minutes to gather the will to stand. The room spun again, and I reached out for the bed frame to steady myself. I had never felt this weak in my life.

As the dizziness passed, I noticed Ryan's normally pristine sheets were covered in grass stains. Looking myself over, I saw streaks of mud covered my legs, but they were the least of my problems.

I had no history of sleepwalking but for the past month. I had been leaving my apartment each night. In the beginning it happened every few days, until it gradually became a nightly occurrence. I had been afraid to tell Ryan and felt guilty for hiding something from him. Turns out, I wasn't the only one keeping secrets.

I made my way to the en suite. My stomach flipped, but I wasn't sure if it was from moving too fast, or if I was on the verge of a nervous breakdown—possibly both. I was a mess. Damp hair clung to my forehead and I stank. I braced my hands on the sink, blinking back tears.

"You're not crazy," I told myself, picking yet another mangled twig from my hair.

I ran the tap, rooting around in the bathroom cupboard until I found a wash cloth. I began cleaning my face, gently dabbing the specks of dirt dotting my cheeks.

Making a conscious effort to ignore what looked like a mix of blood and dirt caked under my fingernails, I leaned in closer to the mirror and checked for any remaining stragglers. The bright bathroom light above stung my eyes and highlighted my dishevelled appearance. I looked like someone had dragged me through a bush, as Kate would say. Personally, I thought it was more of a '*hauled out of a tree, through bushes, and dumped in a murky puddle for good measure*' look.

The gash on my forehead that should have needed stitches was a blotch of purple bruising and a thin red line that had almost healed. It made no sense. I rubbed the dark circles brewing under my eyes, as if willing them away would work. Snippets of strange dreams flashed through my mind. I chewed my lip, biting back the tears threatening to spill.

You're not crazy, but you look like shit.

There was no trace of Luke's hoodie or shirt. Cursing myself at the thought of running naked through the park like a nymph, I grabbed one of Ryan's sweatshirts off the end of the bed, putting it on over the t-shirt he had dressed me in. As I shuffled across the room and reached for the door, the handle turned, and Ryan stepped into the bedroom.

"Eve!" He swept me into his arms and before I could protest, he placed me back down onto his bed.

I flinched at the sudden movement and he flashed me an apologetic smile. "You shouldn't be walking around!"

"But I'm okay."

"No." Ryan met my gaze, his bloodshot eyes full of concern. "You need rest."

I wanted to thump his shoulder, but I had all the strength of a feather. Instead, I huffed and flopped back onto the pile of pillows, cringing at the gentle impact. Ryan pulled the duvet over me, tucking the sides around me as if I were a child.

"Water, please?" I croaked. My throat felt like sandpaper.

Ryan left without a word and returned soon after with a glass of water. By the time he was back in the room, I had already hobbled over to the window. I knew I looked like a pathetic zombie, but the walls were beginning to feel a bit too close. I pulled the curtain across, unlocking the door.

"Can you please get back into bed..."

Ignoring Ryan's pleas, I pushed the glass door open and felt the welcome breeze wash over me. Fresh air filled my lungs and the early summer sun kissed my face as I stepped out onto the balcony. The wooden slats lining the terrace floor were warm under my bare feet.

I took a deep breath and closed my eyes, wishing the light breeze would wash away the events of last night, but it did nothing to unwind the tension coiled in my shoulders. Ryan stepped up behind me and snaked his arms around my waist.

It took me a moment to relax into his touch. Memories of our last time together before I woke up in a park, the tears and the screaming, swam in my mind.

"You are the worst patient ever," he muttered.

I shrugged, flinching at the reflexive motion. "I didn't ask for any of this."

I didn't even know what *this* was.

"You remember what happened?"

I nodded, not trusting myself to speak. I had a hundred questions burning inside, bursting to get out. At the same time, I had no idea what to ask first.

"What exactly happened before I got there, Eve?"

An interrogation wasn't really what I was looking for, so I rolled my eyes.

"Everything. Being in the park. Luke finding me." I felt him go rigid against me at the mention of Luke, but I let it slide and continued, "You two fighting and then him saying I was a werewolf." The last part came out weaker than I expected, my voice cracking.

Ryan's face was out of view, but he seemed deep in thought.

"Let's go get some breakfast," he said, breaking the silence that hung between us.

Breakfast? I mention this ground shattering revelation and he suggests food.

"Seriously?" I twisted in his arms, my tone flat and eyes narrowed. The last thing I wanted was food; my stomach was churning in all the wrong ways.

He nodded, linking my fingers with his and pulling me out of the sun and back into his bedroom. I didn't protest, but the scowl on my face said it all.

"I don't want food, I want answers," I said, throwing myself down on the bed with a groan, immediately regretting the sudden movement. "And a shower."

He sniffed and wrinkled his nose. "That might not be a bad call."

"You're a dick."

"Come on, let's get you cleaned up." Ryan said, chuckling as he grabbed a towel from the cupboard and helped me sit up slowly. "Then we can get some food into you."

"And answers," I reminded him, I wasn't letting go of this bone.

Ryan brushed his lips against mine. "I promise, breakfast and answers."

He grinned, his newfound preppy attitude at odds with his tired eyes. He must have been watching me all night. Unease began to creep into my bones as I nodded. The least I could do was stomach food in exchange for answers.

$$) \;) \; \bullet \; (\; ($$

Nestled in the city centre, alongside Ryan's apartment, was a small café that served the best breakfast in town. Although it was only two minutes around the corner, it took us longer than usual to make our way to the coffee shop thanks to my hobbling.

Parked cars lined the street and colourful flower boxes sat on each apartment window ledge. Couples holding hands, parents with prams and the odd group of kids passed us. Unlike my side of town, there were no drunks stumbling around.

Every time he promised we were nearly there, I had to fight the urge to smack him. Even as a child I was the worst patient.

Not to be dramatic, but I felt like I'd been hit by a bus. *This isn't how finding out you're a werewolf goes in the movies.* Wasn't one of the perks meant to be instant healing?

I plodded down the street, tripping on the uneven pavement as I dragged my feet. Ryan wrapped his arm around my middle. Memories flashed in my mind, of Luke holding me up in the park. I shook my head as I could rid myself of the thought.

Once the scent of freshly baked bread reached me, my shoulders relaxed. It was a welcome relief. I had been battling the noise of car horns and conversations worming their way into my head along with the smell of car exhausts since we left his apartment,

The café was typically busy for a Saturday morning. People talking and laughing filled the seats under the striped awning outside. Ryan held the door with one arm and gently ushered me inside with the other. I didn't mind. Although the sun was shining and fresh air was what I needed, it was in short supply in the city, and the stench of car fumes was making my already unsettled stomach churn.

I watched him as he queued, twining my fingers in my lap. Coffee bean grinders and frothing machines lined the long counter with colourful bottles of flavourings stacked on the shelves behind. A blender started up, and I jumped in my seat, startled by the noise that sounded louder than usual. Conscious of a few sets of eyes on me, I bent down, pretending to have dropped some cutlery, feeling heat creeping up the back of my neck.

Maybe this was a bad idea.

I closed my eyes and tried to focus on my breathing. The legs of the chair opposite scraped the ground, and I opened my eyes to see Ryan's bright blue ones staring back at me.

"All sorted, are you feeling hungry yet?" He asked with a smile, sliding into the seat.

When I glowered instead of answering, his smile slipped, and he shifted uncomfortably under the weight of my gaze.

"You promised me answers," I blurted, the words coming out blunter than I had intended.

Ryan nodded; his hands clasped on the table as if this were some sort of business negotiation. "I did."

I stayed silent, waiting for him to continue. "Seriously, Ryan, stop playing around and explain what happened last night. That guy said I was a werewolf," I hissed the last word, losing what little composure I had left.

"Why don't you say that louder so everyone can hear?" he snapped.

I sat back and bit my lip. Ryan had never so much as raised his voice at me before. As if anyone would even believe a word I was saying. I wasn't even entirely sure I did. We were both on edge.

"Sorry." Ryan shook his head at himself. He reached out for my hand, but I pulled away. "I should have told you sooner."

"You still haven't explained anything." I tilted my chair back, arms folded across my chest as I tried to keep myself together. Breaking down crying in a coffee shop was not the best way to be discrete.

"It's true. You are a werewolf," Ryan said, his gaze level with mine. "Sort of."

"Sort of?" I blanched, lowering my voice again as I leaned in. "What the fuck does *sort of* mean?"

"I'm a werewolf—the kind you've read about or seen in the movies. I can only turn during the full moon phase." His tone lightened into one that got my back up, speaking as if he were teaching a child the basics of spelling. Ryan paused, waiting for me to interrupt again. I didn't. "You're what we call a hybrid, a shifter of sorts. A werewolf that can shift at will."

I chewed my lip. "Did you know? Did you know what I was when we first met?"

"Yes."

My stomach dropped. I had known Ryan for over a year and not once had he mentioned anything about me being a werewolf, hybrid, or whatever I was.

He lied to me.

"Why didn't you tell me?" My voice wavered more than I expected.

"Would you have believed me?"

My mouth hung open. Would I have thought he was crazy? Would I have wanted to believe him? Did I even trust him now? It was one thing Ryan telling me I was a werewolf, and that Luke guy seemed pretty convinced too, but I had no recollection of *being* a wolf. *Besides the recurrent running through a forest dream.* Dammit.

A waiter arrived with our orders just as I slammed my fist against the table in frustration. She gave me a weird look, but at least her presence saved me from having to answer. The waitress slid a plate of French toast drowned in syrup in front of me and handed Ryan his coffee with a sickly-sweet smile. She glanced over her shoulder as she walked away, swaying her hips. I snorted. Ryan frowned.

I still had no real answer, so I opted for more questions. "Did you only get to know me because I was a hybrid?"

"I told you, I recognised you were a hybrid the night we met at the bar."

I shook my head, stabbing at a slice of toast with my fork. "That's not what I asked."

"Yes, I knew that you were a hybrid. I noticed your... scent. You smelled like a wolf, but you were completely oblivious when we started talking." He lowered his voice, leaning over the table towards me. I twitched at the dog reference. "I wanted to protect you. It was clear from the beginning that you had no idea what you were, but I didn't fall in love with you because of what we share."

"A little heads up would've been nice." I gave in to the maple syrup, forcing a forkful into my mouth to satisfy my gurgling stomach. Food was either going to settle it or make me puke.

He nodded, splayed his hands on the table and leaned back in his chair. "I wasn't sure if you would turn... or when you would turn. Hybrids are a bit of a mystery."

"You keep saying that like I'm meant to know what it means."

"It's complicated, but the basics are true. Werewolves are super strong, fast, can see in the dark and rely on the full moon for their powers. The claws you saw me use last night, that's as much as I can do outside of the full moon. Hybrids are not bound by the lunar cycle. They are similar—a kind of variation—but they aren't as strong and it requires a lot more energy and control for them to shift, especially outside of the full moon." Ryan took a slow sip of his coffee before continuing. "We still aren't certain on how the genetics or magic work, it's not common."

My head was bursting with the onslaught of information.

"For you to be a hybrid, one parent had to be a werewolf. That's as much as I know. Your mother must have been human, no werewolf mother would give up their child. It's dangerous—not to mention the trouble they would get in."

I stiffened at his words. "How do you know so much about my parents when I know nothing?"

Put up for adoption immediately after birth, all I had ever known was one foster home after the next.

Ryan shook his head, the pity in his eyes making my skin crawl. "I don't know them specifically."

"How do you know I'm not a werewolf then?" *Not that I wanted to be either option.* I dropped my fork on the plate and harrumphed.

"You're almost twenty. A pure werewolf turns during puberty, but hybrids seem to turn later than that. There are some theories linking it to the blue moon." A strange expression that I couldn't place flitted across his chiseled features, but it went as quickly as it had appeared.

I was glad we had chosen a quiet corner in the cafe because Ryan's explanation sounded insane. Though, for all anyone knew, we could have been talking about a TV show.

"So, I could turn right now?" I wasn't sure if the thought terrified or excited me.

He nodded, twirling a teaspoon between his forefinger and thumb. "Yes, you can, but you need to learn control."

"Wait, am I not stronger if I can turn whenever I want?" I asked, my mind working overtime trying to process everything, despite how crazy parts may have sounded.

Ryan rolled his eyes, savouring his coffee before replying. "No, hybrids are not stronger. Changing takes much more energy outside of the full moon, they heal slower, and they are generally weaker and slower than us in their wolf form."

My questions were multiplying by the second. "How come you didn't turn last night?"

"I was trying my best to control myself around you. That kind of restraint takes time."

I tucked into the breakfast properly now. The nausea was beginning to pass, and ravenous hunger was taking over.

"The next time I can turn will be mid-June." He noticed that I was more focused on cleaning my plate and frowned. "Eve, you need to take this seriously. You could harm yourself or an innocent person if you turn at the wrong time."

"I am taking this seriously. I'm just hungry and tired. Not to mention sore. In my defence, I actually think I'm coping rather well with all of this." I gestured wildly, my mouth half full.

"When you join the pack, you will understand more."

I choked on a piece of crust going down the wrong way. "When I what?"

"Join my pack. It takes practice to have complete control over the change and what you do as a wolf. Instinct can take over and that is not a risk you want to take." He mistook my silence as a cue to continue. "There are various packs throughout Europe.

My father is alpha of the Faolchúnna pack, the oldest pack in Ireland—one of the oldest in the world, actually."

I stabbed the last remaining slice of toast with my fork. "Is Luke part of this pack too?"

"No." Ryan's tone cooled and his eyes blazed.

Any eager buzz of excitement died then and there.

"There was a disagreement some twenty years ago, a faction broke away and formed their own pack—the Crescent pack—which Luke is part of. They are much smaller, and you'd do best to avoid them—especially Luke." Ryan's voice dripped with disdain, only brightening when he referred to his own pack. "When my father steps down, I will take his place as alpha."

"That's the life plan?" I stabbed the last piece with my fork, pushing the food around my plate. "Become the leader? Ditch the normal life?"

He had always talked about taking over the family business. I had thought he meant their law firm, not a pack of mythical creatures.

"Pack life is so much better, Eve, you will understand when you join us. Being the alpha's mate, you will want for nothing."

I coughed, caught between the heat of his gaze and unease in my stomach. "So, I don't get any say in this? I'm automatically joining the pack?"

Ryan nodded, his expression softening. "Of course, you do, but as my mate—"

"Your what?" I cut him off, my voice rising. "You may be my boyfriend but I'm no Bella. I'm not joining anything."

"Having a pack isn't optional, rogues don't fare well. Especially hybrid rogues."

"What is this, some kind of macho possessive werewolf crap?" I stood, sending the empty plate flying across the table into his coffee. It splashed all over his lap. "I can do whatever I want."

Ryan grabbed a napkin and started blotting at his pants, his expression schooled into one of distaste. "Not anymore. You have a responsibility. Without control you're dangerous."

He didn't seem too impressed with my outburst. I wasn't exactly pleased with his plans for me either.

"This is crazy. Do you hear yourself?" I went to grab my bag, but realised I still had nothing with me. My cheeks flushed. "I'm done with this. I need some space."

With that, I turned on my heel and stormed out of the café, leaving Ryan to cover the bill. Without my phone or money it was a forty-minute walk home, but I needed time to think. No way in hell was I going back to beg for a bus fare.

CHAPTER 4

Days later, after being forced to break my self-imposed wallowing, Friday morning lectures followed by labs forced me out of my bedroom. It felt weird being outside on my normal college commute. I had spent the week pretending to be sick, avoiding my housemate and Ryan and spending far too much time on the internet doing a deep dive into Crazyville. I don't recommend it.

My apartment was on the outskirts of Dublin's city centre, close enough for the rent to be ridiculously high but far enough that I still needed to get buses to the college campus. When I arrived, it was awake and bustling. The campus was a mix of old and new with grand stone structures forming the walls of a large courtyard. Farther away stood some taller modern buildings, their presence imposing on the old magic of the college grounds. Students dashed to and from lectures with coffee in hand while others sat in cafés lining the walkways. On the green, groups of students stood chatting and sharing assignment notes.

A breeze swept through the courtyard, and I pulled my sleeves down over my hands, wishing I'd bothered with a jacket. It might have been the beginning of summer, but the chill in the mornings would still linger for weeks.

My phone buzzed for the umpteenth time that morning. With a sigh of defeat, I fumbled around in my bag for it, my fingers numb from the cold. One look at the messages and my shoulders slumped. The texts were from Ryan and a few happy birthdays from friends. I clicked into Ryan's message to find several essays apologising and promising a proper explanation. The last message asked me to meet him after work and that he had booked a restaurant for my birthday. I sighed and shoved the phone back in my pocket; I wasn't ready for that. Every time I thought about the werewolf thing, my head felt as if it was about to implode.

I was making a beeline for a caffeine hit when something nudged my back.

"Happy birthday!"

Still on edge, I squeaked and spun around to see my best friend Kate holding two coffee cups. Her hair fell past her shoulders in electric-blue waves, framing her pixie-like features. Thick eyeliner framed her green eyes, bright with mischief. Dressed in a plaid skirt and a cropped jumper, she looked fantastic compared to my zombie like state.

I pressed a hand to my chest, the thunder of my heart slowly beginning to settle.

"Here." She chuckled and held out one coffee towards me, her cheeks dimpling. "You look like you could do with one, birthday girl."

Part of me wanted to hit her for giving me a fright, but I softened at the taste of the much-needed coffee. "Don't sneak up on people, I could've sent the drinks flying."

"Relax. I didn't sneak, you were away with the fairies. Twenty isn't that old, maybe you should get your hearing checked." She laughed again and took a sip of her drink, motioning for me to do the same. "What's up with you anyway? You've been hiding in your room like a vampire or something."

I sniffed pointedly. "I had a bad cold."

"Uh huh." Kate arched a well-drawn eyebrow. "Boyfriend problems?"

My phone buzzed in my hand and before I could stop her, Kate grabbed it and was skipping away down the path.

"Kate," I huffed as I trudged after her, cup in hand. "Give it back!"

Although she was my best friend, she was also a giant pain in the ass sometimes. Kate was the first girl I had befriended in college. She had advertised a spare room in the city; the rest was history.

I never had many friends growing up–I was a bit messed up as a teenager. My parents died when I was a baby, a car crash they said, so, I spent years jumping between foster homes and worked through my teens until I was officially an adult, old enough to move out and go to university. Once I met Kate, we clicked immediately, and I finally felt at home. She was always there to lend a shoulder to cry on, or to share some vodka.

"Don't be such a grump!" Kate turned toward me, walking backwards while taunting me with the phone. "Now, will you tell me why you're avoiding me, and why you were in such a state when you stormed in the other night before descending into full hermit mode?"

I sped up, gritting my teeth and made a lunge for the phone, but she danced away. "First of all, you're not my mother."

Kate's grin only widened, her delicate features lighting up. She loved nothing more than winding me up. We walked across a path lining the diagonal of the courtyard, passing a small pond with a fountain in the middle of the open space. Kate held the phone hostage over the water.

"Second." I darted towards Kate again, taking the risk and reaping the benefits as I snatched the phone from her grip and scooted several paces away. "I wasn't in any state."

She shot me a withering look and fell into step beside me. I cupped my hands around the warmth of the coffee cup and scowled when my fingers came away sticky. Though the wind had died down, the weather was still unsettled. The late morning sun was pleasantly warm so long as you stayed away from the shadows.

"So, there's absolutely no reason for your delightful mood all week?" Kate bumped her hip into mine, taking a swig of her coffee. I wasn't entirely sure her choice of beverage was just coffee.

I sighed. "I'm not in a mood."

She stared me down. "What is it? You're being weird. Please tell me you haven't let him off the hook again..."

Kate was no fool; she knew me inside out. She was relentless, eccentric and annoyingly observant. When she knew something was on my mind, she wouldn't let go until I spilled. I shrugged and sat down on one of the stone benches. Kate swung her leg over the bench and straddled it, facing me.

She stared at me for a moment, her eyes locking on mine in the most unnerving way. I hated eye contact, and she was the worst for it.

"Ryan's been texting me again." I caved under the pressure of her gaze, the only words I could tell her tumbling out before I could stop them.

Kate growled, slurping at her now empty coffee cup. "I presume you blocked him?"

When I said nothing, she threw her hands in the air. "Eve!" Realisation crossed her pointed features, followed by a scowl. "You were at his house the other night, weren't you?"

"He wanted to explain what happened."

"What happened is I caught him kissing another girl, and he's a snake." Kate said, her words cutting.

I flinched. "It's not about that..."

"What else has he done?"

Lied to me about everything.

Yet here I was, lying to my best friends. I didn't know how to tell her what happened. I couldn't, not when it didn't make sense in my own head.

Frowning, I twirled the paper cup in my hands. "Kate, please, this is about so much more than a girl..."

"Eve, I know you want your fairy-tale ending and all, but you need to open your eyes." Kate scooted closer on the bench, her brow creased.

"You're not listening to me."

Kate reached out and pushed a stray strand of hair behind my ear. "And you're listening to your heart over your head. That only works when you're not relying on a relationship to fix you."

I swallowed. Sometimes I forgot she was two years my senior. For someone who lived her life like it was one big party, Kate was always full of advice. Even if it wasn't what I wanted to hear.

"Says the queen of friends with benefits."

She shook her head, letting the dig slide. "It's different when there are feelings involved. Ryan hurt you, he knew kissing that girl would upset you."

I bristled. "You're hardly an angel, Kate. You play guys off each other all the time. What are we on now? Three?"

As soon as the words had left my mouth, I wanted to snatch them back. My temper was out of control.

Kate glowered but seemed to take the insult with a pinch of salt. "Two actually, Mr. Big Guns had to go."

"Good to know." My nose scrunched as I grimaced. The guy in question didn't have two brain cells to rub together. While Kate thought his muscles were sexy, they only made me wonder how often he took steroids and how on earth he managed to keep up with her appetite. Evidently, he didn't.

"What did Ryan have to say for himself then?" Kate pulled a face at the taste of Ryan's name, clearly intent on deflecting.

I thought back to the argument I'd had with Ryan before the park, before everything hit another level of crazy.

"More lies?" Kate prompted, her expression darkening.

I raised an eyebrow and when she pretended to zip her mouth shut, I took my cue to continue. "He said she was a family friend, and that if he was rude to her, it would cause trouble. It was just a peck."

She broke her pact immediately. "What, because he works for Daddy, he has to let chicks kiss him? Or more? Does he have to sleep with clients? That's one fucked up family business."

Kate was never a fan of Ryan and discouraged me from seeing him from the moment he came into my life. He had tried to win her over by flashing his cash, but that had only heightened her mistrust.

I glowered. "You're twisting his words. I never said I was happy about it; things are just complicated at the moment. Besides, you were drunk at the time, you can't be sure what you saw!"

Kate sighed with pity in her eyes like I was a love-sick teenager who couldn't see the signs. "If you believe that it was an innocent kiss, then you are being naïve."

I bristled, feeling like I was being chastised. "I'm not, I've spoken with Ryan and we are dealing with things."

While I was still furious with Ryan, a part of me held on to the hope that he had good reason to withhold the truth about me being a hybrid. I probably would have thought he was crazy. The fight we had before I changed in the park paled in comparison. A kiss on the cheek wasn't high on my priority list, it was just one more thing on my growing list of problems.

Kate muttered something under her breath, trailing off into her own little rant.

"I don't want to argue about this. You're my friend and who you date is your choice." Kate set her hands on my shoulders, her tone serious. "I'm just saying, make sure you're not staying for the wrong reasons. You don't need him to make you happy. You have me, Craig, your friends. Learn to back yourself."

Part of me wanted to break down crying and tell her everything about the sleepwalking, the werewolf thing, how I needed Ryan to make sense of everything; but I knew I'd sound insane. This was so much more complicated than she could ever imagine.

"I'm not falling back into anything," I said, pulling my friend into a tight hug and burying my face in her hair. "I promise."

The chime of bells rang out from the steeple peaking above some of the older buildings. Kate rose to her feet, brushing down her jeans before pulling me in for a hug. Her head only came up to my chest, but her height didn't stop her squeezing the life out of me. Despite the pressure making me wince, Kate's gesture made me smile for the first time in days.

"Let me know if you're in tonight and we can get pizza?" she suggested, her normal unnaturally peppy attitude returning.

I glanced at my phone as another message from Ryan popped up.

"I'll see."

Kate knew exactly who was texting me and was none too pleased that I might blow her off for Ryan, but she just shook her head and pulled me into a tight hug.

We split up in opposite directions, Kate heading for the arts block. I hurried across the courtyard towards a cluster of tall stone buildings with high-arched windows lining each floor, the wind whipping at my hair. The wide-arched halls were silent, the chatter of students dying out as lectures began. I could hear the distinct northern accent of my lecturer drift down the empty hallway.

Taking a deep breath, I edged the heavy oak door open and snuck into the back of the lecture, flinching as the door swung closed with a bang. The lecturer stopped mid-sentence and glowered like a wolf zeroing in on their prey.

"Thank you for joining us, Ms. O'Connor."

I mumbled an apology, my cheeks burning, and scurried into a free seat at the back. Once everyone stopped staring, I slouched in my seat and held my head in my hands. A headache was still throbbing behind my eyes as I kept replaying Ryan's words and Kate's warning.

I always hated birthdays and so far, this was no exception.

"Now," the lecturer continued, motioning to the slides behind her. "Let's talk about genetic inheritance in female specific disorders."

CHAPTER 5

I spent most of the morning struggling to keep my droop-ing eyes open, switching between periods of checking my phone to see if Ryan had messaged again and cursing myself for wanting to talk to him. The headache had faded, but I still felt like I had run a marathon. The moment class was dismissed, I upped and left, slipping out the back exit before a big queue could form.

The early signs of sunshine had been replaced by rain showers, and a fresh breeze had turned into a wind that blew my umbrella inside out. My damp socks squelched as I trudged down the street, watching people scurry to and from their cars. I cursed as a puddle splashed my legs, tyres squealing as the driver respon-sible sped away.

"Cheers," I muttered, scooting to the wall as close as possible and flinching with each car that drove past.

By the time I turned onto a familiar side street, my jeans were splattered with muck. At the end of the cobbled lane, a neon sign saying *Brady's* lit up the side entrance to the bar. Businessmen who had finished work for the week and students starting the party early were already filtering into the bar, past a stocky bouncer stood at the door barring entry to any teenager trying to give him the slip.

"Jerry." I smiled and gave the bouncer a nod.

Two guys were arguing with Jerry, even though he was twice their size. One of them was too drunk to stand, propped up by his friend who was doing most of the arguing. Jerry shooed them away, instructing them to get a strong coffee before turning to me.

"Eve, how many times have I told you to get a car?" he asked, chuckling as he looked me up and down.

"Too many."

"In you go." He ushered me past the dwindling queue. "Aoibhinn is on tonight too. She might have spare clothes."

"No worries, I have spares in the locker. Learned my lesson during the snow."

Jerry laughed a deep throaty rumble. He turned back to the next punter, a girl who was too young to get in. Fridays were always a long night. I gave him a pat on the back and walked past.

The noise of music thumping and the buzz of conversation rose as I moved through the inner doors, a welcome wave of warmth creeping into my bones. I headed for the staff door near the service area, giving Aoibhinn a nod as she whizzed by with a stack of pint glasses. Fridays always started early in the city, so the bar was busy as usual.

Brady's was split into two parts—a downstairs pub that had a beer garden to the back and a club upstairs that you couldn't pay me to go to. Dim lights hung from the ceiling downstairs, and cosy snugs lined the walls. Not a single table dotted throughout the bar was empty. Beyond the bar at the far end of the room was a bit of space for dancing if they didn't fancy the club. It was a nice spot, but most of the bouncers were too relaxed about checking for ID, which allowed the place an eclectic mix of people past midnight.

I was fond of the place though.

As I got changed in the staff area, I silently thanked myself for leaving a change of clothes in my locker. The dress code was a basic black t-shirt and jeans which did nothing to help my scruffy appearance. I checked my phone briefly and went to toss it into the back of the locker without thinking twice, paused and tucked the phone in my back pocket instead. This shift couldn't end soon enough.

My head was still all over the place when it came to Ryan. The only good thing about our fight was that it helped keep my mind off the sleepwalking issue, and the state I had woken up in. But now and then, sketchy memories of running through the streets and parks came back to me, briefly and disjointed. I felt like I was going crazy.

"Here we go." I sighed, dusting my jeans down and stepping back into the bar.

A manager waved to me from the far side of the room. Aoibhinn was serving a table full of rowdy stags, all of them wearing ridiculous t-shirts with personalised slogans across the back. I gave her a pitiful smile and slid behind the bar to join one of the newer staff members, a scrawny kid with bad taste in glasses who was darting back and forth between customers with shaking hands.

"Hi, Peter. How's it going tonight?"

He glanced up briefly, his eyes wide and panicked as he pulled a pint with far too much head. "Busy."

I laughed and shook my head. Poor Peter looked absolutely frazzled. I remembered the feeling well. Some people took longer to learn the ropes than others.

Still chuckling, I moved to the nearest person at the bar. A handsome man in a well-fitted business suit maybe a year or so older than me caught my eye. Any attraction withered when he waved a fifty euro note in my face. "Six pints please, sweetie."

Nodding, I bit my tongue and placed each drink on the counter after I finished pouring them in record time. I flashed a fake smile, took the note, and slammed his change down making it scatter across the bar.

"I'm so sorry," I lied, moving down the bar to another customer before he could kick off.

From the corner of my eye, I could see Peter still dealing with the same guy as before. A man twice his size, with a full beard and flushed cheeks, who had already had too much to drink.

"No way am I paying you for that, kid. It's a joke. I thought Dublin was meant to be famous for its beer?"

Peter tugged at the collar of his shirt. "I've already pulled you two pints..."

I apologised to the lady in front of me and drifted down to Peter, readying one of my more dazzling smiles. "Can I help you, sir?"

Peter's pale face had flushed red and his glasses were practically fogging up at this point. He looked at me, his eyes pleading. The man he was serving slammed his fist down on the bar. Peter flinched.

"This lad pulled me a shit pint, and I'm not paying for it until I get a real one." His voice was gruff, and his words slurred. He stank of cigarette smoke and bad hygiene.

I examined Peter's second attempt at a pint. In his defence, it was perfectly passable, but this guy had clearly taken a dislike to Peter and had no intention of backing down. Sometimes it wasn't worth arguing.

"That's all right, sir. Let's get you another one." I flashed him a placating smile and poured the two wasted pints down the sink, but not before taking a sip to settle my own nerves.

I tugged Peter's sleeve as I passed, motioning with my head for him to leave and cover the other end of the bar.

"Thanks Eve, you're a lifesaver," Peter whispered.

As he rushed away, I noticed the way his t-shirt stuck to his back and shook my head. Maybe the kid wasn't cut out for this.

"Anytime today, love." That same grating voice came from behind.

I forced my shoulders down and ignored the comment, taking my sweet time to put the glasses onto the wash rack before making my way back over to Peter's customer. The man scowled, his gaze unfocused. I could see him eyeing me as I pulled the perfect pint of Guinness. I set his drink down on the bar, my empty hand outstretched. "That's eight euro."

He picked the pint and took a long sip. "It'll do."

"That's eight."

Ignoring me, he turned and started back towards his friend. As he walked away, I ran around in front of the bar and gave him a pointed tap on the shoulder. "That's eight euro please, *sir.*"

He swung around to leer at me, leaning in and wrapping an unwelcome arm around my waist before I could move out of reach.

"Let's call it quits, love." He sniffed my hair, and I recoiled. "My, my, don't you smell a treat..."

My stomach churned at the stink of beer on his breath. He leaned closer, a predatory glint in his eyes that made me shudder.

I went to shove him away, but before I could, two bouncers hauled him off me. They dragged him towards the door, the drunk man yelling bloody murder as they removed him from the premises. His friends upped and followed him outside, casting suspicious glares in my direction. The bar fell quiet for a moment as everyone stared and then slowly returned to their conversations. Aoibhinn was by my side in an instant, pulling me into a quick hug before ushering me back behind the safety of the bar.

"Are you all right?" she asked, giving the bouncers a thumbs up.

I nodded, my hands shaking as I grabbed a pint of water. I had a love hate relationship with this job. The people I worked with were fantastic, the drunks not so much. If that guy meant what I thought he did, this was a new level of nope.

"That guy had been in here since opening. I warned Peter to stop serving him." Aoibhinn said, giving my shoulder a squeeze before moving off to serve a customer.

For the rest of the night, Aoibhinn stuck close to the bar, asking Peter to take over clearing tables. I felt bad that she was throwing him in the deep end, but I didn't have the energy to manage serving people alone for the night.

By one in the morning, the bar started to die down. Rowdy students took their dodgy dance moves to nearby clubs, and the stags were long gone in search of some action for their weekend in Dublin. All that was left were locals having a quiet night, and they were always happy to leave at closing time. This was my favourite part of the late shift, when the orders slowed, and we could relax a bit while cleaning tables.

As I passed the main doors, I caught a glimpse of a man with blonde hair and a checked shirt lingering outside. Our eyes met as the door swung closed.

Luke?

I dropped my tray on a table and walked to the door, but when I peeked outside the only person out front was Peter.

"Were you talking to someone?" I asked, surveying the empty streets. Across the road, a group of girls teetering in heels cackled and strut towards a taxi.

Peter shook his head, gathering up the last remaining pint glasses. "Nope, just myself."

I frowned and walked back inside, reaching into my pocket for my phone. My hands fumbled and sent the device flying across the bar floor. Cursing, I bent to pick it up.

"Eve, are you sure you're okay?" Aoibhinn asked, pausing by the bar on her way to the kitchens with a crate full of pint glasses.

I jumped slightly and straightened, biting my lip. "Yeah, it's just been a long day."

"Ryan keeping you up all night?" Aoibhinn winked, her freckled nose crinkling a bit as she smiled. Her hair was red, proper ginger, and she was the personification of a stereotypical Irish girl. The yanks loved her.

"Nope," I cringed. "Definitely not."

"Trouble in paradise?"

"Something like that."

As much as I wanted to vent, Aoibhinn was a gossip. I wasn't going to tell her we were fighting—and I definitely couldn't tell her the crazy parts.

She plopped the crate down onto the bar, rattling the glasses. "Eve, you look like someone who has gone all out in Ibiza for a week, not someone who had a fight with her fella."

I shrugged, rubbing my arm, and started wiping the bar down. I needed to keep moving. "Can't sleep lately, maybe that's it."

She frowned. "Maybe. He treats you right, doesn't he?"

"Can we change the subject, please?"

"He better be or he'll have me to deal with. And Jerry." Aoibhinn cocked her head towards the doorway, flashing a grin.

I tried to crack a smile, but whatever expression I managed must have been pathetic.

Aoibhinn's smirk faltered, and she frowned. She glanced at my phone, sighing as she took the cloth from my hand. "Why don't you knock off early, Eve?"

I didn't wait around for her to ask twice.

CHAPTER 6

Ryan had messaged during my shift, asking to meet at his apartment again, but Aoibhinn's words echoed in my mind, and I decided that she was right. I was too tired and not in the mood to talk to him or hear more excuses. I texted him saying as much. All I wanted to do was go home and drown my sorrows in a romcom.

The cobbled stones lining the alley were slick, and rainwater gushed along the side drains. My only company was rats rummaging in the bins and empty crates stacked against the wall. I tossed my broken umbrella in the trash as I passed, pulling my hood up in a futile attempt to keep myself dry. A stray cat stalked towards the rat pit, its stomach low to the ground. It ignored me as I walked past, its attention firmly fixed on dinner. Only dim lights from the apartments overlooking the little lane lit my path.

Behind me, I heard a metal crash followed by a squeal. I turned, but the alleyway was empty. The stray cat stood in the middle of the lane, ears flat and its fur standing on end. It hissed at the shadows and scarpered past me towards the main street. An involuntary shiver ran down my spine. The cat had the right idea, so I began jogging in the same direction.

As I turned onto the busier road, I saw my bus pulling off in the distance.

"Oh, for fuck's sake."

Cursing, I trudged to my stop, sulking under the cover of the bus shelter. The rain pounding the streets forced people to dart between cars and shop doorways. Loose flyers flapped in the wind, and the stench of smoke filled my nostrils. I scowled, shuffling to the far end of the seat.

I huddled up, clutching my bag to my chest and sighed. "Happy birthday to me."

It didn't take me long to give in and flag a taxi to Ryan's place to escape the rain. He met me at the door with a hug, insisting on picking up the fare. My bag and jacket dripped all over the pristine floors, leaving a trail the whole way to his apartment door, but he didn't seem to mind. By the time I had kicked off my rain-soaked trainers, Ryan appeared in his bedroom doorway with a pair of fluffy socks and tracksuit bottoms in hand. He ushered me into the room, moving to the kitchen to give me some privacy to change.

Once I was in dry clothes and the fluffy socks began warming my feet, I breathed a sigh of relief. A knot of tension still tugged at my shoulders, but being dry was an improvement. I scooped my damp hair into a messy bun and gave myself the once over in the mirror, noting the dark circles under my eyes that seemed to have taken up a permanent residence there. The mark on my forehead was almost completely gone.

Ryan's apartment was open plan like mine and Kate's, except his living area was twice the size and you could have more than two people in his kitchen. As I stepped out of his room, the scent of spices had my stomach rumbling immediately. All I'd had was a crap meal deal sandwich before work. At least Ryan was on the same page as me when it came to food. I was not in any state to go out for dinner.

"Hungry?" Ryan turned to me, wooden spoon in hand and a grin plastered on his face. "I didn't think you'd fancy heading back out in that weather."

I nodded, my mouth going dry. "Good call."

What's wrong with me? I'm acting like some kind of nervous schoolgirl.

It was like when I first met Ryan. He had approached me at the bar where I worked, and I'd struggled to string together a sentence. Normally, I didn't care much for pretty boys, but he was hot with an air of mystery about him that drew me in. For our first date, he figured out my favourite meal and brought me to the best place in town. They say the way to a man's heart is through their stomach—it's true for me too. But it wasn't just that. What had made me fall for him were the times he showed up at my apartment with a bottle of wine or popcorn on bad days, and how he would hold me in the night when I had a bad dream. The nights we stayed up talking about our future. That's what made me fall for him. Right now, I felt like I was meeting him all over again, and that terrified me.

"Eve?" Ryan asked, his voice tugging me out of my spiralling thoughts. "Are you ok?"

He had a bottle of wine in one hand and a glass in the other, his brow furrowed.

I shook my head. "I'm fine, please don't ask me again, or I might explode."

His frown dissipated, but the concern never left his eyes. He seemed muted as he poured me a glass. Maybe I wasn't the only one who was nervous.

As Ryan handed me the wine, I forced a slight smile, trying to settle his nerves along with mine. "Thanks, I'm just a bit spacey at the moment."

"That's to be expected." His expression brightened, and he rushed over to stir the curry simmering on the hob. "Go sit down and I'll bring this over."

I walked around the island in the kitchen to grab some cutlery. He spun around to plant a gentle kiss on my cheek as I passed, sending goosebumps up my spine.

Snap out of it, you're still angry. A kiss does not get him out of the doghouse.

Focusing on setting the table kept me distracted, but my cheeks were still burning when Ryan joined me, placing two plates brimming with massaman curry and rice. My stomach roared to life. The food smelled unreal—he had always been a great cook. Unlike me, who relied on pizzas and coffee to survive.

Then it got weird again. Normally, we talked the whole way through dinner, Ryan politely, and me with my mouth full. But an awkward silence hung in the air as I dug in, and not because I was too hungry to talk. I didn't want to have this conversation. His gaze never left me, and the look in his eyes only added to my unease. I couldn't read his expression. It was a strange mixture of concern, anger, and something else that I couldn't place.

I'd always thought he was an open book. Not anymore.

"Why are you looking at me like that?" I finally asked, placing my fork down.

"Like what?" Ryan swallowed, still pushing his food around his plate. "I'm not allowed to look at you now?"

"Like I'm about to break."

"I'm worried about you," he said, wringing his hands un-characteristically nervous. "The way you found out... it was wrong. I should have been there for your first change, to keep you safe. It's so much to take in, and I haven't made this any easier."

I sighed, twisting my fork between my finger and thumb. "It feels so surreal. I'm not sure if I believe it."

The image of that drunk guy in work sniffing my hair resur-faced.

"What's wrong?" Ryan asked, dropping his cutlery. "Why do you look like you've seen a ghost?"

"It's nothing, some drunk guy got angry at work. He said something about me smelling nice and I thought... But he can't be."

A dark shadow crossed Ryan's face as he reached for his phone, fingers hammering the screen. For a moment, I thought the phone was going to end up embedded in the wall, but when he placed the phone back down, he spoke calmly. "Don't worry about that, he won't be bothering you again."

"I don't th—"

"This is real, Eve," Ryan continued, raising his hand. "You need to take it seriously."

I watched as his nails slowly morphed and reshaped into claws extending from his fingertips. My mouth opened and closed like a fish gasping for air. Ryan seemed amused, showing off once more by retracting his claws. Within seconds, his hand was normal.

"That's why it's important that you learn control, so you can remember and control what you do during a change."

The thought made my chest constrict. "I'm not sure I want to remember."

"You will. It takes time to learn, but it will be worth it." Ryan took up his cutlery and placed it on my empty plate, beginning to stack up the plates. "That's why I was talking about joining my pack, it's about learning and having somewhere to belong."

"I've never belonged anywhere."

I cringed inwardly at my own words because I sounded like a whiny little teenager. But it was true, I'd always felt like I was on the outside looking in.

Ryan's expression softened at my words. I watched as he got up from the table and disappeared into his room, ready to launch into a tirade if he was running away from yet another argument. He emerged with a black rectangular box clasped in his hands and stopped by my side, dropping onto one knee.

"Ryan... no. That's not what I meant," I said, tripping over my words as I backed away.

With that, a grin split his face and he burst out laughing, so much so he was holding his belly and his eyes teared up. I waited, mouth hanging open, shifting from looking like a rabbit caught in the headlights to a very confused one.

"It's a birthday present, not a proposal," Ryan chuckled, mischief sparkling in his eyes. "I promise, I got the message loud and clear the other day. I'm not trying to force you into anything."

I eyed the box sceptically, my pounding heart beginning to slow as relief washed over me. Our relationship was rocky at best with all the recent revelations.

He opened the box to reveal a bracelet nestled in navy velvet, an intricate silver chain with different phases of the moon spaced evenly. The full moon sparkled under the light. I couldn't stop myself from smiling as he took my hand and closed the bracelet around my wrist.

"You don't need to make any decisions about joining my pack right now, but I want you to take it seriously. Deal?" Ryan asked, clipping the clasp shut.

I wasn't sure what I wanted to do, it was all so new. Maybe he was right, I did need to at least take the situation seriously.

"Deal."

His smile widened.

"It's beautiful," I said, brushing my fingers across the different moons lining the bracelet. It was delicate, the perfect fit. "I love it."

"I love you, Eve." Ryan laced his fingers with mine, still kneeling by my side. Placing the box down, he leaned in so that his lips were inches from mine and cupped my cheek. "I promise, I never meant to keep the truth from you. I understand why you are angry, and I will do everything in my power to regain your trust, if you'll let me."

Tears pricked the corners of my eyes, his words sparking emotions that I had suppressed since the park incident rising and threatening to overwhelm me. Not trusting myself to speak, I nodded.

Ryan leaned in and captured my lips in a gentle kiss. It felt just like him, just like before. As I lost myself in his touch, I wondered if maybe change wasn't such a bad thing after all.

CHAPTER 7

The next week was a blur of struggling through work shifts and attempting to study when my mind wouldn't focus. Ryan agreed to park the hybrid stuff until after my exams except for a few history lessons, which felt more like myths. I was still struggling to get my head around it. We talked about wolves and packs, but I still felt as if I had jumped into a book and it wasn't my life.

Part of the deal was the agreement that I'd stay at Ryan's each night in case I changed at night. As much as he would have loved to follow me around all day, it wasn't feasible. I promised to remain calm at all times, but I had no *feeling* or whatever of wanting to change. Honestly, I wasn't sure what I was looking out for. It didn't feel real and that night in the park was the only proof I had that Ryan was telling the truth. Skipping work wasn't an option unless I wanted to default on my university fees, and I'd refused Ryan's offer to pay them. So, I forced myself to grit my teeth and push through it.

"All set," I murmured to myself.

Ducking down one of the side streets, the unpleasant scent of rubbish and damp filled my nostrils. It was getting easier to block out constant background noises, but unexpected smells often caught me off guard.

I cut across the city, crossing one of the many bridges lining the river which split the capital in two. The water's surface glistened in the afternoon sun. Tourists and locals enjoying a pleasant weekend occupied benches along the waterfront, though there was always a gentle sea breeze coming from the coast.

Turning onto a familiar street, I spotted Jerry in the distance. The broad man was smoking outside the side entrance, tipping the ashes onto the cobbles. The stench of tobacco caught in the back of my throat.

"Hi Jerry."

He nodded in reply, deep circles brewing under his eyes. It must have been an eventful night. Either that, or he'd had another row with his wife. I was running too late to stand around chatting about his marital woes so I flashed him a warm smile and hurried inside.

It took a moment for my eyes to adjust from the sunshine to the dimly lit bar. Only a few people sat inside on a day like this, mostly lone drinkers and the odd group of men forsaking the sun out of desperation for a better view of whatever football match was on show. Through a small archway leading outside, I could see that the small beer garden was busy, as were any tables out front on the streets.

Good thing this place doesn't do table service.

I sighed in relief as I saw the boss wasn't the manager on shift, quickly dumping my bag in my locker. A middle-aged man with greying hair and a tea towel thrown over his shoulder came over to me at the bar.

"Late again, Eve?" The man smiled, laughter lines tightening with his expression.

"Sorry, Paddy, it's been a rough few weeks."

He nodded, giving me an affectionate pat on the arm and continued on his way to the kitchen with a tray full of dirty beer glasses. "Pop out front and clear some of those tables, will you? It's been packed all afternoon with the weather."

I mustered a smile and grabbed a tray, heading outside. The sunshine beating down on my back made the shift that bit more bearable. I was on my way back inside with a tray stacked full when I picked up a familiar scent. It was a mix of burnt orange and pine that took me far too long to place. I opened my mouth, ready to ask Paddy if the dishwasher was still broken, when I caught sight of Luke ordering a whiskey at the bar. My grip on the tray faltered, and it hit the ground with a loud smash as dishes and broken shards of glass ricocheted across the floor.

"Eve! What's wrong?" Paddy asked, rushing behind the bar to grab a broom.

I shook my head and squatted to clean up the mess, my cheeks burning. "Just tired, sorry Paddy."

Ryan may have agreed to press pause on the werewolf thing, but apparently the universe wasn't on side with that decision. Within seconds, the familiar scent was right by my side, and I cursed under my breath.

"Sorry, I didn't mean to give you a fright."

"Well, you did," I snapped, glancing up in time to see the wounded look on Luke's face.

Paddy came over, broom and dustpan in hand. "I've got this. You take the bar," he said, ushering me behind the counter while he cleaned up the rest of the mess.

Luke resumed his post, propped on a stool and leaning over the bar and his untouched whiskey.

I hovered behind the bar, eyeing Luke nervously. "What are you doing here?" I hissed, all too aware of the warnings Ryan had given me about Luke's pack.

It was still early days when it came to my History of Werewolves 101 lessons, but Ryan had made one thing inherently clear from the start. There were various werewolf packs scattered across the world and each had their own territory. There used to only be one pack in Dublin—Ryan's, the Faolchúnna wolf pack which had deep roots in Ireland. But there had been some kind of argument about twenty years ago and a faction broke away—the Crescent pack. Ryan had avoided delving too much into the how and why, but he had been dead set on one thing, I needed to keep my distance.

Luke took a slow sip of his whiskey, his gaze unwavering as he watched me. He looked curious, intrigued. Everything he wasn't supposed to be, according to Ryan anyway.

"I was warned to stay away from you." I muttered, taking out a cloth and beginning to wipe down the counter to keep my hands busy.

He snorted and took another swig of his drink. "By your boyfriend, no doubt."

I bristled at that, leaning in close so the manager wouldn't hear. "What's your point?"

"Are you sure you can trust him?"

"Why are you here?" I asked, ignoring his question like he did mine.

"I fancied a drink."

Luke looked far too smug for my liking. I couldn't stop thinking about that night in the park. The memory gave the wrong kind of butterflies. I hoped he wasn't looking for his shirt back; I was pretty sure Ryan had torched it.

I ignored the grin plastered on his face, snatching a few rogue glasses off the bar, anything to keep my hands busy, but my brain was working overtime. He motioned for another drink. I reluctantly obliged. All the while, I could feel his eyes on me as I poured his drink and slammed it down on the counter.

"I'm not in the mood for games. What do you want?"

I had tried so hard to push all of this away. So far it had worked. I hadn't shifted or woken up in strange places without my clothes once. I knew I should heed Ryan's warning to stay away from Luke, but I couldn't ignore my curiosity.

"I wanted to check that you were okay," he said, his lilting tone softening.

If one more person asks me that, I'm going to explode.

"Why? I can take care of myself."

"You mean Ryan can take care of you?" He shook his head, raking his fingers through his hair as his brow furrowed. My mouth set in a thin line and Luke took the hint, holding his hands up in defeat. "I'm not here to argue with you. I get that you are with Ryan. I'm not here to steal someone's girl."

"No one owns me, and I'm not interested."

Luke chuckled. "You need to be smart about this. I'm sure Ryan told you how dangerous it is to be a hybrid right now. If he cared for you at all, he would make sure you knew that."

I stared at him, unblinking. From what I'd been told, aside from being weaker and slower than the werewolf standard, hybrids had the upper hand—even if shifting made me feel like I'd been hit by a bus.

Luke twirled the whiskey glass, his expression thoughtful. "You were terrified that night. I wanted to make sure that you are coping with... everything." He looked across at Paddy and lowered his voice. "That you were learning to deal with things."

"How did you know I was a hybrid?" I asked.

What I really should have asked was how the hell he knew where I worked, or how he knew that I would be working this shift.

His intense gaze lingered on my face and I looked down, glancing around the almost empty bar under the pretence of scanning for customers.

"Because you smell like a wolf, you're not a teenager, and you had no idea what was going on."

"Excuse me?" My gaze snapped up, and it was then that I noticed that those eyes, silver mirroring the full moon that night, had been replaced with a soft brown.

Surprise must have been etched across my features because he noticed my second take.

"What? Oh, the eyes?"

I nodded.

"They change around the full moon when I'm fighting a transformation, usually during a stressful situation." Luke leaned in, his hands circling around the now empty whiskey glass. His face was inches from mine, but there was nothing sinister about his hushed tone. If anything, his expression was a mask of concern.

I swallowed hard.

"Finding a hybrid terrified and alone in the park when her pack should take care of her is a stressful situation. Especially when her boyfriend shows up and tries to slice you open for helping," he said, amusement lifting his tone as he recalled the fight.

"I don't have a pack, and Ryan was trying to mind me."

Luke slouched back and folded his arms across his chest, so irritatingly relaxed when we both knew that he shouldn't be anywhere near me. But then again, he was right. Until I agreed to join the Faolchúnna, I had no pack.

"Why haven't you joined yet?" Luke echoed my thoughts.

"Why are you drinking so much this early?"

"Why not?" He countered, the corner of his lips twitching as he smirked.

Was being this hot a werewolf thing? No. Get a grip.

"I haven't much else to be doing at the moment, to be honest." He sighed, his smile slipping as an empty look ghosted his face for a moment.

I frowned. "I don't want to join a pack. I don't want any of this."

"Some of us have no choice..." Luke's brow furrowed as he took a long sip of his drink. He opened his mouth to continue but appeared to think better of it. I guess I wasn't privy to any Crescent pack business.

"Is Ryan going to be the leader of his pack?" I asked, curious despite my reservations.

"He's next in line, unless his uncle takes it." Luke stared at his half empty whiskey glass, his expression darkening. "Not everyone is cut out to be an alpha."

"Do you have a choice?"

Luke cocked his head to the side. "To be alpha? In a sense, yes."

I chewed my lip, reciting the story Ryan had spun me. "I thought it always fell to the alpha's oldest son, or daughter the odd time."

"Yes, and no." Luke leaned in close again and cast a quick glance around the room. Paddy had left us and was probably out back washing up or chatting with the locals outside. "Usually, the alpha's son is the best fit. But in the event that they don't want the title or are deemed unworthy, another alpha will step up. Sometimes, there's a fight if the next leader isn't an obvious choice."

"Is this the same for every pack?" I asked, the thought of Ryan having to engage in some archaic fight to the death sending my anxiety soaring.

He nodded. "For most packs, yes. Your boyfriend's pack goes by the blood thing."

I sighed at that, but my relief was short lived.

"Unless someone in his pack challenges him. It might be tradition, but blood doesn't guarantee status in any pack. That is how his father took over in the first place after all."

At Luke's revelation, my shoulders knotted again. Ryan never mentioned that.

His head snapped up, and he sniffed discreetly for a moment before knocking back his drink and jumping out of his seat.

"Luke?" I asked, my brow furrowed as he grabbed his wallet off the bar top. An hour ago, I had wanted him to leave immediately, but now I wanted more answers. I needed answers.

"I have to go. But if you ever need to talk, give me a shout." He reached out, pushing a crumpled piece of paper into my hand. His fingers were warm against mine. Our eyes locked has his hand lingered there, and I shifted uncomfortably under the intensity of his gaze. "Be careful who you trust, Eve."

With that, Luke strode towards the main doors, almost knocking over Paddy in his rush to exit.

"What the hell?" Paddy grumbled, scowling at Luke's receding back. "Is that asshole some friend of yours?"

I stared after Luke, watching as the doors swung closed. "I don't know."

The rest of the day slid by far too slowly and the heat filtered inside, making the bar stuffy even as the sun began to set. I couldn't stop yawning, the long study days and exam stress beginning to catch up on me. Being the wonderfully kind man that he was, Paddy gave me the nod to leave early. I didn't hesitate to take him up on his offer, starting towards Ryan's apartment just as the last of the summer sun was fading.

I felt a shiver in my spine and the odd sensation that I was being watched, so I took a longer more winding route back to the apartment. There was no odd scent around me, and when I cast my hearing out for any hints, I got nothing. No one was following me, but I didn't want to panic and accidentally shift on the way home. The longer option was worth it, even if I was being paranoid.

The apartment door swung open before I could turn the key in the lock. I pushed the door, stepping inside and heard a footstep behind me.

I turned to see Ryan in the hallway, his hands balled into tight fists. "Where have you been?" Anger contorted his features.

He pushed past me before I could answer, stomping into the apartment and slamming the door behind us. "I'll tell you where you have been—doing exactly what I distinctly told you not to!"

Luke's swift exit suddenly made sense.

"Have you been keeping tabs on me?"

Ryan's expression clouded, dark and furious. He spat each word through clenched teeth. "I told you to stay away from Luke and his filthy pack."

I blanched, dropping my bag onto the floor. "Ryan, have you been following me?"

"Not that I needed to, you stink of him," he growled, anger flaring in his narrowed eyes. "Ever since your change, I always stop by your work to make sure you're safe."

"I didn't tell him to come."

He set his shoulders and took a step towards me, looking more feral than I had seen him since the fight with Luke. "You didn't ask him to leave."

"You're ridiculous, you know that, right?" I scowled, stabbing him in the chest with my finger. "I can't go throwing guys out of bars for no reason. Telling my manager that Luke is from a rival pack isn't going to cut it in the real world."

Ryan glowered, not listening to a word I had said. "There are rules, *pack* rules."

Not this shit again.

"I'm not part of your pack though, I haven't said yes."

Excitement and something else glinted in his eyes. Whatever it was, it made bile rise in my throat.

"It's not a matter of if, it's a matter of when."

"Woah, mate, back it up," I said, battling two sides of myself—the one that wanted to beg Ryan for forgiveness, and the other that was my newfound temper.

Ryan shrugged. He seemed so sure of himself. "You will join eventually. You don't have a choice."

I shook my head, mouth open as I stared at him in disbelief. This possessive streak that had appeared ever since the night I turned was making my skin crawl.

"Why are you making such a big deal out of this?"

"You don't understand." Ryan was looking at me like I was some clueless child, irritating him with disobedience.

"Because you won't explain anything to me," I snapped, throwing my hands up in exasperation.

"I told you before, he is a Crescent wolf."

"Yes, and I get that there was drama, but he hasn't tried to hurt me. He helped that night in the park! What's the harm in talking?"

His expression darkened, and I realised rather quickly that even mentioning or joking about the remote possibility of me joining another pack went down like a tonne of bricks.

"His pack is full of heathens."

"You're not making any sense." I said, quirking an eyebrow at the biblical turn.

Ryan remained stoic, simmering. "Luke's pack left because they had very different beliefs. They didn't care about pack survival or protecting ourselves against the future. This isn't a game, Eve. There are worse things lurking in the dark than werewolves."

"Like vampires?"

"No... well, yes. That's not the point." Ryan sighed and gave me a withering look. "We are not the top of the pecking order and packs cannot function if they do not stick together. Luke's father betrayed the pack."

I frowned, struggling to imagine what horrible thing Luke's father was supposed to have done. The image of his kind, rugged features came to mind. While he always seemed a bit distant, every action until now had been to help me.

"What did he do?"

Ryan ignored my question, but his demeanour softened. He took a step towards me, his body language shifting. "I'm sorry I got angry. I was worried about you. His pack is dangerous."

I snorted derisively. "I know you warned me that wolves can get a little macho and possessive, Ryan, but this is taking the piss."

"Just stay away from Luke and his pack, is that so hard?"

Any warmth that had crept into his voice had vanished. The atmosphere soured once more.

"This is bat-shit crazy, I'm not having this argument," I said, storming past him to grab my duffle bag from his room. When I re-emerged, Ryan was blocking the doorway.

"Move, I'm going back home."

He didn't budge.

"Ryan, I'm not joking. My last exam is on Friday, and I really don't have the energy left for this." I took a step towards him, my body temperature sky rocketing. "Let me go home and do not follow me."

I had fought so hard to keep my temper under wraps. A part of me still refused to accept this warped reality, but the tight knot in my stomach told me it was all true. And if it was, I refused to give into the anger just to get away from Ryan.

"I want to help you, Eve. You need my help."

"What I need is for you to move before I do something we both regret," I demanded, my voice steadier than I felt.

Whatever he saw in my eyes made Ryan move out of the way. He wasn't angry anymore, he was looking at me as if he was not only worried but scared. Scared for me.

"Maybe you should stay away from me," I echoed his earlier words, my voice barely a whisper.

I shoved past Ryan and shut the door behind me. As I started down the street, the clouds above rumbled and rain dotted the pavement in front of me. My emotions were a taut ball of anger, sadness, and confusion all rolled into one. Ryan's wounded expression lingered in my mind, but I didn't look back.

CHAPTER 8

I spent all my spare time in the library, avoiding Ryan and focusing on getting through my last exam. Beyond that, I didn't have a plan. On Friday night, Kate insisted on dragging me to Craig's birthday. It's not that I didn't want to go, I really did, but between the whole wolf thing, fighting with Ryan, and summer semester finals, all I wanted to do was curl up in bed. Kate wasn't buying my excuses.

Craig lived just outside of the city centre in a more suburban area with nice uniform brick houses, well-kept gardens, and nice cars in the driveways. His house stood out for all the wrong reasons. The garden was a mess of weeds and there was a stack of beer crates beside the front door. I could hear blaring music the moment I set foot outside of the taxi.

As soon as we stepped in the door, a guy dressed head to toe in black with a band t-shirt and jet black hair scraped back in a perfect quiff, squealed and pulled me into a tight hug.

"Eve! You made it!"

Kate smirked beside me. "I wasn't going to let her back out over a silly little cold, Craig."

I winced as his arms crushed a bruised rib that was healing faster than it should. He didn't notice, squishing me with pure joy. For a beanpole, he was always stronger than I expected. I extracted myself from the crushing hug so that I could breathe, grinning up at my friend.

"As if anyone would miss one of my parties, especially my birthday twin." Craig barked a laugh, his impish features lighting up. "Now let's get you girls a drink."

He always called us twins because our birthdays were three weeks apart. It warmed that dark side of my heart, the one that never felt like it belonged.

Craig laced his fingers with mine, and before I knew what was happening, he took off down the hallway. I twisted to catch Kate's hand just in time as he dragged me through a throng of students. I had no choice but to dodge drinks and apologise until he skid to a halt in the kitchen.

The counter and sink were overflowing with food and drink. The fridge door hung open, drawers teeming with bottles and ice, and the table standing in the middle of the room was stacked high with beer cans and half-empty bottles of every spirit you could name. Craig bustled about, experimenting like a potions master with whatever was within reach. When he was happy with his concoction, he spun around and held a red cup out to me, a wide grin plastered on his face.

"Bottoms up."

"Nice to see you too." I put the cup to my lips and sniffed, wrinkling my nose as I downed a mouthful.

Craig watched intently, bursting out laughing as I started to cough. I pressed a hand to my chest, glaring at my friend as I spluttered and tried to breathe through the fire licking my throat. A bitter taste lingered on my tongue.

"Why can't you pour a decent drink?"

He shrugged, a playful glint in his eyes. "Because they're no fun."

If it had been anyone else, I would have refused to drink, but Craig's enthusiasm was infectious. His main goal was to make sure everyone was having fun, and he was just the distraction I needed.

While Craig was no bartender, his experiment did its intended job. By the time I saw the bottom of the cup, I was well and truly in a party mood. I spent most of the night laughing and joking with girls from my course, complaining about assignments, gossiping about other students and lecturers—most specifically which students were sleeping with them. All harmless fun that had us falling around with laughter. Enough normality for me to push the events of the last few weeks to the back of my mind and lock them in a box to be dealt with later.

That box was working perfectly fine until I spotted him across the room. Luke was leaning against the wall with a beer in hand, casually scanning his surroundings while a group of guys and girls at least three years his junior vied for his attention. I went slack-jawed. His gaze met mine. If Luke was surprised to see me, it didn't show. His expression remained passive. I looked away and felt my cheeks flush.

What the hell is he doing here? My stomach knotted. When I dared to glance up again, he was prying a petite girl off his arm.

"Eve?" Kate gave me a nudge. "Did you hear about Chris getting with his tutor last week?"

I turned at the mention of my name and shook my head, allowing myself to be drawn back into the conversation.

Kate took a step aside from the group and gave my elbow a tug. "What is up with you?"

I tore my gaze away from Luke and tried to shake some sense into myself, running a hand through my hair. "Nothing, I'm fine."

"Is it Craig's mixing skills again? I told him to go easy on you." Kate frowned and followed my line of sight, a wicked smile curving her lips. "Who is *he*?"

Luke noticed both of us looking his way and winked, earning a scowl from the first-year fawning over him.

"No one you need to know."

Kate made a beeline towards him, hips swaying with each step. I grabbed her forearm and hauled her out of the room, refusing to let go until I was satisfied that she was out of danger.

She huffed and rubbed her arm where my nails had left slight crescent indents. "No need to be like that. If you fancy him, you just had to say."

All I could do was glower and snatch a bottle of vodka off the table. "I don't fancy him, he's a stalker."

No matter where I moved, Luke seemed to follow. Each time I went into a different room, he would appear in the doorway like a shadow I couldn't lose. I promised myself I would enjoy the night and made it my mission to keep Kate away from him. The last thing I wanted was to drag Kate into this mess.

Nothing I did helped shake the unease in my gut. Not even a round of shots could get me back in a party mood, though I kept trying in vain. I was an awful mixture of drunk and sick with worry.

In my attempt to drown my problems, I lost sight of Luke. I expected to feel relieved, but the knot in my stomach only expanded. The room was spinning. Luke was gone. Kate had me on the makeshift dance floor, cordoned off with two sofas, dancing her little heart out. Mine was only half in it. The bass thumped in my chest, and snippets of conversation swirled around me. It reminded me of a bad trip. I focused on Kate, her fingers entwined with mine. A small comfort.

She looked past me and wiggled her eyebrows suggestively. Before I could ask what was going on, I felt a light tap on my shoulder. I spun, my muscles coiled and charged with adrenaline.

"Can I borrow Eve for a moment?" Luke stood between the two couches, a whisky in one hand, while the other lingered in the air still.

"Of course!" Kate all but threw me at him, shooting me a mischievous grin as she danced away and latched onto the nearest guy.

Luke let his hand rest between my shoulder blades and gently nudged me off the dance floor. A tingle ran down my spine at his touch. I grabbed a random drink off the table. Anything to keep my hands busy.

"I wasn't expecting to see you here," he finally said, those gorgeous eyes of his boring a hole in mine. He took a swig of his whisky and dropped onto a chair, lounging as if he belonged there. But this was my territory.

"Why wouldn't I be at a party in *my* friend's house near *my* college campus? Aren't you a bit old for this kind of thing?" My words were slurred, but the liquid confidence was stoking the fires of my temper.

From the wounded expression on his face, he hadn't been expecting such a frosty reception. A pang of guilt hit me. No matter how hard I tried to run away from things, werewolves seemed to catch up to me.

I took a deep breath and pinched the bridge of my nose. "I can't deal with this right now."

"You ignored what I said at the bar."

My head shot up. "Have you been following me?"

"Watching you, yes. Stalking? Let's leave that to your boyfriend."

I opened my mouth to argue, but he had a point. After Ryan's latest antics, the last thing I wanted was to defend him. "You can't keep turning up like this, Luke."

He chuckled, leaning back on his chair, and kicking one leg across the opposite knee. "Who said that I'm here for you?" Luke winked, gesturing to a group of younger boys huddled in the far corner. "I'm here on babysitting duty for one of our baby pack members."

My cheeks burned, and I bit my tongue. Maybe I had gotten too used to Ryan obsessing about me. Perhaps it had gone to my head, or—most likely—I was drunk. "Of course, you are."

Luke looked me over, my body heating under his gaze. "You sound disappointed."

"I'm just confused."

The drink had well and truly taken hold. My fuzzy brain was ticking over too slowly to keep up. There were two werewolves in this room. *And then me, apparently. How was this even possible?*

"That's understandable," he said, those russet eyes of his remaining fixed on me as he tilted his head.

"Is it?" I nursed the cup of vodka in my grip, taking sip after sip to keep myself sane. My hands shook more than I liked when I brought the drink to my lips. "You grew up as a werewolf." Luke shot me a look which told me to drop my voice. I ignored him and continued with my tirade. "You don't know what it is like to have this dropped on you out of nowhere. It's like some bad practical joke. You don't understand at all."

"Fair enough." He fell silent for a moment, staring into space.

I was ready to stand and go in search of Kate when Luke leaned forward, all humour drained from his expression. His fingers wrapped around my forearm, his touch light.

"Eve, I know this situation is not what you expected. It's scary. At the start, it will be, but you can learn to control and embrace your hybrid side."

I frowned, biting the inside of my cheek. "I don't want to learn. I don't want to be a part of this."

Luke shook his head and exhaled slowly, reaching up to brush a stray strand of hair behind my ear. The look in his eyes was one I recognised too well—pity. "You have no choice, but you will figure that out on your own. Just be wise with your choices and trust your instincts."

His grip on my arm loosened. I lingered for a moment before breaking contact and walking out of the room. When I glanced over my shoulder, Luke sat back in the chair watching me with that same troubled expression.

CHAPTER 9

If I wasn't drunk before, after my conversation with Luke, I made it my mission to make sure my alcohol to blood ratio was off the charts. I just wanted to forget everything. I didn't bat an eyelid when a guy with a lip piercing and a face that screamed trouble snaked his arms around my waist, or when he began leading me up the stairs. My rational only decided to pop in for a chat when we were on the landing and he was pressing me against a wall.

"I don't think this is such a good idea," I mumbled, my words slurred.

The guy kept kissing my neck as if he hadn't heard me. I leaned my head back against the wall and sighed into him. The ceiling was spinning, and my stomach was doing somersaults.

I pressed my palms against the wall and tried to slide away, my movements clumsy. "I don't think I'm in the mood."

This time, I was sure he heard, but he ignored my request and pulled me against him, trapping me firmly between his body and the wall. The sharp edges of the door frame bit into my back.

"I need to go," I repeated, trying to shove him off me.

He flashed me a grin, one that didn't meet his cold gaze.

"You don't know what you need." The tone of his voice mirrored the hunger in his eyes.

My stomach sank, and I felt a familiar sensation wash over me—a warning. I planted both hands against his chest, putting every ounce of my shaky strength into the push. He stumbled back a few paces before lunging at me again. Before he could reach me, a blur slammed into his side and sent him flying into the far wall. Then it was me. I was on top of him and a guttural growl ripped from my lips. A shiver coursed down my spine at the sound, an unnerving excitement mingling with the fever rising within. I had an intense urge to clamp my jaw around his neck. The thought alone sent a thrill through me, but at the same time, it made me want to hurl.

He thrashed beneath me, and I stumbled back. I heard voices drifting up the stairs and quickly scrambled to my feet. Faces I didn't recognise stared wide-eyed and cowered as I shoved past them. My skin felt too tight and my heart beat out of my chest. I pushed through people lining the halls, sending drinks flying as I elbowed my way towards the exit.

I staggered out onto the street, vision blurry and one hand gripping the door frame. Fresh air mixed with smoke filled my lungs. My head snapped to the left, and I zeroed in on two guys smoking. One look from me and my wild eyes had them stamping out the stubs and heading back inside while eyeing me nervously.

My body was screaming at me to do something. I just didn't know what it wanted.

The hairs on my bare arms stood on end, a thin sheen of sweat coating my skin. I touched my forehead, and it felt like I had stuck my head in an oven. My feet were heavy and itchy at the same time. I began moving away from the house and broke into a jog. The tightness coiling within me wouldn't ease.

I heard my name ring out and picked up my pace. They called again, Kate's familiar voice piercing the inky night. I sped up until I was sprinting, refusing to turn around, and focused on the unsteady beat as I forced one foot in front of the other. I could smell her, a mix of heady perfume and sweat, hear her feet pounding the pavement echoing in the empty street. She was gaining on me.

"Leave me alone," I cried, trying to run faster, but the heel of one boot caught on the pavement and my ankle twisted. The edges of my vision were blurred and disjointed. My legs shook and refused to move faster, the only thing keeping me moving was the adrenaline coursing through my veins as it tried to take over.

"Eve," Kate whined, puffing out a long foggy breath as she fought to catch up with me. "Stop, you can't outrun me. What happened back there?"

Kate ran competitively for years before college. I hadn't, but for some reason I wasn't out of breath. I was panting for an entirely different reason as I struggled to keep control. Running in heels wasn't in my skillset and I didn't have time to kick my boots off. I tried to put some distance between us, but I felt a gentle hand grip my shoulder. A howl of frustration tore through me. I spun around to face my friend, nostrils flaring. She stumbled back from me, her hand flying to cover her mouth.

"What's going on?" Kate's voice shook, her eyes brimming with tears. "What did he give you?"

She reached out gingerly, as if trying to stroke a feral cat. I shot back, fighting with every ounce of inner strength I had not to snap at her. "Please, go away," I begged through grit teeth, my hands balled into fists so tightly that my knuckles had turned white.

"I can't leave you like this." Kate glanced around for help, concern etched into her delicate features.

But she couldn't help me. No one could. I had no control over this side of myself, my only recollection of shifting was disjointed dreams. I didn't understand it, but I could feel the pull.

As she craned her neck, I could hear more than see the artery pulsing. I felt like a vampire. I could pick up every little detail, a primed hunter, but I didn't want to drink her blood. I wanted to chase her through the streets and terrorise her until I slit her throat. A sickening feeling bubbled up from my core, begging to be let loose.

Kate refused to take the hint, stepping towards me every time I stepped back. The burning fire within me was slowly taking over. I could feel it spread through my limbs, a pulsing excitement eating away at my resolve. My nails cut into my palms, forcing me to uncurl my fists.

Kate's concerned gaze landed on my hands, and her expression turned to one of horror. All colour drained from her face. "Eve?" Her voice wavered as she stared at me in disbelief.

Claws extended from my nail bed. Just like ones I'd see on Ryan.

I wanted to beg Kate to leave, but the words wouldn't come to me. Energy rippled through my body as I stood frozen in place. I tried everything, counting, mentally pleading with my other side not to come out. But my control was slipping.

Kate took a nervous step towards me, despite me shaking my head like a rabid dog. She reached out to grab my arm, and something snapped. I felt myself lose control, catapulting over the edge with nothing to break my fall as I tumbled into the abyss.

She spun and ran like prey. That was the final straw.

I raced after her, snapping at her heels the closer I came to the change. Kate was fast, and I let her wind through the street and parked cars, keeping close enough to tail her but letting her think she had the upper hand. Then I lunged, slamming both of us to the ground. Her petite body hit the pavement first with a crunch that should have made me cry. Instead, an inhumane screech tore from my lips. I was still human, but my claws sliced her arms as Kate thrashed in my grip. I could feel the pull, the inner call that begged me to give in completely to the change.

I leaned into her neck and sniffed, breathing her scent in deeply. Her perfume made my nose wrinkle, but beneath that, the smell of sweat mixed with fear sent chills rippling through my spine. Kate was howling in terror, begging to be released. Her words fell on deaf ears. I threw my head back, running my tongue over my teeth. A bone in my arm popped. I knew what was coming, and the carnal side of me relished it.

A fresh scent behind me caught my attention too late. Before I could react, something knocked into my side, forcing me off my prey and sending me sprawling onto the road. I rolled onto all fours, crouched and ready to spring at a moment's notice. Kate was lying on the ground, her body completely still. She was either out cold or dead, and to my disgust, neither of those scenarios filled me with dread in that moment.

I looked up, expecting to see those soft brown eyes from the park, but it was Ryan's face I saw, his lips curled in a feral smirk.

CHAPTER 10

I must have blacked out again, because I came to in Ryan's bedroom with him stroking my back and murmuring softly in my ear to keep me calm. My stomach constricted as the memories rushed back, blurry but undeniably real. I sprung out of the bed and dashed into the en suite to empty my stomach into the toilet bowl. Besides locking the door before Ryan could move off the bed, I didn't move from the fetal position. My hair stuck to my cheeks, and my back was damp with sweat. The t-shirt I had been dressed in clung to my torso. The chequered black-and-white tiles of the bathroom were cool against my skin, a small comfort in my foreign surroundings.

Ryan's familiar voice drifted in, asking if I was okay. I ignored him, but he hovered outside the door, knocking incessantly.

"Leave me alone." I muttered, gritting my teeth to keep the bile down.

I heard a sigh, closely followed by another rap of his knuckles against the door.

"You can't stay in there forever."

I could and I would. The sound of another stream of vomit landing in the toilet gave him his answer.

"Eve?" Ryan tried to turn the handle. "You need to let me in."

"I can't." I squeezed my eyes shut, struggling to string words into a sentence. "Kate..."

The thought of my best friend had me doubled over in seconds. My body shook and tears streamed down my face, matted hair mottled with vomit clung to my cheeks and neck.

"She's alive."

Relief washed over me, followed by a wave of nausea. My hands shook as I gripped the toilet bowl and retched while simultaneously bursting into tears. Mounting fear and guilt overshadowed the tiny piece of relief I felt.

"Just let me in, and we can talk." Ryan gave the door a shove, and the frame rattled. "You need to calm down, you're making yourself ill. You shouldn't be dealing with this alone."

All I could see was the image of Kate covered in blood, her chest heaving as she fought to breathe, the tears rolling down her cheeks, and the sheer terror in her eyes when she had looked at me. The memory of her gaze going cold and glassy triggered a surge of bile in my throat.

"It's your fault, you could have stopped me. Someone should have stopped me." I said, though it came out more like a whine.

"I tried, and I got there before you went too far."

I was about to explain exactly why that was a lie when my stomach flipped again.

He retreated and silence hung in the air, only my ragged breathing and disturbed thoughts to keep me company. I don't know how long I stayed there, slouched on the floor with my head over the toilet until I was just dry heaving. Even then, every time the image of Kate lying prone on the ground, my stomach flipped all over again.

This was the hangover from hell and had nothing to do with vodka but everything to do with me attacking my best friend like a feral animal. That was the first time I remembered being close to my hybrid state. It was all far too real.

I curled up on the floor and locked my arms around my knees, chest heaving as sobs racked my body. Light footsteps echoed outside the bathroom. The latch wiggled for a moment before falling onto the tiles with a clang. Ryan peered around the door, a screwdriver clasped in his hand. I watched him from under my lashes, my cheeks wet.

Without a word, he walked over and produced a blanket from behind his back, wrapping it around my shoulders and scooping me into his arms in one smooth movement. He carried me back over to the bed.

I looked around, disorientated and dizzy. My gaze swept back to Ryan's face, his brow furrowed with concern. He watched me carefully, his mouth set in a thin line as he placed me down on the soft mattress.

"Help me fix this," I begged, my voice cracking as I choked on my tears.

He shushed me softly and brushed a damp strand of hair behind my ear. "All I have ever tried to do is help you, Eve."

I buried my face in the warmth of his chest, a constant stream of tears rolling down my cheeks. "I need to learn how to control this. I can't... I can't do that again." I coughed, squeezing him tighter to me. "I'm a monster."

"No one will remember what happened. Kate is in hospital, but the doctors say she will be fine. I made sure of it." Ryan said, not delving into any further explanation.

I wasn't in any state to press him further, and I wasn't sure I even wanted to know what that meant. The thought of Kate hurt because of me made my stomach churn. I wanted to be with her, but I was the last thing she needed. I was the reason she was hurt.

Ryan wrapped his arms around me, holding me against him as his fingers traced up and down my spine. It reminded me of things I wanted nothing more than to forget.

"If you join my pack, I can teach you control so this doesn't happen again," Ryan murmured, nuzzling the top of my head. "I'll be there every step of the way."

"Once I learn control, can I go home?" I hiccoughed, curling into a tight ball in his arms.

"It depends on how things go. You might be safer living close to the pack where there's more space."

"You live here though. We'll be coming back, right?" Panic rose in my voice a bit. I didn't want to leave my friends behind. I wanted a life with Ryan, in the city.

"It's not that simple, Eve." He sighed, pushing a strand of hair behind my ear. "You need a pack, it's dangerous to go rogue—especially if you're a hybrid. Some pack members live in the city or scattered around the country, but the majority live in the pack estate. It's not that far anyway, just south of the city."

"I want to live here with you and my friends. I don't want everything to change."

"You can go back to college in September or take a year out. It depends on how things pan out." Ryan said and took my hand, giving it a gentle squeeze. "Working in a bar isn't good for you right now. It's dangerous being around so many people in that kind of environment. I'll take care of things."

"I don't like this," I said, surprising both of us with my honesty. "I don't want to be some kept woman."

He shook his head. "It's not like that, you can move about freely, and once you settle in, we can figure something out, I promise. For now, let's just focus on getting through the summer."

I linked my fingers with his, fighting back tears. It felt like I was backed into a corner with no choice.

"You can't hide from this Eve. You need a pack. All wolves need one." Ryan held a finger up to silence my protests, shifting closer to me on the bed. "Joining the pack isn't immediate, you need to get to know the pack and our way of life. So, any decision you make today isn't binding."

Despite his promises, I felt like I was signing my life away.

"If you don't learn control, you will have another accident. It's only a matter of time, and I won't always be there to stop you."

That image of Kate lying deathly still swam in my mind. I knew deep down that if Ryan hadn't stepped in, she would be dead, and it would have been my fault. I never wanted to attack someone like that again.

"If I agree to meet the pack, I am not agreeing to join," I said, eyeing Ryan cautiously.

"Of course, but you do need to learn control and take this seriously."

My throat tightened, and I bit back tears. "I'll do it."

Ryan smiled, planting a gentle kiss on my lips as he tucked the blanket tighter around me. Cradling me against his chest, he began gently rocking back and forth. Eventually, my eyelids fluttered closed. For the rest of the day, I slipped in and out of broken sleep fraught with nightmares. Each time I woke up, I cried fresh tears. Ryan never once left my side.

CHAPTER 11

Later that week, I found myself in Ryan's car, the boot overflowing with packed bags as if we were off on a holiday. The sun was shining, Ryan had his sunglasses on and was cruising along the road. He rang ahead to tell his parents we were coming but only after being badgered into it. I wasn't comfortable being a surprise. I'd had enough of those.

"Will you please relax?" Ryan asked, reaching out and placing his hand on my knee to stop it bouncing. "You're driving me mad with your twitching."

I sighed, leaning my elbow on the window. "I'm sorry, I'm just nervous."

"Don't be," He said, giving my leg a comforting pat. "I love you, so my parents are bound to."

"Tell me about them again?"

I couldn't sit still, let alone stay quiet.

Ryan chuckled, and I swatted his shoulder, slumping against my seat with my arms crossed. He kept his eyes on the road, laughing at my sour expression.

"Please, Ryan. Just tell me about the pack again?"

"Fine, if it will put a smile back on your face." Ryan relented, placing both hands back on the steering wheel. "The Faolchúnna pack is one of four Irish werewolf packs, the original pack in fact. There's another up north, one in the west and well..." He paused, his eyes narrowing briefly as his tone cooled. "You know the Crescent pack story already."

I only knew the snippets Ryan had told me, but I nodded, not wanting to bring up Luke or start another argument.

"We settled in South Dublin so we could roam the mountains freely. I grew up here with my family and other pack members. My mother, Rebecca, is going to love you." He paused for a moment, his mouth working as if he were battling in his mind about whether to continue. When he did, the words spilled out in one verbal information dump, his tone monotone and detached. "My brother, Jake, drowned when we were kids. Never mention him in front of my father."

I wanted to say something about his brother, but I was at a loss for words. This wasn't the first time Ryan had alluded to having one. He had mentioned Jake once or twice before, but never went into details. Now was definitely not the time to push it.

"My father is the alpha. He's responsible for all pack members and business." Ryan began tapping his thumb on the wheel, his voice warming again and swelling with pride at the mention of his father. "He was away a lot when we were growing up. Damien is by far one of the best alphas we have had in centuries, and I hope to succeed him."

"They sound nice," I offered, not sure his descriptions were doing much to ease my nerves.

He flashed a smile towards me which faltered briefly at my glum expression before being reinstated. "You'll like them, Eve, and they will like you. They know how important you are."

"It's not about liking them, Ryan. I'm turning up on their doorstep like some kind of stray, begging to be taken in."

I wasn't sure if he had ever met any previous girlfriend's parents. He seemed completely oblivious to how awkward it would be. Part of me thought to ask, but he got so prickly whenever I mentioned any ex that I decided against it. Plus, I didn't want to imagine him with another girl, never mind hear about it.

"They knew I would ask you to join the pack. I asked their permission the moment I fell in love with you."

I cocked my head, arching an eyebrow. "Which was when exactly?"

Ryan kept his eyes locked firmly on the winding country road ahead of us. I could see the corner of his mouth twitch as he smirked.

"You're no fun," I whined. Despite my teasing, I didn't succeed in coaxing a proper answer from him.

"I am *plenty* of fun," he quipped, flashing me a cheeky wink and a lopsided grin before turning his attention back to the road.

I wanted to argue, but my nerves had abolished any witty comebacks that would usually come to mind. Instead, I gave up and stared out the window until we reached our destination. The afternoon sun was still high in the sky when we turned onto a country lane littered with blind turns. It was too narrow for two cars to pass and seemed to wound endlessly through the landscape. Tall trees and a ditch marked the edges. My stomach flipped, and I sank into the passenger seat. While the countryside was beautiful in full bloom, I much preferred the city streets I was used to when it came to driving. Thankfully, Ryan seemed completely at ease racing through the sharp bends.

He slowed the car as two tall pillars came into view, marking an obscured driveway. Intricately carved stone statues in the shape of wolves topped each pillar, their eyes appearing to follow us as the car passed.

"We're here."

Lined with oak trees and surrounded by fields full of various livestock, the driveway took us on a winding path until it widened to present a massive, sprawling house. Large stone steps led up to the main doors adorned with plants and hanging baskets. Wild ivy in a mix of purple and green covered the exterior stonework of the building. It was truly magnificent.

Ryan parked in front of the house, his expensive Audi perfectly at home next to an equally showy Mercedes. To either side of the main house were other buildings in the same grand style.

I began counting the windows but only made it to eight before Ryan appeared on the passenger side and held a hand out to me. As if on cue, the front door burst open the moment I placed one foot onto the gravelled surface.

"Ryan, darling!"

A stout woman came running down the front steps, arms outstretched. She had the same hair as Ryan, dark brown curls that were almost black bouncing as she ran. Ryan's mother was like a peculiar cross between Mrs. Weasley and Carrie Bradshaw, dressed in a strange combination of a white blouse, matching trousers, and then a bright pink apron which threw the entire outfit off.

They shared the same striking blue eyes, but apart from the dark curls, that's where the similarities ended.

Ryan turned and stepped into his mother's embrace. She was immaculately put together, but not the posh housewife I had expected. As she came closer, I could see stains on the apron and a small chocolate handprint just above the knee of her sharp white trousers. She was smaller than Ryan and the apron bunched over her stomach slightly, yet she moved with the grace and confidence of a leggy supermodel.

I had completely zoned out when I heard my name creep into conversation.

"And this must be Eve." Ryan's mother released him from the hug, stepping back and giving him a proud pat on the shoulders before turning to me. "Welcome to the pack, dear."

"I—"

"This is my mother, Rebecca," Ryan chimed in with the introductions, redeeming himself quickly after one look at my sour expression. "With regards to the pack, Eve is taking things one step at a time."

Slow, small, very baby-sized steps.

His mother smiled, her cheeks dimpling. Her gaze lingered, settling on the bags under my eyes.

"Lovely to meet you."

She stepped up and pulled me into a tight hug, her head coming to just above my shoulders. "Don't worry, love," she whispered, picking up on my uncertainty. "You will settle in soon enough."

I nodded, doing my best to stay calm, and decided that saying nothing was the best option for now.

His mother pulled away, still smiling as she brushed her spotless apron down.

"Where is father?" Ryan asked.

I followed his gaze towards the farthest window to the right of the top floor, wondering if it was an office. But noting the many floors and trying to count the number of rooms soon had me occupied. The building was beautiful, an old country estate house kept in pristine condition. The white-washed door and window frames added a pop of colour and complimented the ivy tapestry.

Ryan's mother waved a dismissive, well-manicured hand. "He is busy with the business, you know him." She tugged him towards the house. "He will join us for dinner. I made him promise to take the night off," she added, noticing the crestfallen look on Ryan's face.

I hovered awkwardly to one side.

"Come on, dear, let's give you the grand tour." Ryan's mother strode into the house with her arm linked in his, motioning for me to follow. She led the way up the steps and into a large foyer furnished with rich oak floorboards and a wide sweeping staircase as the centrepiece. The stairs split off to either side of the house, giving access to both wings. An enormous but tasteful chandelier hung from the ceiling peaked with large wooden beams. The walls were painted white like Rebecca's suit, a sharp contrast to the dark timber.

I was getting a cramp in my neck from staring. The landing was empty, but I could hear voices carrying from the back of the mansion and the distinct clang of dishes coming from another side. There was no doubt that a house like this needed staff.

She led us down a corridor to the left which opened out into a kitchen. A group of women bustled from one station to the next. Each counter was made of polished marble and equipped with every cooking appliance you could name. While they whirled around, there was an order to the chaos. Clearly the head of the kitchen, a small, round woman with grey hair scraped back into a haphazard bun barked orders.

"This is the kitchen," Ryan's mother said, stating the obvious.

I stepped to the side to avoid a girl whizzing past with a pie balanced precariously in one hand and a platter in the other. "It's magnificent."

Ryan nodded in agreement, feeling obliged to explain what his mother didn't. "We share the duties between pack members. If there is a big event on, we call in caterers, but for the most part, we cook for ourselves."

I glanced around the kitchen, my nose scrunching as I sniffed. The entire house smelled of what I now recognised to be werewolves. It felt overwhelming to be surrounded by so many in one place.

Ryan turned to the woman I identified as the head chef. "Isn't that right, Mary?"

Mary looked up from the dessert she was inspecting, pushing a stray strand of hair from her eyes. I noticed a deep scar running down her right cheek. It was an old wound, long healed, and blended into the creases of her laughter lines.

"Indeed, it is." She looked between the three of us, her gaze lingering on me and her eyes creasing. "Nice of you to pop home, Ryan. Your mother has been missing you."

I chewed my lip, looking anywhere but at her scar. It was rude to stare. Mary seemed like a lovely woman, emanating warmth, but something about her words stuck in the pit of my stomach.

"I was waiting until the right time to introduce Eve to the pack."

Mary shooed a willowy blonde girl away without so much as a glance. "I suppose that's some sort of excuse. It's lovely to finally meet you, Eve." She smiled and turned to Ryan's mother. "Dinner will be ready for six, Rebecca."

Ryan nudged me through the kitchen, leaving his mother and Mary to discuss preparations. As we meandered past the counters, we passed a large oak dining table that didn't quite fit in with the flawless decor.

He followed my gaze and tapped the table affectionately. "My mother did up the main house a few years ago, but this table has been here for centuries. In the old days, we used to hold Pack meetings around it. We didn't want to part with it, so I convinced her to keep it as a dinner table." The tabletop was worn with scratches and grooves dotting the surface, but it had a homely feel about it.

I spun out of the way of a young girl carrying a tray of cupcakes. She was taller than me with kind eyes and mousey brown hair that tumbled past her shoulders. The girl smiled in thanks, her freckled cheeks dimpling.

A stretch of sizeable garden and a patio laden with flowerpots popping in colour was visible beyond the kitchen. Ryan led me towards a set of double doors that would lead us outside.

"Ryan! Come bring Eve to your room, so you can both get ready for this evening." Rebecca's voice rang through the kitchen. "I have some things to attend to before the meal."

He took my hand, and we exited through a different door to the one we entered through. I was already lost. I let Ryan lead the way, too busy marvelling at the art hanging on every wall and the tasteful furnishings. His mother definitely had an eye for decorating.

Taking me up the left-hand side of the staircase, Ryan guided me to the landing and paused there to explain the layout. I stared at the chandelier hanging above the staircase, my thoughts elsewhere.

"My father's office is the last room in the right wing. You'll be staying in my room in the left wing."

I wasn't entirely sure what hid behind the doors lining the corridor we walked down, but I found it hard to believe that they were empty for the most part and only used for guests. That would be such a waste.

"What are the other rooms for?"

"There's a library full of pack history books and records, and I have an office too," Ryan said, chuckling as my eyes lit up.

"Is it just your pack history?"

"Mostly, but there're all sorts of stuff in there, even stuff from the US packs."

I felt a surge of something I'd long kept buried—hope.

"Do you think I'd find something about my parents?" I asked, a nervous chill rising up my spine as I voiced my thoughts.

"I'm not sure. We have tonnes of older records, who knows what's in there," he said with a shrug, changing the topic when my smile crumpled. "Lots of pack members used to live in here before we extended the estate. We get visitors most weeks, and my mother has converted a few for hobbies. I think she hoped that Jake and I would fill the house with grandchildren."

Well, she better not be counting on me. I bit my tongue. Bad-mouthing his mother before dinner wasn't the best idea. Plus, we all had sensitive hearing and although his mother seemed nice, I didn't want to test her bad side.

Ryan's room was halfway down the west wing. The door to his room stood out from the others, the wood stained a dark brown to match the original support beams of the house.

He noticed my eyebrow quirk. "I don't share my mother's obsession with white," he explained, rummaging in his pocket and producing a key.

Ryan unlocked the door which swung open to reveal a room very different to the little hideout. The room was minimalistic like Ryan's apartment and tastefully decorated, but with mauves and cream rather than flashy white. The floorboards matched those in the foyer. I felt a giddy rush as I spotted his bed. Against the right wall stood a four-poster bed complete with netting looped around the posts. It was like a child's fantasy fairy bed but much more tasteful. The wooden headboard and base of the bed were decorated with intricate carvings, some drawings of wolves, and words etched in Latin. There was an en suite to the left, whitewashed to his mother's taste. The outer wall was almost entirely taken up by a large window and a glass door which opened out onto a balcony.

The décor was a bit too extravagant for my taste. I also wasn't too sure about being in the same room. I knew we were still a couple, but we had stuff to work on, and I didn't know how well my resolve would fair when we were sharing a bed.

My face must have been a picture because Ryan's chuckling snapped me out of my trance.

"You like?" His tone softened, and he spun me into his arms, pressing his lips to mine before I needed to lie. "It's all ours."

CHAPTER 12

Ryan wasn't too impressed when he emerged from the shower to see me in jeans and the nicest top I could find. He was in a suit and I was most certainly underdressed. He'd told me it was 'dressy', but guys didn't know what that meant, and I hadn't exactly packed evening wear.

"Now who is making us late?" I asked, half teasing but also growing more nervous with every passing minute.

"Sorry, sorry," he muttered, fumbling with the last button on the crisp white shirt hugging his chest.

Once he was ready, Ryan led the way down the elaborate staircase. Ever the gentleman, he held my hand as if I might go flying in my non-existent heels.

"Well, well, well. Aren't you going to introduce me to your new *friend*, Ryan?"

I turned to see a redhead with porcelain skin and too much cleavage on show. She was a natural beauty, heightened by expertly applied makeup, but she gave off a distinct air of bitchiness. Her red-painted lips parted in a twisted snarl as she looked me over.

"Eve, this is Nadine, one of our pack members," Ryan said, sliding a protective arm around my waist.

"Lovely to meet you." Nadine fixed a too-wide smile on her face, inclining her head politely in my direction before reaching out to place a delicate hand on Ryan's bicep, pulling him towards her. "Shall I join you for dinner?"

"That won't be necessary, it's just a small dinner to welcome Eve," he said, prying his arm free and pressed my lower back, guiding me away from the staircase.

Nadine nodded curtly, her tone cooling. "I'll see you later then."

What the hell was that all about?

Before I could get a word in, Ryan pressed his hand to the small of my back and steered me towards the back of the house. He rapped lightly on a door before escorting me inside. I glanced over my shoulder to see Nadine stalking in the opposite direction, her fingers curled into fists by her side. I'd be asking him about her later.

The dining room was larger than I had expected. A lesson I really should have learned by now––Ryan's family clearly didn't do things by halves. The room was long rather than wide, with a grand dining table that could seat well over twelve people if necessary. There was space at either end of the room to mingle as well as other small tables in the far corner.

Each table place was set, but only three of the seats were occupied. Ryan's mother sat at the far corner of the table opposite a man I didn't recognise. His raven black hair was thinning around the edges and no doubt flecked with grey when it wasn't dyed. The man's gaze drifted to me, his eyes hard and cold. He showed little to no resemblance to either Ryan or his mother.

My eyes were drawn to the head of the table where a tall man in a sharp grey business suit sat, his broad shoulders drawn back. His black hair looked more natural and kept than the other man's, cut short and showing little signs of ageing. He shared his son's chiselled cheekbones and handsome features, though his expression was harder. The way he held himself, even sitting, radiated confidence and status, though I did notice small lines around his eyes and forehead giving away the strain of his role. He was everything you would expect an alpha to be.

"This is Eve," Ryan finally said, breaking the silence while guiding me over to the empty place set beside his mother.

He pulled the chair out and I gingerly took the seat. Rebecca flashed me a blinding smile and gave my arm a gentle squeeze. "You look lovely, darling."

I thought back to how Kate always said it's better to be over-dressed and I never agreed until that moment.

She had the same posh lilt to her accent as Ryan, but I could hear the smallest hint of a country twang. I filed that detail away to ask Ryan about later.

"Thank you, Rebecca."

The alpha inclined his head in acknowledgement, but neither he nor the strange man said a word.

I laced my fingers in my lap, fighting the urge to fidget as the silence lingered. Behind them, a large black iron fireplace crackled, the centrepiece of that end of the room making it feel almost cosy. *Almost.*

Ryan walked to the other side of the table, pausing by his father's chair as if he wanted to address him. He shook his head and continued to the seat facing me.

"Eve," Ryan said, my head snapping up at the mention of my name. "This is my uncle, Nicholas."

His uncle sighed, his eyes narrowing into slits as he watched Ryan take a seat. "Nick, no one calls me Nicholas."

"I would never introduce you with your nickname, that would be inappropriate," Ryan taunted, keeping his tone polite but icy. He reached for a jug of water and began pouring himself a drink, and then one for everyone at the table except Nick. "As the alpha's son, it is my responsibility to introduce pack members correctly."

Nick visibly stiffened. Ryan's father looked between the two, mild amusement sparking in his eyes. "Now boys, behave. We have a guest." The alpha's eyes drifted to mine, intense and unwavering. I struggled to hold his gaze.

Something about Ryan's father felt odd, unlike any other werewolf I had ever met. It wasn't a pull—I didn't find myself drawn to him as an alpha like in the movies—but it was as if I could sense something different, a latent power of sorts.

"Then tell your son to grow up," Nick huffed, swiping the jug to pour himself a drink. He didn't appreciate the slight, and I got the distinct impression that Ryan and his uncle didn't get along. Ryan had mentioned his uncle a handful of times with little affection, but it was obvious that they were always at odds with one another. Right then, they were bickering like brothers.

Ryan growled, and was no doubt about to respond with his own witty insult when his father stepped in.

"I said, that's enough." The alpha snapped, placing a heavy emphasis on each word.

His voice had an air of dominance about it, dripping in disapproval and annoyance at their behaviour. I doubted he ever had to raise it. Both men bowed their heads in apology. They still glared at one another, swapping trading insults for dirty looks instead.

I looked at Ryan's mother, wondering if she would ever step in. She appeared unperturbed by the little spat, as if she had seen it all before. I realised I was gripping the table slightly and re-entwined my hands in my lap. The air in the dining room felt heavy.

"How is the business, father?"

I was grateful that Ryan broke the silence, and even more so when his father gave a proper answer and the two entered a discussion about trading. His uncle got involved in the conversation, much to Ryan's chagrin. I made out something about property in London and taxes but soon grew bored.

To my side Rebecca seemed completely disinterested in the conversation topic, even a little annoyed that they were discussing business at the table.

I took a deep breath. "When did you redecorate the building? It's beautiful."

Rebecca stopped drumming her fingers on the table and turned to me. "Why thank you, darling." Her face lit up, and I knew I had chosen a safe, comfortable topic. "It must be almost twenty years ago now, after the pack split..."

She began telling me about the need for a change and her excitement when Ryan's father had tasked her with revamping the place. I placed my chin on my hand and listened intently, not to the parts about the colour scheme or types of wood, but the little things she let slip about the pack. How Ryan's father had been furious when the Crescent wolves broke away and that he had wanted to make his mark, a statement. She spoke fondly of her husband, her voice full of admiration for him as both a man and an alpha. I filed all the information away for later. Ryan's mother was much more open about their history than her son had been. No doubt her lips would loosen further after a few glasses of wine.

The dining-room door opened, interrupting both parties. The nice girl I had seen earlier in the kitchens and two others brought in trays of aperitifs, setting them down in the centre of the table. I thought they might join us, but they left immediately.

I was about to reach for smoked salmon, my favourite starter, when I caught Ryan's eye. He gave a slight shake of his head, and I dropped my hands back in my lap. No one else seemed to notice. They all waited until Ryan's father had made his choice and started filling his plate. Once he finished, Ryan and Nick did the same. When they were done, Rebecca set about filling her plate and Ryan gave me a little nod to follow suit.

It appeared there was a pecking order.

The main course soon followed, and they repeated the same protocol. Alpha first, then Ryan and Nick, women last. A threat of tension hung between Ryan and his uncle as they tucked into their food. When Ryan had told me about the hierarchal order, I had wrongly presumed it only applied to when we were in our wolf forms. I had never expected it to extend to normal meals.

It was a constant reminder that I was at the bottom of their hierarchy, an outsider.

Now and then, I felt Ryan nudge my foot under the table and catch my eye to check if I was all right. For the most part, I talked to his mother, while the men discussed business and other pack concerns.

We were waiting for dessert when Ryan's father finally addressed me directly. "So, you want to join our pack?" He pinned me with that intense stare of his. The conversation about spring flowers with Rebecca that I'd been faking my side of died. I knew I couldn't fake anything around the alpha.

My eyes widened as I struggled to come up with an answer. His question had caught me completely off guard. I looked to Ryan for support, but he refused to step in, giving a minute shake of his head. Though I could feel him silently willing me to come up with an answer. His father watched me for a moment, and I got the distinct impression that he expected even the smallest of replies.

"I-I'm still thinking about it. This is all very new to me."

The knot in my stomach tightened.

The alpha tilted his head to one side, his stoic expression unnerving. "Why the hesitation?"

"Ryan said a wolf needs a pack," I began, choosing my words carefully as I squirmed with unease under the weight of his gaze. I knew fear wasn't a reason that would go down well. Being out of control wouldn't be an acceptable answer either, so I made one up. "He has told me so much about your pack, the history and your achievements as alpha. I don't believe joining a pack is a decision to be taken lightly."

Nick snorted, and I heard the dull thud of a kick under the table. He winced, his lips setting in a thin line. I wrung my hands under the tablecloth, my palms stinging at the bite of my nails as I clenched my fists and tried to wrangle control of my nerves.

"Finding out that I'm a hybrid, it's a lot to take in. It would be stupid for me to rush into making any big decisions without giving my options careful consideration."

I looked to Ryan, hoping my answer was acceptable, but he was watching his father.

The alpha sat back in his chair, placing his hands together under his chin as he reflected on my answer. His cool expression gave nothing away. "You want our protection while you *consider* your *options*?"

Fuck. Guess that was the wrong answer.

I hesitated, glancing at Ryan for some kind of hint. His face remained passive. "Yes," I said, my voice coming out far more confident than I felt. "I want—I need to learn control."

Nick began to growl but turned it into a cough as Ryan's mother shot him a look before beaming in my direction. The alpha studied me intently.

"Well then." His father clapped, flashing an uncharacteristic toothy smile and placed his palms flat on the table. "It's a full moon and the pack will hunt tonight in celebration of the summer solstice. You must join us."

Tonight?

The blood drained from my face. Ryan paled and opened his mouth to argue, but one look from his father and Ryan's mouth snapped shut.

Shit.

After the invitation, I struggled to stomach my dessert. I forced myself to nod and smile at Rebecca's ramblings until Ryan finally excused us. My vision swam, ears ringing as terror took hold. With each step my chest tightened, and I struggled for air. I was having a full-blown panic attack, but Ryan didn't stop walking, his grip firm on my hand as he led us back up the stairs to his room.

Once we were safely inside, I spun to face Ryan. "Tonight?" I shrieked, placing a hand on my chest as I tried to force myself to take a deep breath.

"I thought you might get a day or two to adjust, but it's the solstice this week, so the pack spends the full moon weekend celebrating. It's important that you run with the pack, if you're even considering joining..." Ryan looked stricken as he explained, but that didn't stop my temper from flaring.

He had promised this was on my terms, and this was anything but. My heart thundered, my face a picture of pure terror as I stared at him. He knew I wasn't ready. But what choice did I have? I had to be ready.

"I'm going to try to talk my father around, stay right here," Ryan said, giving my shoulders a squeeze. His normal cool demeanour was frazzled, and panic shone in his eyes. "I'll be right back."

"Ry—" I began, but Ryan cut across me and kissed my cheek.

"I'll fix this," he promised, striding out of the room before I could protest.

Being alone was the last thing I needed. Flashbacks of the night I woke up in the park and of the night I attacked Kate resurfaced and refused to leave the forefront of my mind. A familiar sense of alarm surged at the thought of having to shift. I had no control over it. What if I couldn't make the change? Not only that, but the thought of being surrounded by werewolves wasn't something I was ready to deal with. When I had agreed to come to stay with the pack, I was thinking baby steps, not throwing myself off a cliff.

When pacing the room stopped working, I sank onto the bed, palming my chest and talking to myself in an attempt to subside an oncoming panic attack. At the sound of the lock clicking open, my head snapped up. For a split second I thought it was Ryan and relief surged, but it was short-lived. It wasn't Ryan.

Nick stood in the doorway with two wine glasses on a marble serving tray, his broad shoulders taking up most of the door frame.

A Cheshire smile lit up his face as our eyes met. "Eve, the alpha sent me up with something to settle your nerves before the run."

"Where's Ryan?" I asked, eyeing him cautiously. Everything about the man gave me the heebie-jeebies.

"He won't be long." Nick waved his hand dismissively, setting the tray down on top of the chest of drawers before carrying both glasses over and joining me on the bed.

I attempted to subtly scoot sideways to widen the gap between us. Nick's lips thinned as he handed me a glass.

"There's nothing to worry about. We go for a pack run every full moon. It's a great way to meet everyone, and you don't have to be a part of the pack. We invite guests from time to time." Nick sipped his wine, staining his lips red. "I know many of us are interested to have a hybrid join the hunt."

"Hunt?"

There it was again. *Hunt what? Deer? Foxes?*

"Yes, we are wolves, after all."

I nodded, trying not to give away the guessing game going on in my head, resolving to ask Ryan once he got back. I didn't want him to find out that I couldn't control my shift, I could only hope that the collective magic of the pack would make it easier. This was going to be disaster.

"I must go help the alpha," he said, the mattress squeaking as he rose to his feet and strode towards the door. Before he disappeared from view, he threw one last glance over his shoulder that sent chills down my spine. "When we all run as one pack under the full moon, it's truly magical. The alpha wants us all downstairs in ten minutes."

I shuddered, tiptoeing over to the door and peeking into the hallway to make sure he was gone. When I strained my senses to hear, all I could pick up was the distant echoes of Nick's footsteps and my hammering heart. Once I knew the coast was clear, I released a breath I didn't even know I was holding and closed the door.

Sinking back onto the bed, I clutched the wineglass in my hand and sniffed the contents. It smelled of rich red wine and maybe a little spice. Rolling my eyes at myself, I took a sip of the wine and sighed as the liquid burned the back of my throat. Maybe Nick was a creep, but he was right, I did need something to take the edge off.

CHAPTER 13

I was sitting on the bed with my legs crossed, a little bit calmer thanks to the wine, when Ryan came back into the room, his eyes downcast. It took one look at his face, at the tension in his jaw and the set of his shoulders to know that his father was still insisting that I join the hunt.

"Going on this hunt doesn't mean you have to join the pack," Ryan said, as if reading my thoughts. "You can still walk away from this."

From us.

The unspoken words made a lump rise in my throat.

Ryan gave my hand a squeeze, his palm clammy. "I'd love to give you more time, I know this is a lot all in one go. It's not the way I wanted things to go."

Kate's image resurfaced in my mind along with the fear I'd felt the night I attacked her. I never wanted to be out of control again. The thought of turning with an audience made me sick, but the chance of seriously injuring someone I cared about felt worse. At least with Ryan and his pack, I would be safe.

I nodded, slowly rising to my feet, feeling like a deer on ice. "I'll do it."

He pulled me flush against his chest, his lips crushing against mine in a feverish kiss that did nothing to settle my nerves.

Ryan briefly explained the order of events before we left his room. It was some sort of ceremonial run for the Summer Solstice that took place in the mountain woodland. I was a taut bundle of fear and nerves, and the only thing keeping me from bolting was my grip on Ryan's hand.

He led me out of the house and down the front steps. The hard stone was cool under my feet. I'd decided to spare the heels I was wearing, shoes and socks seemed pointless if we were going to shift. It was dark outside, and the full moon hung high in the sky, casting a soft glow over the buildings. Ryan's parents, along with his uncle and some pack members I did not recognise, stood by the large water feature in the centre of the driveway. They all wore black as if attending a funeral.

Small goose bumps rose on my skin against the night breeze. Only his mother looked remotely pleased to see me. The rest watched with an excitement that sent a chill through my spine.

I took a deep, shaky breath and wrung my hands. Ryan pulled a black handkerchief emblazoned with the pack crest, a wolf's head in one corner, from his pocket. He stepped behind me and slid it over my eyes, tying it at the back. Everything went dark.

The blindfold wasn't a surprise. What followed was.

They bound my hands. This time the touch was gentle, careful. I assumed it was Ryan again. Part of me wanted to punch him for not telling me about this part. But he had told me I needed to be strong and show no fear, so I rolled my shoulders back and resolved to do just that. Then I remembered him saying shifting would shred clothes. Wiggling my fingers and twisting my wrist, I touched a piece of the material binding me. Silk. I breathed a sigh of relief.

A hand pressed to the small of my back, gently nudging me forward. When I didn't move fast enough, the pressure increased until I began walking. At first, the gravel was sharp under my bare feet and I winced, but soon I felt the welcome coolness of grass blades between my toes. With no spatial awareness and no clue where we were going, I had no choice but to trust the person leading me. I hoped it was Ryan, even if I was furious at him for not mentioning that I would be *bound* as well as blindfolded. I wanted to ask for reassurance, but I could hear his parents talking in hushed tones nearby as we walked. I heard other voices, too, ones I didn't recognise. Their words were far from kind.

After some time, I felt small twigs under my feet. Soon after, an arm gripped my bound wrists and pulled me to a halt.

A chill began seeping into my bones and not just from the cloudless night. The knot in my gut was somersaulting like a circus performer. I resisted the urge to talk to Ryan. I could smell him behind me, and I hated him for staying silent. No one spoke to me. I threw my senses out and heard various unfamiliar voices murmuring with excitement. *Mongrel... Get what she deserves... Son is a joke...* My heart thundered. I stopped trying to listen and resolved to block the background noise.

"Welcome, my brothers and sisters, to the opening of the summer solstice celebrations." A voice I recognised as the alpha's rang out crisp and clear. All whispered conversations came to an abrupt halt. "Tonight, we begin with the first hunt in the lead up to the solstice moon."

I rolled my shoulders, stiff and uncomfortable from the way my wrists were bound behind my back. I started pulling at the bindings in what I thought was a subtle way but soon received a stinging slap to my palm. It took all my willpower not to make a sound. That didn't feel like Ryan. There was something distinctly feminine about the rebuttal.

What the fuck?

Before I could get a word out, the alpha's voice boomed again.

"Tonight, we will celebrate what makes this pack the strongest in Ireland. We are formidable, fortified by strong family bonds lasting centuries. We bow to no one. Loyalty is the glue that binds us. Without that, a pack is nothing. Without his pack, an alpha is but a figurehead. But you, my family, have stood by me for many years now and shown your unwavering support."

A few whoops came from the crowd along with murmurs of agreement. I could feel them growing restless. Feet shuffled and heartbeats thrummed with excitement at the alpha's rousing speech.

"I know there has been much unrest over the last few years. Despite cutting out poisonous roots, we have some brothers who lost their way, whose loyalties strayed. But they are naïve and mistaken." At the mention of betrayal, growls ripped through the pack. Ryan's father paused for a moment, letting the werewolves rile themselves up. "There is only one pack who has lived on this land for as long as time. I promise I will continue to fight for this pack and ensure that werewolves, the superior race, have a bright future."

I couldn't see his father's face, or those of other pack members, but I could almost feel their crazed smiles. It was clear why Ryan's father was alpha—he commanded respect and obedience. What made my stomach lurch was the similarity between his speech and those that I had read in my history lessons about war and dictatorships.

"On this night, we celebrate what makes the Faolchúnna pack so special. A show of our strength and refusal to shake traditions, for tradition made us who we are, who we will always be. Nobody can rival us. I promise I have so much to show you in the coming months, plans to ensure that the entire world knows that we are not to be trifled with."

A hand tightened around my wrists and shoved me forward. Twigs and stones ripped the soles of my feet. I bit my lip, stumbling in the direction they pushed me.

"Tonight, we have a special guest." The alpha's voice was right beside me then. I felt his bony hand grip my shoulder like I was a bold pup. "She shall be our summer offering and lead the hunt under this glorious full moon."

I stiffened, the blood that had been previously rushing to my cheeks now completely draining from my face.

"Father, you s—" Ryan began, but he was cut off before he could finish.

At the sound of another slap, I whipped my head in his direction, panic surging.

"Are we ready to begin the hunt?" Ryan's father asked the pack, his voice rising. Roars rang out from the crowd as they reached fever pitch. Growls ripped through the pack, and my spine tingled. They were all shifting. My blood ran cold.

I tried to shift too, but where I normally felt a fire inside, there was nothing. I searched for the magic, the pull, but all I felt was a lingering residue that was just out of my reach. While I had pretended to be strong until this point, when I realised I couldn't shift, all pretence went to shreds. My hands shook more with every passing moment and a bead of sweat ran down my back.

"Ryan?" I turned my head, squinting as if it would help me see, desperately searching with my senses but he was farther away now. I kept calling for him over the wolves howling with excitement. Tears pricked my eyes, soaked up by the blindfold to save me the embarrassment of them streaming down my face. Ryan wasn't coming.

"Let the hunt begin!" Before I had a chance to prepare, rough hands shoved me forward and this time there was no hand at my back to guide me. I didn't need another push, every bone in my body screamed *run*.

So, I ran, putting one foot in front of the other as I bolted blindly into the forest. Despite being unable to shift, I still ran faster than before, but I was no match for a wolf pack on my tail. My feet throbbed, my mind racing as I stumbled through the undergrowth.

For the first while, I heard nothing but the frantic beat of my heart in my ears and my rasping breaths. No one was following me. As I slowed, a howl pierced the night. Gut instinct told me that was the whistle and that the game was only just beginning.

I tripped and fell, my chest and shoulders scraping against the forest floor. I felt a sharp stone digging into my leg as I struggled to my knees. The pack roared in the distance, but I paused, shuffling around until I could grip the stone in my right hand. I began slicing at the silk binding my hands, cutting my wrists in the process as I hacked at the restraints. My palms were slick, and the stone slipped too many times, but eventually I felt the silk give way. I tore my wrists free and ripped my blindfold off. I had seconds to take in my surroundings before I scrambled to my feet and ran.

The forest was pitch black, but one thing I hadn't lost was my ability to see in the dark. Not that it helped much. I had no idea where I was, I couldn't hide from werewolves. I pushed on, my feet numb as the forest floor ripped through them. At least now I could swat away branches and jump over fallen logs before they tripped me. Maybe I had a chance with the lead they had given me. *Was it a kindness from the alpha or an opportunity to prolong my suffering?*

Howls came from two different directions. The pack must have split up. I continued running blindly in the same direction until I came to a stream, skidding to a halt. But I stopped too late, the riverbank giving way under my weight. I slipped down the muddy bank and fell face first into the river. Cold shot through my body and I gasped for air, swimming to the surface. I thrashed, and my foot touched off something hard. Once I realised my feet could touch the riverbed, I stopped splashing, and found that the river was shallow enough for me to stand with my head just above the surface and the current was weak where I had fallen in.

"Come on Eve, think," I wheezed, struggling to catch my breath. Once the initial shock had passed, the water became bearable, though my teeth chattered.

I glanced between the edge of the river bank within my reach and the far side of the river that was lined by trees and thick undergrowth. Then I remembered one of those outback shows I had watched about surviving in the wild. How prey would go through streams to shake off predators, to break the trail. I kicked off the grainy riverbed and began swimming across the river, away from the direction I had come.

As I shoved through reeds slicing at my arms and clambered onto the river bank, a shrill howl echoed in the night. I crawled over to the nearest tree and slumped at its base, peeking around to see a group of wolves pacing along the riverbed. They seemed confused, frustrated even. A large wolf, with grey flecks in his coat glinting in the moonlight, turned to another beside him and nipped their neck sharply. They whined and shrunk back at some unspoken command.

I wanted to step out, to gloat that I had outwitted them. Content that I was out of sight and downwind, I let my head fall back against the tree and sagged with relief. After the alpha's speech about superiority, I—a hybrid—had outsmarted them as if they were nothing but beasts. Then again, I wasn't entirely sure if they could swim. I had never tried to swim as a wolf, but I knew dogs could. I laughed, a manic sound, and burst into tears.

A twig snapped to my right and two wolves emerged from the shadows.

CHAPTER 14

I leapt to my feet, wincing as the adrenaline still coursing through my body begged me to change. It stung, like something inside me was trying to claw its way out. The wolves advanced on me, their heads low to the ground and their hackles raised. Both had dark coats which shone under the light of the full moon, each movement causing muscles to ripple across their back. Spittle dripped from their open jaws.

I swallowed and backed up until my back hit another tree, looking around for an escape, but they were advancing from two directions. I was trapped. The only way out was another dip in the river, and I could tell I wouldn't make it that far before they pounced. A human can't outrun a wolf, never mind a werewolf.

Every move closer, every snap of their jaws made my heart hammer in my chest so hard I thought it might burst. My breath came in shallow rasps. More howls sounded in the distance. I debated calling for Ryan, but I couldn't risk drawing more attention to myself.

When I was just about ready to take another leap of faith into the river, the air surrounding the two wolves shimmered, and they shifted back into their human form. I froze, watching wide-eyed as the alpha and Nick rose to their feet in one fluid motion. They seemed completely at ease at their lack of clothing, and while it was uncomfortable, the masks of anger contorting their features was much more unsettling.

I averted my gaze, keeping it above shoulder level as I tried to inch my way around the tree trunk to the left so that I would have a better line if I needed to sprint towards the river. No matter how hard I searched for that feeling, the adrenaline surge I had recently become used to wasn't there. I couldn't feel the magic, the curse, whatever it was. All I felt was a searing pain surging through my limbs, as if my body was fighting itself. One glance towards my desperate exit plan gave me away, and Nick rushed forward.

Two strides was all I managed before he was on me, pinning my arms behind my back with one hand before grabbing a fistful of hair with the other, wrenching my head back.

"Get off me!" I yelled, despite my better judgement. "Ry—"

Nick released my hair to clamp his hand over my mouth. I bit down on his fingers but aside from a minor flinch, all it earned me was a backhand across the face that made my ears ring and stars dance in my vision.

The alpha towered over me, wiping his hand on his bare chest as if he had just touched a stray dog. A low growl, muffled by Nick's grip, ripped from my throat. The alpha's eyes creased and he chuckled, waving a hand and motioning to Nick. "Let her speak, she's not stupid enough to scream again."

Nick obeyed, muttering under his breath as he removed his hand from my mouth. "Hybrid scum."

I caught the tiniest glimpse of Nick examining the bite mark on his hand with disgust before he gripped my jaw and forced me to turn my attention back to the alpha, who was watching with the most chilling look of amusement.

"Now, Eve," the alpha stepped forward, clasping his hands as if he were in some sort of business negotiation—not butt-naked in the middle of the forest. "It seems my son may have misled you to some extent."

My mouth was dry, and I didn't dare speak. The icy tone of his voice made it very clear that this was a monologue, and I was not welcome to interrupt.

"Being a hybrid is not special, it is a curse to our kind. My son can get too ahead of himself. He is not the alpha, he does not decide who joins the pack—I do." The alpha leaned in, a bead of sweat dripping from his brow onto my cheek. "He will eventually realise that this silly experiment of his, a hybrid and a werewolf won't work. This is real life, not some Shakespearean romance. I thought he had potential, but you seem to have gotten in his head."

Shakespeare didn't write romance, he wrote tragedies. But I didn't dare correct the alpha.

I strained to get away from Nick, but his grip only tightened, my arms twisted behind my back to the point I thought a bone might snap.

"Keep your head down and stay out of trouble. Don't even think about trying to run," the alpha ordered, reaching out to pinch my jaw in between his finger and thumb, forcing me to maintain eye contact. "You may have no family, but if you step out of line, I know who you hold dear. Don't think I won't hesitate to punish my son either."

I swallowed, tears streaming down my cheeks.

"Do I make myself clear?"

At a nudge in the back from Nick and the alpha's unwavering stare, I found myself nodding in agreement mutely.

The alpha smirked and clicked his fingers, motioning for his brother to release me. As he did, I collapsed to my knees, my shaking arms doing little to break the fall. I watched Nick fall into step beside his alpha, walking towards the thicket of trees.

"One last thing," the alpha said, pausing to look over his shoulder. "This should be obvious, but do not breathe a word of this incident, or anything I have said, to Ryan. You're a smart girl, keep it that way."

He didn't wait for my response. Through the tears clouding my vision, I noticed shadows moving just beyond their retreating figures. There was a soft flash of light as the two men shifted back into their wolf form, bolting off into the distance. I stared not at the retreating wolves, but at the silhouette of another wolf, its coat burning orange, illuminated by the moonlight.

The red wolf emerged from the shadows, its head and shoulders low as it stalked towards me. For a second, my heart leapt, and I thought it might be Ryan. But the wolf lifted its head and curled its lips back in a vicious snarl, revealing a sharp set of canines dripping with blood. The wolf's metallic eyes narrowed at me, its prey.

That's not Ryan.

In that moment, I wanted nothing more than to be able to shift.

Tears of desperation stung my eyes as I looked around for an escape route, but there wasn't one. Glowing sets of eyes became visible in the undergrowth. I counted eight and gulped. The pack advanced towards me from all angles, cutting off every exit. The red wolf stood out from the others with its russet coat. Not only that, but there was also an air of power and arrogance about their movements. They circled me with such intent and malice that I felt a chill right down to my core.

The wolves had me surrounded. I cast a desperate glance at the river, but the hunger in that wolf's eyes told me they would gladly drown me.

I turned and bolted along the river's edge but barely got up to speed before the red wolf lunged at me. My body slammed against a tree trunk and something snapped. I screamed in pain and a chorus of howls echoed in unison, several more wolves emerging from the shadows. They stalked towards me, fangs bared, their lips curled back in a vicious snarl. The wolf nearest grabbed my leg and whipped its head around, throwing me to the rest of the group. Running on pure adrenaline, I kicked out at them, struggling to fight them off while also fighting the pain that burned within me. My fight-or-flight senses were in full swing and to my body that meant one thing, shift. But I couldn't and the pain of resisting made me cry out.

They snapped at me, shoving and tossing me around like a wounded deer. I never gave up, using all my strength to kick at them and claw at their eyes each time they tried to bite me. I quickly realised that the wolves weren't trying to kill me immediately. They were *playing* with me. They toyed with me like a cat terrorises its prey. Each time they let me get up, I never managed more than two steps before they dragged me back onto the ground.

The red wolf sat back for some time, watching them torture me, before finally deciding to join in.

I watched in vain, backing up gingerly as the red wolf advanced on me. Something about their body language told me they were finished playing games. My fear was confirmed as the wolf sank back on its haunches and launched at me, its jaw aimed for my jugular with perfect precision.

Sharp fangs grazed my throat, but the bite never came. I felt a whoosh of air and a loud yelp echoed through the forest. I opened my eyes to see the red wolf on the ground trapped on its back. A dark wolf stood over them, almost black in the moonlight. I recognised him in an instant, I could feel him.

Ryan.

My heart fluttered and my stomach lurched all at once.

Ryan towered over the red wolf, his teeth bared. The wolf swatted at him playfully, trying to lean up to lick his muzzle, but Ryan let a feral snarl rip from his lips. The red wolf shrank back in surprise, whimpering. He stepped away and looked around the small clearing. All the wolves dropped their head in a slight bow and began to retreat. The red wolf lingered, and our eyes locked, their gaze burning with an intense hatred. One growl from Ryan and they bolted into the darkness after the rest of the pack.

CHAPTER 15

R yan carried me back home in his arms after the hunt. Every inch of me wanted to fight him, but I was too weak. I curled into a ball, my face buried into his bare chest as quiet sobs shook my body. When we returned to the manor, it was empty, only the sound of Ryan's bare feet on the stairs stirring the silence. He placed me down once he manoeuvred our way into the bathroom.

The cool tiles stung the scrapes on my feet, and I hissed.

Ryan kissed the top of my head before rushing out of the bedroom, returning with a first aid box in his hand.

"Eve?" He spoke softly, as if I were a feral kitten he was afraid would scarper. "We need to get those cuts cleaned up."

I nodded numbly, allowing him to sit me on the edge of the bath. The sting of each cut and the ache of my muscles was the only thing allowing me to keep a grip on reality. My mind was locked in a nightmare reel of the wolves attacking me, the alpha's face inches from mine, his words echoing.

"I'm so sorry, Evie, please talk to me," Ryan pleaded, his voice cracking.

I let his voice draw me back to the present. My legs were a patchwork of bruises and cuts, the large gash on my leg leaving bloody streaks all over the tiles. No doubt I looked a picture with panda eyes and my make-up destroyed.

Ryan's face paled at the sight of my wounds under the harsh bathroom light.

"Why?" I whispered, feeling a lump in my throat rise as tears threatened to spill again, but I had cried the well dry.

"I don't know who did this to you, it was supposed to be a normal hunt," Ryan said, anger seeping into his words.

"What do you mean, you don't know? You saw your father announce the hunt."

I glanced up at him from under my lashes. His jaw was set, twitching every now and then, and his eyes burned with concern and fury in equal measures.

Ryan sighed, raking his fingers through his mop of ebony curls. "It wasn't meant to be like that. Someone gave you night-shade."

"Night-what?" I snapped, not even realising that I was speaking aloud.

"Nightshade. It's an herb that's lethal to humans... but not to hybrids. It affects them differently. All it does to you is block your ability to shift for a while."

"Oh, that's all? Lucky me." I glowered at him, eyes narrowed, and he squirmed under my gaze. "You said there aren't that many hybrids. How would you know how it affects me?"

"There have been rumours."

"Well, I'm glad someone was so sure it wouldn't kill me."

He flinched at the venom in my words, but I wasn't finished, I was only getting started. "Is it normal?"

"Is what normal?" Ryan repeated my question, his tone erring too close to sounding fed up for my liking.

"Having some sort of sacrificial lamb?" I growled and made a poor attempt to get to my feet, ignoring the wounded expression on his face.

He groaned and buried his head in his hands, beckoning me to stay still. "You're going to make your leg worse, please sit down."

"Not without an answer."

Ryan's jaw twitched, his mouth set in a thin line. "Fine. It's an old tradition that we haven't done in years. My father promised it would be a normal solstice hunt."

"Why did he do it then? Because I'm a hybrid? What kind of fucked up archaic game is this, Ryan?"

"There are old hunting rituals that we don't do any more, a kind of symbolic offering thing," he admitted, biting his lip in a way that would normally make me melt. But I was beyond that. My temper blazed.

I arched an eyebrow. "Clearly your pack does."

"That's not how things were supposed to go. You were meant to shift with us and join the hunt. We usually use game as an offering."

"Why did you let me do it?" I snarled, catching sight of my reflection in the bathroom mirror.

My face was contorted in anger, my eyes were narrowed and cold. Damp hair clung to my shoulders, and my limbs were flecked with a mixture of dried blood and dirt. I was a patchwork of bruises. Tiny cuts, along with some bigger ones that were still bleeding, covered my body. I didn't recognise the person staring back at me. She looked like something out of a horror movie.

"I swear, I would never put you in danger or let them hurt you." His eyes searched mine, begging me to believe him. "The pack... some wolves just can't accept hybrids. But I will sort it!"

So, it was personal.

"Well, you were too damn late, Ryan. They *did* hurt me," I spat, clenching my teeth as I forced myself to stand.

I turned sharply and let out a carnal scream of frustration as my injured ankle buckled, my balance giving way. The other leg was still weak from the attack.

Ryan leapt to his feet to help me sit on the edge of the bath as I fell back. "You need to calm down."

I knew deep down that he was trying to be helpful, that he was right, but my temper flashed, and I insisted on attempting to stand again, favouring the ankle which was probably sprained.

"Why? It's not like I can shift right now, is it?"

"The nightshade will wear off in a few days or so."

"I fucking hope so. How else am I supposed to protect myself?"

He flinched at the look I shot him. "I won't let anything like this happen again, I promise."

"This isn't normal. Hunting people like prey is not normal, whether they are werewolves or not." I swayed but gripped the sink to keep myself upright, running on pure adrenaline. "They were going to *kill* me."

"They wouldn't have." Ryan reached out to grab my arm. I tried to snatch it away, but his grip was firm. He looked at me with those wide, pleading blue eyes. "I will find out who gave you the nightshade. They will pay," he spat the last words, slipping an arm around my waist and squeezing me tight to his chest, his penitent gaze sweeping over the bruising on my arms. "I promise."

"I don't want to be part of this pack," I said, my lower lip trembling. I was swinging from blind fury to wanting to collapse in a puddle of tears. I didn't want any of this; I never asked to be a hybrid.

Somehow being in his arms was making the anger dissipate, reminding me of how I used to feel with him. Safe.

He nodded, holding me tight until I stopped fighting him and relented. "I understand, I will talk to my father in the morning."

"No!" I froze, panic rising in my voice. "No, you can't tell him."

Ryan frowned, pulling back and brushing back my hair so he could see my face properly. "Can't tell him what? Did he say something to you?"

I thought about telling Ryan what his father had said, how they had practically set the wolves on me, but his father's threats echoed in my mind.

"Nothing... he didn't say anything," I said finally, shaking my head as if trying to brush off the thoughts.

Ryan studied my face for a moment, not quite buying my story. When tears started to spill down my cheeks again, he sighed and wrapped me in a hug.

"For now, we need to get you cleaned up," Ryan said, releasing me for a moment to flick on the shower, before guiding me under the steady stream of hot water. "I will always make sure you're safe, Eve. I got to you as soon as possible. I lost your scent at the river."

The initial touch of the water stung, and I sucked in a breath, but the warmth slowly began seeping into my bones. I let my eyes close for a moment as Ryan pottered around, rustling in the first aid box.

"I was trying to shake them off."

"You did a great job, but when you tried to ditch them, I lost your scent too. I promise I was right on your tail."

Ryan pressed a cotton bud doused in disinfectant to my leg and I hissed, jerking my leg away. That was one way to change the topic.

"This will sting, but I don't like the look of that one on your calf. Hybrids heal fast, as far as I know," he said, kneeling down with his hand hovering over a deep cut on my right calf, "but better safe than sorry."

The moment he began cleaning the wound, I growled and grit my teeth. The calming effects of the shower didn't outweigh the pain.

"You'll be sorry if you keep that up," I snapped, struggling to keep still as he probed the cut.

He chuckled, relief washing over his features as I started to sound more like myself.

It took all the self-restraint I had left not to prance like a horse and let him see to the cut. The alcohol stung like a bitch, but Ryan was gentle, and by the time I thought I was just going to have to kick him off, he straightened up and threw the bloodied gauze in the bin.

"It should heal okay on its own," Ryan said, a hint of a smile ghosting his lips. "I can't imagine you would tolerate stitches right now."

"Thanks." I mumbled, emotions still swinging like a pendulum.

It was crystal clear that the alpha didn't really want me here, but Ryan did. I needed to learn control, but after what had happened, I didn't want to join Ryan's pack. I'd never been one to stick around where I wasn't wanted. I remembered the red wolf, the way it had looked at me, the anger burning in its eyes as if it wanted nothing more than to rip me limb from limb. I wasn't unaccustomed to being disliked as the new girl—bouncing between foster homes had given me a tough skin, but this was another level. I needed to learn the rules of the game at play before I risked telling Ryan what happened.

CHAPTER 16

"**Y**ou've got this," I whispered to myself, brushing a stray strand of hair back into place as I studied my face in the mirror.

Apart from deep circles brewing under my eyes and a small cut lingering on my cheek, I looked semi respectable. It had been over a week since the hunt; I had missed the solstice run altogether. Since that night, I'd been hiding out in Ryan's room resting and healing for the most part, and then making countless excuses, wallowing. But I couldn't hide away forever. If I was to step out of here, I was going to fake confidence and refuse to let them get under my skin. Getting dressed and showered that morning made me feel more human, more—myself.

I could still sense that gentle pulse inside begging me to change so I could heal faster, but I pushed the feeling down, locking it away. Though the presence of nightshade in my system seemed to have dulled, I couldn't be sure that it was enough. Trying to change and failing hurt almost as much as changing itself. As much as I wanted to try, I knew failing again would push me right over the edge. I'd spent so much time crying, there were no tears left in the tank.

After several pep talks in my head, I convinced myself to open the door. When the hinges creaked, it took every ounce of resolve I had left not to bolt back inside to the safety of Ryan's bedroom. I descended the stairs one step at a time, leaning on the banister as I favoured the bad ankle. The usual noises drifted from the kitchen, but for the most part the house was quiet, empty.

Morning sunshine filtered into the foyer. I flinched as a teenage girl walked towards me, a pile of laundry in hand, but she didn't seem to notice me, rushing past as if I weren't there at all.

"You are a hybrid, Eve," I muttered once the girl had passed, desperately trying to find some fight. "The full moon is over, they can't change. You can... normally."

Casting a quick glance around to make sure no one had heard me talking to myself, I continued towards the kitchens. During the family dinner, I had noticed an adjoining room and what looked like a second exit to the gardens. I needed air. Maybe if I snuck out that way, I could avoid running into anyone.

I eyed the doors leading towards the back of the house and took a leap of faith, hoping that the dining room was empty. I breathed a shaky sigh of relief when I realised it was and tiptoed around the table. The door swung open to reveal a spacious room widely devoid of any furniture. In the far corner, there was a home bar with gaudy gold accents and then to the left, a door I presumed led towards the kitchen. The floors were white marble and spotless. Between two large bay windows, a set of patio doors opened onto the garden lawn. I knew Ryan had mentioned they held parties and pagan celebrations, but this was obnoxiously over the top.

I stepped outside and tilted my chin up, letting the morning sun wash over my face. The breeze was light and warm, barely making even the thinnest of trees sway and rustle. Beyond the initial picket fence and bushes, I could see the grounds stretching right up until the forest edge at the base of the mountains.

Nestled on top of a hill, the house gave me an excellent view of the surrounding land. Past the garden, a scattering of red-bricked houses peaked out from between trees. Ryan had mentioned pack members living here while learning to adapt to the change, but this was becoming a permanent thing. The estate was the perfect location for a werewolf pack, backing onto the mountain forests. Surrounded by fields and shielded by trees in every direction, it was completely secluded.

Worried that someone might spot me from the kitchens, I started towards the end of the garden and slipped through a small gate. I found myself in a flower garden, surrounded by an array of colourful flowers, topped off with arches of climbing roses, standing in full bloom.

I wandered through until I found an archway leading out onto a wide, gravelled path that wound between the houses. There were no designated gardens, but trees and high under-growth gave the families some level of privacy.

It was a wolf pack's dream home and more. I had seen none of this during my last ill-fated foray outside. It looked different in the morning light, almost welcoming. The view really was beautiful.

A twig snapped behind me, and I flinched. I spun to see a tall redhead, slim but with curves in all the right places, with skin the colour of ivory watching me.

"What do you think you're doing?" she asked, absolute dis-dain dripping from every word. The girl looked me up and down with a mixture of pity and disgust. I recognised her by voice alone from the hunt, but her name escaped me. She was one of the pack members who had bayed for my blood. My stomach flopped.

I tried to think of a witty response, but my mind went blank. "I'm walking."

Her expression darkened, eyes narrowing. "You shouldn't be wandering around unsupervised."

"I'm not a *dog*. I can walk where I want. Ryan said I was free to explore while he was at work."

She stepped out onto the path in front of me, one hand resting on her hip. She was in white shorts and a low-cut string top, even though it wasn't warm enough for so little clothes. Somehow, I doubted she chose her outfits based on the weather.

"Ryan should have known better. It's not safe for you, mutt," she sneered, flashing her teeth.

I stiffened at the insult, struggling to keep my temper at bay. I wanted to shift and show her exactly why I was better, that a hybrid was something to be feared. But my body was sluggish, and I could still feel the after-effects of the nightshade. I suppose I should have been thankful that it didn't kill me like it would a normal human, but it temporarily killed my ability to shift, something I never expected to miss.

She eyed me as if she wanted to torture or dispose of me in equal measure. I watched her scarlet waves blowing in the breeze.

Her name finally came to me.

Nadine.

"I don't think Ryan would appreciate you speaking to me like that, Nadine." I stepped forward, squaring up to her. "I might not be able to shift, but she didn't know that. "I'm with Ryan and as far as I know, pack rules are an eye for an eye."

"You think you're worthy of being his mate?" Nadine snorted. A few pack members had paused to watch. Her face was a portrait of pure hatred and, if anything, the small crowd that had gathered made her ten times less likely to let this go.

I was never going to agree to some archaic mate pairing, but I needed to be smart, so I played along. Just because she knew the alpha, didn't mean she knew anything about me or my relationship. "He wants me to be his mate, ask him yourself."

"You will never be good enough. You are a mongrel, nothing more."

"As if you know what Ryan thinks of me."

"Ryan knows me very intimately," she purred, and looked off into the distance with a fond expression.

Blood rushed to my cheeks, and my mind spun at her words. Memories of Kate's claims that she had caught him kissing a redhead, the entire reason I had fighting with him the night I changed, came flooding to the forefront of my mind. *Did Ryan sleep with her?* I knew Ryan had past partners, but if it was a pack member that I would have to deal with, he should have told me. He would have told me... wouldn't he? Unless he didn't want to ignite that argument.

Nadine's gaze snapped back to me, her face smug. "Did he not mention me?"

A chorus of laughter rose from her audience.

"He didn't mention Christmas?" She pressed.

I swallowed, pushing away the seeds of doubt that had already been planted.

"Ryan mentioned Christmas, but you didn't make the cut," I said, my voice coming out stronger than I expected. Maybe I was getting better at the whole fake it 'til you make it thing.

Her pretty features twisted into an ugly scowl. I heard a small laugh come from one onlooker. One dirty look from Nadine, and he made a swift exit from the scene.

"You will soon find out what he really thinks of you, mongrel," she spat, turning on her heel and stalking back towards one of the red brick houses.

Once Nadine was a safe distance away, the crowd dissipated. I didn't recognise anyone. A few people among them appeared genuinely curious, kind even, others watched me with the same distaste that Nadine shared. I was like Marmite.

Because I wasn't up for a game of Russian roulette, I made my way back towards the main house, hoping that I didn't run into any more trouble. As I got closer, I heard the distinct sound of Rebecca's voice and raucous laughter from a bunch of women in the patio garden. From the cackles that echoed, they were well on their way through a bottle of wine. No doubt the finest kind.

I decided to take a detour. At the top of the vast sprawling lawn leading to the kitchens, I clocked a small bunch of girls congregated in deep conversation at the doorway. Exhaling slowly, I set my shoulders and started walking towards the door.

The whole time, I had to keep telling myself that I was all right. I was sick of being treated like some kind of freak.

The girls fell quiet and watched as I came closer, but none of them glared or began hurling insults. I took that as a win. They stayed silent and moved aside to let me pass. Once I was in the kitchen, their chatting started up again and from what I could hear, they were only curious. I breathed a sigh of relief and kept walking.

The kitchen was busy with chatter, always ticking along. I saw Mary over by the oven. She caught my eye and gave me a nod, ushering the girl she was speaking to away.

When the girl stood there, gaping, Mary slapped her arm. "Stop staring, Maddison. There's nothing to see here, go get the herbs I asked for."

Maddison dropped her head and scurried off toward the gardens.

Just as I was about to leave the kitchen, Mary called after me. "Eve, pet. Come get something to eat."

My stomach rumbled as if in reply. The last few days had taken their toll. "I suppose I could manage something."

Mary smiled, the scar on her dimpled cheek stretching. She motioned for me to take a seat at the table and went about readying food for me.

"How are you feeling now?" she asked, setting down a ham sandwich and a plate of crisps. A child's meal if there ever was one—comfort food. It was exactly what I needed. My stomach growled in agreement as I popped some crisps in the sandwich and took a bite.

"Mostly sore but better," I said between bites, suddenly ravenous. "I still can't shift, but I can feel it coming back slowly."

Mary chuckled as I wolfed down the sandwich, handing me another two slices. "It's good to see you at least have your appetite back."

It dawned on me that all the little treats and food in bed that Ryan had been bringing me wasn't his doing.

"Thanks, by the way, for the food packages."

"Nonsense, can't have you starving now, can we? I knew you would eventually show your face again." Mary pulled out the chair beside me and plopped into it with a sigh. "They scrapped that tradition years ago—and it should have stayed that way. I'm sorry you had to go through that."

"Me too."

Mary frowned, wiping her hands on her apron. "Don't let them get to you, sweetheart."

My chewing slowed, and I looked up, struggling to fight back an unexpected surge of tears. I had thought there were none left. "Thanks," I whispered, not trusting myself to say any more.

"These days..." Mary shifted in her seat, looking off into the distance. "The pack is struggling. Many of them refuse to change and would prefer to stay in the dark ages. It's a dangerous time."

"How so?"

"You will understand in time. If you are ever in trouble, you come to me," she said, her blue eyes sparkling with a fierceness I never expected. "No matter what."

I chewed my lip, unable to hold the intensity of her gaze. "I will, thank you."

The kitchen had emptied to some extent; only a handful of girls lingered.

"Fiona, come over here and take a break. You've been on your feet all morning, pet." Mary motioned to a slight girl cleaning dishes with her back to us. I tensed, but when Fiona turned to join us at the table, I noticed it was the same girl with the kind eyes who had smiled at me on my first day.

"Mary feeding you up?" Fiona chuckled, her voice soft and melodic. She was tall and willowy, with long limbs. Yet there was an understated grace to the way she walked which put me to shame.

I nodded, taking another bite of my second sandwich. "I was hungry," I explained, a sheepish grin tugging at the corners of my lips.

Mary had returned to pottering around the kitchen, boiling the kettle and picking out mugs for the three of us. I wished this had been my first meal in the pack and not that horribly forced dinner.

Fiona watched me, curiosity sparkling in her eyes. She was too polite to ask whatever was on her mind.

"What do you want to know?" I had questions of my own.

Maybe if I let them get to know me, I can get some answers.

She dropped her head, blood rushing to her cheeks. "Sorry, I didn't mean to stare."

I knew exactly what she meant. I glanced at Mary, conscious of the questions brewing about her scar.

"What's it like?" Fiona asked, looking at me as if I was a Kinder Surprise egg. "Does it hurt when you shift?"

I realised that Fiona had never met a hybrid before. *Was I really that rare?* "Apparently it only hurts when I fight it."

Her lips curved into a wide smile. "I was the same when I was learning!" she said, as if we were trading stories about something like shopping, not shifting into our wolf forms. I supposed this was her version of ordinary, a world that wasn't normal to me yet. I still had no control. There was a significant adjustment period that I was struggling to navigate. Every time I thought I had a foothold, I slipped.

Mary returned to the table, expertly balancing three cups of tea. "Milk? Sugar?" she asked, handing me a pink mug.

Once she had readied the brews, she took a seat opposite Fiona and me, her expression growing sombre. "Eve, I have to say, not all of us feel the same way as those who hunted that night."

I swallowed, not sure I wanted to have this conversation again. My blood was still cooling from the run in with Nadine.

"I skipped the hunt once I saw what was happening," Fiona chimed in, tracing the lip of her cup with her thumb, her pretty eyes sombre. "My mother went, though I begged her not to."

Mary patted the girl's lap. "Some wolves would follow their alpha off a cliff. Too many."

"So how do things work around here?" I asked in a poorly disguised attempt to change the topic.

The questions tumbled once I let the first past my lips, though I managed to keep the more controversial ones to myself.

Mary shrugged, her face brightening. "I look after the kitchens. We used to have staff, but that didn't end well. Especially since there became less of us, we are fairly self-sufficient. The men handle most of the business, trading and whatever. It keeps the money flowing."

Didn't end well? I struggled to keep my expression passive.

"You could help out in the kitchens. Nadine never bothers us," Fiona suggested.

I blanched. How did she know about Nadine?

"I saw you guys fighting from the hill." Fiona rushed to explain, winding a long strand of hair around her finger. "Well, at least it looked like you were arguing. She rarely has anything good to say."

My shoulders relaxed. Mary looked at Fiona as if she was about to tell her off for speaking ill of Nadine. Instead, she shook her head with a wry smile.

"Stay away from that one, she's nothing but trouble," Mary warned me, her tone growing serious. "Her family is well respected by the alpha, so you don't want to get on her bad side."

As if the alpha doesn't already hate me.

With that, Mary got up from her seat and dusted her apron down. "Now, I wish I could stick around here gossiping all day, but these wolves are a hungry bunch." Fiona went to stand, but Mary laid a firm hand on her shoulder. "Not you, stay here and keep Eve company for a bit."

Mary walked over to the ovens and began speaking to a girl harbouring a tray of sunken pastries. Once she was out of earshot, Fiona leaned in to whisper in my ear. "Mary's right, Nadine isn't someone you want to mess with. Her dad is best friends with Nick and the alpha."

She sat back, painting a smile on her face, but her eyes were dark and serious. Only when I nodded did Fiona's mood genuinely seem to lighten. "Will you join the pack?"

"I don't think so... I mean I haven't decided," I said, toying with my sleeve. The alpha's threat was fresh in my mind. "I have to go back to college in September. I'm hoping to have more control by then."

Fiona's brow furrowed. "But the pack stays here."

"Ryan lives in the city though?"

"Yes, but that's only allowed on business." She placed her palms flat on the table, still timid like a wild rabbit, but there was a certainty in her voice. "Most pack members live here."

Maybe pack members were okay with that, but I wasn't prepared to enter into a cult. I started to correct her, but the naïve expression she wore made me shut my mouth. Fiona was lovely, but she couldn't possibly understand.

I agreed to pop down for a chat soon. Mary put Fiona in charge of showing me the ropes, 'to keep me busy' in her words. I got the distinct impression she knew I wasn't keen on sticking around.

CHAPTER 17

Spending every waking moment of the day with Ryan wasn't possible, but I wasn't in the mood to play happy families with his parents, so I stuck to the kitchens mostly and spent the rest of my time in the library. I remembered Ryan letting slip about all the records and history; it didn't take me long to badger him into giving me access. Apparently it was only for pack members, so he told me to be sneaky. I had a feeling he thought it would just be a rap on the knuckles if I got caught. I wasn't so sure.

Bookcases stacked full of mostly handwritten texts detailing everything from moon phases to the earliest werewolf settlements in Ireland and Europe stretched up to the ceiling. There were filing cabinets practically overflowing with folders and papers piled high, records of births, deaths, and all other sorts. Nothing was catalogued. I quickly found out there was no order to the madness, but trawling through the books and papers kept me occupied and helped pass the days. Reading the historical accounts first-hand was much better than Ryan's attempt at teaching me.

I spent the majority of my time sitting back in a comfy armchair that I had positioned beside the only window, angled so I could curl up reading, looking out across the estate. Under the afternoon sun, it was picture perfect, but something never sat right with me. Staying hidden away like this didn't feel normal.

It was as if they were dead set on keeping the pack separate from modern life.

I was flicking through an old book with yellowing pages when I stumbled across a hand-drawn section on family trees detailing the lineage of the McKenna family and their rise to alpha status.

Ryan's family stretched over centuries. Beside each name was a birth and death date, but that wasn't what caught my eye. The alpha lineage was highlighted in red, overlaid on the family tree. Ryan's father hadn't been next in line to become alpha originally; his cousin Cormac had been. There was a small asterisk beside the cousin's name along with the lettering 'deceased', both his parents were marked the same way. A sibling was linked on the tree, but their name was scribbled out. The alpha line then jumped to Damien.

Something is off here.

I bookmarked the page with a sheet of paper and gathered the book under my arm, walking over to one of the many cabinets. I had figured out that this one held some—not all—birth and death records. I dug through the folders until I came across the death certificate for Cormac's father. The cause of death was ruled as a car accident. The mother's was the same. Poor kid. Only his sister Ester wasn't marked as deceased. Why did he die so soon after his parents? Had he been involved in the accident? Who had done up the certs was another question. Could you bring werewolves to a normal coroner, or did they have their own doctors?

Rummaging further through the files, I came across Cormac's name and pulled out his death cert. My stomach sank. Most of the injuries listed and the cause of death were redacted, and not in a professional way either, like a kid had gone at it with a sharpie.

I moved back to the desk, running back and forth between filing cabinets as I tried to find more information. I'd been looking for information on my parents and came up with nothing, but this was more worrying.

The door creaked and I jumped, spilling the folders in my hand onto the floor, sheets of paper fluttering to land in a haphazard circle around me.

"Ryan!" I hissed in both surprise and relief, pressing my palm to my chest to try ease my hammering heart.

He chuckled, holding his hands up in defence. "My bad, didn't mean to scare you."

"I thought you wouldn't be home 'til later?"

"It is later. You must have been off in your own world." Ryan gestured to the window. Dark shadows were beginning to stretch across the room. "Anything interesting?"

I crouched down and busied myself shoving papers back into their folders. "Nope, just got caught up reading some old myths."

Ryan went to help, but I gathered up the folders and dropped them on top of the cabinet, quickly turning to him with a smile that made my cheeks hurt. I wasn't sure what I'd stumbled across but telling Ryan just didn't feel right until I figured it out. The alpha disliked me enough as it was.

Since when are you the girl who hides things?

"So, do you fancy going tonight?" Ryan asked, snapping me back to the present.

"Tonight?"

"Yes, tonight," he said, pulling me into his arms. "I know shifting scares you, but you need to practice before the hunt tomorrow night. I was holding off until the full moon."

I groaned inwardly. "Not all of us need a full moon," I teased, trying to lighten my mood.

"No but shifting isn't draining for hybrids during a full moon." He rolled his eyes, tugging me towards the door. "And it means I can change too."

The curiosity of seeing Ryan in his wolf form properly while not being attacked and the urge to learn control won out. It didn't mean I was looking forward to the hunt, I was dreading it. But so long as I stuck to Ryan and avoided nightshade spiked drinks this time, I would be safe. As much as the alpha had scared me, I didn't want him to know that.

CHAPTER 18

O nce dusk had fallen, we drove up the winding mountain roads towards the denser parts of the forest. Ryan thought it would be best if we went somewhere secluded. I focused on the countryside flashing past us on the road, trying to steady my nerves. He eventually pulled the car up on a grass verge of what seemed like the middle of nowhere to me. Tall trees surrounded us, stretching into the night sky. To our right, a dirt path, wide enough to block cars from entering but easy to walk through, blocked by a metal gate, led into the forest.

"Come on, it's now or never." Ryan reached across and gave my leg a quick squeeze that did nothing to dispel my nerves. "The stronger the pull of the moon, the easier the shift is for hybrids."

I stayed rooted in the passenger seat until he walked around the bonnet, opened my door, and practically lifted me out of the car.

"I can get out by myself," I growled, swatting him away.

He shook his head, his brow pinching with impatience. "We don't have all night, Eve. You're the one who said that you wanted to learn."

"In my own time."

"We don't have time, and you can't keep putting it off."

"Says the man who put off telling me I'm a hybrid," I scoffed, surprising even myself with the amount of venom in my voice.

"This temper is part of the reason you need control." His lips thinned and I noticed the slight twitch of his jaw before he turned on his heel and stalked around the gate.

I followed with my arms folded across my chest, deliberately trailing behind. The grass was damp, soaking through the toes of my runners, further souring my mood.

Ryan took no notice of my sulking, reaching behind to take my hand to make sure I kept the pace and didn't try to bolt back to the car.

Above the inky silhouettes of the treeline, the dim light of the full moon pierced the canopy. Shadows danced on the forest floor below, and the distant sounds of small animals foraging disturbed the silence. An uneasy mix of anticipation and dread swashed around in my stomach. We walked deep into the forest, only stopping when Ryan stepped out into a large clearing. Swaying trees cast long shadows in the moonlight. There were no tracks in the clearing, no well-trodden path. I had no idea how far we had walked, but it was definitely far enough. We were alone.

I stood there awkwardly as Ryan turned to face me. He took the hem of his t-shirt and pulled it over his head. I could see the muscles of his chest ripple, but I stared intently at a tuft of grass, playing with loose threads on my sleeve. I couldn't resist a peak.

We had talked about this when he suggested I bring a change of clothes, and I had naively asked why. As if I wasn't familiar with the naked part, as if I didn't know that shifting meant your clothes went poof, as if I had never seen his gorgeous body before. The feeling of sheer terror mixed with anticipation and the sight of Ryan topless was the oddest combination.

"You're going to have to lose the clothes, and the bracelet. They won't survive the shift," Ryan said as his hands moved to his belt, drawing my eyes to the deep v there, and panic surged in my chest.

"I'll be right back," I said, backing up several steps before turning and running back into the thicket of trees with my tail between my legs.

"Don't be silly," he yelled, the sound of his voice closely followed by the clang of his belt buckle hitting a rock. I could only assume his pants dropped too, but thankfully we were no longer in each other's line of sight.

I felt like it was my first time all over again. We had seen each other naked plenty of times, that wasn't the issue, but the thought of Ryan seeing me shift was giving me palpitations. I didn't want him to see that ugly, raw side of me that I wasn't ready to accept.

I rubbed my forehead, muttering to myself. "I can do this."

My hands shook as I fumbled with the zip on my dress. If I was being completely honest with myself, I didn't know if I could do this. One thing I knew for sure was that I would never be able to concentrate if we were both stark naked, and I was intent on doing this alone the first time until it stopped being weird. I would prolong the awkward as long as possible.

By the time I was kicking my clothes into a pile, I could hear Ryan tutting and pacing in the clearing. He kept shouting for me to join. Ignoring him, I knelt down on the ground with my legs folded beneath me and my palms braced parallel with my shoulders. The grass was damp and slick against my fingers, but the cold was a welcome break from the heat burning within me. While I was mentally struggling with wanting to change, my body was begging me to listen. Just being outside under a full moon, surrounded by nature and the scent of another wolf nearby had that side of me raring to go. Although I had been focusing hard on keeping it caged, the change didn't come naturally. There was a war of wills between my mind and my instincts. Ryan had warned me that the more I fought the urge to shift, the more painful it was. This time, he hadn't lied. I stayed crouched and panted, willing myself to shift while fighting the sheer terror of losing control. But I had to shift. My back arched and the joint in my elbow snapped with a loud pop that made me cry out.

"Eve!" Ryan's voice was strained and closer this time.

"Go away." I groaned and grit my teeth, digging my nails into the soft earth as claws extended. The sensation made my stomach lurch.

Ryan's footsteps stopped, and I turned my attention back to each of the bones in my limbs as they warped and snapped in quick succession, but not quickly enough. Each time, a burning white fire of pain ripped through my body. I was damp with sweat, limbs shaking so much I thought I might collapse. The change continued, relentless and irreversible once it had begun. I squeezed my eyes shut, tears streaming down my cheeks. My howls of agony rang through the night, slowly morphing into those of a wolf's as the shift completed.

I blinked slowly, my vision swimming into focus. My eyesight had improved since that night in the park, but as a wolf, it was like I had my own high-definition filter. Objects that should be shrouded in a blanket of darkness were crisp with clear outlines. I glanced around slowly. The movement felt odd, disproportionate—foreign almost. If the sensation of having my nose stretch out was strange, moving my paws felt even more peculiar. While I knew how to crawl, walking on all fours was a different ball game. This wasn't my first change, but I had been out of control and had no recollection of those nights. While there was an element of adjusting that came naturally, it took a few minutes of pacing in circles and catching glimpses of a furry tail for my conscious brain to catch up.

Ryan stayed true to his word, hovering by the edge of the clearing until I inclined my head in invitation. He was still in his human form—with only boxers to hide his modesty—but it felt more normal than I had expected. He took slow steps towards me, his eyes wide and a smile playing on his lips. "You did it." Ryan reached out and scratched behind my left ear. The sensation was odd but comforting, kind of like getting your hair stroked.

I was still terrified of my capabilities, but despite everything, I felt comfortable in this skin, as if I were born for it. I suppose in a sense that I was.

"Now to do it all over again." Ryan chuckled, as if it were a game.

My head snapped up, snout smacking into his open palm. I sneezed at the contact and retreated, making a mental note to practice that too as one leg caught the other.

"Eve, to gain full control you need to change until it's instantaneous." Ryan stayed where he was, arms folded across his broad chest. A bored expression had replaced any initial wonder that had shone in his eyes, unimpressed by my reluctance.

I fully understood my hesitation. Maybe it wasn't like this for werewolves the first time; perhaps it only hurt hybrids. It had taken every ounce of my resolve to fight through that pain. The thought of having to do it again—even just once—before I had a week to recover made my lips curl back over my canines and a low growl rip through my throat.

Ryan held his hands up to placate me. "I know it hurts, Eve." His expression softened, and he closed the space between us. "It's horrible. They don't call it a curse in the movies for nothing. But the more you shift, the less painful it will become. If you gain control, it will stop hurting altogether."

I cocked my head to the side and ran my tongue over my sharp canines. He hooked his thumb in the waistband of his boxers, and I immediately looked the other way. When I opened one eye, I saw Ryan lurching forward, the air shimmering around him as his body shifted. I shuffled back and in a matter of seconds, there was a large black wolf in front of me, its coat gleaming under the moonlight. He didn't howl once, nor had his face contorted into a mask of agony like mine. The potential of it being so painless and easy was tempting. I knew I had no choice but to learn. I couldn't bear going through the pain again, but if it meant in the long run that I could shift as I pleased and enjoy this side of me fully, it was worth it.

We both shifted back to our human form. Ryan waited patiently while I fought with the change. I ended up on all fours, dry retching as my body struggled to adjust. He even held my hair back.

Once I could stand without my legs shaking too much, Ryan gestured in front of us. "Again." A hint of amusement seeped into his tone, but I pushed it aside.

I covered my modesty. He didn't. My cheeks flushed. I should have been embarrassed, and I was nearly positive that there was spit in my hair, but Ryan was unfazed. He watched me with the strangest expression, a mixture of excitement and something I couldn't place. After some protesting, I did as he instructed, enduring the burning agony until I was back on all fours. But twice wasn't enough. Each time I changed back into my human form, Ryan told me to shift again. I lost track of how many times I called to my wolf side, of how long I spent curled up on the forest floor crying and screaming. Unlike the night I attacked Kate, I felt like I was working with my inner wolf and not against it. Ryan coached me through each transition until it came faster. Ryan hadn't been lying; the pain lessened each time, but it still hurt like a bitch.

I lay on my back, panting, four paws stretched above me. My tongue lolled out to the side, and the stars spun above me.

Ryan had fallen silent, no longer spewing words of encouragement or criticism. There was a soft rustle in the grass and as I rolled onto my side, the black wolf was watching me. He was taller and broader than me in his wolf form. I wasn't sure if it was a male-female proportion thing, a werewolf-hybrid thing, or if it was just because he was taller in general. As a wolf, I couldn't ask. That was the most frustrating part. Most of the time Ryan had been yelling at me, I spent howling in pain and couldn't speak. Every time I was in my wolf form and he had asked me to change back, I wanted to curse him. I soon found that nipping his arm gave the same satisfaction.

I watched him curiously, taking in the point of his ears and the slope of his features. During the hunt, I had been too terrified to notice the details.

He was almost jet black but not quite, more a dark brown masquerading as the night. I tucked my haunches beneath me and pushed myself to my feet, slowly padding over to his side to measure up. I was definitely smaller.

Ryan swung his head to look at me, the blue of my eyes reflected in his. Unlike mine, his matched the silver of the moon. I was a light brown to match my human hair colour. My ears flickered back and forth. I remembered what Luke had said about grey eyes and made a mental note to ask Ryan later.

He nudged my neck with his wet nose, a low rumble sounding from his chest. I nuzzled his jaw, the movement almost a reflex. Even if my brain was struggling to communicate, my instincts were there.

Ryan spun on his heels and yipped, bounding towards the tree line. He paused briefly at the edge of the clearing, checking to see if I was following. I loped after him, the soft turf cool and giving way under my weight with each stride. It took me a few moments to shake off the hundreds of different scents bombarding my senses and focus on where I was going, dodging low-lying branches and trees by the skin of my teeth. It was easier once I got into a rhythm, my instincts and muscles working in perfect tandem. The freedom of the wind rushing past as we bounded through the undergrowth was a feeling I could never thoroughly explain. We disappeared under the cover of the forest, racing in the moonlight.

When we finally got back to the house in the early hours of the morning, the sun was just about to peak over the estate. Going for a run had loosened up my muscles but left me exhausted. Ryan had to help me up the stairs, and we laughed each time I tripped. I realised it was the first time I'd laughed properly since the hunt.

The halls were quiet, dark shadows stretching across the landing. As soon as he opened the bedroom door, I rushed to flop on the bed. He returned from the bathroom to find me curled up under the covers and half asleep.

"Goodnight, Eve," Ryan murmured, leaning in and brushing his lips over mine.

I froze and my eyes fluttered open. There was so much we still needed to talk about, that I needed to forgive. While it felt amazing to gain control of my wolf side, I felt like I was losing control in every other aspect of my life.

Ryan stared down at me, his eyes shifting between blue and silver, a mix of emotions crossing his face. He lingered there before kissing me again, and this time his lips were hungry against mine.

CHAPTER 19

The summer sun beat down on the city, and large Victorian buildings cast shadows across one side of the street. I was nervous but excited when Kate texted to say she was back in the city. Several weeks had passed since the incident; she had gone to stay with her parents in the country while she recovered, and I was dying to see her. Ryan suggested somewhere in public where I'd be less likely to shift if seeing her upset me. Plus, I was close enough to his office if I needed him. He dropped me outside my favourite spot, a little café down a side lane, quaint and full of character, unlike most of the coffee chains taking over the city. A little bell rang as I eased the door open and the same barista that used to serve me every day popped behind the counter. She knew my favourite off by heart. I took a seat outside, under the warm shade of a canopy jutting out onto the street. With its large front windows and turquoise walls, the little coffee shop stood out against the crowd.

"Fancy seeing you here."

A familiar smooth lilt, a mix of Dublin and the midlands, that I would recognise anywhere broke my reverie. I looked up to see Luke dressed in a plaid shirt and jeans despite the heat, standing over me

I pushed my sunglasses onto the top of my head and frowned. "Luke? What are you doing here?"

"I could ask you the same thing. I thought you had joined the dark side."

"Who told you that?"

Luke shrugged. "Packs talk. Even the ones like yours where people aren't supposed to." His gaze travelled to my arms where the faintest white line could still be seen on my wrist, one of the last remaining marks. "What happened?"

It had been a month since the hunt, but I still had a small handful of scars, a constant reminder.

I reached behind and grabbed my denim jacket off the back of my chair, slipping it on. "Nothing, I haven't joined any pack. I'm still learning."

His eyes narrowed. "Eve, what's wrong?"

Everything. My boyfriend's pack is living in the dark ages, the alpha hates me, he may have killed his cousin...

"Why does something have to be wrong?"

Luke sighed, running a hand through his sandy hair. "Call it a hunch."

"Nothing is wrong. I'm fine." I held his gaze but began playing with the hem of my shirt.

He took the seat opposite me without asking. "I'd know nothing about women if I believed that."

I stuck out my tongue, and he returned the gesture with double my enthusiasm.

"You said it yourself. Most werewolves don't like hybrids," I said, surprised his little birds hadn't told him the full story. Or maybe they had. It would explain why he showed up out of the blue. "Why are you even here?"

He threw a parcel he had been holding onto the table between us. "I had business in town, and my dad said I needed to spend less time in bars." His joking tone didn't hide the truth shining in his eyes. I had seen him knock back whiskey before.

I nodded, swirling the teaspoon in my coffee.

Luke changed tact. "Yes, it is hard being a hybrid, my sister was one, I know it isn't easy, and that a lot of werewolves won't accept you as part of the pack."

My eyes widened, and I tried to do my best not to fixate on the fact that he spoke about his sister in the past tense, my mood souring as I realised rumours about the hunt had spread. "Then you know what happened."

"I know some of it. Ryan's pack are scared to gossip."

My shoulders relaxed slightly. "They're not *his* pack yet, his father is the alpha," I said, taking a sip of my coffee and licking the foam off my lips.

Luke sighed, leaning back in his chair. "It may never be his pack if his uncle has anything to do with it."

I frowned. Before I could ask any more, the barista came over and interrupted, asking Luke for his order. I expected him to refuse, but he ordered a coffee and turned to face me again with a lazy smile. He sprawled in his seat, hair tousled as if he'd just gotten out of bed.

"You need to be more careful, Eve," Luke said once the barista had left, leaning forward. "Never let your guard down. Ryan can't always be there to protect you."

He did know.

"I can't fight other pack members, especially when they all gang up."

"You're a hybrid, don't forget what that means. You can turn when they can't, when they are weaker and more vulnerable." Luke lowered his tone and sat up as the barista brought over his coffee. Once she was a safe distance away, he continued, "Don't let them underestimate you. Make sure they know that whatever they do to you during the full moon, you'll give it back threefold."

"I'm not sure Ryan would appreciate me causing aggro."

"Ryan isn't the one in danger," Luke said, his expression hardening. "Besides, if he truly cared about you, Ryan would want you to defend yourself. Whether or not it annoys his father." The words stuck in his throat.

"Why does every conversation with you have to be so life or death?" I asked, cradling my mug in my hands. "Can't we just talk about nice things?"

He chuckled, his laugh deep and hearty. "Nice things?"

"Well, I'm not supposed to be talking to you at all. So yes, nice things. Normal things."

A shadow crept across the table, followed by a voice that made my heart ready to burst. "Eve?"

I spun in my chair to see Kate, dressed in tiny denim shorts and a crop top that showed off her bellybutton ring, paired with a pink blouse that billowed in the wind. She was beaming from ear to ear despite her injuries. Aside from a few bruises along her collarbone and neck, and one arm in a cast, she looked much better than I had expected. When her eyes met mine, Kate didn't skip a beat. Relief washed over me, followed by a wave of guilt. *How much of this was Ryan's doing? Was it a healing thing?*

Kate looked from me to Luke, eyeing him with an equal mix of confusion and blatant interest. He flashed her a grin, and I leapt out of my seat, almost knocking my coffee over in my excitement to get to my friend. I flung my arms around her, trapping her in a tight hug.

"I missed you," I whispered, my face pressed against her shoulder. I was at least a head smaller than Kate, something she loved to point out.

We stepped apart and Kate smiled, fixing her blouse. "I missed you too. How is Ryan's family?" She looked at me like nothing had changed. I had a million excuses planned, but apparently, I didn't need one. She had no idea what happened or that I'd vanished straight after attacking her. The confused expression on her face made a lump rise in my throat.

"Good. Great." I shrugged, sitting back down and looking between the two. "This is Luke, my... friend."

Kate visibly brightened, her gaze glued to Luke's face—and his body. I rolled my eyes and gestured to him. "Luke, Kate is my best friend from college."

Luke nodded and held out his hand. "Lovely to meet you."

I thought Kate looked as if she might melt at his accent alone. It was embarrassing. She went to pull a chair over from the table next to us, but one look from me had Luke spring into action.

"I should leave you two ladies to it. I have business to attend to."

He scooped the parcel off the table, along with my phone, and ushered Kate into his seat before leaning over and pulling me into a one-armed hug. All very casual.

"You have my number if you ever need to talk, try not to lose it this time," Luke whispered in my ear, his breath tickling the nape of my neck as he pressed my phone into my hand. His fingers brushed my wrist and he flinched like he'd been electrocuted. "What the hell?"

"Are you okay?" I asked, my brow furrowing.

Luke didn't reply, he frowned and reached out to examine my wrist and the delicate bracelet encircling it. I pulled my hand away before he could make the moment even weirder.

"Thanks for the chat." I said, trying make things look as normal as possible for my friend's sake, but my voice rose an octave.

"Right, yeah." Luke nodded, seeming to snap back to reality as he stepped away from our table and into the throng of people walking along the street. When he flashed me a wide grin over his shoulder, his eyes sparkled with mischief. "See you around, mutt."

I slumped into my seat. Something about Luke always stuck with me. He was so carefree, cheeky even, but there was a haunted look that never completely left his eyes. He always had a habit of popping up when I least expected him. I unlocked my phone, to find a new contact in under the name Lucy. I bit my lip as it curved into a smile.

"So, who was that?" Kate asked, jolting me out of my thoughts.

I waved my hand dismissively, accidentally signalling for the barista to come and ask if I wanted another coffee. I ordered anyway. I needed a caffeine hit, if not something stronger. "He's no one, just a friend."

Her eyebrow quirked in disbelief. "Sure, if you say so. He looks like more than a friend to me."

"He's only a friend, Kate, you can shag him if you want." I rolled my eyes, refusing to bite. The words stuck in my throat, and I most definitely did *not* want Kate to go there, for her own safety of course.

"I would. So would you," Kate teased, curling a ringlet of hair around her index finger and grinning as she stared off into the distance, her mind clearly running away with itself.

"No, I wouldn't. It is possible to be friends with a boy."

"He's more than a boy, Eve, or are you blind now?" she smirked, her gaze skimming over the few bruises still on show. I had never been any good at make-up.

"I fell when Ryan tried to take me mountain climbing," I rushed to explain as I caught her staring, unable to tear my eyes off her cast. "What happened to you?"

Kate shrugged, not overly concerned. "Messy night out."

"When?"

"A few weeks ago, at Craig's birthday. You'd know if you hadn't run off with that asshole." The words rolled off Kate's tongue with ease, but her expression remained relatively impassive for someone who seemed to have no clue about how she ended up in a cast.

"Ryan," I corrected her, letting the insult slide for the sake of keeping her on track. "What happened after I left?"

"It's blurry, but I'm pretty sure someone slipped a pill in my drink. Some guy was trying it on with you, and he didn't take rejection very well, so I kicked his ass and we got in a bit of a fight. It's fine."

I swallowed, my voice cracking. "You don't look fine..."

Kate noticed the tears pricking my eyes and reached out for my hand, linking her fingers with mine. "I promise, the doctors said the bruising will heal, and the arm will be right as rain. That guy deserved to get his ass kicked."

When Ryan had said he'd sorted it, I didn't think he would have used any version of the truth. *At least he made Kate think she was the hero.*

"Do you have his number?" Kate asked, interrupting my brooding thoughts and plans to ask Ryan about how exactly he made everyone, including Kate, believe that version of events.

"Who's number?"

She rolled her eyes and gave me a deadpan stare. "The hot blonde?"

I shook my head, ignoring her Cheshire Cat grin. "You're not shagging him."

"I knew you wanted him for yourself!"

"No," I said, my tone firmer than I expected. "I just don't want to lose a friend because you go through men like wildfire."

She folded her arms in a huff. "I do not."

"You would eat him for breakfast!"

She lifted her sunglasses and winked. "He can have me for breakfast any day."

We both broke into a fit of giggles.

"You're disgusting," I hiccupped between laughing, tears rolling down my cheek.

It had been so long since I had a proper conversation with a friend. It all felt so normal. Except it wasn't. Luke could eat her, just not in the way Kate was daydreaming. I sobered. I needed to be more careful. Kate wasn't a part of this world, and I didn't want to put her in danger. Not that I believed that Luke would hurt her, but I wasn't so sure about Ryan's pack. I couldn't risk Kate becoming a part of this side of my life. It was too dangerous.

CHAPTER 20

W e talked for hours about everything from boys to exam results. When the café closed, we moved on to the nearest bar and kept talking, with a few drinks thrown in for good measure. Kate was getting our third round when my phone rang.

"Hello?"

Ryan's voice blared down the line. "Where are you?"

"I told you, I'm with Kate." I laughed, watching my best friend chat up a group of guys at the bar for free drinks. "I'll be back later. I can grab a taxi."

I wasn't entirely sure I could give someone directions to the manor drunk, let alone sober, but I could always crash at Kate's.

"You should have been home hours ago. It's Friday."

His voice rose and I winced, holding the phone away from my ear.

"Yes, I know what day it is, *Ryan*." I rolled my eyes, trying to communicate to Kate with one hand not to order another sambuca.

"Then you should also know this is the first night of the lunar celebration for the month?"

My mouth went dry. *Shit*. "Ryan, I'm sorry I forgot."

The pressure of the hunt with his pack had been weighing on me for weeks now, but vodka had a funny way of washing away my worries. It still felt like only yesterday that Nadine had mauled me.

"Are you drunk?" he hissed, sounding absolutely furious. "We only shifted the other night, how much of a reminder do you need?"

"No, I'm not drunk. I've only had a few."

"I'm coming to get you."

The line went dead.

Ryan didn't even ask where I was or how to find me. Within half an hour, he texted to say that he was outside the bar. When I didn't answer the text immediately, he appeared in the doorway. The thunderous look on his face warned me arguing wasn't an option. Plus, I didn't want Kate getting involved. Some friends from college had joined us, and two cute guys were fawning all over her—she wouldn't miss me too much. I said a rushed goodbye to them, promised to see Kate again soon, and followed Ryan outside.

He was already back in the driver's seat. I hopped in the passenger side and flung the door shut. Ryan looked less than happy to see me. Without a single word, he slammed his foot onto the accelerator, and I scrambled to put on my seatbelt.

"I'm sorry," I said, trying to break the awkward silence hanging between us.

Ryan's grip on the steering wheel tightened. "You can tell the alpha that."

I gulped. "Don't be like that."

"Like what, Eve?" His head snapped to look at me, his expression dark and unreadable. "You asked to join the pack. This isn't all fun and games."

"Hey, I've already gone through my fair share of crap." I scowled, slumping back in my seat. "And I haven't asked to join the pack."

I watched the way his jaw tensed and sighed. When it came to arguing, he had the worst temper. It was impossible to talk him round. The only time I remembered seeing him this angry was the night in the park and there was only one common denominator. Luke.

He sped around a corner, tyres squealing. His knuckles were white as he gripped the steering wheel. "Do you think I can't smell him all over you?"

I blanched, sobering up on the spot. "Luke came to me. I was only there to meet Kate."

Ryan stared at the road, a manic anger flashing in his eyes, as if he wanted to wrap the car around a tree. "If I smell him on you again, it will be the last time you get to meet her."

He sounded just like his father.

"What the fuck, Ryan? Where is this coming from?" I wrenched the door handle down, but it wouldn't budge—not that I was going anywhere at this speed.

He knew I wasn't great with cars. I'd told him about the nightmares. I was only a baby, I had no memories of the crash my parents died in, but that didn't stop it haunting my dreams.

Ryan wasn't finished ranting, and his foot pressed even further on the accelerator. "There is more to being part of the pack than turning up when you feel like it. You're embarrassing yourself and me."

"As if they even want me there," I spat, crossing my arms. "You can't tell me who I can and can't see."

"If you're staying with my pack, you need to start playing by the rules."

The last few weeks had been rough and today was the first day I had felt remotely normal again. I wanted to press rewind on my life, to go back to before and get out of this crazy mess, but that wasn't an option.

"I was having fun with Kate." I hated how childish he made me sound.

"You don't get it. You can change whenever you want, but we can't. The full moon is sacred to us. By flouting this, you are only highlighting how different you are."

"I *am* different!"

He shook his head, staring darkly at the road ahead. "Maybe that's the problem."

I stared at him open-mouthed, wondering where exactly the guy who I'd been sharing a bed with had vanished to.

When we arrived, the lights in the manor house were off. Ryan headed towards the back of the estate. Although we walked together, we were at least a foot apart at all times. I could see fire in the distance, beyond the red brick houses. As we drew nearer, I could hear shouting and the hum of conversation. The entire pack was there, either sitting near the fire in their human form or in small scattered groups with plates on their laps. It looked like they were just finishing up a meal.

Ryan's father strode over to us, imposing as always in his black suit. I swallowed, beginning to feel queasy. Butterflies and alcohol didn't mix well.

"You missed the dinner." It was a statement, not a question.

"I'm sorry, father. I had some business to attend to. It won't happen again." Ryan hung his head, and I followed suit, trying to look suitably chastised.

The alpha looked between us and scowled, muttering something incoherent before stalking away.

I breathed a sigh of relief, looking to Ryan, but he was already moving in the opposite direction. Not recognising many faces and wary about being alone, I followed. There were three large bonfires burning in the clearing and several tables piled high with food and wine. As we got closer to one, I noticed a deer carcass on top of the carefully built wooden pyre. Ryan picked up a glass from a table and took a sip, his lips red as he smiled, and handed a second glass to me.

"Truce?"

Seriously?

I frowned, eyeing the glass with disdain. "No nightshade, right?"

"Of course not."

Ryan knocked back his drink, a wide grin plastered over his face. The crazed look in his eyes had vanished, and that scared me even more. How could he just switch from zero to a hundred like that? Was it fear of his father? Then I remembered his temper that night in the park. The way he could flip like a switch meant that I was always on my guard. When we met, he was the perfect boyfriend, always polite and calm. I didn't know how to deal with this new Ryan.

Forcing my shoulders to relax and faking a smile, I took a sip of the rich red wine. As the liquid hit the back of my throat, I gagged. A metallic taste filled my mouth and the scent of fresh blood flared in my nostrils. There must have been an herb in the drink masking the smell, but once it passed my lips, I could tell it was blood.

He bowled over with laughter, like a jock watching a teenage girl struggle to down her first drink. I paled and spat the contents out on the ground, wiping my mouth with the back of my arm. The taste lingered.

"What the hell? Please tell me that isn't human blood."

He looked less than impressed at my little show when it splashed his shoe. "It's deer blood, don't be so dramatic."

Bile rose in my throat and I gagged, struggling to keep the contents of my stomach from making a reappearance. I heard sniggering behind me, and my temper surged. Deciding to take Luke's advice, I set my glass down on the table and turned slowly to face the culprits, a group of two guys and one girl who I recognised as a friend of Nadine's. I stalked towards them, letting the tips of my claws extend.

"Do we have a problem?"

The tallest guy stepped forward, eyeing me up like a piece of meat he wanted to spoil and then slaughter. "No problem here. We aren't the ones trying to fake it."

I let a low growl escape my lips. Maybe it was Dutch courage from my drinks with Kate, or maybe I was finding my feet. Maybe I was just pissed off. He was twice my height, but I squared my shoulders and poked him in the chest with a clawed forefinger.

"Do you want to come say that to my face in a few days? Some of us don't need to hide behind the full moon to be brave," I said, mirroring the bitchy tone I picked up from the queen bee herself. It seemed to do the job.

They shook their heads, glancing over my shoulder towards Ryan and then to my clawed hands. I saw the bigger guy's eyes flash silver for a moment, but a crowd was gathering, and he clearly had second thoughts. They backed away, retreating to one of the other bonfires.

I reluctantly walked back over to Ryan, who had the most sadistic grin lighting up his features. He nodded in approval. "Nicely done."

"You aren't off the hook either, this isn't a truce," I snapped, giving him a thump in the chest for good measure. "You don't get to speak to me like that."

Ryan nodded, but I wasn't looking at him. I caught sight of the alpha watching me over his shoulder. His face was a mask of displeasure. Ryan threatening to stop me seeing Kate was one level of crazy, but what the alpha had threatened was worse.

As much as it stuck in my throat, and I wasn't finished arguing with him, I pulled Ryan into an overzealous hug. "I'm sorry," I said, placing a kiss on his cheek in perfect view of his father. "I didn't mean that, I'm still struggling with my temper."

Ryan accepted my apology far too easily. He stayed glued to my side for the night, only leaving me briefly to get another drink. This time, it was water, and I was more than grateful to wash out the last hints of metal lingering in my mouth. I glanced at the now cremated carcasses atop the pyres and shuddered. One thing I was yet to do was kill as a wolf. Not that I was a vegetarian or anything, but the thought of taking down an animal and eating it raw was difficult to stomach. I knew as part of the hunt lasting the weekend that was what I would have to do.

"It will be fine so long as you give into the wolf side." Ryan followed my gaze to the charred remains. I hoped he was right.

He squeezed my arm and led me away from the dancing light of the bonfires and towards the entrance to the forest. I wriggled out of his grip once we were out of the alpha's sight. A worn path in the undergrowth, lit only by the full moon casting shadows through the forest canopy, led us to a group of werewolves, all with broad chests and heavy-set shoulders. They were definitely all male. Several of them stood in a wide ring, surrounding two werewolves in the middle, squaring up to each other. One was a sandy brown, with a shaggy coat, and a deep red patch on his flank. The other was slightly larger with half an ear. Both wolves had saliva and blood dripping from their teeth and were panting and growling as they circled one another. Tension hung heavy in the summer night. The wolves watching kept the outer boundary, snapping at their heels if they came too close.

We stopped a couple of feet back, but the wolves barely seemed to notice us. If they did, they made no effort to acknowledge our presence.

The darker wolf made the first move, lunging at his opponent with his fangs bared. They leapt at each other, becoming a tangled mess of limbs and snapping jaws. Blood sprayed on the grass near us.

I watched in silence, disgusted but also enthralled by the skill with which they fought. Even in their wolf form, it was clear they were both making calculated decisions, learning from their mistakes, and seeking out their competitor's weaknesses. They were both talented, and although the smaller of the two was less experienced, he far outmatched the other wolf in terms of speed and recovery. But the older wolf had technique. There were clear pros and cons to both, and I found myself enjoying watching their bouts.

I twisted, turning to Ryan. "Who won?" I whispered, not wanting to disturb the next fight or draw attention to us.

He smiled, his thumb tracing circles on the small of my back. "That one was a tie. We only fight to the death when someone is contesting the alpha."

"Oh." I remembered what Luke had said earlier that day and shivered.

An unnerving bloodthirst shone in Ryan's eyes as he turned his attention back to the next match.

I filed the information away to add to my research. I needed to know how his dad had become the alpha—something about it didn't sit right with me. I'd planned to ask Ryan, but given his recent tool-like behaviour, that was a no-go.

As I watched the wolves and their intricate dance, I discovered that I liked the idea of fighting more than I ever thought possible. Not for the blood sport, but for the power and confidence it would bring. As Luke had said, I needed to be able to protect myself.

"Can I learn how to fight?" I asked Ryan as we walked back to join the crowds surrounding the bonfires.

"No, you have me to defend you."

I frowned. "Would it not make sense, since I'm a hybrid?"

"There is no need for you to learn how to fight, Eve. I'm always here," he replied, his tone growing bored.

"What about when you're not here?" I stopped, pulling Ryan to face me. "What if someone attacks me when I'm alone?"

He shook his head. "You are a hybrid. I think you made it clear tonight that you are not afraid to hammer that point home. Give them a chance to adjust. Change takes time."

Ryan began walking again, hooking my arm in his as he led us towards his family. I detached myself from him immediately, attempting to be subtle. Nadine stepped out from behind Ryan's father, as if appearing out of thin air. She beamed at Ryan, but when her gaze fell on me, she reverted to the usual look of disdain. Ryan may have been convinced that I was safe in the pack, but at least half of the members still looked at me like they wanted to rip me limb from limb. I needed to learn how to fight and I knew just the person to teach me.

CHAPTER 21

Less than a week later, I watched Fiona's mini fade off into the distance while I lingered in a derelict business park. She had dropped me off on the outskirts of north Dublin at the address Luke had given me. Talking her into helping me had been easier than I expected, especially when I had explained that I wanted to be able to defend myself against Nadine. There was no reason the alpha should find out. As long as I kept Ryan happy, I was fine, although, we still hadn't cleared the air after that argument. He was frosty, stressed out, and nothing like his normal self. I felt as if I was living with a stranger.

I frowned and glanced up at the building again, a grey warehouse whose walls had seen better days. *Was I in the right place?* The addressed matched the location pinned on the map app on my phone, so I slumped against the wall and waited. When I was ready to give up, tyres squealed in the distance. Moments later a black car turned into the carpark. Luke flashed me a welcome grin as he pulled up in front of me and cut the engine.

"You're late."

He didn't make any move to get out of the car, rolling down the window instead and motioning for me to join him. "Hop in."

Against my better judgement, I joined him, and we sped off in the direction he had come. This was exactly how girls got murdered. But Luke didn't drive far, only to a neighbouring business park.

When I looked to him for an explanation, he simply shrugged. "I didn't want to get you in trouble if Ryan did something stupid like read your messages and decide to show up."

I had no arguments there. It was the same reason I'd deleted any messages to Luke.

Is this what my relationship had become? Lying and sneaking around behind his back?

We pulled up in front of another warehouse, but this time signs of gym bunnies in shorts and guys with rippling muscles plastered the windows. "Seriously?"

Luke caught sight of my sceptical expression and laughed. "I promise it will make sense when we get in there."

As I followed him to a back entrance, he held the door open and ushered me through in front of him. I could hear the clang of weights hitting the floor as we descended a flight of steps bringing us to a large room where a boxing ring took centre stage. It was empty but for a bald man re-racking dumbbells and muttering to himself.

"Are you kidding me?" I spun to face Luke, throwing my hands in the air. "You promised to teach me to protect myself."

Someone cleared their throat behind me. "You need to learn to fight as a human first."

I turned to see the bald man, a head taller than me, with a physique that could only be described as that of a brick. My mouth dropped and Luke chuckled.

"This is Benji, the owner of this boxing gym," Luke explained, doing some sort of a private handshake with Benji and clapping him on the back.

I looked between them and rubbed my temples. Benji was obviously a werewolf too, and I cursed myself for not paying enough attention to notice his scent, though the stench of sweat in the gym gave me some excuse.

Feeling sheepish, I shut my mouth and let the two chat for a moment before Benji excused himself, leaving me alone with Luke.

"He's right, you know," Luke said, shrugging his hoodie off to reveal those muscles underneath. "You need to learn to fight as a human before you can defend yourself as a wolf. Two must become one."

"I just thought..." I sighed and shook my head, throwing my jumper on top of his hoodie. Deep down I knew Luke had a point. I'd felt the connection. There was no rushing this. "You're right."

My arms looked like twigs compared to his. Luke's idea of a warm-up left me looking like a tomato and ready to puke up my breakfast. At first, I was embarrassed, but I was quickly too exhausted to care. He barely broke a sweat while teaching me the movements and ordering me around. Even though he was bossy, he did it in such a way that made me want to try harder.

I rolled onto my back panting and took a swig of water. "You might be a good teacher, but you're also an ass."

"I'll accept the second part of that." Luke laughed. A look ghosted his eyes but vanished as soon as it came. He reached for the water bottle in my hands and tossed it aside, his hand still outstretched. "Come on, time to fight."

My jaw dropped. "What was all this?" I motioned to myself, hair stuck to my forehead and my skin a bright shade of pink.

"The warm-up." Luke flashed me a grin that made my heart skip a beat, his eyes sparkling with mischief.

I took his hand, and he pulled me to my feet. Less than a second later, he swept his foot out and caught me behind the knees. I yelped and landed on my ass with a thud.

"What the hell?" I yelled, kicking out at his ankle.

Luke dodged with ease and held his hand out to me again, an impish grin on his face, but his gaze was serious. "Lesson number one, never let your guard down, not with anyone."

This time, I refused his offer, huffing as I stood up with no help and backed away cautiously. Luke took up a defensive position, hands balled into fists above his chest. I followed suit.

"Lesson number two, strength and speed can always be overcome with intelligence," Luke said as we circled one and other.

I kept my eyes trained on his hands and my focus on my feet, wary of what was coming next. Sure enough, Luke came at me again, but this time I was more prepared. I parried the first punch, the second caught me in the ribs.

"Why can't we use gloves?" I winced, rubbing my side.

Luke stepped towards me, ready with another warning blow that glanced off my shoulder. He danced away, clearly having fun.

"There are no gloves in real life. I thought you wanted to learn how to fight properly?"

We went back and forth sparring, and although I knew Luke never used his full force, I was guaranteed a few bruises in the morning. Every couple of rounds he would pause and teach me a new move. When he stepped behind me to perfect my right hook, a shiver crawled up my spine. His breath was hot on my neck as he explained the technique to get maximum power behind my fist. I nodded and bit my lip, his words going over my head.

"Make sure that your feet are set, one leg out in front," Luke said, nudging my left calf forward with his foot so I was in a split stance. "This will help you put all of your strength behind the punch."

As he held my arm and showed me how to follow through with the movement, I was glad he couldn't see my face or the redness burning in my cheeks. Not that he could tell, I knew my entire face was beetroot from all the movement. He could smell me though, in all my sweaty glory.

"Maybe we should call it a day," Luke said, and I felt an unexpected wave of disappointment as he stepped away from me.

I realised that he must have taken my distracted silence as a sign that I wanted to stop, but I was just getting the hang of things. "I think I can do more after a little rest."

He nodded, grabbing a water bottle and flopping on the ground. I followed suit and sat cross-legged opposite him, my breath coming in short pants. In between sips, I pressed a hand to my chest and gulped, trying to fill my lungs. When I looked up and caught him studying my face, blood rushed to my cheeks again unbidden. The thoughtful expression he wore piqued my curiosity.

"What's your pack like?"

Luke paused, scratching the back of his head. "You already have a pack."

"I don't have a pack," I said, pressing the cool bottle to my neck and sighing with relief. "Humour me, please?"

"It's different. We left years ago because we didn't agree with their methods or the direction in which they were going. Ryan's father was power hungry and short-sighted." Luke watched me for a reaction but continued, an intensity creeping into his tone. "We value loyalty and family, what a pack is meant to be. There's no place for modern politics in my family, and we don't care for archaic induction ceremonies."

Luke looked at me, curiosity burning in his eyes. I rolled my shoulders, my lips curving into a smile. His pack sounded different—nice. Especially the last part.

"Why don't you want to be the alpha?" I asked, blurting out the question that had been there since our first real conversation. Luke was a lovely guy. He had buckets of charm and a laugh that made a girl melt, but there was a darkness that lingered around him.

His expression cooled, but when he spoke, there was no anger in his voice, only the pang of regret. "I let my pack down many years ago when my sister, Alice, disappeared." He got to his feet and took my hand, pulling me up so we were standing noses inches apart. "Like I said before, not everyone is cut out to be an alpha."

We lingered like that, his gaze locked on mine in some kind of unspoken dance, his hand resting on my hip. I looked away first.

The moment Luke shuffled back from me with his hands raised in a block, I knew training had resumed. He rushed at me again and again until I started getting better at dodging even unpredictable attacks. Once I cleared my head and let my heightened senses take hold, things became easier. I still ended up on my ass more times than I cared to remember, but the survival instinct was there.

One... two... duck. Three. Hook.

I watched Luke send his fist towards my shoulder and ducked just in time so that his fist connected with air. Luke chuckled and swung his left arm towards my side, but I spun away from that too. Uncontrollable spinning had slowly become planned, and I began anticipating some of his swings. When I turned to face Luke and launch an attack, a wide grin lit up his face, and he was so busy smiling at me that my fist collided with his stomach, right below his ribs.

"Got you!" I squealed in delight, dancing away from him before he could retaliate.

But Luke was bent over, caught in an odd mix between bellowing laughter and breathlessness.

I frowned and walked towards him, staying on my toes in case it was a trick. "Are you all right?"

"I'm fine," he said, coughing and spluttering with laughter. "You just winded me a bit, that's all."

"You don't look winded." My eyes narrowed as I watched him laugh and rise to his feet. "You look amused."

He shook his head, straightening himself slowly. "I'm not amused, I'm pleased."

I folded my sweaty arms across my chest and arched an eyebrow, panting as I tried to catch my breath. "Pleased?"

"Yes, with you." Luke placed his hands on my shoulders, those gorgeous eyes of his sparkling. "You have more fight that I expected, Eve. Never lose it."

CHAPTER 22

By the time I caught a bus back to meet Fiona, dusk had already set in, a blanket of darkness replacing the earlier sunshine. Luke had offered to drive me, but I didn't want to push my luck. Boxing had been fun. Being out of pack territory had me feeling more like myself, but I knew Fiona was less than happy about the situation. Sure enough, she was waiting for me under a dull streetlight, her mousy features creased with worry.

"What kept you so long?" Fiona snapped, practically dragging me towards her car. If looks could kill, Luke would have been six feet under.

"I'm sorry, I thought we agreed to eight?"

She gripped my wrist, her fingernails cutting into my skin. I winced, my head reeling as I watched Luke's car disappear off into the night. Fiona only released her grip on me once she had bundled me into the passenger seat of her mini, slamming the door before storming around to the driver's side. I glanced at my watch which said eight, bang on the pre-agreed time. I specifically chose the afternoon to meet Luke because they were less likely to notice me slinking back this late.

Fiona kicked off the engine and pulled out onto the road without so much as a look my way, or in the direction of on-coming cars, before pulling out and ramming her foot down on the accelerator.

"What the hell is going on, Fiona?" I snapped, scrambling for my seatbelt.

The evening with Luke had me in such a good mood. It was the first genuine fun I had since finding out what I was—and here was Fiona, pissing lemons all over it.

Fiona scowled, pointing to the glove compartment. "There's perfume in there, don't stop until you're choking on the smell."

Seeing Fiona like this scared me. I didn't think she had bad moods, let alone a temper.

"Fi—"

"Perfume, now," she snapped, focusing on the winding country road ahead of us.

I did as I was told, rummaging in the glove compartment until my fingers closed around a glass perfume bottle. A tentative test spray had me spluttering. It was not my kind of scent.

"Why are you freaking out?"

"You need to look at your phone more often. Ryan got back from work early, he was wondering why you weren't back at the manor."

"The *manor*?" I scoffed, chucking my bag down between my legs, which were still shaky from the boxing. Who knew it was so tiring?

Fiona swung her head to give me a dead pan glare. "Yes, the house. Whatever you want to call it."

"What did you tell him?" I asked, her demeanour quickly souring my mood.

"I told him that you asked me to drop you off to meet Kate, and that you didn't tell him because he got mad last time."

"How'd he take it?"

Fiona rolled her eyes at me.

"That well, huh?" I groaned, flopping back in the seat, toying with the lid of my water bottle.

Shit.

"I warned you they wouldn't approve of this, Eve," she snapped, an iciness in her tone that I never imagined possible. "They hate the Crescents. You're playing with fire."

Fiona took the next corner at full speed, and my stomach lurched. I watched her pained expression, those soft features scrambled into a mask of panic. She was always so softly spoken and kind, this had come out of nowhere. She looked petrified.

All I could do was hope Ryan hadn't told the alpha. From the small bit of research I'd managed, pissing him off wasn't on my list of things to do. I still needed answers before I could tell Ryan what was going on. At least Fiona hadn't said I was meeting Luke. That would've blown things up.

Two familiar pillar statues shone in the headlights and I gulped.

When Fiona turned to me again, her expression was grim. "You better pray he believed me, otherwise we're about to get burned."

When Fiona dropped me outside the house, the front door was closed, and everything seemed normal. I'd half expected Ryan to meet me on the steps, but there was no sign of him. Fiona said a rushed goodbye and drove off towards her end of the estate. I would have loved some backup, but it wasn't fair to involve her. She had lied for me too much already.

I opened the front door to an empty foyer, only the distant sounds of metal clanging in the kitchen and some quiet conversation echoing. I frowned. Ryan wasn't one for sulking. He was explosive—more so than I had originally thought. I'd been pumping myself up for an argument for the entire car ride, fully expecting him to be waiting for my arrival. He had a habit of confronting me head on, so where the hell was he?

"Ryan?" I called out, but no one answered.

I'm not entirely sure what I was expecting. This wasn't a game of hide and seek.

Once I knew the coast was clear, I nipped back outside to grab the bag of clothes I'd stashed in the bushes and tiptoed upstairs. Before I even opened the bedroom door, I knew it was empty. Normally I'd be able to hear Ryan pottering around or the faintest beat of his heart from outside, but all I could hear was silence. I had the quickest of showers, tying my damp hair up in a ponytail and gathering all the dirty clothes up. There was a laundry basket in our room, but I brought them all down to the laundry room myself after dousing them in body spray. Fiona was the one who did the washing anyway, and she wasn't going to rat me out.

By the time I finished covering my trail, I was exhausted but grateful that I got the chance. Wherever Ryan was, if he didn't believe Fiona's cover story, he would have a hard time proving his theories.

As I rounded the top of the staircase and stepped onto the landing, I heard a bang come from down the hall in the opposite direction of the bedroom. I remembered Ryan saying his father's office was the very last one in that wing. Common sense told me to go back to our bedroom, but my curiosity won out, and I followed the direction of the noise. I kept my footsteps light and my ears trained, ignoring my heart thumping in anticipation.

I'd almost reached the end of the corridor marked by a large glass window, when one of the doors burst open and Nadine fell out onto the corridor, her grating laugh echoing. I leapt, cursing in surprise. I caught sight of Ryan's name on the doorplate as it swung open completely.

"Eve," Ryan said, stepping out into view, his voice tight. "I thought Fiona said you wouldn't be back until later."

I shot him a strained smile. "And I thought you were at work."

Nadine watched the exchange with far too much pleasure, her eyes lighting up. She opened her mouth to butt in, but Ryan held his hand up to silence her.

"Nadine was just returning my phone. I left it at the office, and she was kind enough to fetch it for me," Ryan explained, earning a sideways glare from Nadine.

She pressed her tongue to her cheek, steely eyed and ready to argue.

"I thought girls weren't allowed at the office?" The words left my mouth before I could claw them back.

"Do I look like a secretary?" She smirked, adjusting her too-low cut top. "Plus, I can't have Ryan ignoring my messages."

"Maybe you should take a hint."

"My father needed urgent papers delivered, that's all," Ryan said, keeping his expression perfectly schooled.

I didn't believe him for a second but let it go. I was in no position to go digging for secrets.

Ryan closed the door behind him, locking it and placing the key in his pocket before turning to us, giving Nadine a pointed look. "Speaking of which, don't you have something to do?"

An ugly scowl twisted her features as she turned and stalked away from us, heels clacking on the wooden floors. Once she was out of view, he turned his attention to me.

"So, what's this I hear about you running off to meet Kate?"

"Back it up," I snapped, half-ready to snatch his phone and see if Nadine's words had any weight, but I swore I'd never be that girl. "First of all, you don't get to ask me that. I told you, she is my best friend, I'll see her when I like it. Second, fancy telling me what that bitch was doing in your office?"

Ryan sighed and pinched his nose, his expression pained. "I told you, she was dropping my phone in. Stop trying to twist this around on me."

"It's not twisting, it's a perfectly valid question. You're being shady."

"*I'm* being shady?"

"Yes," I said, struggling to keep my voice down. "You've been flipping out at me. That night you picked me up from the bar you were out of line. You're working all the time, and then I catch that cow stumbling out of your office. You barely speak to me anymore, yet you're the one who dragged me here."

"You came here to learn control." Ryan growled, stepping towards me until my back pressed flush against the wall. "You came here by choice. Don't say I forced you."

"Yes, to learn control, not to be mauled by your pack, threatened, or kept under house arrest," I bit back, shoving him firmly in the chest and back out of my personal space.

"Who threatened you? Nadine?" he asked, his brow furrowing, completely missing the bulk of my point.

I wanted to tell him his father was a psychopath, that his pack was seven shades of fucked up, but a Nick shaped shadow appeared down the hall.

"Everything okay here?" Nick asked, walking towards us.

We all had werewolf hearing, there was no way he hadn't heard me.

I cursed under my breath and gave Ryan another shove until I was happy with the distance between us.

"Nick, this is none of your business," Ryan said, his dark gaze moving from me to zero in on Nick. He set his already tense shoulders, squaring up like some kind of testosterone fuelled teenager. "Please, stay out of things."

"There's nothing to stay out of," I hissed, shoving past both of them and striding down the hall.

Ryan made no attempt to stop me, too busy launching into an argument with Nick that I wasn't planning on sticking around to hear. I didn't head back to the room. Instead, I sought solace in the library in the hope of finding some answers. The way Ryan had been acting, I wasn't so sure he didn't already know the truth. The only thing keeping me from packing up my things and heading to Kate was the worry that the alpha might follow.

CHAPTER 23

R yan wanted me to meet him for lunch, so I didn't have to rely on Fiona for cover, which was probably for the best. She wasn't a natural liar. Each time she drove me to meet Luke, it stressed her out. We'd been meeting almost twice a week. I wasn't half bad at fighting now, and the breaks were doing me good. The city was buzzing when I stepped out of the taxi and onto a street crammed with people, some strolling and others in business suits power walking. I handed the driver a fifty euro note and told him to keep Ryan's change.

"What time do you call this?"

The familiar voice broke through the throng shortly after his scent filtered to me. I spun to see Luke lounging at the side of the footpath against the wall. He was in his signature shirt and jeans look, getting in everyone's way but completely oblivious.

"I thought we agreed to meet in the bar? How did you even know I was being dropped here?" I babbled, caught off guard.

He shrugged, a sly little smirk curving his lips. "I have ways."

"Now who's the stalker?" I muttered, grabbing his arm and pulling him through the crowd and down one of the many side streets.

Luke followed at his far too chill pace, but I kept tugging him along until we were deeper into the north side of the city, still surrounded by people but away from the business area.

"I told you we needed to be careful. Ryan's pack don't like me as it is."

"So you've said, yet you insist on sticking around because of what—your boyfriend?"

I stiffened, Nadine's vicious smirk fresh in my mind. I'd been seeing less of Ryan as the weeks went on. He was spending more time at work, I was spending my days with Fiona and Mary in the kitchen or running off to meet Luke. There was nothing but tension back in the house—Ryan's half-hearted apology and the promise of a fancy lunch hadn't been enough.

"Besides, you wouldn't be about to find the bar without me," Luke said, rolling his eyes at me as if I were being dramatic.

"Can we go inside somewhere, please? Or go practice?"

"We are going to practice, just a different kind."

My interest piqued. "I get to change this time?"

"Nope, not yet, eager beaver." Luke began striding down the street, and I scurried after him. "Besides, since when do wolves shift in bars? Have you hit your head?"

I scowled, sick of the back and forth. "How am I supposed to learn to protect myself if I'm not practicing as a wolf? I understood the boxing angle, but my main perk is that I can change whenever. It's the only thing I have over them."

"There's more to being a wolf than just walking the walk. Body language, instinct, and your best weapon—using that brain of yours."

"If you say so."

Luke didn't wait around for my little pity party. As he walked deeper into the city and began disappearing amongst the crowd, I huffed and followed him using my nose until I caught up. Even on a weekday, downtown was bustling with tourists and locals alike. When I weaved my way to Luke, the corners of his lips curved in a smirk. I scowled but fell into step beside him.

"Can I at least know where I'm going or are you planning to keep the dark and mysterious thing going?"

He arched an eyebrow, and laughter bubbled from his throat. "I'm blonde."

"You're a pain in the ass, you know that?"

Luke chuckled, mischief sparkling in his eyes. "You're not the first woman to tell me that."

"I'm sure I won't be the last either," I muttered under my breath, scuttling alongside him. Each step he took was worth two strides of mine, I had to speed walk just to keep up with him.

"What?"

Sighing, I shook my head and placed a light hand on his arm to stop us from being separated as he took a sharp left. "Nothing."

He led me farther along the side streets of the city, past apartments and shops that I didn't recognise. Here the bricked walls were covered in graffiti and wilting posters. Small neon signs flashed, and people gathered in groups cast suspicious looks in our direction. I kept my head bowed and huddled closer to Luke as he strode forward with confidence, even earning a small nod from some groups.

"Are you taking me to a drug den?"

Luke choked on a laugh and almost tripped over a curb at the same time. "No, I'm not." He watched me for a moment, a thoughtful look on his face. "You remind me of her sometimes."

"Of who?"

"No one." Just like that, the ghost of an expression vanished, and his normal lopsided grin reappeared. "Come on, we're almost there."

True to his word, after another few turns and a handful of winding streets, Luke stopped us in front of a rusted metal door. We were in a run-down alleyway that reminded me of work in a strange way, with its mountain of black bins and the odd scruffy cat eyeing me. The door was firmly shut and the weathered handle, old paint flaking with rust and corrosion, looked as if it hadn't been opened in years.

I shot him a sceptical look. "Seriously?"

"Not everything is as it seems, Eve." He flashed that signature smile again and rapped the door with his knuckle three times as if we were in a fantasy film and this was some sort of hidden passageway. "That's your lesson for today."

Unamused and flushed from all of his speed walking, I watched the door. Nothing happened.

"Luke, I—"

"Shush. Just wait."

With a huff, I did as I was told and kept my eyes glued to the door. Slowly, the handle began to blur and turn. At the same time, the door frame started pulsing, and the entire structure morphed into a modern glass automatic door complete with a black carpet right before my eyes.

"Act normal." Luke leaned down to hiss in my ear.

He clasped my hand in his, and all I could think of was how clammy my palms were while trying to pick my jaw off the floor. I squeezed my eyes shut, but when I opened them, the new door was still there, the glass gleaming in the early morning sun. Luke watched me closely, his nose crinkling as he forced back a laugh. I must have gone white because he gave my hand a gentle squeeze that made the butterflies in my stomach flutter.

Luke took a step through the automatic door and I followed, one foot moving in front of the other as if I were on autopilot. We entered a narrow corridor with steps descending into a dimly lit tunnel. Luke led the way, keeping his grasp on my hand the entire time. I could hear something thumping in the distance and tensed as an unfamiliar scent reached me. It smelled for all intents and purposes like death.

"What the hell is that?"

I noticed his shoulders tense as his grip on my hand tightened and took that as a not-so-subtle queue to shut up. The corridor opened out into a bigger room with two large double doors intricately engraved with what looked like a mixture of pagan and Celtic imagery at the end.

"ID?"

A voice came from my right and I jumped, my nails digging into Luke's wrist. I spun to see a tall man with piercing amber eyes staring down at me. He was flawless, his chiselled cheekbones and shoulders accentuated by his fitted black suit. He made Luke look like a scruffy teenager in comparison. This guy oozed class. My breath caught as I spotted another Adonis in the opposite corner.

"Miss?" Their expressions darkened, reminding me far too much of the way Nadine, looked at me during the first hunt.

I pressed a hand to my chest, my heart was hammering for all the wrong reasons. My body was screaming fight or flight, and I knew Luke could feel it too because his grip was like a vice now.

"Sorry, she's never been to this spot before," Luke said, his voice brimming with confidence as he slid his arm around my waist. He faced the first bouncer and his eyes flashed silver, nodding to me. "Babe?"

The bouncer turned his attention to me, his lip quirking up to reveal a single fang. Fear knotted my shoulders. If it hadn't been for Luke's grip on me, I would have bolted out the other side.

In my state of panic, my claws pricked my fingertips and protruded the skin slightly. I glanced down and the bouncer's gaze followed, a fleeting glimpse of surprise lighting up his cold eyes. Luke pulled me into his side as the bouncer leered at me, running his tongue across his fang in a most seductive, but sickening way.

"Are we done here? You were told to quit singling out werewolves," he snapped, taking a step forward so his chest was touching the bouncers. He was a head shorter, but Luke was brimming with confidence. "Or do I need to talk to Darius again?"

"No sir, not at all," the bouncer spat, bowing out of the way with a sneer. "Enjoy."

I was prancing like a horse by the time Luke led us through the doors, my stomach doing somersaults. The sound of electric guitars and drums filled my ears. We had entered an enormous room with a stage, where a band appeared to be doing a sound check. The room was one big circle with a dance floor in front of the stage and a three-sixty bar lining the walls, only breaking for a staircase that led upstairs.

No one took any notice of us as we walked through. Staff continued stacking glasses and cleaning up. A multitude of scents filled my senses and did nothing to settle my nerves. I leaned into Luke, keeping my voice low. "You never told me we were going to a vamp lair."

"It's not a vampire lair and those goons aren't vampires, they're demons," Luke whispered, cupping my elbow in his hand and guiding me up in the winding stairs. "Though there probably will be vampires up here."

If they were demons, what the hell did vamps look like?

My mind flashed through every single vampire movie, but I didn't have to wonder for long. We emerged into a well-lit room, airy, with pristine timber flooring and tasteful turquoise walls decorated with silver designs. At the very end of the room, a large bay window stretched the length of one wall, and wrought iron chandeliers dangled from the high ceiling, flames dancing. To the side was a counter with every pastry you could imagine. The sound of coffee machines hissing echoed over the thrum of conversations and the scent of vanilla lingered in the air.

"An underground Starbucks?"

"Sort of, I guess." Luke chuckled, steering me towards a table by the window. "But without the hipsters."

He had to pull my seat out because I was so busy staring. The clientele looked normal at first glance, but when I looked closer, there were subtle tells; a pointed ear, a shimmer in their outline, lavender eyes, the glimpse of a set of fangs whenever they spoke or laughed. They didn't stay in distinct groups, they mingled and chatted amongst one another.

"Hey, Lukey boy."

His head snapped up, and he groaned.

A small redhead sauntered over to us, her flaming gold eyes lighting up at the sight of Luke, who was squirming under her gaze. She was dressed in a tight-fitted cocktail dress with heels that were far too high for this hour of the morning. Her dimples deepened as she slung a casual arm over his shoulder and cooed in his ear in an American drawl. "Fancy seeing you here this early, honey. Swapping whisky for espresso now, are we?"

"Good, thanks Kallie," Luke said, gently prising her arm from around his neck, but she slithered back like a snake. He grit his teeth and removed it a second time, his voice strained. "This is Eve, I don't think you two have met."

Kallie's gaze flickered to me and her cat eyes narrowed into slits. She pursed her lips, her hands pinching her waist as she jutted her hip out. "Oh, and who is Eve?"

"A friend," Luke said firmly, meeting her bitter stare with one of his own. "We have a lot to discuss, so if you wouldn't mind?"

Clearly not one to take a hint, Kallie hovered by Luke's side and turned her nose up at me. "Who let her in anyway? I can smell her from a mile away."

I stiffened, and Luke nudged my leg under the table. No one else in the room seemed to pay attention to Kallie's little display.

"She's a friend, so back off. This is neutral territory." He scanned the bar, discreetly nudging Kallie out of his personal space. "Where is Jonas?"

"He'll be back in a moment. I'll tell him to come take your order."

"Thanks Kallie."

She swayed on her tiptoes, glowering at Luke. When he twisted away from her to lean closer to me, Kallie threw her arms up and stormed off, her heels clicking on the wooden floorboards.

"What is it with redheads and me?"

Luke barked a laugh, lounging back in his chair, completely relaxed once again. "I don't think this one is you, it's me she hates."

I arched an eyebrow, toying with a napkin. "Really? She looked like she wanted to eat you up."

"We had a one-night stand years ago that's going to haunt me forever." Luke kept one eye on the bar, raking a hand through this hair. "I was blackout drunk and Fae are... trouble. That wasn't the welcome I wanted for you."

"It's okay, I've had much worse." I shrugged, and he grinned, which made a smile dance on my lips. "What is this place?"

Before Luke could answer, a handsome young man with tight fade and a jawline to die for appeared by our table. He wore a deep emerald waistcoat and matching slacks that complimented the rich bronze of his skin. The look in his eyes told me he had years on Luke, but he barely looked past his mid-thirties. Either he had fantastic genes, an amazing plastic surgeon, or he was some kind of immortal.

"It's a safe zone for those of the underworld to relax and be themselves," the waiter explained, handing us a menu and tweaking his bow tie. "All are welcome here so long as they play by the rules, which are mainly no business and no attacking each other. Here, vampires, werewolves, Fae, demons—we all get along."

"Good to see you, Jonas." Luke smiled warmly and reached out to shake the man's hand.

"No witches?"

I laughed, but Jonas' jaw stiffened and all humour in his eyes vanished.

"No, witches are not welcome here. They monitor the place and we tolerate their politics, but that's it."

I swear, if there was a competition for putting your foot in your mouth, I'd be a world champion.

"Sorry, Jonas, she's still learning the ropes. Only a baby really," Luke cut in, rubbing my arm with his thumb when he noticed the panic in my eyes.

"It's fine, I'm just a bit on edge with the extra visits lately. What with everything going on, they're constantly sticking their noses in," Jonas said, scowling at thin air. When he looked at me again, his expression brightened, and the friendly sparkle in his eyes returned. "Now, where did Luke here pick up a beauty like you?"

"In a park, would you believe it?" Luke laughed, shooting me a playful grin.

I thumped his arm, making him double over and laugh harder.

"What? It's the truth," he insisted, pretending to nurse his arm where I'd hit him.

Jonas watched the exchange with a curious expression. "Well, she seems nice, so don't scare her off."

"I'm just showing her around this world, helping her get used to it."

"Just be careful, you know she's with the Faolchúnna pack?"

At Jonas's revelation, whispers stirred throughout the room and all eyes were on me. I could feel their gaze burning a hole in the back of my head, and I shrank in my seat.

"She isn't a member, she's just learning. We welcome everyone here." Luke raised his voice, not that it was necessary. Everyone was listening in on the conversation, and no one was trying to hide it.

"So long as he doesn't turn up, it's fine. Hybrids are more than welcome here, Eve. Any friend of Luke's is a friend of ours," Jonas said, making sure that everyone in the room could hear. Whatever sway he had in this place, they lowered their heads and the gossiping stopped.

"Now, Eve, what can I get you?"

"A latte please?" I squeaked, my heart still hammering in my chest. By that point, I'd shredded the poor napkin all over the table.

"Of course." Jonas smiled, giving my arm a reassuring pat. His touch was cool but not as inhuman as expected. "The usual for you, Luke?"

"Please, thanks for looking after us."

"Anytime. Welcome to The Dark Night, Eve." Jonas winked and took our menus with a flourish, striding away.

Once he was out of earshot—or so I hoped—I propped my chin on my hands and sighed. "At least he doesn't hate me."

"It's not you." Luke sat forward in his chair, perching on the edge. "Ryan's pack isn't popular with this crowd. They're too close to the witches. People don't trust them."

I nodded, struggling to process everything. Between realising that *this crazy world* was real and extended beyond werewolves, along with finding out that I was automatically in their bad books for even knowing Ryan, it was a lot to take in. I think my mind was slowly getting used to massive revelations, though because I didn't faint, I took that as a win.

I looked around the room, examining the various tables. The vampires were obvious, especially the women. They had text-book flawless complexions, but the biggest giveaway was the sultry way in which they moved, even in the simplest of tasks. I could tell some Fae by their pointed ears, or maybe that was me being presumptuous. Now that Jonas had spoken, they seemed to have lost interest in me.

"Why are you showing me this?"

"Because you won't survive in this world being cooped up like an expensive China cup." He chuckled, the melodic sound making me sigh. "An important part of fighting is knowing your enemy, understanding them, being able to predict their next move."

"I don't have an enemy—not that I know of. Maybe Nadine."

"Everyone has an enemy, Eve. If you don't have one yet, you will."

I frowned and looked around the room, watching Jonas bustle about behind the counter readying our orders. "Do humans know?"

"About this place? Not really. It's supposed to be a safe zone for our kind," Luke said, tilting his head and tapping his chin with his fingers. "Yes, some know. The government knows magic exists and there are humans, especially ones involved in wolf packs with hybrid children, or those born without magic, that are still a part of this world. Humans believe what they want to, it's easy to cover our tracks if needed. But if something big happens, which it has, it takes a lot to put them off our scent."

"Like what?"

"Let's just say not all the catastrophes in this world are man-made." Luke sighed, slouching back in his chair again and gesturing to the room. "Now, time for your lesson. Tell me the species of every person in this room. You have three guesses for each."

"What happens if I get them wrong?"

His lips curved into a wide grin. "You'll see."

CHAPTER 24

onas insisted on escorting us to the exit. Although Luke had said everyone was welcome, it was obvious that associating with Ryan was social suicide there. I squinted and used my hand to shield my eyes as we stepped back outside. The afternoon sun beat down and while the alleyway was empty, the moment all three of us were clear, the door morphed back into its dilapidated state. Jonas and Luke lingered by the exit, deep in conversation. I hovered like a third wheel, leaning my back against the wall and tilting my head up to catch a small patch of heat. Admittedly, I was only half trying to mind my own business, but with enhanced wolf hearing, I couldn't help but overhear.

Luke towered over Jonas, who I now knew was a vampire thanks to my lesson. Luke's shoulders were tense, and both of their expressions taut. To any bystanders, it looked as if they were arguing, which wouldn't be outside the realm of possibilities. Apparently, the theory that vampires and werewolves don't get along wasn't a complete myth.

"I told you I needed to get him alive," Luke hissed, dipping his head and lowering his tone. "You promised your guys wouldn't hurt him."

"I'm sorry, accidents happen. This guy wasn't going down without a fight, and my coven couldn't risk him running back to the witches." Jonas sighed, wrapping his bony arms across his chest. "I know you need the intel, but if the witches catch you sniffing around again, you will end up like Alice."

Luke's hands balled into fists. I pricked my ears and focused in on their conversation, despite my wavering morals. My eyes remained trained on the cars flitting by the side street entrance.

"Don't say that, we don't know what happened to her." The pain in his voice made my heart twist. After a brief pause, Luke sighed and scuffed the gravel with his foot. "You know they are hiding something. If you cared for her at all, you'll make sure this trail doesn't go dead. It's the first news we have had in years."

"I promise, I'll keep on it," Jonas said, and I snuck a quick peek in time to see him give Luke's arm a gentle squeeze.

Luke nodded, his mouth set in a thin line. "I'll continue doing my part too. Let me know if you hear anything."

At that, Jonas pulled Luke into a hug, and I looked away. I kept my head down, trying to look as inconspicuous as possible, but Luke barely seemed to notice me as he walked past. When he didn't wait, I bounded after him, slowing when I noticed him wringing his hands. Silver flashed in his glistening eyes when he finally turned to me.

"Are you okay?" I asked, wanting to reach out to him. I hesitated. "Luke?"

He shook his head, his jaw twitching. "No, but I'll be fine. Let's get you back to where you need to be."

I wanted to help, to cheer him up somehow like he always did with me, but I couldn't find the words.

Luke turned to walk away but paused mid-step and spun on his heel to face me. He reached out for my hand, his eyebrows bunching together as he frowned.

I tried to ignore the way the pace of my heartbeat rocketed as he twined his fingers with mine, appearing spaced out but also firmly fixated on my wrist at the same time.

"Where is it?" he asked, his voice distant and disconnected.

I blinked slowly in confusion. "Where is what?"

Luke traced his finger across my wrist, and I went rigid as a shiver travelled down my spine. "Your bracelet."

That morning as I was getting ready, when I went to put on the bracelet, it didn't feel right. My relationship with Ryan was unravelling, and somehow the moment we shared when he gave me the bracelet felt tainted.

"I—eh, I must have forgotten to put it on," I mumbled, not quite ready to spill my guts.

But I didn't need to.

A knowing ghost of a smile tugged at the corners of his mouth as he released my wrist, his anger dissipating as he started towards the exit of the alleyway and motioned for me to follow.

Luke left me a few blocks away from Ryan's office block. He looked as if he was on the edge of falling apart and could barely look at me when we said goodbye. I wanted to comfort him, to tell him that whatever it was would be okay. But the haunted look in his eyes had returned, and if the morning had taught me anything, it was that I was completely out of my depth in this world. What advice could someone like me possibly offer an alpha in the making? None. So, I kept my mouth shut.

Ryan's office building was a glass tower block that reflected the river and the autumn sun. It was an enormous chunk of metal really, but I suppose some fancy architects found it pretty. As I stepped through the rotating doors, trying my best to make sure I didn't trip as businessmen powered through, I admired the sheer wealth of the place. Royal red carpets criss-crossed the marble floors to guide visitors towards the reception and large screens covered the walls with high-definition images swirling and changing in sequence. In the centre, a spiral staircase ascended towards the roof of the building, branching out to the different floors. It was magnificent, huge, and so over the top, it was perfect for Ryan's father and their business.

I felt out of place in my jeans and top but that seemed to be a constant in my life now. As a hybrid, I didn't seem to fit in anywhere. With my shoulders back, I walked over to the reception desk where I was greeted by a tall girl in a pencil skirt with legs that went on forever. Her makeup was flawless, and there wasn't a hair out of place in her perfectly preened bun.

"Can I help you?" the receptionist chirped, her pointed nose scrunching as she gave me the once over. "Do you need directions?"

No. Do you need me to rearrange your face?

"No, thank you." I flashed her a fake smile, biting back the first words that came to mind. "I have a lunch appointment with Ryan McKenna."

She drummed her manicured nails on the desk, staring at the computer screen for a moment before looking up with a smirk. "I'm sorry miss, Mr. McKenna is otherwise engaged."

Lately, I would have been happy to waltz away and not have to deal with Ryan for the rest of the day, but this girl had gotten under my skin, and I so wasn't in the mood.

"You should check again, or I could ring him myself, perhaps?" She paled as I produced my phone and flashed her his number. "I'm sure he would like to know why you have rearranged his schedule without notifying him."

"I—I'm sorry," the receptionist stammered, casting a panicked glance up the stairs.

All colour drained from her face, and I followed her gaze to see Ryan's father, the alpha, striding towards us. He zeroed in on me, and I noticed his posture stiffen. I had no doubt that I also resembled a ghost at this point.

"Eve, how lovely to see you," he said, reaching out to shake my hand. I was too stunned to reciprocate, but he shook my limp hand, regardless. "How can I help you?"

"I'm supposed to be meeting Ryan for lunch now."

I swallowed and watched as the alpha eyed me carefully, his hands clasped across his stomach and his expression impassive. Reading people had always been something I prided myself on, but I could never read Ryan's father. He was impossible to predict and knowing what he was capable of terrified me.

The receptionist gaped at us, only remembering to shut her mouth when the alpha leaned down to peer at the appointment book.

"Ah yes, it seems he had an urgent meeting to attend across town," he said, flashing me a wide smile that didn't dent the ice in his eyes.

"I don't mind waiting."

Shut up, Eve.

"No, that won't be necessary." The alpha stepped closer, his nose crinkling and his posture stiffening for the briefest of moments. "You should go back to the house, shower perhaps, and I will explain to Ryan that you stopped by."

I gulped, and my heart started hammering in my chest. Of course, he smelled Luke. I was an idiot for thinking that just because we didn't get all sweaty, his scent wouldn't linger.

The alpha placed a hand on the small of my back and slowly but firmly began guiding me towards the exit. "You should arrange to meet somewhere else next time."

It didn't take much for me to read between the lines, but just in case I was too stupid, he decided to hammer the point home.

"This is no place for hybrids," he said, pulling me to a halt by the door and staring at me, intensity burning in his eyes. "It would upset our clients."

Every answer that came to my mind would land me in trouble, so I sidestepped and reached for the door. A hand closed around my arm and the alpha pulled me back towards him, glowering down at me. "Do you understand?"

I bit my lip, chewing until it was raw, and nodded. "Understood."

CHAPTER 25

Since my lunch trip had been ruined, I convinced Fiona to drive me in for more sessions. She always dropped me to the false address, and sometimes I got the bus under a different excuse. We kept the times sporadic, and Ryan was none the wiser. I always showered thoroughly before he was home. When I wasn't learning to fight, which I found surprisingly enjoyable, I spent my time going for runs in the forest, practising the change, annoying Mary in the kitchens and exploring.

The sun was setting over the mountains as I stepped outside for my evening walk. I always attempted to avoid Nadine's house, but I could see her fiery curls from the path, eyes narrowed as she peered out at me. I gave her the finger, and the curtains snapped shut.

That day, rather than heading to the forest, I took a right after the first batch of red brick houses and started exploring this side of the estate instead. There were barns, and rhythmic banging came from some sheds, metal on metal and sometimes on wood.

Further on, I passed an old man with greying hair, one eye a pale blue. In front of him, there was a large easel and a half-finished picture of the view by the river. He was painting from memory. Ryan had told me his paintings sold for a good sum in the city.

"Hi Billy," I called out, raising my voice more than usual so he would hear me. Not only was his eyesight going, his hearing was fading too.

Billy lifted his free hand to wave, grinning to expose a missing front tooth. Ryan refused to tell me the full story, only that it was the reason Billy's whisky access was rationed.

Until now, I had never walked past this point. It had taken me some time to become brave enough to walk through the area. I felt like the new girl in the gym, too scared to intrude on the *man zone*. But as the rest of the pack had begun adjusting to my presence, I had chanced it once a fortnight ago. When nothing bad happened, bar one wolf whistle, I had come back a handful of times since to continue exploring.

At the back of the sheds, there was an old garage with a corrugated roof. Most of the time it was locked, but now and then, there would be a flashy vintage car outside being cleaned. The pack had their fingers in many pies. I drifted off the main path, wandering through the high grass lining the area leading up to the forest treeline. I smiled, the gentle breeze making a stray strand of hair tickle my nose. When I looked back towards the main part of the estate, I noticed a small cottage far to the right of the garage, farther away from the other buildings. Nestled behind a slight hump in the mountain, the hill completely obscured the bungalow if you were looking in that direction from the main path.

The sun was slowly dropping in the sky, but I decided to have a quick look before heading back home. I picked my way through the long grass until it levelled to reveal the little cottage. Whitewashed walls covered in ivy wound up old wall terraces that must have once held climbing roses. The thatched roof was weathered but in good condition. In one corner, the thatching looked fresh, as if someone had fixed it up recently.

I skirted around the outside of the building, peering in each of the windows. Most of them were still intact, but one at the back had a crack in the glass panel. All I could see inside was an old kitchen that clearly had been vacant for years, and a dining table coated in dust.

The front door was bright red to match the brick houses, but the paint was peeling to reveal the white base. The stiff rusted brass knocker whined as I tried the handle.

After three tries, the door swung open to my surprise, and I stumbled into the room, kicking up a puff of dust in my wake. I coughed and covered my mouth with my forearm as I waited for my eyes to adjust to the darkness.

The kitchen cupboards were bare, dust particles danced in the sunlight, and the furniture had the faint scent of damp. Despite its neglected appearance, I could appreciate the charm the little cottage would once have had. From the little square window, I could see trees lining the forest edge.

As I walked further inside, my foot caught on a bump in the rug. I frowned and bent down, rolling the mat back slowly to reveal a square trapdoor cut into the floorboards. No dust wafted from the carpet, and when I went to lift the latch, the trapdoor squeaked but opened with relative ease.

I cast a nervous glance around the room to make sure I was alone before ducking through the hatch and proceeding down a short flight of steps. The lump in my throat only grew as I stepped out into a hallway lit by three dim bulbs hanging from the ceiling.

Relief washed over me as the first door handle didn't budge for me. I looked back at the stairs, cursing my newfound curiosity.

"This is why girls die in horror movies," I muttered to myself, moving to the next door, but there was nothing wrong with the doors. Each one was mahogany to match the dark floors. A sinister feeling took up residency in my gut, and it was not shifting.

The second door was locked too. I gave it a shove, and the door rattled but still held fast. A bang echoed moments later. I paused, and the noise came again from farther down the corridor. I cursed under my breath, but before I knew it, my feet were taking me past the doors towards the end of the hallway.

As I passed the last door, a turn to the right came into view. I thought about going back up the stairs but the bang came again. This time, I could have sworn I heard a voice. My heart thumped in my chest and the adrenaline screamed at me to run, but something inside made me walk farther.

The turn led me down a darker hallway, and the wooden floor abruptly gave way to raw stone, almost like an extension that was never finished. There were two doors lining each wall, all with padlocks. A dull thud echoed, and the fifth door marked a dead end. My body was on autopilot, one foot moving in front of the other. I felt like a backseat passenger as I found myself standing in front of the door. A voice rang out, clearer this time, and the door shook, the door handle rattling against the padlock.

"Let me out!" A girl's voice echoed through the door, not pleading but demanding and fearless.

Fists pounded the door, and I jumped back, my hand hovering over the padlock. I tugged on the lock and the banging stopped. There was no sign of a key nearby, so I braced my thumbs through the loop of the lock and pulled as hard as I could. My palms were slick and slipped against the metal.

Cursing, I slammed my fist into the lock. I winced—the lock stayed intact, albeit with a dent now.

Someone sniffed. The voice came again, but this time it wavered. "Who are you?"

I followed suit and focused, my brow furrowing as I picked up a familiar edge to the scent that I couldn't quite place.

I fumbled with the lock, my hands shaking, but despite my best efforts there was no way I could unlock the door without the key. "I'm Eve, I promise I'll get you out of here."

I had no place promising her anything. I was no hero, but it felt like the right thing to say.

The lock wouldn't budge, I was heading into full panic mode. I slammed my fist into the door frame, and it splintered slightly. For a moment, I considered tearing the door down piece by piece. While I couldn't do that by hand, maybe there was something upstairs that could.

"I need to go get something to pry this lock open, but I will be back," I promised again, hoping I sounded more confident than I felt.

There was a rustle as someone slumped against the other side of the door, followed by a soft sob. "Please, don't leave me here."

I hovered by the door, the erratic pounding of their heart and mine drumming in my ears. My mind raced as I shoved away and began sprinting back down the hallway the way I had come. My foot caught on the steps as I took them two at a time, slick palms slipping on the rail. That would definitely bruise. I cursed and picked myself up, climbing out of the hatch.

As I set foot upstairs, I found myself face to face with Ryan's uncle, his beady eyes staring down at me.

"What do you think you're doing?" Nick demanded, grabbing me by the collar of my shirt, flinging me onto the dusty mat like a naughty child with more strength than I had expected.

I landed on my back with a dull thud. Nick's usual gloomy expression had twisted into a mask of fury, glaring at me through the glasses propped on his upturned nose.

"I'm sorry," I stammered, coughing as I struggled to my feet. I briefly considered saying that I saw nothing, but one look in his eyes told me that if I was going to lie my way out of this, I needed to be smart. "I heard someone calling for help."

Nick didn't offer to help, clenching and unclenching his fist by his side. He towered over me, fury emanating from every inch of his body. The man who had never spoken more than a handful of words to me was now ready to read me the riot act.

"You insolent brat. What have you seen?" Nick growled, not bothering to wait around for a proper answer.

"N-nothing, all I heard was a voice." I did my best to seem bewildered. It didn't take much effort, I was terrified, and my mind was spinning.

Nick nearly sent me sprawling on the ground again as he stormed past and disappeared down the hatch. I heard muffled yelling and the slam of metal before he reappeared. He cast me a look of utter disgust as he began closing the latch.

"Stupid girl, you have no business being here." As soon as he finished locking up, he kicked the carpet back over the hatch. Each movement was stilted. He was shaking with anger. "You're lucky it wasn't the alpha who found you here."

"I'm sorry, I didn't know..."

Nick reached out, his long fingers closing around my wrist in a vice-like grip. He marched towards the exit, hauling me along with him. I squirmed, my eyes stinging as I tried to wriggle free. His grip remained firm as he ignored me and began locking the front door.

"I assume your pitiful excuse for a boyfriend left this unlocked," he said finally, spitting on the floor. "Useless as always."

My first instinct was to contest the inaccuracy of his statement, but one look from Nick and my mouth clamped shut. We were at the cusp of a full moon, and while I could outrun Nick, I had no chance of outrunning the entire pack.

Unimpressed by my silence, Nick released his grip on my wrist and shoved me up against the cottage. Uneven rocks tore at my shoulders as I strained against him. He kept his arm firmly braced against my neck to the point where breathing became difficult. I caught sight of a claw in the corner of my eye and my blood ran cold.

"Listen very carefully, mongrel," Nick spat, his words dripping with venom. He pressed his face up against mine, so close I could taste his breath. "No one is to know about what you found here. And you needn't think about running to Ryan, he can't save you."

I couldn't scream even if I wanted to, with his forearm squeezing down on my windpipe. I was gagging for air. No one would listen anyway. Ryan was still at work, and most of the pack hated me. I was a fool for getting too big for my boots.

Nick leaned closer with each word, the pressure on my neck gradually increasing. "If you speak of this to anyone, I will ensure that everything and everyone that you love is destroyed. And then I will hunt you down and treat you like the hybrid scum you are. Do you understand?"

"Yes," I croaked, my throat rasping as I struggled in his grip.

He held me there a moment longer. My eyelids fluttered and the forest surrounding us blurred.

"This will be our little secret." Nick leaned in, his breath tickling in my ear.

With that, Nick released me, and I slumped against the cottage. He turned on his heel and stalked away, whistling to no one. I clutched my chest, the sky spinning, and the ground rose up to meet me.

CHAPTER 26

When I came to, dusk had dulled the sky, and I knew I had to tell Ryan despite Nick's warning. Avoiding everyone, I hailed a taxi on my phone to pick me up at the entrance of the estate to bring me straight to the office building. Thank fuck for smart phones and GPS. When I rang Ryan on the way, all I got was his voicemail, but this couldn't wait. Not even the alpha's threats the last time I turned up would stop me.

Sick of the games, I made a beeline for the receptionist. It was the same snotty girl as last time, strutting around in her Louboutin's.

"I'm here to meet Ryan for dinner," I lied, leaning over the front desk and painting a sickly-sweet smile on my face. "He's expecting me."

The receptionist clicked her mouse a few times and rolled her eyes, mirroring my fake smile. "There's nothing in his diary."

"Check again."

"I'm sorry, Miss. Mr.McKenna has no appointments right now, and he specifically asked not to be disturbed," she said, loving every minute of refusing me again.

She wasn't a werewolf, so I wondered if she knew about Ryan and the other pack members. There was only one way to find out.

"I think you need to give him a ring and let him know I'm here," I growled, flashing her a glimpse of a fang.

She arched an eyebrow, tapping her pen on the counter and nudging my elbows off of the pristine glass. "Like I said, Miss. He gave clear instructions that he was not to be interrupted under any circumstances. You are free to wait here until I can contact him."

I wanted to wipe the smug look off her face, but I stepped back from the counter and glanced towards the stairs. Although they had placed security outside, there was no one in the foyer but the receptionist and a handful of businessmen chatting in the lobby. I lifted my head up and started walking towards the staircase as if I belonged there.

"Miss! You can't go up there unsupervised!"

Ignoring the receptionist's squawks and secretly hoping this got her in trouble too, I made my way up the spiral staircase to the first floor. Unlike the reception, the floor here was glass and see through, so I could still see the receptionist throwing a strop at the desk she was bound to. The lobby was busy with people strutting back and forth, paying no attention to me whatsoever. You'd think a girl in jeans would stand out in an office, but when people have their noses glued to paperwork or their phones, they miss what's right in front of them.

I noticed a lift opposite the stairs, and speed walked towards it, pushing the button repeatedly. When the bell dinged and the doors opened to reveal an empty lift, I exhaled a shaky sigh of relief and stepped inside. The floors were numbered one to seven, so I took a gamble and guessed the top floor. I couldn't imagine Ryan having an office on any other floor. As the lift passed each floor, I prayed it didn't stop and that Nick or Ryan's father would appear. Being trapped inside this metal box was torture enough.

The top floor was empty. Expensive paintings hung along the interior walls of four different corridors branching off from the foyer. At my back were the lifts, to my left, right, and up ahead a corridor. Pristine white walls made everything look the same and with corners obscuring whatever lay beyond, I was at a loss.

I backed up into a corner beside the lift, hiding myself, deciding to trust my nose instead. I inhaled slowly. Ryan's familiar scent mingled among countless others.

At least I have the right floor.

I zoned in on Ryan's scent, struggling to pick it apart from the others. It wasn't as simple as it sounded when your primary brain was human. Distinguishing smells took time and effort to learn. I sensed it was stronger to my right, so I opened my eyes and started walking in that direction, entering a winding hallway lined with different offices.

My breath caught as I picked up another unwelcome scent, shortly followed by the sounds of footsteps and a high-pitched giggle.

"Are you fucking kidding me?" I muttered under my breath, plastering myself to the wall and peeking around the corner. "I'll kill him."

The corridor was empty, but I could see a single office door ajar and shadows moving in the sliver of light. Absolutely sizzling, I peeled myself away and tiptoed around the corner, following the rising laughter and hushed whispers. I didn't need to focus my hearing to pick up on what was being said. They weren't trying too hard to be quiet.

"I promise, I'll keep her in line."

Ryan's voice, a soft purr I hadn't heard in a while, reached my ears.

"I shouldn't even be telling you this," Nadine murmured, confirming what I had feared. "Your father asked me not to say anything."

Liar.

"Disobeying your alpha for me? How bold." Ryan teased, his husky voice thick with passion. "Now, did you come here to talk business or is there something else I can help you with?"

I heard the distinct rustle of clothes and fought the urge to bolt.

"Ryan! We can't do it in your office," Nadine gasped, her giggle making my skin crawl.

"As if that's stopped you before. I've had you on that desk more than once."

My stomach lurched, and I struggled not to empty my lunch all over the spotless floor. That uneasy sense of dread that had lived in the pit of my gut for weeks reared its ugly head in triumph. *I was right all along.*

I shuffled closer, my trainers treading softly, but I needn't have bothered. No one was paying any attention to me, and they obviously didn't care who saw. *Fucking exhibitionists.*

Ryan's name was etched on the door along with the title 'Vice President'. I scoffed and leaned forward, craning my neck to see inside the office. They were on the desk, on the floor, hands and legs everywhere as they made out like sex-starved teenagers. Nadine's skirt was up around her hips and I didn't even want to think about where Ryan's hands were. Her moans echoed down the hallway, and I simultaneously cringed and gagged.

Nadine's bra hit the door frame right beside me. I didn't need a second invitation to leave. Biting my cheek, I bolted back the way I had come and hammered the elevator button. I passed the alpha on the stairs, his eyes gleaming with satisfaction as they locked with mine. I shoved past and strode through the lobby, refusing to stop until I was at least two blocks away. Only then did I allow myself to fall apart.

I'd had my suspicions for a while. Before I found out I was a hybrid, we had been on the rocks. I trusted Ryan when he led me to his pack. Despite the lies and growing distance between him, I'd stayed loyal to him against my better judgement. That made this betrayal a hundred times worse. One thing was sure, though. I couldn't trust him what I'd found out.

What if he is in on it? What if he has been in on this all along—the alpha's threats, Nadine attacking me? What if it has all been a lie?

There was only person I wanted to call.

"Kate," I said, my voice cracking at the sound of her voice down the line. "I need you."

Kate was waiting for me when I got to the apartment, wineglass in hand. At the sight of my best friend, I broke into tears. She took one look at me and sighed, her brow furrowing and concern shining in her eyes as she ushered me inside without a word and set the glass down, pulling me into her arms. Craig followed over from the couch and wrapped his arms around us, planting a wine-stained kiss on my cheek. We stood there for what seemed like forever, me bawling my eyes out as they held me close and Kate cooed in my ear. But nothing she said could make things okay again, and I couldn't even tell her the full story. All the shit I'd never asked for had been taken to a new level. I was sick and tired of everything.

"Come on," Craig said, gently prying me off Kate and guiding me towards the couch. He sat on one side and patted the cushion beside him. "Tell us what he did."

I was snivelling so much, I struggled to get a word out. When I eventually managed to speak, my voice was a hoarse whisper. "You were right... I caught him cheating with that Nadine girl."

Kate flopped onto the armchair beside us and let out a string of curses, a flowery mix of English and some Irish curses her grandmother had passed on. When she finished, she took a deep breath and exhaled slowly, as if mentally trying to talk herself out of beating the shit out of Ryan. "I didn't want to be right, but I knew what I saw that night."

Craig shot her a warning look no doubt intended to stop the 'I told you so' speech.

"I know, and I wish I'd believed you. I just didn't want it to be true."

She rummaged around in her handbag, handing me a tissue with a sombre smile. "Here, you look a right state."

"Thanks, I feel like someone ran over my chest and then reversed for good measure," I mumbled, dabbing at the tears that weren't quite ready to stop flowing.

"He might be an asshole, but you love him." Craig sighed, knocking back a mouthful of wine and immediately filling me a glass.

I shook my head, sniffling. "Not anymore."

"Feelings don't disappear overnight," Kate said softly, handing me the glass as Craig continued to top them up. "It takes time."

The pity shining in her eyes made a fire rumble in my belly. "They might not disappear, but when you've been through what I have, feelings definitely change."

"Did he..."

"No. Nothing like that."

Craig's shoulders slumped with relief. "Then what?"

"Besides the cheating? It's complicated. Let's just say staying with his family was a nightmare, and he's been lying to me this whole time."

She shook her head, unable to keep up with my riddles, but happy to let me rant. I wanted so much to tell them the truth, to confide in my best friends, but it was dangerous. I was dangerous. It was up to me to get myself out of this crazy situation, not them. Kate would walk through fire for me. If I told Craig, he'd jump straight in the middle and get hurt.

"I feel like such an idiot." I sighed, clutching my glass to my chest as I slumped back against the couch in defeat. "It's so obvious now."

"Hindsight is a wonderful thing," Craig said, snuggling up beside me. "You can't blame yourself for not being able to see the future. Whatever he has done, none of it is your fault."

I ran my fingertip around the edge of the glass, the vibration causing a low hum, and stared into the pool of liquid as if it might give me the answers I needed. "That doesn't make me feel any better about loving a monster. What does that make me?"

"Human." Kate said, leaning forward to link her fingers with mine.

A choked sob escaped my lips at her words. Craig reached out to wrap his arm around my shoulders, giving me a gentle squeeze.

"It takes time, but you will move on, and we can help with that," Kate promised, a small smile curving her lips at the prospect of me coming home.

It broke my heart not to jump at the chance.

Tears stung the corner of my eyes again. "I can't. I have some things to sort out there."

The wounded look on Kate's face cut like a knife. I wanted to move back in with her, forget everything that had happened. The thought of going back there made my stomach churn.

"You can't go back there," she said firmly, her grip on the stem of the wineglass tightening so much I thought it might snap. "Not after he's betrayed you like that."

Craig shook his head, nudging Kate with his foot. "Quit it. If I'm not being a drama queen, you don't get to. This is about what Eve needs."

My brain was working overtime trying to process everything that had happened in the last few hours. I was unsure about so many things, but one thing I knew was that I had a promise to keep. Whoever that girl in the basement was, she needed my help. I couldn't just barge back in, though, I needed to be smart about things.

"It's not about him... I wish I could explain. I made a promise to someone else that I have to keep."

Kate eyed me carefully, her emotions warring with each other. It was clear that she wasn't happy with me going back, but she eventually sighed in defeat. "Fine, but then you're moving home, and we'll forget he ever existed."

"Gladly."

Her expression brightened, and she rose to her feet, refilling my wine before walking to the kitchen and rummaging around in the cupboards until she found a packet of popcorn. She came back over to the couch, brandishing another bottle of wine.

"Right, we don't need to think about any of that tonight. Let's get you settled," she said, filling my half-empty glass to the brim again. "Craig, sort the snacks. I'll grab a duvet and we can have a movie night like old times."

Craig pulled me close for a hug and then sprang into action, his long legs eating up the floor of the small apartment as he made a beeline for the fridge.

The well of tears threatened to erupt all over again. I stared at my friends, having forgotten what it felt like to have them around, people who constantly watched my back. The bond I had with Kate especially, knowing we would do anything for each other, I'd missed it. She was the closest thing to family I had.

"Kate?"

She stopped midway to the bedroom, her cerulean hair tumbling over her back as she turned to look at me. "Yeah?"

"Thanks, for this," I said, swallowing the lump rising in my throat. "I've missed hanging out."

She smiled, her cheeks dimpling. "Me too. I'm always here, no matter what."

CHAPTER 27

Ryan was waiting for me at the front door. I gulped, thanking the taxi man before forcing myself out of the car. I didn't want to go back into the house, but running away to my old life was no longer an option. The stakes were too high. Nadine appeared like a thorn at Ryan's side and tugged on his sleeve. He shrugged her off, but she leaned in, whispering something in his ear as I approached the house. His smile thinned at whatever poison she was spewing. Her hand lingered on his arm as she hovered. Ryan inclined his head and whispered to Nadine, who then retreated, her dark gaze never leaving me until she was out of sight.

"What was that all about?" I asked innocently, watching her back as she disappeared around a corner.

Ryan shook his head and raked his fingers through his curls, his expression brightening. "Nothing to worry about. Nadine's just making a nuisance of herself."

"That's one hell of an understatement," I replied, keeping my voice steady, wishing I could wipe that silly smile off his face.

I wanted to scream at him, lose my temper altogether and tell Ryan exactly what I thought about his web of lies. More than anything, I wanted to know why. How much of our relationship had been a lie? But I couldn't risk telling him the truth about what I'd found, I couldn't trust him. He wasn't the man I had fallen in love with.

"Are you all right?" he asked, concern sweeping across his features.

"To what do I owe this welcoming party?" I countered, not in the mood for niceties.

"I was worried when you didn't come home last night." He pulled me into his arms, nestling his chin on top of my head. "I'm so glad you're okay."

I swallowed as bile rose in my throat, dread settling in the pit of my stomach. "Why wouldn't I be?"

"Nothing. Don't mind me," he said, releasing me from the embrace. His hands settled on my hips where he gave what was supposed to be a reassuring squeeze. "Go settle in and I'll tell Mary to bring us some breakfast."

My body turned rigid at his touch. "I'd actually rather jump in the shower and go read for a while."

Ryan didn't seem to notice. "We can have lunch together then."

He took my lack of a response as a yes, pressing his lips to my cheek before striding off towards the kitchens. It took every ounce of control I had not to recoil, not to give him the stinging slap—or punch—that he deserved so much.

The moment I was alone, my shoulders sagged, and I exhaled slowly. I started up the stairs, yesterday's events replaying on repeat in my head. My footsteps echoed in the empty house, and I wondered what it was like back when the pack lived as one, before they split. Ryan's pack was three times the size of the Crescents, but something about the house in which the alpha stowed his family away felt empty.

As I rounded the top of the stairs onto the landing, an un-welcome scent caught my attention. I pinched the bridge of my nose and grit my teeth, a wave of frustration washing over me. I turned to see Nadine lounging on one of the window seats, a low-cut dress with a plunging neckline grazing the ground. *Why hadn't I noticed that earlier?*

"What do you want?" I demanded, skipping the niceties.

Nadine uncrossed her legs and rose to her feet, her every movement irritatingly graceful. Red curls tumbled over her shoulders, and with her pale skin and the black dress, she looked like some kind of succubus. She wasn't far off one.

"I heard you got in trouble for sticking your nose where it isn't wanted, mutt."

I froze, my mouth drying up. *How much had she told Ryan?* I shook my head and rubbed my temple.

"He doesn't know," she said, as if reading my mind, a sadistic grin curving her lips.

"Know what?" I asked, playing dumb, but she didn't bite.

Nadine stalked towards me, her voice lowering to a snarl only meant for my ears. "That you went digging for dirt and found that mongrel."

I gulped.

She grinned. "That Nick caught you and made sure you would keep your filthy trap shut."

I bit my tongue so hard it drew blood. "I've kept my word."

She traced a delicate finger along my jaw, a single claw extending. "I know, you wouldn't be that stupid." Nadine paused, pressing her nail against my chin just enough to draw blood. "Would you?"

"I told you, no one else knows."

Nadine watched me for a moment, eyes alight with the same delight of a cat playing with their prey. This time, she had the upper hand. No matter how much I wanted to pull those hair extensions out and run her through the window, I had to keep my cool until I had some sort of plan.

Satisfied with my response, she eventually retracted the claw and withdrew from my personal space. "Good. Don't forget what will happen if you do spill the beans, mutt." Her melodic voice dripped with disdain.

I nodded, swallowing the metallic taste in my mouth and wiping the blood off my chin with my sleeve. Before I could answer, footsteps started up the stairs. We both turned towards the noise and fell silent as Ryan appeared, a glass of wine in each hand. He looked between us, frowning as he caught sight of Nadine. Anger flashed across his features, but he quickly schooled his expression.

"Nadine? What are you still doing here?"

Ryan spoke to her like she was an irritating business associate, and judging by the scowl twisting Nadine's pretty face, she wasn't pleased in the slightest. "I was just going."

Clearly, I wasn't the only one biting my tongue.

They shared a look I couldn't place before Nadine turned on her heel and stormed away, her hips swaying with each step. She disappeared into one of the many spare rooms, the loud slam of a door following her exit.

"Why is she hanging around?" I asked, wondering why she seemed to have taken up residence so close to me all of a sudden.

Did he know I saw them?

Ryan shrugged and stepped onto the landing, leading us in the opposite direction. "Her father is away on business. She kicked up a fuss about something, and my father decided to offer a spare room to keep the peace."

"Uh huh." I chewed my lip, half waiting for the evil bitch to re-emerge.

"Don't worry about her, it means nothing. It's just politics."

It went far beyond politics, but that was a conversation for another day. It sounded like Nick had just landed me with a watchdog.

CHAPTER 28

It took every ounce of my resolve not to cancel my training session with Luke that week. I had spent my time hiding out in the library and the kitchens, avoiding Ryan as much as I could. I even pretended to have a stomach bug when he tried it on, and then hay fever. I'd never been so happy to see mother nature arrive. Lying was draining, but I couldn't leave without answers. Every time he touched me, it made my skin crawl.

Since Ryan had started getting suspicious, Luke and I decided to meet at the Dark Night, the last place Ryan would think to look. By the time Luke showed his face, I was on my second drink. I had never coped well with nerves, but Jonas had kept me company while I waited, offering a distraction. Between his kind words and the Dutch courage, I was feeling a bit more like myself.

"This isn't exactly part of the lesson plan," Luke chuckled, sliding into the seat beside me. His hazel eyes sparkled with mischief.

Jonas made his excuses and winked. What was up with everyone today?

I rolled my eyes and downed the last mouthful of my beer. "Call it improvisation."

Luke shook his head and swirled a set of car keys around his index finger, his expression a mixture of anticipation and excitement. "Are you ready to start then?"

"As ready as I'll ever be." I sighed, hopping off the bar stool and slipping a tip on the counter for Jonas before following Luke outside.

He had parked around the corner. I should have known we would have to go somewhere since shifting in public was a no-no, but a weird feeling of nostalgia hit me as I slid into the passenger seat of his car. I'd missed him. "Where are we off to then?"

"My place." Luke flashed me a lopsided grin and slammed his foot on the accelerator.

It only dawned on me then that werewolves seemed to have zero fear when it came to speeding and no road sense whatsoever. I guess the rapid reflexes made up for it, but still.

He wasn't lying, but we didn't end up at his house. Instead, we stopped off in the middle of nowhere down a deserted back lane. When I stepped out of the car, the welcome sounds of waves crashing and the scent of salt filled my senses.

"We're going to the beach?" I asked, arching an eyebrow.

Luke chuckled and led the way along a grass trail surrounded by towering sand dunes on either side, which soon faded into a well-worn path. The sun beat down on the back of my neck, and I welcomed the fresh sea breeze washing over me.

"Why are we grumpier than usual today?" Luke asked, walking ahead of me as we picked our way towards the beach. "Got out of the wrong side of the bed?"

I let out a small snort. "Something like that."

A dark understanding flickered in his eyes and he looked away, moving a few paces ahead of me until the path opened out onto a rocky strand. The beach was deserted with no houses or buildings in sight. Even so, it felt too exposed.

Luke caught me frowning. "It's a private beach, the land surrounding it is owned by an old family friend. No one comes here, and if they do, there's a thicket of trees that can lead us back to the car under cover," he explained, setting down his bag of what I presumed were spare clothes. "Don't worry."

I sighed and followed suit. If only it were that simple.

Luke shrugged off his shirt so that he was left in a t-shirt and jeans, casual as always. As he took up a defensive stance, the muscles in his arms rippled. I copied his arm placement, looking scruffy in comparison in my tracksuit. But the same way guys couldn't comprehend high heels, fighting in skinny jeans wasn't for me unless it was a necessity.

We circled one another for a while, Luke sprinting at me to land a hit and then dancing away. He dodged each of my attempts, barking orders that made my head spin. There was nothing natural about my movements—they were slow and predictable.

"Focus," he barked, his fist grazing my shoulder yet again.

I cursed under my breath and weaving away from him, trying to stay on the balls of my feet like I was instructed. But each bounce seemed to jumble my thoughts even more. There was no way I could focus.

Refusing to give up, I lunged forward and struck at his stomach with every ounce of energy in me. Luke saw me coming and stepped back, letting me follow through on the punch and stumble forward. I lost my balance and ended up on my knees, leaving a small hole in the sand as I punched the ground in frustration.

"Ugh. I can't do this."

"You can," Luke said, standing over me but not offering any hand up. "Back on your feet."

I growled. My arms shook under my weight as I forced myself up, hair stuck to my forehead, my top was sticky with sweat, and I wanted nothing more than to collapse on the ground. But I was also filled with a fire that had no exit route, instead staying pent up in me and ready to explode.

Luke set his feet wide and crouched in a defensive position with his palms raised at chest level. "Again."

Before I could get two strides in, Luke scooted out of the way. He sighed and slapped his thighs, wiping some sand off. "Eve, get out of your head. Push whatever it is to the back of your mind and focus."

I nodded, biting my lip as I watched him set his stance. This time, I tried to stalk towards him, keeping my gaze locked with his to avoid giving my intentions away. Sand slid beneath my feet as I jumped and spun, swinging my leg around. I had aimed perfectly for his ribs, or so I thought, but his hand shot up and grabbed my ankle before I could land the kick.

"I give up!" I yelled, yanking my leg out of his grip, unceremoniously falling on my ass.

Cursing, I leapt to my feet and brushed the sand off myself. My movements were disjointed and rough, and my shoulders were shaking as I tried to force a shallow breath into my lungs.

"Eve, what the hell is going on?" Luke stepped towards me, his frown deepening.

It wasn't just a question, it was an order. The passion in his voice caught me off guard. The happy-go-lucky side to Luke that I knew had been replaced with a serious one. I had caught glimpses of it before, when he was brooding or knocking back whisky. During those fleeting moments, I saw him staring into space. This was different.

I shrugged, worrying a rock with the tip of my shoe. "Nothing."

"You're a terrible liar."

"You don't know me." I kept my eyes downcast, my fingers still curled into fists. Ever since I found out I was a hybrid, I had lied to my best friend, to Ryan—not that he didn't deserve it—and now I was lying to Luke. I hated it.

When I looked up again, Luke was towering over me, wearing the same worried expression. "You know you can tell me anything."

I bit my cheek, thinking back to all the training sessions, to lying on the boxing ring floor laughing so hard I got the hiccups, and the drinks we would go for after. With Luke I could talk about semi-normal things. Life didn't always have to revolve around the pack or the crazy things that came with it.

He tilted my chin up to look at him, but I tore my eyes away. "Not this."

His hand traced my jaw with his fingertips, sending a chill down my spine. I let my eyelids drift closed and leaned into his touch. He tensed and the movement stopped.

"Who hurt you?" Luke all but growled, his body rigid against mine.

My head snapped up. Luke's expression darkened as he examined the bruises, pulling his hand away when I flinched.

I had never been a whizz with concealer. Part of me wanted to stay mute like I had with Ryan to keep him safe, but the fire burning in Luke's eyes told me he wouldn't buy my lies.

"Tell me, Eve. I can help."

"You can't." I exhaled slowly, taking a step back in case he lost the plot completely. "I found something—someone—yesterday. Ryan's uncle caught me snooping."

Luke's frown deepened. I could see a storm brewing, but outwardly he seemed incredibly calm. "What someone?"

I studied his face and the concern shining in his eyes cracked my resolve.

"Yesterday, I found a girl locked up in an abandoned cottage on the manor lands. She was begging for help, but before I could, Nick caught me and h-he..."

A muscle ticked in Luke's jaw, his chest muscles tensing as his grip on me tightened. I could feel the anger emanating from every inch of his body. It matched mine. So, I told him everything right up until Nick knocked me out, everything about Nadine and the alpha's threats. The words tumbled from my mouth—once I started, I couldn't stop. He stayed silent the entire time, only his face betraying his emotions.

"I had no idea anyone was trapped there though," I finished, out of breath and choking on my words.

Luke stared at me for a long moment before running his hand through his hair and rubbing his face like he was trying to wake up from a nightmare.

"You can't tell him." Luke broke the silence, his voice a hoarse whisper. He cleared his throat and took my hands in his. Unlike Nick's, his grip was gentle but firm, as if he were afraid I would disappear right before his eyes. "You can't tell Ryan that you know."

I shook my head. "I haven't... I don't think I will."

Luke's gaze was intense and unwavering. "I know you believe that despite all his flaws Ryan cares, but I am telling you, there is no way he doesn't know about this."

My brow furrowed.

"He is the alpha's son, Eve." Luke squeezed my hand, his voice pleading but certain. "Nothing happens without the alpha knowing, and I guarantee you that Ryan would have his nose in this. He's a pathological liar."

I didn't need as much convincing as Luke thought. Walking in on him and Nadine in the office and overhearing them had been the last nail in a very battered coffin. Yes, I still loved Ryan, feelings didn't vanish overnight, but he had shattered my trust. Try as he might, there was no piecing together the jagged shards that remained.

"I don't know what they're up to, but I promise I will find out. Until I figure this out, do not go back there."

I chewed my lip, looking at Luke from under my lashes. The burning intensity in his eyes made my stomach uneasy.

"I promise I won't go back to the cottage or tell Ryan. You don't have to worry." I needed to stop making promises I wasn't sure I could keep.

Luke stepped back from me and threw his arms open, his lips stretching into a wide smile that lit up his handsome features. His expression brightened, but the troubled look never left his eyes. "Let's try something different."

I wrapped my arms around my middle, hugging myself as his warning echoed in my mind.

Luke unbuckled his belt and began stripping off his jeans until he was down to his boxers. My jaw fell open, but I quickly snapped it shut and bit my lip. We went from zero to ninety in seconds, and I was completely bewildered as to where this was headed. "What are you doing?" I sounded so naïve, and the moment the words left my mouth I wanted to snatch them back.

He chuckled, completely at ease despite being mostly naked. Images from the night we met came flooding back—Luke topless and his arm around my waist. I was standing there like a noodle, fully clothed.

"Are you going to join me or just enjoying the view?" Luke teased, bursting into a fresh fit of laughter at my blank expression. "Relax. I meant we should shift."

I did relax, but only slightly. It had taken me ages to let Ryan see me naked, let alone vulnerable. That's why the betrayal hurt so much. He knew how hard it was for me to trust. I reached for the hem of my shirt and pulled it off anyway, silently praying that all the hard work was paying off. I wiggled out of my tracksuit and tossed it aside. The sports bra and underwear could stay. There was a line, and this was it. I could cope with shredding them. Luke was obviously on the same wavelength.

As I dropped my clothes to the ground, I caught him staring at my body with a hunger that reflected my own. I shook my head and shivered. *Focus*. The air between us shimmered as Luke shifted seamlessly into a sandy wolf standing over a pair of shredded boxers. His tongue lolled to the side as he trotted over and nudged my leg, his full height stopping just below my ribs.

I scratched behind his ears, a small smile playing on my lips. His coat was soft. Silver eyes stared up at me, encouraging me while he backed away to give me some space.

Seeing Luke change already had my wolf side primed and begging to come out and play. It was also ten times easier to concentrate when Luke was already in his wolf form rather than half naked in front of me. I tried to forget that I was in my underwear and focused instead on the magic within, on the tingle travelling up my spine and down my arms all the way to my fingertips. The warmth and fire burned inside, calling to be set free. I closed my eyes and exhaled slowly. When I opened them, I could feel the coarse grains of sand under my paws.

I pawed the ground, slowly padding towards Luke. The sand gave way under my weight, but not half as much as it did in my human form. Once I got used to the foreign feel, I pounced on Luke just as he always did in the boxing ring. We both tumbled to the ground, sending up a puff of sand. Within seconds, I found myself face down in the sand with Luke pinning my throat, his grip gentle.

I broke into a sneezing fit when he let me up, snorting in the most unattractive way imaginable—for a wolf. Luke yipped, his eyes wide with amusement. He had been right, fighting and balance in my wolf form was the same dance, just a different playing field.

We played back and forth, Luke sending me flying more times than I cared to admit. By the end of our play fighting and him dunking me in shallow rock pools, my coat was covered in sand and my ego wounded. I shook my fur out, spraying Luke with a murky mix of sand and salt. He swung his head towards me, his lips curling back. Luke launched off his haunches and pounced, sending me onto my back. He stood over me, one paw braced against my shoulder and his jaw at my jugular. I could hear both of our hearts hammering. I wiggled and feigned submission. As soon as he released my throat, I clamped my jaw around his neck and flipped us.

A shout echoed in the distance. Without thinking, I shifted back to my human form, adrenaline still pumping through my veins. Luke did the same, and I found myself kneeling over him in the most awkward of positions. Our eyes locked and heat rushed to my cheeks. He reached up to brush my cheek, his touch feather light. I leaned in, head tilted, but as my lips neared Luke's, a twig snapped in the distance. I detangled myself immediately and leapt to my feet.

My t-shirt was on in record time and when I turned, Luke was in his jeans and shirt like nothing had happened. He gave me a strange look, as if I were a puzzle he just couldn't figure out. I stuffed my feet into my runners and felt my cheeks warm again.

A face appeared over the sand dunes and I tensed, still very much in fight-or-flight mode. Luke waved his hand dismissively. "Relax, they won't have seen anything."

I rolled my eyes and stood up. "Good to know."

"The worst they will think is that we were hooking up on the beach in broad daylight."

I didn't let my mind wander towards what might have happened if no one had interrupted us. I couldn't.

CHAPTER 29

Luke dropped me in the city a few blocks away from the Dark Night, his words still ringing in my head. There was too much to process. The guilt intensified with each passing day I spent with the pack, eating away at my nerves. Knowing that poor girl was trapped nearby made me sick.

I had to push those thoughts to the back of my mind or I would fall apart. Raindrops danced on the path under the flickering streetlamps. Cars whizzed past with their blinding headlights, and thunder rumbled in the distance. I pulled my hood up, keeping to the inside of the footpath to avoid getting drenched by a puddle.

Rain pounded the pavement, and I cursed myself for insisting on Fiona collecting me on the far side of town, but it was safer that way. I couldn't risk Nadine figuring out where I had been.

"You're an idiot," I muttered to no one.

The street was quiet bar a few people dashing from one doorway to the next, the night sky a murky grey. Heavy rain battered the umbrella I'd packed that morning, and the breeze picked up. A storm was brewing, and I needed to get to Fiona before it kicked off.

A rush of wind blew my umbrella inside out, and I paused under the cover of a shop canopy, watching people dash to and from their cars. I eyed the narrow street to my left. The wind rattled the awning and sent a bucketful of water spilling over the edge that missed me by an inch. I decided to take a shortcut.

My spine tingled with an itch I couldn't shake and unease writhed in the pit of my stomach. Each time an alleyway ended, I dashed across a main road and ducked under the cover of another side street, winding my way through the city towards the south side. I caught sight of a figure striding between cars behind me, seeming unperturbed by the raindrops pelting the ground. When I looked back again, they were gone.

A spoke on my umbrella had snapped, but it still did the job despite one side flopping against the wind. As I started down an alley between two buildings to my right, the rain lightened. Dublin was a maze of small streets that I knew inside out. I trudged along, my trainers slapping in puddles. There were no lights but the streetlights dimly illuminating the entrance and exit to each cobbled side street. My damp hoody clung to my back, water sloshing in my trainers with each step. I heard a thud behind me and glanced back to see that I was alone.

Stones scattered behind me and I spun, the umbrella barred across my chest like a sword, ready to attack. But the alleyway was empty. I shook my head and pinched the bridge of my nose as I inhaled deeply. "Calm down."

My umbrella was wilting, so I threw my make-shift weapon in a trash can as I passed. It landed with a thud and sent a rat scampering over my feet. I squealed and stumbled back against the wall, not daring to move until the rodent was out of sight. My heart hammered in my chest, and I felt a familiar magic warm my core.

"Not today," I whispered, resorting to the chant that had gotten me through so many of Ryan's lessons. "Mind over matter."

I started down the alley again, stuffing my hands into the pocket of my hoody. My fingers were numb, and a chill was starting to eat into me. As I turned down another narrow opening, I passed the sign of a familiar bar. My shoulders sagged with relief, and I sped up. Fiona wasn't far.

There was a splash behind me, but this time I didn't turn around, fighting the instinct. I picked up the pace, as the sound of footsteps became clearer. A chill ran down my spine, spurring me into a jog, but I refused to shift. I splashed through the puddles and took a sharp left that not many people knew about, hoping to shake my chaser off. I cast a quick glance over my shoulder and saw a black figure running behind me. They weren't fooled.

Unadulterated fear surged through me as I started sprinting, skidding around corners and knocking over beer kegs as I went. My chaser kept pace, their footfalls steadily gaining. How were they so fast? They sped up in sync with me and sounded closer than ever.

I leapt over a stack of trash bags but lost my footing on the slick cobbles. My legs slid from under me, and I fell forward on both hands. A sharp pain shot through my right wrist, and I winced. I scrambled to my feet, but icy fingers clamped around my ankle and pulled me back. I went down again, this time without my arms braced. Landing on my shoulder, I didn't even stop to look at my attacker, twisting onto my stomach and clawing at the wet ground.

"Get the fuck off me!" I growled, kicking out at my attacker to free my leg. "You have no idea who you're dealing with."

I felt a string as something sliced into my calf and cried out. When I spun to lunge at them, I saw the distinct glint of a claw extending from their hand as they dug deeper into my flesh. A chill ran through me when I realised it was me who didn't know what I was dealing with.

There was no time to freeze. I snapped my gaping mouth shut and kicked again, this time with more intent and well-aimed at their wrist. The attacker lost their grip and that was all I needed to roll out of their range into a crouch. They sprung into an attacking position and turned to face me to reveal silver eyes flashing, their hood shadowing their features.

"What do you want from me?" I demanded, trying to stop my voice from shaking.

Their lips curled back into a feral grin. "We want you dead, hybrid scum," they said, their voice cold and masculine. Their broad shoulders had been a dead giveaway.

I blanched, and my blood ran cold. They knew what I was.

"Who sent you?" My voice wavered, and I hopped back a few steps, trying to keep the distance between us.

"You were warned," he hissed. Metal glinted in the light and this time, it wasn't his claws.

I had no idea who he was, but I wasn't going to hang around to find out. Casting a glance behind me, I knew I couldn't outrun him, but what choice did I have? The nearest main street wasn't too far away, so I thought about crying for help like a damsel in distress, but I didn't want to involve an innocent bystander. This guy clearly had no qualms about slicing people open. My body begged me to change, but fear coursed through my veins. I didn't trust my control in the city and I couldn't risk being seen.

Relying on pure adrenaline, I turned and stumbled towards the bright lights in the distance, the wound in my leg throbbing with each stride I took. My attacker was gaining in no time, and I was running out of options. I put on the breaks without warning, digging my heels in and ducking into a ball. He didn't stop fast enough. This time when he leapt, it was his foot that caught and brought him crashing down.

The attacker's hood slipped to reveal a blonde buzzcut and an angular face. The man staring back at me was no older than I was, but he had a deep scar on his cheek that caused one side of his mouth to curl in a permanent snarl.

He was on his feet as fast as me, unfazed by his fall. We lunged at each other at the same time. My claws extended, and I swiped at his torso, aiming for his unprotected side. An easy target. Blood spilled wet on my hands. He howled and threw me off, sending me crashing into a metal bin lining the alley. I groaned as I felt the familiar sensation of bones snapping, and this time, I knew it was my ribs.

The scent of blood filling the air made me gag, but before I could react, he had reached me, his claws slicing into my skin. A fresh jolt of pain ripped through me. The edges of my vision blurred, and my body convulsed. Panic set in, instinct took over.

A new kind of pain swept through me as the change took hold, contorting and shifting into my wolf form faster than ever before. My attacker stumbled back, the blood draining from his face. I swayed briefly, my leg still weak but no longer bleeding. I lowered my head and tensed my haunches, ready to lunge. A feral growl ripped from my lungs, the vibrations causing me to wince.

My attacker stared wide eyed for a moment, frozen in place. I took a menacing step forward and growled again, the rumble echoing through the narrow street. His mouth opened, but nothing came out. He looked up at the sky, at the waning crescent moon, and cursed. Pride swelled within me.

"Dirty hybrid scum," he hissed, spitting on the floor in front of me. "You'll never be safe."

His gaze moved to something behind me.

"She will always be safe," a familiar voice rang out, firm and certain.

I turned and did a double take. Ryan stood behind me, dressed head to toe in formal business attire. He looked dapper as always and well groomed, and completely unfazed by the scene before him.

The attacker stumbled backwards, sheer terror in his eyes. If he was terrified of me, Ryan was his worst nightmare.

"Eve is under my protection," Ryan said, gesturing to me as if he were giving an office presentation. "You've made a big mistake. Leave, now, before I make you regret it."

The attacker nodded and bowed his head, murmuring a half-apology.

"Make sure to tell them all no one is to touch her." With that final warning, he dismissed the attacker, who gladly limped away out of sight.

CHAPTER 30

O nce I was safely in Ryan's car, I couldn't stop thinking about what the attacker had said. If the alpha, or Nick, had sent them, they knew I had told someone. *How could they know? Had someone followed us to the beach?* Even Ryan seemed to know who *they* were.

Luke wasn't answering any of my messages. Ryan caught me staring at my phone, so I stuffed it back under the blanket draped over me. My jeans lay crumpled on the floor, damp and stained red, along with my shredded t-shirt and a bra that I would rather have salvaged. I was completely soaked, and even with the blanket a chill had set in. Ryan noticed me shivering and turned up the heat. I dumped a bloody tissue into the pile at my feet and pressed a fresh one to my leg. It wasn't pumping blood, but there was too much coming out for my liking, and I was beginning to feel light-headed.

A hiss escaped my lips as I increased the pressure on my leg. Ryan didn't bat an eyelid.

"Why did you do that? Why did you step in?" The words tumbled out of my mouth before I could stop them. Maybe it was my brain's way of distracting me from the pain.

"You should be grateful," Ryan said, completely ignoring my question.

"I can defend myself."

He chuckled, and I clenched my fist, wishing with every fibre of my being that I was in a position to jump out of the car. With my leg bleeding all over his fancy leather seats, that wasn't an option.

"Speaking of that, who taught you how to fight?"

I bit my tongue. Now it was my turn to ignore his questions.

"Ok, let's try again. What were you doing out there?" he asked, keeping his eyes firmly focused on the road. It was an innocent question but weighted with double meanings.

"I wanted to pop in to work to see Aoibhinn, but she wasn't around." The lie came to my lips all too easily. I never thought I would become a natural liar.

Ryan nodded, but his shoulders tensed, and a vein throbbed in the side of his neck. His silence set my teeth on edge.

"What were you doing there?" I countered, hoping to take the heat off.

"Work."

Both his work and the bar were a thirty-minute walk away.

"How did you know where I was?"

"Your scent."

I wrinkled my nose. Whenever he talked about wolf things, it still made me think of a dog.

"Speaking of scents," Ryan continued, his voice turning icy. "Why do you stink of that lowlife?"

My heart somersaulted, and I frowned. My clothes shouldn't have smelled of Luke too much because they had spent most of the time on the floor. Plus, now they were destroyed, and I was completely drenched and sticky with blood.

How could he smell anything?

"What are you talking about?" I replied, calling his bluff.

Ryan twisted to face me, his eyes flashing. The car swerved. "I can smell him on you. Luke."

He stared me down, unwavering, daring me to lie. I glanced down at the bloody pile of clothing at my feet and groaned inwardly.

A wheel clipped the curb, and I yelped, hissing as my hand slipped off the wound. Visions of us smashing into a tree flashed through my mind, and I gulped. Ryan turned his attention back to the road and corrected the car with ease.

"I ran into him on my way to the bar," I said, choosing my words carefully.

There was a fine line between Ryan losing his temper and him wanting to wrap the car around a lamppost.

He drummed his thumb against the steering wheel, mumbling under his breath. I double checked my seatbelt as the car sped up. Ryan kept his focus on the road rather than turn it to me.

"Don't you think that's odd?"

I frowned, not quite sure where he was going with this. "What?"

"That you run into lovely Luke and then as soon as you leave, you're attacked?" His voice was thick with hatred as he mentioned Luke's name.

Anger surged inside of me and I fought to stop myself from blowing up at Ryan. Luke had been the one helping me while Ryan's uncle threatened me, and his pack did God only knows what to hybrids. But I couldn't tell him any of that, so I bit my tongue with great difficulty and sank back in the seat in defeat.

Ryan glanced over at me, displeased by my lapse into silence. "You don't think Luke would do that?" he pushed, looking for a reaction.

I rubbed my forehead and closed my eyes, warring with my temper. Protecting Luke and our secret was the important thing. *I would love to wipe that smug look off his face.* "No, I don't think he would."

He snorted, chuckling to himself. "He's not the hero you think he is."

"Nobody's perfect."

Ryan shook his head. "You're being naïve."

"Excuse me?"

"Did he tell you what happened to his sister?" he began, and I arched an eyebrow, curious as to how he planned to paint himself in a better light. "That he killed her."

My head shot up and my temper surged, my instinct screaming at me to defend him. But a small seed of doubt nestled in my stomach, and I wondered how much I knew about anything. I thought of Luke, his kind eyes and the pain that had ripped through him just talking about Alice, racked with guilt. Yes, I could tell he was a killer. He was born to be an alpha after all, but he spoke of Luke's sister as if she were still alive.

"What do you know about Alice?" I asked, wishing I could stuff the words back into my mouth as soon as they left. So much for lying low.

Ryan stiffened, his voice becoming edgy. "Who is Alice?"

For someone with so many pack secrets, Ryan was a terrible liar.

"Luke's sister, the one who died. You seem to know a lot about her." Now it was my turn to rile him, and I relished in it.

Ryan turned to look at me, those brilliant blue eyes of his stone cold and emotionless. "I know she was a hybrid and a stupid girl who stuck her nose into things that were none of her business."

Any sick pleasure I got out of seeing Ryan wound up dissipated immediately. He turned his attention back to the road, his lips set in a thin line. I gulped and wrung my hands. My teeth began to chatter, so I pushed the heating up to full blast. Ryan didn't so much as look at me again. His knuckles were white as he gripped the steering wheel, and he took the corners like a rally driver.

My phone buzzed in my pocket. We both heard it. I slipped it out and held the phone to my side so Ryan couldn't catch a glimpse, though he clearly knew it was Luke. Ryan clenched his jaw and swerved around another corner. Luke had texted to say he got home okay. My heart stopped hammering, and I exhaled in relief. At least he was safe.

We lurched to a stop in front of Ryan's family home. He appeared at the passenger door before I could blink, scooping me into his arms like a damsel and carrying me up the steps. He was stiff against me, anger radiating from every inch of his body. I was in no fit state to kick up a fuss as each step he took made me clench my teeth. He set me down on my feet inside the front door, and I wobbled, clutching a bruised rib.

"Stay here," he ordered, hurling the door shut. With that, Ryan stormed off yelling orders at anyone who passed. I heard his father's voice booming in the distance.

He ripped through the house like a hurricane, doors slamming, yells echoing down the hallway. I was grateful that the brunt of his anger didn't seem to be directed at me. I wasn't sure if Luke's scent set off his disproportionate territorial ego, or if maybe a small part of him was angry about me being attacked because he still cared. It was anyone's guess.

I huddled inside the doorway, my bare bloodied feet marking the pristine white floors. Cold began to set into my bones, so I wrapped the blanket tighter around me. I wanted to bolt upstairs into the shower. In fact, I wanted to run a mile in the opposite direction, but Ryan had ordered me to stay put. While I was in no mood to obey his orders, I didn't know who was lurking in the shadows.

Ryan strode back into the foyer, the last person I wanted to see following hot on his heels. The chill seeping into my bones turned me into a rigid block of ice. Nick, the alpha's henchman, wore a smart black suit, his thinning hair slicked like a wannabe mafia boss. He watched Ryan with an expression of disgust before his eyes met mine.

Nicks lips curled back in a predatory sneer. "Look what the cat dragged in."

I glowered and Ryan shot him a dirty look. "Someone from a rival pack attacked her," he snapped, gesturing to my blood-soaked jeans. "Find out who it was."

"I don't take orders from children."

The vein throbbing in Ryan's neck almost popped, his face flushing red. "I'm not asking."

"I can't promise much, she's a hybrid after all." Nick shrugged, brushing off my injury like I was a broken bird Ryan had picked up on the streets. "Get her cleaned up or your mother will lose the plot."

With that, Nick stalked off towards the dining room.

CHAPTER 31

Nadine's presence in the main house meant I spent as much time outside as possible. She followed me like a shadow I just couldn't shake. It quickly became clear that Nick was using her as some kind of watchdog or snitch. Any conversations I had with Fiona or anyone else were monitored. She played the part with a malicious grin and took sadistic pleasure in ruining my days.

Meeting up with Luke was difficult with Nadine on my case constantly. It took weeks for Fiona to come around to the idea of bringing me into the city again, the attack had spooked her. Fiona and I leaving the pack for the day seemed like a normal shopping trip. While Nadine tried to make excuses to follow us, we lost her on the back roads. She was used to being driven, and Fiona, though deceivingly timid, was fit to be a Formula 1 driver. Today, the roads were slick with rain, but she hugged the corners and flashed me a toothy grin, unfazed by the conditions.

The rain was steadily growing heavier as Fiona pulled up right in front of my old haunt, Brady's.

"Right, this is you," Fiona said, shooting me a stern look. "I'll text when I'm outside to collect you."

I rolled my eyes. "Yes mother."

"Stay out of trouble," she warned, her lips twitching in amusement.

That little hole in my heart, the inner child my counsellor once called it, throbbed slightly. I'd never met my mother. Until Kate, and then Craig, I didn't have anyone who really cared about me. Fiona's gaze softened as I swivelled around and pulled her into a one-armed hug, the most her cramped mini would allow.

Before I got too emotional and the rain could get any worse, I grabbed my bag and pulled up my head before hopping out of the car and running for cover.

Paddy was standing outside the bar under a canopy, chatting to a new bouncer I didn't recognise. He gave me a tight hug and a quick kind word before I ducked into the bar. After I'd told Luke about the minor alleyway incident, we decided that meeting in a public place filled with humans was the safest bet.

As I scanned the familiar surroundings, the worn couches, and the bottles lining the bar, I felt a slight pang of regret about leaving my job without so much as personally handing in my notice. What kind of girl lets her boyfriend sort that? An coward, that's who.

Luke was hiding in the far corner, huddled in a snug and pouring over a half empty glass of what could only be whisky. A breeze blew in as the door swung shut, and Luke's head snapped up, swivelling to look at me. He had deep circles around his eyes and his fingers drummed the table impatiently, but when he noticed me his face lit up.

Looks like I'm not the only one not getting any sleep.

I smiled, and he returned one in kind—it was all terribly polite and awkward. Peter popped up behind the bar, balancing a stack of glasses against the inside of his elbow—a trick I had taught him.

"Eve!" He set the glasses down and rushed over to serve me, a goofy grin spreading across his face. "What can I get you?"

"Rum and coke, please." I watched Peter as he moved around with an air of confidence that hadn't been there before. It was nice to see him growing into the role.

"How have you been? Paddy misses having you around. We all do."

My heart twisted and I sighed, flipping a beer mat between my fingers and resisting the urge to shred it. "I miss you guys too."

"Will you be back in September?" he asked, making sure to give me a double shot.

"No, I don't think so." I shook my head and shifting from foot to foot, praying he would let the subject drop.

Peter's smile crumpled a bit. "How come? Don't you have college?"

Why did bartenders have to be so chatty? I rubbed my face and sighed. Lying to people sucked.

"I think I'll have to take a year out. Family stuff." I forced a smile for his sake and straightened my shoulders. "I might be back the year after."

His expression brightened at that, and he placed my drink down on the bar with a flourish, swatting my hand away when I reached for my purse. "It's on the house." With that, he winked, scooting away before I could argue and returned to cleaning tables.

I was still chuckling to myself when I sat down opposite Luke. In the time it had taken me to order a drink, he had drained his.

"What's so funny?" Luke asked, looking up as he swirled the empty glass between his finger and thumb.

"Nothing, really. It's just mad how people change." I shook my head and turned my full attention to Luke, brushing a stray strand of hair behind my ear.

His blonde hair was swept back and tousled from him continually running his hand through it. I counted three times, and took a sip of my drink, watching him fidget.

"Are you all right?" I asked, and his brow furrowed.

Luke was on edge, shifting restlessly in his chair and playing with his glass until it slipped across the table with a clatter. I arched an eyebrow and he sighed, setting the glass upright again.

He stared at me with an intense burning in his eyes that had me squirming in my seat.

"I found out something," he said, leaning across the table to close the space between us. His knee brushed mine under the table. Neither of us moved away. "They're hunting hybrids."

I choked on my drink, bursting into a coughing fit. Tears rolled down my cheeks as I tried to catch my breath, pressing my hand to my chest. When I finally spoke, it was a hoarse squeak. "Who's they?"

"The Faolchúnna pack."

I thought back to the night of the ritual, when Nadine had been raring to slit my throat. They had been good—too good—at hunting and far too ready to kill a fellow wolf, especially since I wasn't one of them.

Luke got Peter to bring over a glass of water and waited patiently for me to stop spluttering entirely. "From what I could gather without drawing any suspicion is that they have been looking into a way to ensure their pack survival and strength by using hybrids." He watched my reaction carefully. When I paled but nodded, he continued. "They want all the perks of a hybrid but with the strength and instincts of a werewolf. Whatever their plan is, it won't end well."

My blood ran cold, and my stomach lurched. I wanted to scream and cry all at once. This notion was insane, never mind the fact that I was very likely a part of their sick plan. I sank back in the couch and groaned. "Is Ryan involved?"

Luke shrugged, his expression darkening. "I have no definitive proof, but Ryan and his father are up to something. They have been spreading their twisted theories to other packs."

"Are you sure he's involved?"

He scowled and knocked back a mouthful of whisky. "Why are you so sure that he's not?"

I wasn't. I just really hoped he wasn't because it meant I had only ever been some kind of sick prize to him.

"You're hiding something from me."

Luke sighed and spread his hands palm down on the table, rolling his shoulders. "I'm not. Ryan isn't as innocent as you would like to believe. A long time ago, we had a run in, and I know he had a hand in what happened to Alice."

"You never told me what happened."

"Alice was my younger sister who disappeared when she was sixteen…" Luke's voice dropped, and pain reflected in those glassy eyes. He took a sip of whisky between each sentence. "My family just presume she is dead, but I don't believe it. We never found a body."

I swallowed a lump in my throat. There were no words.

"I was meant to mind her while my parents were away. I had a few friends over for drinks… a girl." He shuffled awkwardly, guilt etching into his features. "Alice tried to sneak out, and I caught her. I knew she was meeting someone from the Faolchúnna pack, and we had a row. She stormed out."

Luke drained his whisky, flinching as it stung the back of his throat. "After my friend left and Alice still wasn't home by midnight, I felt bad and went looking for her. But I was too late…" He rubbed his eyes with his sleeve, quickly composing himself, but a sadness echoed as he continued, "I'll never forgive myself."

"I'm so sorry." I squeezed his hands, at a loss of what else to say. "What does this have to do with Ryan?"

He stiffened and withdrew his hand. "Ryan was the guy she was meeting."

My hands shook as I pushed my hair back, cursing myself for being so stupid. "I'm an idiot."

Luke's expression warmed, and he shook his head, stretching his back as if it would rid him of his demons. "No, you're not. You have a good heart."

"Just no brains," I said bitterly, earning a chuckle from Luke.

He seemed to like the change of subject, composing himself far quicker than I would have imagined possible. How he couldn't see his potential to be alpha, I would never understand. Then it dawned on me.

"That's why you won't lead the pack, isn't it?"

"I thought we were done with this," Luke groaned and pinched the bridge of his nose. "They don't know, okay? I was disgusted with myself for letting her go that night, and I always will be."

I bit my lip, feeling like I had overstepped a line.

"I never told them she was meeting Ryan, or that I saw her sneak out. Now that's the end of that," he said, stealing a sip of my rum.

I went to motion for Peter, but he held my hand. "No, I need a clear head for this."

"Uh huh," I said, watching him drain my glass too. "Nick has Nadine on my tail."

Luke looked bewildered.

"One of his minions, the one who tried to gut me during the ritual."

"Of course," he muttered, his voice growing thick with emotion. "You need to be careful, Eve. Whatever they're planning, whether Ryan has involved you or not, being a hybrid isn't safe right now. I'm not having you end up dead as well."

"What am I supposed to do? Hang around?"

Luke shook his head and reached out, his fingers closing around my hand. His skin was warm against mine. "No, if you try to leave now, they'll follow you."

"What else do you propose I do?"

I wanted nothing more than to run.

He sighed, biting his lip. "We need to know what's going on..."

I swallowed hard. "What are you saying?"

"As much as I don't like you staying there, you're our only chance to get to the bottom of this, Eve. I would never put you in danger. If you don't want to stay, I'll get you out, but if you ca—"

"I'll stay," I interjected, my voice wavering. "I'll stay to find out what's really going on"

He squeezed my hand and held my gaze, his husky voice softening. "Once we know what we are dealing with, I promise we will get you out. We don't know who that poor girl is, or what else they have planned."

"I'll lie low and keep to myself until we find out more. There might be some clues around the house. Ryan must know something."

"You need to be careful," Luke said, cupping my hands in his. "Don't do anything to raise suspicion with Ryan or his father. I would never forgive myself if anything happened to you."

The way he looked at me made a weird feeling rise in my stomach. "I won't draw any attention to myself."

He visibly relaxed a fraction. "I'll see what I can find out on my end. The quicker we can get you out of there, the better."

"What are you going to do?"

Luke grinned, but the worry never left his eyes. "I have my ways, contacts and stuff."

"And stuff?"

He laughed, a melodic sound that sent chills through me. Even when he was being serious there was a sense of beautiful calm that he exuded. I needed that.

"I can't tell you all my secrets, Eve."

I sighed and shot him a rueful look. Out of everyone in my life, I had only known Luke a handful of months, and I had gotten to know him under the strangest of circumstances. Yet somehow he was the only one I could trust with this secret, one that was so much bigger than just us.

CHAPTER 32

Sneaking into the library was risky, but I needed answers. Whenever the alpha and his minions were having meetings, or when I knew Nadine was off seducing Ryan, I hid out among the bookcases.

So far, I'd turned up nothing of interest. I'd stuffed the death certs I'd found relating to the alpha's cousin into a folder and was slowly building a case—except it was flimsy at best and filled with holes. The cousin's death cert might have been redacted and deemed a suicide, but that didn't sit right with me. The alpha had made it very clear that there was nothing he wouldn't do for his pack, for himself.

The one piece of information I really wanted to find, any information on my parents, was nowhere in this hellhole. Of course, my name wasn't listed in the birth records either, and the woman who'd given me up at birth in the hospital hadn't given her my name according to my social worker and the notes I stole from him in my early teens. There was nothing to go on.

Having given up on the filing cabinets, I stared at the bookcases papering the walls, stacked to the point they were overflowing. I started on the one nearest me, avoiding the history books and putting any books straight back that were just general information about werewolves. Flipping through dusty notebooks was giving me nothing but sneezing fits until I came across some sort of diary. As I picked it from the shelves, a thin, folded sheet of paper popped out from between two pages and drifted to the floor.

I bent down and unfolded the piece of paper to reveal a death certificate. It wasn't just the name 'Luke McKenna' that caught my eye, but the cause of death—his heart was ripped out.

Something about the name was familiar.

My suspicions were confirmed when I flipped back through the notebook detailing the pack history. Luke McKenna was the previous alpha, Damien's uncle. I remembered reading that Luke and his wife died in a car crash. His son, Cormac, should have been next in line, but he died shortly after.

Stepping over opened boxes and some book stacks, I started through the filing cabinet. It didn't take me long to find the other death certificate for Luke McKenna. Tucking the notebook under my arm, I held the two certs up next to one another. They were identical except for the time of death, the car crash one claimed the alpha died hours later.

"Why would you have two death certs?" I wondered aloud as I crouched down and spread out the documents alongside the diary and the Faolchúnna pack on the floor.

If one is a fake.

A steady sense of dread was building. My gut instinct told me the hidden death certificate was the real one. The previous alpha didn't die in a car crash—he was murdered.

I flipped through the diary again, only to find it was some sort of doctor's journal. Whoever it was, they were clearly a pack member. There was nothing else incriminating, just their own notes on patients, except that their last entry was dated the day before Damien became alpha.

Cormac's death cert was redacted, but there was no way him dying within months of his father was a coincidence. Damien's rise to becoming alpha was surrounded by death.

The sound of humming reached my ears, followed by footsteps growing louder. With no time to grab anything else, I panicked and stuffed the full version of the previous alpha's cert

in my pocket. Just as I touched the handle, the door swung open
to reveal a more dishevelled Ryan than usual. Shadows nested
under his eyes, and his tousled hair looked like he'd gone for a
run in gale force winds. Even his tie was off centre.

"Can we talk?"

Talking to him was the last thing on my to do list.

"Ryan, I'm really not feeling great," I said, the lies fluent at
this point. "Can we talk tomorrow?"

I sidestepped past him and started down the hall, subtly
pushing the folded paper deeper in my pocket. I didn't need to
look back to know Ryan was wearing the same wounded look
that he had for days.

Every night, I'd either faked being asleep when he got in or
stayed at Fiona's until late. Anything to avoid talking to him.
When he wrapped his arms around me at night, it made my
skin crawl, but I had to stick it out until I found the answers we
needed. Ryan wasn't stupid. He knew something was wrong,
and I was quickly running out of excuses. I'd even hid in the
bathroom for hours one night pretending to be sick out of
desperation.

By the time I had calmed my frayed nerves, I was halfway
down the stairs. I caught her scent first, then I heard the unmistakable noise of her strut growing closer. Nadine waltzed into
view, a Cheshire Cat grin lighting up her face as she stopped at
the foot of the stairs, one elegant hand on her hip. I didn't even
bother hiding my disappointment, I was so over this game of cat
and mouse.

"I hear there's trouble in paradise." Nadine sneered, her eyes
sparkling at the thought.

"Based on what?"

"The walls have ears."

"Of course they do," I muttered, pausing to give my leg a rest
as I reached the last step. It was almost completely healed, but
it still gave the odd niggle. It would heal faster if I shifted for a
long period, but Ryan wouldn't allow that. Plus, I was trying to

keep a low profile, and pissing off the pack would not go down well.

I caught her watching and rolled my eyes. For such a pretty girl, the pleasure Nadine took in seeing others suffer twisted her features in the most unattractive way.

"Do you have a point Nadine, or are you just stalking me?"

She scowled and I tried to stifle a laugh. "With that attitude, I don't blame him for getting sick of you. It was bound to happen, eventually."

I think it upset her that the last comment drew no reaction from me. I had seen her sneaking out of his office on more than one occasion the past few weeks. Nadine was desperate to keep her claws in Ryan. I had far bigger things to worry about.

Giving her a dead pan glare, I turned, and for once it was me walking away. Nadine didn't like that. She came scurrying along beside me, her words dripping in my ear like venom.

"Now that he's done playing with you, there's no need for you to stick around. I can take care of him," she continued, rambling, her eyes flashing with anger when I continued to ignore her. She eyed me with a mix of disgust and bewilderment, the faintest of lines creasing her brow. "Where are you going?"

"To kill some time." I sighed, turning to face Nadine, a girl that had once terrified me. Now I felt nothing. "As for Ryan, you can have him."

I'd thought about going for a walk, but my best bet to stop Nadine following me was the kitchens. When I stepped into the warmth of the kitchen, Mary was in full swing. She hovered over the girls, barking orders like an army captain. Dishes stacked high with a buffet style breakfast littered the counters. Rebecca must be having guests over.

It was only as I was pulling a chair out and the leg scraped the floor that Mary looked up and noticed me.

"Eve!" She bustled over, her hands covered in flour. By the time she came to help, I had already flopped into the seat.

"You shouldn't be straining yourself," Mary scolded. She grabbed a passing girl with a tray full of fairy cakes by the elbow. "When you've sent them in, get Eve here a slice of toast."

I went to stand, but Mary placed a firm hand on my shoulder and pushed me down.

"Mary, it's been a fortnight, I'm fine."

She rolled her eyes, swatting me with a tea towel. "I told you to rest."

The girl rushed away and joined the queue carrying trays stacked high with cakes as they filed out of the kitchen towards the back patio. Sunlight flickered through the kitchen window, the autumn sun beginning to wane. Mary followed my gaze.

"It's Rebecca's prissy party, or whatever they're called."

The faint hint of a smile tugged at the corner of my mouth. "Council board?"

"Yeah, them. She's organising the harvest celebrations."

I nodded, feeling a small pang of sadness followed by relief washing over me. Ryan had mentioned the party, how they would have fancy dinners, hunt together and dance the night away. I had been looking forward to it, but now I wanted nothing to do with them.

"How's the leg?" Mary asked, drawing my attention back to the present.

Even just mentioning the stab wound made the area itch. "It's pretty much healed."

Ryan had insisted the pack medic stitch me up after the attack. The wound had healed quicker than a human's but slower than it would for a normal werewolf. The doctor probably could have done more, but his bedside manner had left a lot to be desired. He had sneered when I asked about scarring. I don't think he enjoyed treating hybrids, but Ryan wouldn't allow me go to the hospital. Luke had flipped out when I had messaged explaining I was patched up so poorly.

The mousy girl from earlier interrupted my thoughts, placing a plate of jam and toast down in front of me and a coffee for Mary she never asked for but gratefully accepted.

I stared at the toast, pushing the food around my plate. "Mary, do you know anything about Nick?"

"Nick is Ryan's uncle. I don't speak to him much. Spends most of his time with Damien dealing with pack business. They've always been close as brothers despite the age difference. Although, I think Nick fancies himself as alpha someday."

My stomach grumbled as I forced a bite of toast down. The sweet taste of fresh jam tempted me to take more, and before I knew it, I had devoured the entire plate.

She watched me, nodding in approval. "What has you asking questions like that anyway?"

"I was wondering about how Damien became the alpha when he wasn't next in line. And then Cor—"

"Damien became alpha after a very dark time in our pack's history," Mary cut me off, her expression darkening. "You need to stop digging, Eve."

I swallowed, caught off guard by her warning. *Did she know something?*

"Just keep out of the alpha and Nick's way and neither of them will bother you."

"If only it were that simple," I mumbled, earning an odd look from Mary. "Don't mind me."

"Eve." She shifted in her chair, stretching to crack her back. The sound of each bone clicking echoed in the kitchen. "I have never pried or stuck my nose into your business with Ryan. I turned a blind eye to all those times you talked Fiona into helping you meet up with Luke."

"I didn't." The outright lie slipped from my lips.

"You're asking questions about dangerous people," she warned, leaning back in her chair and staring off into space.

"You would be wise to put your head down and leave things be. You've already fallen out of favour with Ryan."

"As if you even like Ryan."

"He offered you some protection." She sighed, wringing her hands in the dirty apron tied around her hips. "Now you have nothing."

"I can protect myself."

Mary simply held a hand up to silence my argument. "If you have gotten yourself into trouble, you need to tell me what is going on."

I looked down, my cheeks heating. "I haven't, I was just curious."

"You're a terrible liar." Mary shook her head, absently tracing the scar along her jaw.

But she was wrong. I had been lying through my teeth for weeks to everyone. Where I felt little or no guilt lying to Ryan, Mary had a talent for making me feel like she could see inside my soul each time she looked at me. "I found out some stuff, something that upsets me, and I can't get it out of my head."

She gave me a blank look.

"I can't tell you anything," I mumbled, toying with the hem of my sweater. "I don't want you to get caught up in this mess."

Mary snorted, throwing her head back with a throaty laugh. "They can try."

My heart hurt at the bubbly sound. She was the closest thing to a mother figure that I'd ever had. "I wish I could tell you, but I can't."

I gestured to my leg and Mary's expression grew stormy. She looked from me to my leg and then back again. She thumped her fist on the table, making the cutlery jump. "I knew this wasn't a random attack."

"Shush, Mary. Please, I can't have Ryan digging. It's so much more complicated than just me."

Mary pursed her lips, her brow furrowing deeply. "I can't read between the lines when I don't know what book you're in, let alone what page you're on."

"It's something about hybrids," I relented, keeping my voice low. "I'm not sure how deeply Ryan is involved, but I know for sure that the alpha is. Whatever they're planning, it's not good news."

She began playing with a knife, worrying a dent in the already worn table. "I'm not going to lie to you. The alpha has never come across as well intentioned, and while I don't know what they are planning, it doesn't surprise me in the slightest that it involves hybrids."

I watched her in silence. Mary was an old battle axe, full of witty comebacks and a force to be reckoned with. When her worried gaze locked with mine, she aged ten years and looked like a different person. The difference was fear.

"What have you gotten yourself into, Eve?"

"I don't know."

CHAPTER 33

So many answers lay in the past, but I knew the key was in the present. Each day Ryan spent at work, I searched high and low for clues in the house. Every drawer, every envelope, I left nothing untouched. When it came to rooms that would raise suspicion, I used an expensive bottle of perfume I stole from Nadine's room to hide my trail. I even snuck into Rebecca's bedroom and spent an hour wading through her walk-in wardrobe searching for answers, but I came up with nothing but envy for her designer shoe collection.

Deciding to go back to square one, I emptied a box of paper onto Ryan's bed, rummaging through the contents. The only suspicious item I found was a receipt for a strip club and indisputable proof that he was a terrible gambler.

A knock on the door made my heart stop. I jumped and spun, hurriedly stuffing the overflowing box back into place on the shelf.

"Sorry, I didn't mean to scare you." A sheepish Fiona stood in the doorway.

I shook my head, flopping down onto Ryan's bed with a loud sigh. "It's fine. I thought you might be Nadine."

"No, she's out getting her dress altered for the party."

Fiona closed the door behind her and walked over, her long honey-coloured waves swaying as she sat down beside me. She moved with so much grace, I always felt like a turnip in her presence.

"Of course she is," I muttered, rolling my eyes at the images materialising in my mind of Nadine being an absolute nightmare in a boutique.

"Are you not getting a dress?" she asked, as if we were talking about a prom and not a posh party Ryan's pack put on purely to schmooze politicians and further their agenda. I wasn't safe among these wolves as a hybrid, a bunch of humans were walking into the lion's den blind. I had no doubt any politician or high society member who became problematic would vanish under suspicious circumstances.

I shrugged, staring blankly at the ceiling. "I doubt I will be going."

From the corner of my eye, I saw Fiona's smile falter for a brief moment. "Oh."

"I might, things are just a bit up in the air." I sat up to face Fiona, pushing a strand of hair behind her ear. "I promise I will do my best to be there. Even if I'm not, you will still have a wonderful night."

Her expression brightened, and I felt a pang of guilt. I had no right to make that promise.

"Is Tim going to be there?" I asked, trying to change the conversation to a lighter subject. Tim was a pack member, a tall guy who was a bit too strait-laced   for my liking, but he had a kind face, and Fiona lit up every time she spoke about him.

"He asked me to be his date this morning," she gushed, her rosy cheeks flushing at the mention of his name.

"See? You'll have a great time." I smiled, giving her arm a light squeeze. "So, stop worrying."

Fiona nodded, casting her gaze around the room. There were still half empty boxes on the floor and random drawers sat open. "What are you doing, anyway?"

"Ryan is... He lied to me about something, and I just want to find proof."

A frown shadowed her pretty face. "About what?" She noticed the lacy underwear beside the bed that I had clocked the moment I had entered the room. "Is it to do with Nadine?"

I chewed my lip. "Sort of."

"He might keep what you're looking for in his office?"

"In the city?"

"No." She shook her head and ran a hand through her golden mane, the bangles on her wrist jingling. "I guess he would keep some stuff there, but he's been using the office here more lately."

Why didn't I think of that?

My head snapped up and Fiona had my full attention. "Oh, really? He never mentioned that," I said, trying to keep my tone calm and breezy.

Fiona caught sight of my wry smile and groaned. "Don't look at me like that."

I bat my eyelashes, doing my best to feign innocence. "Like what?"

"Like you have a plan that involves me."

"I have a plan, but I promise it only involves you a teeny tiny bit." I grinned, scooting closer to Fiona on the bed. "If I get caught, I'll take the blame."

She shook her head, her freckled nose creasing. "I know you think Ryan is up to something, but part of his job is knowing stuff that the rest of us don't need to be involved in."

"You mean lying, hiding, scheming?" I said flatly, softening my tone at the sight of Fiona's wounded expression. "I think he's using me Fiona, that's all I can tell you without getting you in trouble."

Fiona rubbed her temples and sighed deeply, meeting my level gaze. "Okay, what's the plan?"

I broke into a smile, despite the pang of guilt I felt for roping Fiona into helping me. The last thing I wanted to do was endanger anyone, but I needed answers.

"Ryan must be hiding something in his office. I need your master key."

Fiona led me past the landing stairs and down the opposite wing of the house where Nadine had taken up residence. I remembered that Ryan's office was the very last one in that wing, facing his father's. True to her word, Fiona stopped at the end of the corridor beside a large window. One door had an engraved sign reading 'Damien McKenna', the door opposite had Ryan's name etched into the wood in a far less fancy sign.

I hovered as Fiona unlocked the door to Ryan's office. It swung open to reveal a spacious room lined with bookshelves, and a large oak desk in the middle backing onto a wide bay window that overlooked the gardens.

"I'll be by the stairs. I have some laundry to stack," she said, placing the key into the palm of my hand.

"What if someone comes?" I asked, guilt beginning to creep in.

She shrugged. "I'll whistle?"

I didn't want to get Fiona in trouble, but I looked more worried than she did. Then again, she wasn't racking up secrets like they were going out of fashion, and they say ignorance is bliss.

Fiona disappeared as she eased the door closed behind her, leaving me alone. I stared around the room and began taking books off the shelves, dust rising into the air as I flicked through their pages. They were clearly just there for show. I scanned the bookcases for any sign of a hiding spot before walking over to Ryan's desk. His two framed university degrees hung on the wall, along with some graduation and other college pictures. In the photos, he was smiling, and if I didn't know any better, I would have said he looked happy, normal even.

I rifled through the papers on his desk. They were mostly business statements that looked like gibberish to me. There was blackmail on nearly every pack member—even Nadine—and more dodgy death certificates. I shuddered. Ryan may not have had the respect of his pack, but he had creative ways to keep them under his thumb. Not for the first time that week, I found myself questioning my judgement.

There were three drawers under the desk, the first for stationary. The second had condoms inside and was instantly slammed shut. The third wouldn't budge. I grabbed a pen off the desk and started picking at the lock, but I was no thief. The drawer wasn't opening.

A shaky whistle echoed from down the hall—Fiona's warning. If Ryan caught me snooping, one of those death certificates could be mine. I snatched the set of keys off the desk and cast a panicked glance around the room for somewhere to hide. The whistle came again, and this time it was shrill. With my dodgy leg, jumping out the window wasn't an option. While we had come up with a warning plan, we forgot the escape plan, and I had no excuse to be in Ryan's office. Out of options, I pulled the chair out from the desk and slipped underneath. The face of the desk didn't quite reach the floor, but it would do the job. Unless it was Ryan and he planned to sit down, then I was screwed.

As I curled up underneath, I could hear Fiona making stilted small talk. As they drifted closer, I focused on picking out the other voices. The first had the unmistakable air of arrogance of Ryan's father, the alpha. I closed my eyes as Nick's voice carried towards me. My heart leapt in my chest.

There was no sign of Ryan. I crossed my fingers, toes, everything, that they would just go into the alpha's office. I sucked in a breath as the door handle rattled.

"He needs to stop messing about, brother," Nick snapped with none of the respect he normally showed.

I heard a door creak open across the hall, and my shoulders relaxed an inch.

"Since when do you tell me how to raise my child?"

"Ryan is supposed to be the next alpha. He can't keep behaving like a kid. He needs to grow up and take responsibility."

Damien chuckled. "He is still a boy, we all make mistakes."

"Those mistakes could cost us everything."

"He knows his role. Ryan's just bending the rules to see what he can get away with. I wasn't too dissimilar at that age."

A floorboard just outside the office creaked. I tensed and held my breath.

"He needs to keep her on a shorter leash," Nick grunted. Footsteps entered the room, and he sniffed. "See? It stinks of mongrel in here. The boy is letting her run riot."

A second step of footsteps echoed Nicks. My heart hammered in my chest, and I prayed they wouldn't pick up on it.

"I thought you dealt with her snooping?" Damien asked, his tone icy.

"She's not as stupid as you think." He paused for a moment before lowering his voice. "I think she knows something. She's been going in and out of the estate far too much."

"What could she possibly know?" The alpha scoffed.

"What if she knows about the hybrids?"

"You better hope that she doesn't. You told me this was under control."

"I assure you, she is being monitored carefully," Nick said, nervously scuffing his toe against the floor. "I have her word."

"Her word means nothing," the alpha spat. "Does Ryan know?"

There was a pause before Nick answered. "No, as far as I know, he still thinks she's loyal."

"Perhaps if we told him the full story, he might buck himself up and treat her like a hybrid rather than a pet."

"He's in love with her," Nick replied dryly.

"No, not anymore. She's been sniffing around some Crescent wolf and evidently doesn't know when to quit. I've had enough."

Nick snorted. "There's nothing special about her. I know Ryan said she could help lure others in, but there's no way he could pull that kind of deceit off. He's not that smart."

"Where did you find her that night?" Damien asked, speaking about me as if I were some stray dog.

"Coming out of the hatch."

"So, you don't know what she found then?"

Nick swallowed. "No."

"You should have led with that. It changes everything."

The alpha sighed, and his footsteps moved away, echoing in the hallway. Nick followed and shut the door behind him.

"Come, we should discuss the next steps."

Once they closed the door across the hall, both voices became inaudible. I shouldn't have been one bit surprised that the alpha's office was soundproofed, but it did really impede this whole eavesdropping thing. I realised I had been holding my breath. My shoulders drooped, and I pushed my hair out of my face, exhaling slowly. I crawled out from under the desk, pushing the chair back into place.

I glanced around the room to make sure I hadn't missed anything, ignoring the building urge to bolt. They could come back at any moment, but I would never get the chance to check Ryan's office again. Poor Fiona was probably having a coronary while they'd been speaking.

"One more try," I muttered to myself, grabbing a letter opener and prying at the locked drawer, to no avail.

Then I remembered the keys and tried some of the smaller ones. I was about to give up when the last key I tried clicked and the drawer came free. Not expecting it to budge, the force sent me stumbling back. I teetered for a precarious moment before reaching out for the windowsill, steadying myself. I breathed out slowly, shaking with adrenaline.

"That was too close."

I rubbed my forehead and tiptoed over to the drawer. There was precious little in it, just a handful of photos and folders, so I went through them first. They were medical records, but I recognised none of the names. Except mine. I froze, and my heartbeat rocketed in my chest.

My mouth was dry as I began flicking through the photos. One showed two boys playing in the rose garden–one was clearly Ryan, the other shared his impish grin. The edges of the photo were worn and smudged with fingerprints. His brother. The rest were family photos with little meaning, a few that Nadine must have added to the collection herself, and then one of a teenage girl with blonde hair and round chocolate brown eyes. There were more girls, but nothing tied them together, and none were familiar to me. I swallowed, hoping the pit of worry in my gut was wrong, and stuffed the brown-eyed girl photo into my pocket.

A quick glance through the folder told me nothing I didn't already know. It was just more proof that Ryan wasn't innocent in the slightest. I placed everything back in place, and I shut the drawer gently, drumming my fingers on the desk surface. I was a fool.

As I turned to leave, I caught sight of Ryan's car in the driveway. My body was so chock full of adrenaline at this point, I thought my heart might burst out of my chest. I snatched up Fiona's keys and was about to make a beeline for the door when I noticed Ryan leaning across the driver's seat talking to someone. My blood ran cold.

Opposite Ryan sat a young man, no older than us, with short bleach blonde hair and a distinctive scar that twisted the corner of his mouth up. This time, he was dressed in a smart steel-grey suit and looked every inch the respectable businessman, nothing like the thug that attacked me, but I would recognise him anywhere. For a naïve moment, I thought about telling Ryan, but I saw money exchange hands and my chest tightened.

How did I ever think he wasn't involved?

I sat in the centre of my bed, hugging my knees to my chest and staring at my phone. Time slipped by, and I spent what seemed like forever mulling over my ever-growing list of mistakes and bad decisions. I really hoped that this wasn't one. When I heard a loud ring, I leapt forward and snatched the phone off the bed. My hand shook as I pressed it to my ear.

"Eve? Are you all right?" Luke's husky voice came through the line. Even when he was stressed, it had a calming effect that I couldn't explain.

"Yes. Well, no, not really." I was struggling to string a full sentence together.

"Spit it out, one word at a time."

"I found something," I whispered, casting one ear out to see if anyone was stalking the hallways.

Luke inhaled sharply. "You weren't meant to be looking."

"I know, but I searched Ryan's office," I said, toying with the sleeve of my sweatshirt. My palm was slick against the phone. I could hear Luke's breathing change, but when he didn't protest, I explained what I had overheard, and how I had seen Ryan meet with my attacker outside of the house.

There was a smash and then cursing from Luke's end. I jumped but stayed silent. Luke let out a long string of colourful language, and there was the sound of more things hitting either the floor or a wall. After more banging, he eventually came back to the phone.

"I'll kill him," Luke growled.

"Not yet," I found myself saying, surprised that I would even consider that. I'd changed. "There's something else. I found some photos, most of them were normal, but there were a few random head shots of different girls. I know I sound like a jealous weirdo for saying it, but something just doesn't feel right. There were medical records too—including mine."

"Maybe the photos match the records?" he suggested and once again, I felt like a dumb ass.

"Excellent point. I never thought of that." I frowned, rubbing my forehead as I struggled to wrap my mind around everything. "My photo wasn't there though."

Luke's line buzzed, breaking down briefly. A second voice sounded in the background.

"Eve, I have to go deal with something."

My heart sank.

"Promise me you will stop looking. It's too risky. I'll call you later and we can work something out," Luke said, pleading with me. "Please, stay safe."

Before I could respond, the line went dead. At least I didn't have to lie.

CHAPTER 34

R yan invited me to a family dinner that night. While my immediate response was to slam the door in his face, I told him I still felt sick. It wasn't a complete lie. He said he would take Nadine instead, as if it might make me jealous. At least that meant he didn't suspect that I had been in his office.

I paced my room like a caged animal until I heard them settle in for dinner. With that, I grabbed the backpack I had stuffed full to the brim and made for the door. Voices drifted from the dining room, and Nadine's raucous laughter rang out as I padded down the stairs, one light step at a time. Trays scraped and dishes clanged from the direction of the kitchens. A lump rose in my throat as I thought of Fiona and Mary, and how good she had been to me.

An all too familiar feeling of unease nestled in the pit of my stomach as I snuck out the front door, pressing it shut without a sound. I slipped away like a ghost, hovering briefly to stare up at the house with a strange sense of regret.

Stars twinkled in the sky above me, and the crescent moon hung low as I made my way past the gardens, beyond the perfect red brick houses. The autumn air was crisp, frost coating the grass. It was a gorgeous night, and I wondered, not for the first time, how a beautiful facade hid a multitude of sins.

The grounds were quiet. Everyone was either at the dinner or sitting oblivious in their little homes. I began jogging, my breath coming in quick puffs that hung in the cool night air. As the cottage drew closer, the feeling of dread in my gut grew tenfold. As I stopped in front of the cottage, I dropped by bag by the door, quickly checking my phone.

They had installed a huge padlock since my last visit, but I had come prepared. I pulled a large bolt cutter out of bag and turned to the door. That afternoon, I had snuck into the shed and helped myself. After all, what's theirs was mine according to pack rules—not that I would ever join, the one good choice I'd made since coming here. The lock snapped off and fell to the ground with a satisfying thud.

My hands shook as I pushed my way inside. Kicking the carpet up revealed that the hatch had been locked too, but thanks to my trusty bolt cutters, it was easily dealt with. I stuffed it back in the bag, took a mini torch, and pulled the hatch up. Each step echoed as I descended the steps. My palm was slick against the handrail and the light shook in rhythm with my hand.

A bang rang through the empty hallway as my bag caught on the rail. I froze. A cry rang out. It was faint but there. I glanced above me, where the hatch was shrouded in shadows. A pool of darkness lay ahead. My feet were heavy, but I pressed on. The voice grew louder until I reached the same door that had been haunting my dreams.

"It's you." The girl's voice drifted through, shaky and unsure.

I stepped up to the door and hefted the bag off my shoulder. "Yes, me again. I'm sorry I didn't come back sooner."

Something shuffled on the opposite side of the wall. "I heard yelling," she said, sounding so small.

"Ni—someone caught me last time, and they weren't too pleased."

"Nick?"

I cursed under my breath, trying to keep my voice as steady as possible as I took out the bolt cutter. "Yes, he wasn't too happy about me snooping around."

"And Ryan?"

My already frazzled nerves frayed just that bit more. "He doesn't know I'm here."

"Are you sure? He was so angry last time..." she whispered, terror seeping into every word.

I swallowed hard.

"Can you move back from the door, please?" I asked, feigning as much confidence as I could muster. "I'm getting you out tonight."

There was sniff followed by a soft shuffle.

Crouching down, I examined the new three bolt system as if I had any clue what I was doing. At a loss of any solid plan, I clamped the torch between my thighs and set to work with the cutter, trying to shatter the bolts. For a moment, I worried I had brought the wrong tools, but eventually I felt one of the bolts beginning to give. I put all my strength into squeezing the cutter. Sweat beaded on my brow and I was panting with the effort, but I didn't give up. Metal clanged on the floor as the first bolt splintered.

"Tell me about yourself," I said, wiping my sleeve across my forehead.

"I don't know what to tell you. I've been here so long..."

My brow furrowed as I braced the pliers and gave a good tug. "Who brought you here?" Even as the question left my lips, I knew the answer would make my skin crawl.

"Ryan did, a long time ago."

I gulped and swallowed down the bile that rose in my throat, cursing as my sweaty hands slipped on the pliers. In a fit of temper, I slammed the bolt cutter on the ground and swung a kick at the wall hard enough to make my foot throb.

"Sorry."

I sighed, pinching the bridge of my nose as I pushed the tears away. "It's not your fault, you've done nothing wrong."

"He brings me food, as do a few others," she hiccoughed, pausing to gather herself. "I think it's been a few years, but they never tell me the time. It's all my fault I ended up here anyway."

"How so?"

"Because I'm a hybrid."

I resisted the urge to scream for fear of scaring the poor girl senseless. Instead, I picked up the pliers and went to town on the bolts with every ounce of strength I had. I should have known. There was a familiarity to her scent that I had never noticed before. I was the worst werewolf ever.

Only when the second bolt crashed to the floor did I stop to take a breath. I braced my hands against the door, sweat soaking the back of my shirt and panting.

"How did you end up here? What did Ryan do?"

"I thought he was a friend, more maybe. I was stupid," she said, echoing the very thoughts circling in my mind. "We met up a few times but then one night, we were supposed to go on a date, and he never showed. I waited for a long time, but when I turned to leave, someone attacked me and it all went black. When I woke up, I was here."

"They kidnapped you."

"I guess."

At least she had no choice, I thought bitterly. *I entered the lions' den of my own stupid free will.*

I stepped back and reached for the bolt cutter, holding it poised above my shoulder. Anger boiled in my veins, gearing me up for round three.

"What's your name?" I asked, taking a swing at the last lock.

"Alice."

The bolt cutter clattered to the ground, and all the blood drained from my face. I should have known.

CHAPTER 35

I steadied myself against the walls, my ears ringing. Another wave of nausea washed over me, and I retched until there was nothing left. Tears rolled down my cheeks unbidden. I wiped my eyes roughly with my sleeve and let out a long string of curses.

"Are you all right?" Alice's voice rang out, snapping me back to reality.

"I'm fine," I lied, hands shaking as I picked the bolt cutters off the floor.

I felt numb as I began working the lock, clenching my jaw to bite back the tears while my heart hammered in my chest. I pushed it down, locking every bit of sadness and betrayal in a box and throwing away the key. Now was not the time to fall apart. Amidst all the shock and confusion, pieces started to fall into place. Alice was the girl in the picture, and I knew those eyes because they were Luke's.

Alice shuffled behind the door, sniffling until she wound herself up and broke into a soft sob.

"I'm sorry for yelling," I said, wiping my forehead with the back of my hand. "I'm Eve. None of this is your fault, and I'm a hybrid too."

"You're a hybrid?" Alice asked, her voice cracking as my heart did the same. "You need to go, it's not safe."

I braced my foot against the door to give myself more power and pressed down on the bolt cutters, my fingers stinging from the force. My breath came in short pants. "I need to get you out of here."

"You don't understand," Alice pleaded, becoming shrill. "They want more hybrids."

My brow furrowed, but I kept working on the lock. It was the only thing stopping me from going full scale volcano. "Why?"

"Ryan wouldn't tell me everything, but it's to do with their bloodline. They've been studying the genetics, know the were-wolf bloodline has gotten weaker over the years in packs that refuse to mate with humans, because there's no fresh blood. It's a weird mix of science and magic. Outbreeding is what's needed, but they refuse to encourage it." She sniffed, and her voice drew closer. "They need to strengthen the pack, and they think hybrids are the key."

"But they hate hybrids," I spat, growling at the bolt as it began to bend. "They clearly don't want to accept them as part of the pack, despite half pretending to tolerate me."

Alice fell silent for a moment. When she spoke again, her tone was solemn. "They don't want to accept us, they want to use us. From what I could tell from something Nick let slip, the pack plans to use hybrid genes to strengthen the bloodlines and destroy us in the long run."

The bolt cutters slipped off the lock, and I went with it, my shoulder hitting the door with a thud. "What do you mean use us?" I asked, only half listening. I immediately clamped the pliers straight back on, shaking as a bead of sweat rolled down my spine. The last lock was scratched and misshapen. *A few more goes and I will have it.*

"Like dogs."

I paused and looked up at the door, frowning. "What the hell are you on about?"

"Breeding."

Ryan's voice came from behind me, echoing in the empty hallway. The lights blinked into life and my heart froze. I gripped the pliers so tightly my knuckles turned white, spinning on my heel to come face to face with Ryan.

"Get out of here, Eve!" Alice shrieked, the door rattling as she fought to get my attention.

Ryan's lovely lips twisted in a malicious smirk at her pleas.

"Breeding?" I squeaked, my voice rising an octave with each word that followed. "What kind of freak are you? This isn't some scientific experiment."

He brushed a stray curl back into place, not ruffled in the slightest. "Isn't it?"

I picked my jaw off the floor and resisted the urge to run him through with the bolt cutters. "No, it's not. Hybrids are people too, Ryan, not some sick means to an end."

"You don't understand. Werewolves need to survive, we must strengthen the pack."

When Ryan said *we*, I was more than certain it didn't involve me anymore.

I shook my head, tightening my grip on the only weapon I had. "You're crazy."

Ryan laughed, the sound ringing hollow. "That's just the anger talking."

"No, you're bat shit crazy."

His eyes narrowed. "Have some respect. You're the one who has been caught sticking your nose in something that's none of your business."

"None of my business?" I shrieked, quickly losing what hold I had left on my temper. "This involves hybrids, so actually, it is definitely my fucking business. Your messed-up plan is not happening."

"Don't be stupid, Eve."

"That's exactly what I've been doing, Ryan. I've been stupid to believe you," I hissed, bracing the pliers across my chest in a defensive stance Luke had taught me. "You might think I'm a fool, but you can't lie your way out of this one."

"I wasn't planning to." Ryan shrugged and stood between me and the exit, feet planted and looking every part the alpha. But I could see what Luke had meant—Ryan was a blind follower, not a leader.

I scowled. "Really? You lie about everything. You even had me attacked when you thought I was getting close to the truth!"

He blinked, a brief look of surprise crossing his features before the darkness returned. "You needed to learn a lesson."

"Crazy," I muttered, turning to fiddle with the lock again. "Absolutely fucking insane."

Alice's sobs distracted me enough for Ryan to get close and grab my shoulder, his claws slicing into my skin as he propelled me backwards, sending me flying onto my ass. I scrambled to my feet, but he threw me up against the wall and pinned me there, his fingers closing around my throat.

"Don't you dare speak to me like that," he growled, his lips curling back in a feral snarl.

I gulped, my feet scuffing the ground as I struggled to balance on my toes. Ryan's eyes burned with an intense hatred that I could barely fathom as he looked at me.

"You've caused too much trouble, Eve," he said, tracing the line of my jaw with his finger. "It's a shame. I really liked you."

Alice began hammering the door with her fists. A single tear rolled down my cheek at the thought of the timid girl trying to protect me. I willed her to stop, terrified about what Ryan would do to her when he was done with me. The thought of Luke finding out that his sister was alive and losing her all over again made me choke on a sob.

Ryan smiled, the darkness in his eyes growing. I cursed myself for letting him see me vulnerable. "You should have just kept your nose out. We could have been so happy."

He shifted his thumb off my windpipe.

"What, so you could use me as a prize bitch?" I croaked, gasping for air.

"Despite what you believe, I did love you." He closed his grip on my throat again, as if it were all my fault. "But you chose to trust that pathetic excuse for a werewolf over me. Walking around with his scent all over you with no respect. You made me a laughingstock."

My phone buzzed in my pocket, and Ryan scowled, retrieving it with his free hand. I kicked out at him and earned a slap across the face for my effort.

"Stop being such a pest," Ryan snapped, bringing the screen to his eye level.

My heart sank, cheek stinging.

"Lucy?" A sneer contorted his features. "How original."

Ryan tossed the phone at the far wall and the screen shattered. The display flickered for a moment before going black.

I winced, and my throat burned as I desperately struggled to force air into my lungs. Alice thumped against the door again, and I used his momentary distraction to twist the pliers in my hand and aim it between his legs. When the metal collided with its target, Ryan howled and fell to his knees. As he crumpled to the floor, I ran.

"I promise I'll come get you, Alice," I yelled, not risking a second to turn back.

With each step, guilt compounded in my soul, and streamed down my face. The steps creaked and whined under my weight as I took them two at a time. I hauled myself out of the hatch and shut it behind me, wedging one bar of the pliers through the metal loop. I could already hear Ryan's voice growing closer, and I knew the makeshift barrier wouldn't hold for long. I raced outside, glancing around to see if anyone had followed Ryan to the cottage.

Adrenaline coursed through my veins, and it took mere seconds before my body shifted and contorted. My wolf side took over, and I chose flight. I snatched my bag off the ground, catching sight of Ryan's hand emerging from the hatch. With the strap clamped firmly between my teeth, I took off at full speed into the forest without looking back. The crescent moon cast a strip of light across the undergrowth as I ran. Being a hybrid might just have been what saved me.

CHAPTER 36

I ran for hours, sticking to fields and under tree cover where I could. When I got to the coast, I ran freely across the sand under the shelter of darkness. My paws were raw by the time I stumbled upon the edges of the city. When I finally skidded to a halt, my lungs burned in my chest, my legs trembling. I stayed at the forest edge, watching as car headlights flashed by. A train horn sounded in the distance. The weight of my bag had my jaw numb for well over an hour.

Gingerly, I made my way over to a tree and slumped against it. I closed my eyes and relaxed into the magic, the tiredness seeping into my muscles as I shifted back into my human form. A light sheen of sweat covered my body, and the grass was wet under my toes.

"Naked in a city is not a good look for you," I muttered to myself, barking with laughter that soon became a sob.

Still crying, I bent over my bag and rummaged for my clothes. Changing to a wolf hadn't been part of the plan, but I had always known I wasn't going back to the house that night. I had planned to leave with Alice. Guilt bubbled in my gut, but I forced it down. *I will go back for her.*

I changed into jeans and a t-shirt, the clothes sticking to me as I tried to pull them on as quickly as possible. Once I was dressed, I threw my bag over my shoulder with a heavy sigh and began walking towards the lights. I climbed the barrier lining the motorway and stood at the edge, one arm hugging my middle against the cold. Cars whizzed by, splashing my jeans and ignoring my outstretched hand.

An empty taxi eventually pulled up, and I climbed in, shivering so hard my teeth chattered. The driver, a burly old man with a thick black moustache, turned around to me. He had kind brown eyes that made me bite back a fresh wave of tears.

"Where to, love?" he asked in a thick inner-city accent, flashing me a welcome smile.

"I don't know."

Once I had finished sobbing, I asked the taxi driver to drop me at my old apartment. I didn't know Luke's address, I had no plan, and there was only one place I could go. I wasn't sure how I would explain things to Kate, but right then, I needed a friend. The driver talked the whole way there, asking about the boy who 'broke my heart'. As I told him my story in riddles he would never understand, he said no man was worth crying over. Familiar streets filled with weekend revellers dashing between taxis and clubs began flashing past.

"We're here," the driver announced, pulling up beside the curb. "Are you sure that this is the right spot?"

I nodded, rummaging in my purse to hand him the only money I had. "It is, thank you…" I frowned, trying to read the name on his taxi plate in the dim light.

"John," he said with a kind smile.

I swallowed. "Thanks, John."

His smile wavered, and he placed his hand over mine, curling my fingers closed around the note and pushing my hand away. "You're more than welcome, pet. Don't worry about the fare, it's on me."

For a moment, I thought the pity shining in his eyes would push me over the edge. All the sadness in the world welled in my heart, and I struggled to bite back the tears. I murmured my thanks and climbed out of the car, afraid that if I stayed any longer, I would start crying again.

With my rucksack slung over my shoulder, I wound my way up the stairs one shaky step at a time. The constant running was catching up to me. I wiped my bleary eyes and made a beeline for the apartment, my heart warming as the battered door came into sight. Our names were etched in the wood just below the room number. Images of Kate and I falling about drunk, carving our names and making fanciful promises to one another flashed through my mind. That night, we kicked up so much noise we woke the cranky woman across the hall. She had run us into the apartment with a sweeping brush. A small smile curved my lips at the memory.

I stopped outside the door, slapping the palm of my hand against my forehead. "Keys, Eve."

Sighing in frustration, I rapped the door with my knuckles and waited. A sliver of light crept from under the doorway, but that never guaranteed Kate was home. Global warming was never high on her priority list. No one answered, so I knocked again, tapping my foot against the grimy carpet.

"Of course you're not here," I grumbled in a temper. That wasn't fair. Kate had always been there for me, and I had practically deserted her these past few months.

I shook my head and tried the flimsy handle. I was ready to give up and ring Craig when the door swung open with a creak, the lock loose. My brow furrowed in a deep frown. Leaving the light on was one thing, Kate wasn't exactly an Eco-warrior, but not locking the door in this part of town was another thing altogether. We always made sure to lock up when we went out, even if we were drunk as a skunk. We didn't have much, but what little we had, neither of us could afford to lose.

The apartment was empty, the bare light bulb in the kitchen casting warm yellow light across one half of the living area. I stepped inside and pushed the door shut behind me, the lock not clicking into place. Unease settled deep in my gut as I slid my bag off my shoulder and dumped it on the couch.

"Kate?" I called out, but no one answered.

Her bedroom door stood ajar. I edged it open slowly, my heart thumping erratically in my chest. Clothes covered the floor space and were thrown across the bed. It looked like a bomb had gone off, but that was nothing unusual. Every girl makes a mess when getting ready for a night out. I tried to remember what day of the week it was, but I had lost all sense of time. Not that it mattered, Kate's motto was 'every night is a party night', closely followed by 'chicks need dicks'.

I walked back into the main living area. It didn't look like Kate would be home anytime soon, so I padded into the kitchen to ease my grumbling stomach. I had underestimated the toll all that running took on me, and I would pass out soon if I didn't eat something.

My foot caught on something, and I tripped forward with a shriek, smashing into a kitchen cupboard as I hit the ground. I rolled onto my back with a groan, rubbing my side gingerly. "What the hell?"

Kate was sprawled on the kitchen floor, her beautiful wide eyes staring up at the ceiling, clutching the gaping wound in her stomach. Blood pooled on the floor around her, staining her electric blue hair. Someone screamed an agonising banshee wail. A blurry figure burst through the front door, but my brain didn't register them as my gaze remained fixed on the body in front of me.

My best friend. Dead.

Slumped on the floor, with tears rolling down my cheeks, I realised that the person screaming was me.

It was only when someone shook my shoulders that I stopped screaming. I looked up to see the old lady from the corner apartment peering over her spectacles with sympathy. Another neighbour crouched beside me. I shoved them away, crawling towards my best friend. My heart shattered.

Kate was deathly still, but there was no sign of that peaceful look people often spoke of. I gently pulled her body onto my knees, cradling her head in my lap like I used to when we watched movies all night. As I moved her, a kitchen knife clattered to the ground. The small part of me still functioning picked up a familiar scent, and if I'd had anything left in my stomach, I would have puked then and there. Her killer wouldn't have needed a knife and hadn't been concerned about getting caught—they just wanted to make sure I got the message loud and clear.

I closed my eyes, sobs racking my body as guilt engulfed me. Blood soaked my jeans, and a steady stream of tears rolled down my cheeks as I held Kate to my chest, humming our favourite song.

"Miss? You need to come with me."

I looked up from under my lashes, blind with tears. This time, it was a Garda trying to move me, his blue uniform bringing me a thimble-sized bit of comfort. Behind him, a handful of people stood talking in the doorway to a female officer. I recognised the old sweeping brush lady and choked on a sob. I had no idea how much time had passed or when the Guards arrived. They pulled me to my feet and led me towards the door. I snatched up my bag, and although the officer tried to argue that it was evidence, I became inconsolable and refused to let it go. After a tug of war, I slipped the photo of Alice into my pocket and eventually surrendered the bag.

As the officer paused to talk to his colleague, I glanced back at Kate, and a fresh wave of tears overwhelmed me, followed by a guilt I knew would never leave me.

"It's okay, sweetheart." The female officer appeared by my side, gently rubbing my back. "We need to get you out of here and into some clean clothes. Can you tell us what happened?"

I shook my head, fingering the loose threads on my sleeve. Dried blood caked my hands and patches stained my jeans where I had held Kate. The Garda's face swam in and out of view, her words a distant echo. Every breath was a struggle, my chest constricting. I lost my footing and collapsed against the wall outside the apartment, sliding down to my knees.

"I've got you," she said, crouching on the floor beside me. "I need you to take deep breaths for me, in and out."

The thing was, I didn't want to focus on my breathing. I wanted to run, but I couldn't. As I fought the urge to turn into the very thing that had gotten Kate into this mess, I focused on the Garda's words, taking shallow ragged breaths and palming my chest, desperately trying to slow my breathing. It felt as if the world was going black, and a part of me wished it would, but a darker part of me wanted revenge.

Eventually, my breaths came in short puffs and began levelling out. All the while, the officer held my hand and chanted slowly. I tried to look at her badge for a name, but my vision was blurry, tears staining my cheeks.

"Good, you're doing great." She smiled, her cheeks dimpling. The pity in her eyes made me turn away. "Eve, I know this is really difficult, but time is everything right now. You need to tell me what happened to your friend."

I gulped, still working on filling my lungs with air as a sob rose in my throat. "I don't know, I just found her like this."

"Why did you come over? Your neighbours say that you have been gone for months."

Lying didn't come so easily with Kate's dead eyes seared into my mind. "I-I was staying with a friend for the summer."

"And you chose today specifically to come back?"

"Yes," I said, my voice barely a whisper. I searched the ceiling for answers, staring at the cracked paint, wondering if I would crack too. "It was a surprise."

"Do you know who did this?"

I shook my head, sick of the lies and the secrets, but the police would never understand. I was playing a game I didn't even understand anymore. As the Garda piled on the questions, she was slowly gathering me to my feet and leading me out of the apartment block one step at a time. Her words felt distant and surreal. I zoned out and lost myself in the darkness of my thoughts.

CHAPTER 37

I spent that night at the Garda station, going over and over my story until I got so frustrated I thought I might shift in the interrogation room. The only reason I didn't was a numbness that had seeped into my bones and had taken up residence there. I stuck to my original story, lying repeatedly, swearing that I had been staying with a friend and popped by to see Kate as a surprise. My only saving grace was that I hadn't picked up the knife—all those detective movies Kate and I had binged finally paid off.

At an all-time low, I begged them to throw me in a cell for the night, even debated lying and saying I was guilty. But my timelines were wrong. Apparently, Kate had been dead for hours by the time I arrived. She died alone, bleeding out. I think they always knew I was lying; I couldn't talk about Kate without crying and had puked in my holding cell from the shock. Once my alibi was confirmed by dash cam footage from the taxi, the Gardaí ended their questioning.

They confiscated my bloody clothes, eventually returning the rest of my belongings, as they released me back into a world I no longer wanted to be part of. I was on my last set of spare clothes with a twenty euro note and a photo of Alice to get me by.

On my way out, the guard on reception offered me a phone call. It had taken me several tries to guess Luke's number, but eventually I got hold of his voicemail and left him a garbled message. It was only after the call that they informed me I wasn't allowed back into the apartment. I had nowhere to go, and Luke had no way to find me.

The low autumn sun was rising over the city as I stepped outside. People raced to work, life rushing past me as I wandered the streets aimlessly. A single raindrop splashed on the nape of my neck, closely followed by more until it became a downpour. Winding through the streets, my hood pulled up to hide matted hair more than for shelter, I headed down a familiar alleyway. The city was only beginning to wake, my only company a lone cat that bolted at the sight of me.

I stopped in front of an old, rusted door, my hand shaking as I reached out to trace the corroded door handle. Nothing happened. Every time I had come here, Luke's presence had seemed to open the doorway. Alone, I had no idea how to get inside. I tried the handle. It creaked under my grip, but the door remained unchanged.

"Come on!" I growled, kicking the door and immediately regretted my decision as my foot collided with the metal. I winced and the door frame rattled. "Please, Jonas... Anyone. I need help."

I hated how broken I sounded, the way my voice cracked and my throat constricted as I fought down panic and grief that threatened to overwhelm me. No doubt I looked like I had been slumming it for days now. There was still caked blood under my nails that refused to budge. I was a mess.

Sighing in defeat, I turned on my heel and trudged back in the direction I had come. There was a rustle behind me, followed by a polite cough. I turned to see Jonas standing in front of the entrance, his expression torn.

"Eve, you need to go," he said, arms folded across his chest. He hovered by the door, his gaze darting between me and our surroundings, zeroing in on my hands as his nostrils flared. "It's not safe for you to be here."

I stepped towards him, a lump rising in my throat. "I have nowhere else to go."

"I wish I could let you in, I really do, but they will kill me if they knew I was even talking to you." Jonas frowned, running his hand through his hair. "Ryan came here, looking for you. He has warned us that if anyone helps you, the pack will kill them."

I swallowed. Part of me was angry and wanted to blame them, to call them cowards for not helping, the other half knew what Ryan was capable of.

"He has the witches on his roster, Eve. We can't risk it."

"Can you at least give Luke a message for me?"

Jonas sighed, wringing his hands. "I can try."

"Tell him Ryan has killed Kate," I said, choking on my best friend's name. "Tell him...tell him Ryan knows everything and that I need his help."

"I will do my best to get the message to him." Jonas stepped back towards the door, jumping as something banged a few streets away. "I have to go."

"Wait, Jonas—" Before I could finish my sentence, Jonas had vanished before my eyes. "Fuck!"

I screamed in frustration and shoved a tower of old crates, flinging into the alley wall. The stack collapsed, sending rats racing across the cobbled ground and the noise echoing in the alley. The panic in Jonas' eyes had told me everything I needed to know. Ryan would not let me leave with pack secrets. The only way to shut me up was to kill me. I followed the rats back towards the dimming streetlights and fell into step with the commuters rushing to work. No one paid attention to the scrappy looking girl. Blending in and staying in public was the only chance I stood at evading Ryan.

When my feet grew tired, I reluctantly dipped into a random coffee shop. Now that I was sure Ryan was watching my usual haunts, I had to be careful. I thought about going to the bar or maybe visiting Craig, but anyone who knew me was in danger.

The thought of him grieving Kate without me forced me to bite back more tears. I never knew it was possible to cry so much.

Nursing my coffee to keep my hands warm, I sat in the corner seat and stared out the window wondering how it had all gone so wrong. Rain pelted the streets, sending people scurrying indoors. To my left was a young couple giggling and talking about their future together. I felt cold inside, as if a lump of ice sat where my heart had once been. Across the room, a mother was trying to teach her child to drink properly from her cup, but the kid ended up with a cream moustache, and she broke into a fit of laughter. The love that sparkled in her eyes made the icy numbness grow. I used to wonder when anyone would look at me like that, but that had been when I still believed in fairy tales.

I hid in that coffee shop for as long as I could, spacing out my drinks as much as possible and always ordering the cheapest thing on the menu. The barista, noting my dishevelled appearance, stopped asking me to pay once I was down to coins. I looked pitiful with my hair tied up into a messy bun and mascara streaming down my face, and I had no doubt there was a slight tang from my wolf run hanging around too, but I was acceptable enough not to deter punters. So, I stayed huddled in my corner, stomach grumbling and far from satisfied with the one measly sandwich I could afford.

When shadows crept up on the streets outside and the cafe slowly emptied, I knew my time was almost up. Some while ago, I had finally stopped shivering, but that was to be short lived. I had been drifting in and out of fitful bouts of sleep throughout the day. My mind was wide awake, but my body begged for rest.

Someone cleared their throat and my head shot up, the strange surroundings slowly coming into focus. The barista stood over me with a cloth in hand. She was a pretty girl with doe eyes and a kind face.

"I have to ask you to leave, we are closing up in two minutes," she said, glancing at the ground and shuffling her feet.

I forced a faulty smile. "It's fine, thank you so much for letting me stay here all day."

The barista nodded with a small smile in return and moved away to clean the other tables, humming to herself. I gathered my few belongings and patted my pockets to reassure myself Alice's photo was safe.

Once again, I found myself wandering the streets. Dusk had fallen and the pubs along the river were in full swing, music blaring into the night. I took a shallow breath, pausing as I came to the epicentre of the city. I hugged my arms around my chest, desperately hoping for a sign, but I was alone.

A man to my right wolf whistled, and I froze. It wasn't safe for him or me. I had been walking around in a daze, leaving aimless tracks throughout the city that would hopefully confuse Ryan. I couldn't sit still all day like a duck waiting to be slaughtered.

"Think smart," I told myself, stamping my feet against the pavement in an attempt to keep the cold at bay.

My message to Luke had been a quick rant, I couldn't even remember what I had said. I knew that I had mentioned Kate, the blood, and the police station. *The police station.*

I spun and started walking back the way I had come along the wide main street. The station was on the other side of the city, but I didn't have any better ideas. My feet throbbed from all my walking, but they kept dutifully pounding the pavement. Ignoring my bruised body, I set my jaw and kept moving forward. I focused on this sole destination, pushing aside all the pain that threatened to overwhelm and drag me under.

I cursed myself for wandering so far. Taxis whizzed by, but not everyone was like John, and most would turn me straight into the police for fair dodging once we arrived. Thankfully, the rain held off, but a mist had settled which made my damp hair stick to my neck and give me chills. Girls staggered down the streets in skyscraper heels, followed by guys in too tight jeans. Although Dublin was always lively, the weekends were another level. I missed those days when all that mattered was silly gossip and who was buying the next round of shots.

I felt like I was going around in circles. When Pearse Street Garda Station came into view, I breathed a sigh of relief, but it was short lived. Two Gardaí stood outside, arguing with a man who was staring past them and spewing abuse at the air. Beside him a girl sat sprawled on the steps, her skirt hiked too far up. Some things could never be unseen. I didn't envy them one bit.

Tiptoeing past, I pushed the heavy wooden door and stepped back into the brightly lit waiting area. My bloodshot eyes stung as they adjusted. The room was overflowing with a mix of teenagers and people too strung out on their drug of choice to see straight. I walked up to the screen, but the desk was empty. In the background, I saw the small female officer from earlier that day. I tapped the glass tentatively, and she spun around, ready to launch a tirade. When she looked at me, recognition shone in her eyes and her expression softened.

"Has anyone been looking for me?" I asked, cringing at the desperation in my voice.

"No, I'm sorry." She shook her head, gathering up a handful of papers.

A man stepped into view, gruff with a curly beard and a pot-belly. "Eve, isn't it?" He stepped out from behind the desk, and I recognised him as one of the detectives who had interviewed me. "Carl, we spoke last night."

I nodded, stepping closer to the screen as Carl approached.

"Some fellow did come looking for you this morning, around midday maybe," he said, rubbing his beard as he flicked through a list of names. "He seemed really worried about you."

My heart leapt, and I felt the first hint of something bright stir inside me. I craned my neck, but I couldn't decipher the scribbles.

"He was a nice-looking lad, tall."

Luke, he must have traced the call or rang back. Maybe I wasn't such an idiot after all.

"Blonde?" I asked, hope swelling.

Carl's brow furrowed in thought, but then he shook his head. "No, dark brown hair, almost black."

I gulped for air, my chest constricting as if someone had knocked the oxygen clean out of my lungs. My heart started hammering in a not so good way and my stomach flipped.

"Ah, here it is," Carl said, tapping his finger against the list. "Ryan."

"Did you tell him where I was?" I asked quietly, tears stinging the corner of my eyes.

Carl's frown deepened. "No, of course not, we didn't know where you went." He crouched down to eye level, his eyes sparking with concern. "Are you in some kind of trouble, sweetheart?"

I desperately wanted to say yes, to beg him for help and protection, but this was out of their league. I was out of my depth.

"I'm okay," I lied, the waver in my voice betraying me. "Just, if he calls around again, tell him I'm on my way back to his apartment."

I had no intention of going back to Ryan's old apartment, a place that once held so many memories was now a stark reminder of how easily I was fooled. But if it would keep Ryan occupied and give me a chance to figure things out, lure him off my trail, it might buy me some time. The officer nodded; his expression grim.

Before Carl could ask any more questions, I turned and hightailed it out of the building. I barrelled out the door, blind with tears, straight into someone's broad chest. I wheeled backwards, but before I could hit the ground, firm hands closed around my arms and pulled me back to my feet. Dazed, I looked up to see a familiar face. Then the tears came in earnest.

CHAPTER 38

Luke stared at me, eyes wide and worry lining his features, his expression a mixture of shock, sorrow, and happiness. He crushed me against his chest, stroking my hair and whispering soothing words in my ear as tears soaked my cheeks. His skin was warm against my face and his comforting scent filled my senses.

"I thought Ryan had taken you too." Luke's voiced wavered, his usual air of confidence stripped back to reveal something I had never heard in him. Fear.

I coughed, burying my face in his chest as I finally gave in to the pain. Sadness washed over me, a constant wave of emotions bombarding me. The image of Kate swam in my mind, and I couldn't get the sight of her dead body to leave me.

Luke peeled me away, reaching up to cup my cheek. I hiccoughed and blinked through the tears, staring up at those cognac eyes of his that made my stuttering heart flip.

"Never do that again. Ever," Luke said firmly, his expression deadly serious. "You are never to pull a stunt like that again, do you hear me?"

I nodded, chewing my lower lip. "I'm sorry."

"Don't apologise." Luke shook his head, his tone softening. "Just promise never to go rogue again. Not without me."

"I promise."

My nose was still running like a tap, but the tears had finally subsided. I sat huddled in the passenger seat of Luke's car,
watching the streetlights flash by in a daze. He had bundled me
into the car and insisted that we got as far away from Ryan as
soon as possible. I had tried to explain in between sobs that I
needed to tell him something, but it was not the right time to
tell him about Alice while we were speeding down a motorway.

I glanced over at Luke, his chiselled features half cast in shadow. His jaw was set in a hard line and his hands were strangling
the steering wheel. The silence that hung between us served as a
constant reminder of how much I still needed to say.

"Hungry?" Luke asked, keeping his focus on the road.

My stomach rumbled in response. "Apparently I am."

The brief conversation lapsed, and I returned to staring out
the window. Each time my eyelids fluttered closed, Kate's empty
stare haunted my thoughts. I slipped in and out of consciousness until I felt the car roll to a halt.

"Eve?"

I blinked slowly and rubbed my eyes, Luke's face coming into
view. A jacket I didn't remember was tucked around me. It
smelled of Luke's cologne. Cars were parked either side of us,
and a dodgy lamp flickered overhead.

"Come on," Luke said, a small smile playing on his lips as he
reached across and unbuckled my seat belt. "Let's get some food
into you, it'll perk you up."

We stepped out of the car into a large sprawling carpark in
front of a brightly lit service station. Beside it was a food court
standing out against the starless sky with blinding neon signs.
The gentle hum of the motorway sounded behind us as Luke
steered me towards the lights, his hand gently pressing on my
lower back. A tingle ran down my spine.

"Any preference?" he asked, pausing on the sidewalk.

I looked around at our grand total of three options namely, a pizzeria, burger place, or a cafe. My stomach growled again. "Pizza."

"Good choice." Luke nodded in approval and fell into step beside me.

The pizza parlour was empty, just like the car park. Apart from a few truck drivers and odd balls like us, not many people would choose this as a pit stop at this hour. Luke chose a seat in the far corner tactfully obscured by a large, fake plant. From his vantage point, he could see anyone who walked in. A small part of me had forgotten what we were running from, but the memory of Kate's mangled throat popping into my head was a stark reminder.

"So, I probably should have asked this before," Luke began.

I swallowed, fidgeting with the zipper of my hoody.

"Are you a pineapple kind of girl?"

"A what?" I looked up from the menu, my expression blank.

Luke chuckled, his tone teasing as he slowed down his words just for my benefit. "Do you like pineapple on pizza?"

"Ew, no. Definitely not." I wrinkled my nose, earning a bark of laughter from him. "That's gross."

"Good to know you're not one of those heathens." He sat back in his chair, slipping into his usual casual demeanour, but when I watched closely, I caught his gaze flicking towards the door and his body stiffen on the rare occasion someone walked through.

I had every intention of telling Luke about Alice, it was on the tip of my tongue, and I had hyped myself up to the point of saying it when the waiter arrived with our pizzas. Luke smiled and mine faltered. I felt sick, but my stomach was howling to be fed, and I couldn't run on fumes for much longer.

Luke had insisted on ordering a half and half pizza, but he ended up having to let me eat some of his too, even if I offended him by picking off the peppers. Only when the buttons on my jeans were ready to pop did I admit defeat.

"Someone was hungry." He laughed, arching an eyebrow as I slouched back in my seat, fit to burst.

I glowered but was too drained to argue. Each time Luke cracked a joke, and I almost smiled, a wave of guilt came crashing down. My best friend was dead. I understood now what people meant when they said their world had been turned upside down. It felt like a never-ending nightmare, and I wished it wasn't real. Now I was going to have to rip Luke's world apart too.

"What's wrong?" Luke asked, his brow furrowing in concern.

Obviously, I wasn't very good at hiding my troubled expression. I shook my head, willing the words to leave my lips, but I had become mute.

Luke leaned in and closed the space between us, his hand swamping mine. Every touch was a gentle, careful, but deliberate movement. "Are you ready to talk about what happened?" His troubled eyes locked on mine, and he offered a small smile of encouragement.

I licked my lips, as if it might loosen them, and took a long shaky breath. "I tried to get her out—the girl, I mean."

He nodded. "I pieced that much together from Jonas' message and your voicemail from a police cell."

"I was never actually in a cell," I corrected him, finding my voice, and Luke smiled. "I lost it with Ryan, after I found those records and called you. I was so angry."

He listened intently, his gaze never leaving my face. Once I began talking, the story just tumbled out. I wasn't sure if I made any sense and often thought I might burst into tears, but I told Luke about how I had snuck out and tried to get the girl out, tools in hand. How Ryan had caught me and hauled me out. How I had run away and found my best friend with her throat slit in my apartment.

When I mentioned the part about Kate, the hairs on Luke's skin rose and fire flashed in his eyes. It made me want to cry all over again, seeing my anger reflected in him, recognising the urge to protect her. There was something else too—not only sympathy but understanding. He had lost someone too. Upon that realisation, I got stuck on my explanation and fell silent, tugging nervously on my sleeve.

"What about the girl?" Luke said, as if reading my mind. "Is she still there?"

I nodded meekly, conscious of my palm slick in his grip. "I promised I would come back for her."

"We will, but we need to figure out a plan. This is much bigger than just our packs being at war."

That was the logical route to take and the most sensible course of action. A true alpha's plan. It didn't stop me from wanting to run back there to ease the guilt. But Ryan's pack was strong, and we still only had half the story. While he was being practical now, I had no idea how Luke would react to the following words, he was always so calm but fiercely protective. One thing I knew for sure was that the moment he knew, he would no longer want to play the long game.

I took the deepest of breaths. "Luke, there's one more thing I need to tell you."

Luke sipped his drink, slurping the icy leftovers, looking up at me expectantly. His hand still cupped mine, our fingers interlinked. I slid my hand free and began digging in the front packet of my bag, holding something to my chest before placing the photo of the brown-eyed girl onto the table and sliding it towards Luke.

"Her name was Alice."

CHAPTER 39

Luke stared at me in shock, his mouth hanging open, not uttering a sound. I watched in silence as an array of expressions crossed his features, as if he wasn't sure what to feel. He stayed frozen like this for some time, and I waited with bated breath, wondering when the volcano would blow. Eventually, he slammed a twenty down on the table and jumped to his feet. The chair skittered back, metal scraping the floors, and he took off towards the exit without a word. I hesitated. The waiters watched us with silent curiosity. I prayed that it was the most exciting part of their evening as I scrambled to my feet, picking up the photo of Alice before hightailing it after Luke.

When I burst through the doors into the car park, I wasn't sure what I expected to see. My shoulders sagged with relief when there was no sign of a big sandy wolf throwing his weight around. Luke was kicking a trash can and spewing a never-ending list of curse words, many of which were completely new to me. He thumped the bin, denting the metal frame until it fractured and cracked down the middle. Then he moved onto a wall, his knuckles stained with blood.

I only dared to step in when I saw him starting towards a car window. "Luke!"

Luke's head swung in my direction, his beautiful face contorted with rage, his hooded eyes flashing silver. Blood spattered his shirt, and his hands were raw and red. He looked like something from a horror movie, but behind all of that anger, there was pain.

"I know this is a lot to take in," I whispered softly, taking a tentative step towards him. "But you can't lose it here, not now."

There was a confidence in my voice that caught me by surprise. I was still reeling from the past forty-eight hours, and my heart had been shattered into a million pieces, but I couldn't bear seeing Luke fall apart too.

"She's alive, Luke." I took one last stride to close the distance between us, reaching out to twine my fingers with his. The metallic scent filled my senses, causing unpleasant and raw memories to surge, but I pushed them away.

Luke stared down at me, his eyes wide and panicked. "Are you sure?" he said, his voice strained.

I nodded and pressed my hand to his heart. It was beating out of his chest. "She's alive, she helped distract Ryan."

Luke's breathing hitched, and the silver in his eyes blazed once more before subsiding, replaced by hope. "I thought I'd never find her." With that, he lost all composure and fell apart in my arms.

The sight of him so vulnerable was the last straw. I wrapped my arms around Luke and held him as we cried, mine tears of sorrow and his tears of joy.

"She's alive, and we will get her back," I whispered.

It took me a solid hour to convince Luke not to barge in on his own to get Alice. He knew deep down it was a bad idea—we both did. I felt his anger as powerful as the burning revenge in my heart for Kate. Both of us were tightly coiled balls of fury, desperate to retaliate. We were hurting, but walking in alone was a death trap. At least he agreed he was no use to Alice dead.

As Luke drove us through the night, I quickly realised that I was far more nervous to meet the Crescent pack than I was about Ryan's. Back then, I didn't understand much, and I hadn't turned up to their doorstop with a massive bombshell about a daughter they'd been mourning.

Luke pulled into a small town just off the motorway. We were well beyond Dublin, and the estates held a suburban feel with red bricked houses and neat little gardens. The morning sun stretched across the green, piercing a thin fog. A few joggers passed us by, but the households were still asleep. I expected Luke to pass through the estate to the outer edges of the town where I had seen fields and forests in the distance.

Instead, he pulled into the driveway of a large corner house, parking between two other cars. I frowned. He undid his seatbelt and turned to face me, arching an eyebrow at my muddled expression.

"Don't worry, they won't bite." Luke tried to smile, but the panic didn't leave his eyes.

I shook my head, looking around at the decorated garden plants and flowerpots lining the windows. "It's not that. I'm just... surprised."

"About?" He mirrored my puzzled look.

"This. The house. Here," I said, feeling ridiculous as the words left my mouth. "It's not what I expected."

He shot me an odd look, amusement twitching the corner of his lips. "We don't all live in fortresses hidden away from humanity. This is my family house, not the pack house. We are all spread out in different areas, living normal enough lives with plenty of normal friends."

Luke got out of his side, walking around the bonnet to open my door. I pried myself out of the seat and held out his jacket.

"Keep it, you still look cold," he said, pushing my hand away.

"What about during a full moon?" I asked, nervously tugging at the loose threads on the cuff of his jumper as we walked up to the front door.

Luke rang the doorbell and scuffed his toe against the welcome mat as we waited. "We all meet up to go camping or go for a run, and then back to mine for a barbecue depending on the weather."

I nodded as if that was normal. I'd become used to archaic celebrations and hunts that made my stomach lurch, but here, there was none of that, no big, crazy ceremonies. I tried to peer inside, but there were two vertical windows either side of the door made of tempered glass. As a shadow approached, my heart began to beat out of my chest. Luke cocked his ear and reached out to place his arm around my shoulders. It didn't help settle my nerves one bit.

The door swung open to reveal a small woman dressed in grey tracksuit bottoms and an apron with 'The Real Alpha' embroidered across the front, with a tea towel tucked under her armpit. She had auburn hair thrown up into a messy ponytail and freckles dusted her cheeks. She didn't hesitate before throwing her arms around Luke, hugging him tightly before releasing him and wrapping me in a warm embrace. It wasn't the reception I had expected. Far from a courtesy hug, it was a full-on bear hug that squeezed the air out of my lungs.

"Luke, darling, I'm glad you're home all right," the woman said, beaming as she stepped back and appraised me. "And this must have been the reason you were tearing out the door in such a state last night."

Luke cleared his throat, tugging on his shirt collar. "This is my mother, Helena." He motioned to his mother, and then returned to my side, giving my arm a reassuring squeeze. "And this is Eve."

I forced a smile, my brain still doing mental somersaults trying to process too much at once. No doubt Luke was in the same boat.

"Ah, I've heard too little about you, Eve," Helena said with a wink, her cheeks dimpling. The freckles peppering her nose reminded me of the picture tucked in my pocket. "My Luke is always so private."

"Mam, I need to talk to you and dad about—"

Before Luke could get any further, a young boy who shared Helena's fiery hair came hurdling around the corner and sprinted towards him.

"Lulu!" The boy screamed with happiness, skidding into Luke's leg and latching onto him. He couldn't have been more than five years old.

Luke laughed, his expression softening as he looked down. "Shouldn't you be in your uniform, Max?"

"No," Helena cut in, prying her son off Luke's leg.

Max shook his head fervently and wriggled in his mother's grip. "No school for me."

"Max said he was feeling poorly, but he looks just fine to me now," Luke's mother teased, poking her son's nose and earning a high-pitched giggle.

Luke barked a short laugh, his gaze sobering. "Mam, I really need to talk to Dad about something important." He lowered his voice, but even little Max frowned at the grave tone.

"He's still in the shower." Helena looked between us, her brow furrowing as Luke and I shared a knowing look. "Just your father, or the whole pack?"

I shuffled my feet, dread settling in the pit of my stomach.

"I would like to tell you and dad first, in private," he said, casting a half smile in my direction that turned out more like a grimace.

Helena's frown only deepened. She set Max on his feet and ushered him down the hall. Luke brushed his fingers across my wrist and nodded for me to follow. I fell into step beside him as she led us into a living room with worn leather couches and a cosy fireplace. I couldn't stop gaping at how normal it was.

"Sit here, and I'll fetch your father," she said, taking Max by the hand and leaving us in the room alone.

Luke hovered by the fireplace, and I perched myself on the edge of a couch, setting my rucksack on the floor. I watched him closely, noting how his shoulders tensed and his jaw set, lips drawn in a thin line. All joking had vanished, replaced by a seriousness I had never expected from him, but somehow fit him perfectly. He was in line to be alpha after all, even if it was the last thing he wanted.

He picked a photo frame off the mantelpiece, holding it delicately in the palm of his hand while tracing his fingertips across the image. I caught a brief glimpse of a tear before he swiped his cheek.

"She was so happy," he finally said, his voice cracking.

I chewed my lip, not sure what the right response was. He walked over to the couch and sat beside me, clutching a photo of two children playing on a swing set. The boy shared his sandy hair, and the girl had her mother's fiery locks and the same brown eyes as Luke.

"She still could be," I said quietly, slipping the photo of Alice from my pocket and pressing it into his empty palm.

He exhaled a shaky breath. "I thought she was gone. For years I searched but found nothing."

"Alice is alive. We just need to figure out how to get her back."

"I don't know if I could ever look at her again. It's my fault she went out that night."

I shook my head, placing my hand on his knee. "No, she was a teenager, and she was going out whether you let her or not. How were you supposed to know what Ryan would do?"

Luke's expression darkened at the mention of Ryan, his hackles raising. "He hates hybrids, just like his father does."

"How come Alice is a hybrid, and you're not?" I asked the question that had been on my lips for some time.

"My mother died giving birth to me. I never met her," Luke explained, his eyes glassy. "Then dad remarried, mix werewolf guy and a human girl, and you get a hybrid. At least, that's the simplified version, but it didn't matter to us—we don't live in the dark ages."

I blinked slowly, trying to hide my shock. Most of the time, I suppressed my heightened sense of smell, only focusing on it when I needed to. Otherwise, all the different scents would overwhelm me, but having been around humans my entire life, Helena never registered with me.

"We really need to work on that nose of yours," Luke teased, noting my surprise, though his heart wasn't fully in it.

I rolled my eyes. "I think we have bigger things to deal with than my nose."

He nodded, shifting uncomfortably in the seat. "I don't how to tell them this." Luke sighed, running a hand through his hair and shaking his head. "They're going to freak out."

"Probably."

He sighed, exasperated. "Is that seriously your advice?"

"There's no right way to say it."

"What do I say then?"

I shrugged and gave his knee a squeeze, looking up into his warm brown eyes filled with worry. "The truth."

CHAPTER 40

When Luke left the room to tell his parents about Alice, a stunned silence followed. Then there was screaming, closely followed by something smashing and a lot of yelling. I could only guess that Luke had told them the *whole* truth, including the part where he knew she was going to meet Ryan.

Max sat on the couch beside me playing on a Gameboy, completely oblivious to the drama unfolding in the next room. He would never have met Alice, though he knew to point her out in pictures to me. As a child, he had no comprehension of the range of emotions his parents must have felt—even I could only imagine.

Something crashed and shattered in the kitchen. Max looked up with a bewildered expression.

"It's okay, Max. I think someone just dropped a cup," I said, offering what I hoped was an encouraging smile.

He simply blinked and returned his attention to the game. I sighed and sunk back into the couch, rubbing my temples.

Ignorance is bliss.

I found myself watching Max, wondering how much he knew about his sister. Did he remember Alice? How much did he notice her disappearance tearing his brother apart?

Once Luke re-entered the room, everything was in full swing. Helena rushed about the house like a hurricane, readying food and barking orders at anyone who would listen. They even made

Max help with the cutlery. I was roped into helping and got the ear taken off me for dropping a carrot. Luke shot an apologetic glance in my direction, but I didn't mind. The woman was entitled to feel her feelings.

"The pack will be here for midday."

I turned to see a man standing in the doorway, an inch or so taller than Luke but with the same blonde hair and kind eyes. Dressed in a semi-casual shirt and jeans, he looked like a more polished version of Luke, but with more wrinkles, bright blue eyes, and a fully fledged beard.

"You must be Eve," he said, turning to face me with a smile that matched his son's. "I'm Thomas."

I nodded, my cheeks heating as I shook his outstretched hand. There I was peeling carrots in his kitchen, bold as brass when I had rocked up on his doorstep and turned his world upside down, but besides a worn frown line and worry in his eyes, Luke's father appeared calm. He oozed a familiar confidence that put me at ease.

"No one calls him Thomas," Luke said, sidling over to me. "It's Tom."

A deep laugh rumbled in his father's chest. "Only friends call me Tom."

I must have gone as white as a ghost because both of them burst into laughter. They shut up abruptly when Helena glared daggers in their direction.

"Don't worry, Eve, any friend of Luke's is welcome here." With that, he walked over to his wife and placed a hand on her shoulder, which she immediately swatted away.

"Love, you need to calm down."

She spun and glowered at her husband, wooden spoon in hand. "My daughter—the one I mourned—is alive, and you are *laughing.*"

Luke and I looked away, busying ourselves preparing food. Max stood watching them intently.

"Yes, because our daughter is alive," he said firmly, prising the spoon from her grasp, "which is cause for celebration."

"She's trapped with that psychopath, and they have done God only knows what to her," Helena shrieked, her voice rising with each word.

"Don't for one moment think I am not angry, love. I am furious, and they will pay." Tom's tone hardened, and he sounded every inch the alpha. "We will bring her home."

At her husband's assurances, Helena collapsed into his arms, her facade breaking and tears rolling down her cheeks. Tom held her against him, stroking her hair and murmuring words of comfort in her ear. "I laugh because she is alive, and that alone brings me hope and happiness. Even in the darkest of times, we must find a reason to smile."

We dropped our tools and Luke took Max's hand, heading towards the door to allow them some privacy. The alpha raised his voice, even though we could already hear every word. "The pack will gather, and we will decide on what action to take. Alice is coming home."

Pack meetings for the Crescent wolves were very different to what I was used to. I wasn't hidden away or treated like an outcast. Instead, they greeted me as an old friend. I noted the mix of unfamiliar scents—the odd hybrid and even other humans besides Helena. Each pack and family member knocking on the door would either hug Luke or fist pump, depending on their mood, and then Luke would introduce me as his friend Eve—not the hybrid Eve—a friend. "How many are there?" I asked Luke, whispering out of habit. The house looked fit to burst.

"Thirty or so. It just looks like more because you're used to grander things," he teased, squeezing his seat closer to mine.

His leg bumped mine, and I smiled. "I like this better."

We sat around the kitchen surrounded by pack members laughing and catching up, as if this were some party. I watched them, counting them in my head and trying to compare them to the Faolchúnna pack, but they were different in so many ways. Thinking back to the full moon events, there must have been at least sixty plus werewolves, excluding the ones sent away on business. I shuddered and chewed my lip. Even if the Crescents were missing some pack members, how would Luke's pack ever take them on? Ryan's pack outnumbered them almost two to one.

The chatter died down as Tom stepped into the room, wearing a sombre expression that was more suited to the situation at hand. "Can I ask all children to go play outside, please?"

There was a unanimous groan and rush of complaints from the children, but they began traipsing out the back door, bar one teenager that must have been on the cusp of turning. He was still in his uniform and had no doubt argued his way into being allowed to come.

"Please, Dad." The boy turned towards his parents, scowling like he was asking to stay out late to play with his friends.

His father looked at Tom, who shook his head. "I'm sorry, this is serious. We need you to keep an eye on the children."

A soft murmur rose in the room. Helena ushered the boy out and locked the patio door behind him. Once closed, the children's voices became muffled, and I realised they'd sound-proofed the house. Smart.

Tom took a seat at the head of the kitchen table, his wife hovering by his side, shifting from one foot to the other. I offered my seat, but she shook her head with a weak smile and placed a hand on her husband's shoulder. Looking around the table, it seemed like the heads of each family had taken a seat while the others stood around the kitchen. People had already helped themselves to the piles of food stacked in the centre. Even Luke had gone back for seconds, but my plate remained empty, nerves eating away at my stomach.

Complete silence fell as Tom cleared his throat. As Luke rested his hand on my thigh under the table, I cast a sideway glance in his direction, noticing the tension in his jaw as he watched his father. He looked like he needed more reassurance than me.

"Thank you all for coming on such short notice, especially on a school day," he said, earning a soft chuckle. "But we have had some news—news that is a double-edged sword. Alice is alive."

People gasped, some burst into tears, and the volume in the room shot up. Questions came from every direction, so many I couldn't keep track of what was being said.

Tom's voice rang out among the chaos as he slammed a fist on the table. "Please, be silent until I can explain. We only received this news this morning from my son and his friend, Eve."

Tom looked at me and nodded.

I froze, realising he expected me to speak. Luke nudged my side and stood, all but dragging me up beside him. Everyone's eyes locked on us, and I felt my cheeks flush.

"Eve is a hybrid, and she was tricked into potentially joining the Faolchúnna pack," Luke began, his explanation earning a low growl from one corner, but he continued. "She alerted me to the fact they were holding a young girl captive. Together, we began trying to uncover the truth and discovered that they were hatching plans to use hybrids to ensure their pack survival, intending to eradicate hybrids altogether."

Shouts of disapproval at their intentions sounded and my heart warmed, unexpected tears pricking the corners of my eyes.

"Two nights ago Eve bravely tried to rescue the girl alone. However, she was caught by Ryan McKenna and had to flee to save her own life," Luke continued, the entire pack now focusing on me. The look in their eyes ranged from curiosity to approval and made my heart swell all over again. "Before leaving, Eve found out the girl's name. Alice."

Luke nudged my side as whispers ran through the pack. I gulped, my mouth dry like cardboard.

"I—I didn't know until last night that it was Alice," I stammered, coughing and finding my voice as I went on. "I promised that I would come back for her."

"Why should we trust you?" A lone voice rang out.

I paused. They had a point.

"Because Ryan murdered my best friend as a warning," I said in a low growl. "I have no loyalty to Ryan's pack. They lured me in just like Alice, and I was disgusted when I found out the truth." My voice cracked, but I pushed on, biting back tears. I felt Luke's fingers brush mine. "I've no reason to lie. We all know I would have ended up just like her if I hadn't uncovered the truth."

After Luke and I took our seats again, a deafening din began. Tom sat back and spoke quietly to his wife, allowing the pack to discuss and process the revelation. Now and then, I would catch someone's eye or pick up their voice, but unlike what I was used to, none of it was malicious. No one looked at me like I didn't belong here. Given the news I had turned up with, they were taking things well, all things considered.

"You did well," Luke said, swivelling in his chair to face me, his knees touching mine. "They like you."

"I think them liking me is the least of our worries," I mumbled, my face heating.

Luke shook his head, reaching out to push a stray strand of hair behind my ear. "No, it's important. They could have not believed us. It's a lot to ask with very little proof."

"Why did they believe us then?"

"Because no one would risk the Faolchúnna's wrath for anything less than the truth. You're a hybrid, and we all know their pack would never accept someone like you among them, let alone divulge you in their secrets," Luke said, his honeyed eyes locked on mine. "This was the easy part though. Coming up with a plan that works will be the hard one."

Tom rapped on the table and the conversations died out, everyone in the room turning their attention back to him as he stood and wrapped an arm around his wife's waist.

"I understand this is a lot to take in," he said, sharing a knowing look with Helena. "But time is of the essence, and I do not want my daughter suffering any longer. We need a plan to get her home."

Solutions and theories came from every direction. Some good, some bad, and one downright stupid.

"Why don't we just storm the place?" a burly man with a thick black moustache asked, his voice thick with anger.

"They outnumber us. This is a rescue mission, not a suicide mission," Luke interjected coldly.

Suggestions along the lines of kidnapping and ransom sounded, but as Tom quickly pointed out, he refused to stoop to their level.

Tom sighed, bracing his hands on the table. "We need to be smart about this."

"We need to catch them off guard," I muttered to myself.

Tom watched me, a thoughtful expression on his face. "Tell us what you think, Eve."

I balked when I realised he had heard me and looked to Luke for a way out, but he shook his head and flashed an encouraging smile. "Go on."

"You're outnumbered, so your only chance is to strike while they don't expect it. Each full moon, they celebrate with a hunt in the forest, away from where Alice is held. They are throwing a big hunting party for the harvest moon. If we split them like a herd and pick them off one at a time, we can keep them distracted while some of us go straight to Alice. Only then do we stand a chance."

Tom nodded in approval, and no protests came from the pack.

"What about the alpha and Ryan? Will they hunt during the harvest?"

"They won't, not when they know I found Alice. They'll hold on to their best fighters," I agreed, chewing my lip. "But one thing Ryan will hunt is me."

Luke tensed to my right, his fingers digging into my thigh. "No."

I turned to him, placing my hand over his under the cover of the table. "If I can distract him and some of the stronger fighters, you will be able to get to Alice."

"He will kill you," Luke growled, his expression pained.

"Not if I can keep him distracted long enough for you to get Alice and come back to rescue me." I squeezed his hand and set my shoulders, turning to the rest of the pack. "I'll be wolf bait."

Chapter 41

I spent the night tossing and turning in a strange bed. Closing my eyes just brought up memories of Kate, of her laugh, her smile, her dead eyes staring up at nothing. I remembered her teaching me to cook over the summers, the rows we would have over her disappearing on nights out, then all the times we snuggled up in bed to watch Rom-Coms and whine about boys, knocking back wine until we passed out. How she had held me through the night and wiped away the tears I cried over Ryan. She had sworn she would kill him if he weaselled his way back into my life. She had said he was trouble, and now more than ever I wished I had listened.

I stared at the ceiling for as long as I could without going crazy. The day's events swam around in my head on repeat, and I couldn't stop worrying about our plan. I was dreading going back to the Faolchúnna pack lands after everything that had happened. The mattress springs squeaked in protest as I sat up and let my back rest against the headboard. Shadows danced in the corners of the small room. The walls were covered with family photographs; in each one, Alice was sporting a toothy grin.

They had left the room relatively untouched, everything ti-died away into the wardrobe and drawers. A sliver of moonlight seeped between the curtains, illuminating my bag in the corner under the window. Luke had gone back to the apartment, but

I couldn't face it. I wondered silently what phase the moon was in, having lost all sense of time the last few days.

A light rap sounded at the door, and my heart leaped. The door clicked open a crack and Luke's head peeped around. His eyes widened when he saw me awake, an apologetic smile playing on his lips.

"Come in," I whispered and shuffled up on the bed, pulling the covers up to my chest.

Luke tiptoed across the room, catching his leg on the corner table and cursing. "Shit. Sorry, I thought you were asleep."

"Didn't anyone ever tell you it's creepy to watch girls sleep?" I arched an eyebrow, stifling a laugh as he nursed his knee.

"You weren't asleep." He grinned, taking a seat beside my legs. "Besides, if you had been sleeping, I'd have left you like that. You're less sarcastic when you're busy snoring."

I smacked his arm. "I do not snore."

He wiggled his eyebrows but didn't argue further. As Luke glanced around the room, his expression sobered, and he swallowed. The mood inside the room shifted. I reached out and gave his arm a gentle squeeze.

"We will get her back soon," I whispered, wishing I sounded more confident.

Luke sighed and ran a hand through his hair, his eyes locking on mine. "What you did today was brave, Eve. You didn't need to do that."

"Yes, I did."

"No, you didn't." He shook his head, his brow furrowing. "The pack really respects you for what you did. They believe you tried to save Alice before, and they all want to help this time. We will bring her back no matter what."

"Keeping Ryan out of the way is the key. If I can catch him and the alpha when he's just home from work, before they link up with the rest of the pack, it'll give you some time."

Luke frowned, his eyes growing dark. "I don't like the idea of you taking on their best fighters all alone. I know I trained you, but it's a death sentence."

His attempt at a joke fell flat.

"That's why I won't be fighting them," I said, wringing my hands and hoping that was exactly how it would play out. "Ryan is easy to lure into an argument, and once his temper flares, he loses sight of everything else. I just need to keep them distracted."

"He could kill you."

I forced a slight smile, swallowing as Kate popped into my mind again. "He can try."

Luke locked his jaw, gritting his teeth. "I don't like it. We should find another way."

I felt his hands ball into fists, gripping the sheets, and I held up a hand to stop his rant. "There is no better way."

"There are plenty of other ways that don't involve you being bait," Luke said, shooting me a pained look.

"Those options risk others getting hurt in my place, and I am not willing to put anyone else on the line."

He shook his head in dismay, looking like he very much wanted to put a hole in the wall. "Don't make him so angry that he loses sight of his feelings for you."

I nodded, biting my lip as I refused to make any more promises. The way Ryan had treated me the last few times we were together and given his relationship with Nadine, I wasn't one hundred percent sure that his feelings for me were that strong anymore. Luke wasn't keen on the idea as it was, so I kept that doubt to myself.

"As soon as you get the chance, come and find me. Once we have Alice, we need to get out of there. My father doesn't want to start a war."

"What about you?" I asked, seeing the anger in my own eyes reflected in his.

"They started one the moment they kidnapped my sister."

The next few nights, Luke's words haunted me as much as Kate's memory. We spent each day talking over the plan and the possible variations with his father and other pack members. The morning before the full moon, I walked into the kitchen to find a large map, held down on three corners with paper weights, covering the table. Luke sat on one side and his father stood on the other, stroking his beard and holding the map in place with his thumb. Tom's face lit up as he noticed me.

"Ah, Eve!" Tom smiled and ushered me over to a spare chair. "Glad to see you're awake."

I found myself seated opposite Luke, his hair tousled, sipping a coffee. Beside me sat a small blonde woman called Liz, whose piercing blue eyes saw right through me. She smiled and nodded politely. Liz was like aunt to Luke. She had a key to the house and popped in almost daily. I'd found out the hard way when I came down early one morning for a glass of water and saw her rummaging in the fridge for food. She gave me such a fright that I'd dropped the empty glass, and between the noise of the glass smashing and Liz's reaction, the entire house woke up.

"What were you saying, Tom?" asked a man to my left in his late forties with greying hair. Darren was the alpha's best friend with absolutely no patience to speak of.

Tom rolled his eyes and began pacing around the table, arms folded. "This is a blueprint of the Faolchúnna territory. As far as I know, it is up to date."

Liz cooed and pored over the map, her eyebrow arching sharply. "Queen bee certainly has a big enough bedroom after the revamp," she remarked. She was a slight woman but had a fierce temper and a foul mouth that I had witnessed regularly during my short time with the Crescents.

"They have built quite the little community," Tom agreed, bitterness in his voice. "But we will avoid any altercations indoors. The plan is to get Alice and leave immediately."

I leaned in and examined the map. The main house was correct, but other things were missing or misplaced. "This is wrong," I said, pointing to where the cottage should have been. "There are buildings nearby the cottage, used for crafting and god knows what else. There are also a few other buildings to the east."

Tom followed my hand as I gestured, making rough notes with a pencil as I went. "Good, that actually gives us more cover if they are all preoccupied with the hunt."

"Do I want to know what they hunt?" Liz asked, her glasses shifting as her nose wrinkled.

"Deer, at least when I was there."

Darren muttered something under his breath, and Liz scowled.

"What if Eve gets cornered?" Luke asked, his honeyed eyes lingering on mine.

Tom stood behind Luke, his arms braced on his son's chair. "She knows not to antagonise him too much, just enough to keep him talking."

"And if she can't? If the alpha twigs something is going on, he'll kill anyone in his way." Luke was like a dog with a bone.

"Then she lets the alpha and Ryan go, they will be late and unlikely to interfere before we have Alice. If they do, we should be able to keep them at bay."

Luke's lips thinned, his eyes darkening. He was not on board with this plan one bit. "Why don't we just sneak in some random night outside of the full moon and try to rescue Alice?"

"Because I tried that, and it didn't work," I said and all eyes at the table turned to me. "If you think he will leave her unguarded again, you're underestimating him. They must have video surveillance there or something because both times a pack member caught me in the act."

Tom stroked his beard while his son tried very hard to bite his tongue. I felt bad going against Luke, I knew he just wanted to protect me. But this wasn't about me, this was about keeping my promise to Alice.

"We've talked about the cameras. Josh has that covered. Right?" The alpha said, gesturing to a guy Luke's age beside him with dark hair and his nose stuck in his laptop.

"Yes sir." Josh gave his alpha a faux salute, barely glancing up from his work, his eyes darting across the screen as he worked on whatever coding prep was needed to hack into the Faolchúnna's security system. His fingers raced across the keyboard, causing the white rugby jersey that popped against his bronze skin to stretch across his broad shoulders. He was a tech wiz and one of Luke's closest friends.

Luke had briefly introduced me to Josh and his other best friend, Dylan, the night we told the pack about Alice. They seemed nice and seeing Luke joking around with his friends had been weird, they all seemed so *normal*. As if his friends, the pack, were just one giant happy family.

Tom shook his head with a wry smile. "Does anyone stay back from the hunt?"

"Rarely. The alpha stays back if there's something going on, Ryan leads the hunt in his absence."

"Are you sure they will start without Ryan there?" Darren asked, lounging back in his chair in a way that instantly reminded me of Luke.

I wondered if that was where he got it from.

"They have started without him before when he was late because of me. Nick will gladly step up in Ryan's absence," I explained, trying not to let too much anger seep into my words. "So long as we delay Ryan and the alpha, the hunt will begin without them. We can split the Faolchúnna pack into pockets that are easier to manage."

Darren nodded, but Luke stood, the legs of his chair scraping the tiles and bumping Tom's knee. "I don't like this. It leaves too much to chance."

Tom stiffened and laid a hand on Luke's shoulder, firmly pushing him back into the seat like you would a bold child. Luke growled.

"We cannot risk a full attack—they outnumber us. If we need chance on our side, so be it. You want your sister home as do I, so we need to be smart about this. If anyone finds themselves in a fight they can't handle or outnumbered, back down and alert the pack."

Luke stayed silent, simmering. I had no doubt he was dying to punch someone, most likely the alpha—which wouldn't be his wisest move.

"According to Eve and our sources, only a select few know about Alice. I think if we successfully draw out the hunt and split them off along with Eve's distraction plan, we should have no problem getting Alice out without causing too much drama," the alpha said, every word oozing with an infectious confidence. "We do not want any unnecessary altercations. We are bringing my little girl home, not starting a new vendetta."

The main players around the table nodded, but Luke remained stiff, staring at the map so intently I thought it might spontaneously combust.

"We'll make a Crescent out of you yet," Tom declared with a smile, giving me a hearty pat on the back that nearly knocked the air out of my lungs.

I laughed and met Luke's gaze. He half-smiled, the worried look etched into his features only making the dread in my stomach surge.

CHAPTER 42

The pack members disbanded for the day after many pointed looks from Helena muttering about lunch being ready and wanting her house back. Only Luke, Tom, Darren, and myself were left around the table. While Max was running rings around himself in the garden, Helena drifted in and out of the room, having turned to cleaning to keep herself occupied, or maybe she was just sick of all the planning. Much like Luke, she was both itching and apprehensive to take action.

"So," Luke began, his mouth half full with a bite of his sandwich. "Eve has one more thing she needs to tell us."

Darren and Tom were busy tucking into their lunch, but they looked up, all eyes on me.

I whipped my head around to glare daggers at Luke. The night before, I had shown him the papers I'd stolen from the house, and told him my theory about the Faolchúnna alpha, but I wasn't ready to share it with everyone else. Hadn't I brought enough bad news to their door?

Tom sat back in his chair, munching on his sandwich, looking far too relaxed for someone plotting to save his kidnapped daughter.

"Go on," he said, giving me a small smile of encouragement that did nothing to stop the tension coiling in my shoulders.

"I found something," I managed, placing my sandwich back down on the plate. I'd managed one bite, but thanks to Luke, my mouth had gone dry. "Something about Ryan's family."

"About the alpha," Luke interrupted, happily wolfing down his lunch.

Maybe he was happy that for once my bad news didn't concern his own family, or because it validated every warning he'd given me about Ryan and his father.

Darren, who had been engrossed in his food, leaned forward in his chair and propped his elbows on the table. Now I had his full attention.

"I was rooting around in their library, hiding from Ryan and Nadine most of the time," I began, tugging the sleeves of my borrowed hoodie down to cover my slick palms. "There were all sorts of books in there and filing cabinets too. I was originally looking into werewolf history, but then I noticed that some of the files were old medical ones."

Tom paled, and I noticed Luke and him share a brief look before everyone stared at me again. I was getting really sick of being the centre of attention.

Luke nudged my leg with his knee, and I sighed, trying to explain things as simply as possible.

"When I was looking through one of the books, I noticed Damien wasn't next in line to be alpha based on the whole bloodline thing. His cousin was. The cousin's death cert was redacted, b—"

"Cormac."

Tom rose to his feet, the legs of the chair scraping the tiled floor. "His name was Cormac, and he was a good man."

"I didn't—"

Luke cut me off, placing a reassuring hand on my forearm. "Dad, what's wrong? Who is Cormac?"

A myriad of expressions crossed Tom's weathered face until one took hold, and he clenched his jaw.

"No one, we will discuss this another time," he snapped, pacing in a circle and firmly shoving his chair back into place, his hands balling into fists by his side. "We are to focus on getting Alice home, do you understand?"

I wasn't sure who he was talking to, but it was as if he was reprimanding all three of us at once. We nodded in unison, Darren looking stunned by his best friend's reaction.

Tom turned and stalked out of the room, slamming the door with such force that the house shook in his wake. Even Max peered in the window from the garden, his little brows furrowing in worry. Luke smiled and waved at his little brother, who happily returned to his game as if nothing had happened.

But something had happened. Gone was the calm Tom I had gotten to know over the last week, the strong, composed alpha. From the shock written all over Luke's face, I could tell this outburst was completely out of character. We both turned to Darren for answers, who was shaking his head and dropped the last piece of his sandwich onto the plate.

"Well, what the hell was that about?" Luke asked, gesturing to the door his father had almost splintered.

Darren leaned back in the chair, running his hands through his hair and stared at the wall opposite him as if it would give him the answers. "There's stuff you don't know about when the pack split apart," he explained with a resigned sigh. "You know that Damien and your father had a fight, and that it was because of Damien's archaic views and the plans for the future of the pack. What you don't know, is that when the pack split, your dad contested Damien's right to become alpha."

Luke's jaw dropped, as if he were a kid finding out the tooth fairy wasn't real.

"What, like fighting for the status of alpha?" I asked, thinking back upon the books I'd read while holed up in the library and what Luke had said what seemed like forever ago.

"Something like that."

"Why wouldn't dad tell me the full story?" Luke leaned forward in his chair and braced his hands on the table, holding his head. "If what Eve discovered is true and Damien wasn't next in line... if he killed someone..."

Darren shrugged, deep lines etched into his forehead like the conversation was ageing him. "It's complicated, and we were never able to prove anything. So much happened back then. Between the alpha's death and trying to stop Damien, it was a dark time for the pack."

"I have a right to know," Luke said, his voice a mixture of anger and disappointment.

I stared at my lap, wondering why I seemed to have a knack for kicking open giant cans of worms. Maybe if I stopped asking questions, I might stand a chance. Then again, if I had done that that, I could have ended up like Alice.

"Luke, you're a good kid—man," Darren corrected himself, slowly rising to his feet and pacing around the table until he was standing behind us, his hands resting on Luke's shoulders. "You will make a fantastic alpha someday, but you still have so much to learn."

If he didn't notice the visible stiffening of Luke at his words, Darren must have felt it, but he continued and with each word, it became clear to me why he was Tom's right-hand man.

"You're a hothead," Darren teased, tapping the side of Luke's head affectionately. "With a good heart but a temper, and you can make rash decisions. You were told as much as you needed to know. It is not the job of an alpha's son to shoulder the burden and secrets of our past until you are ready to lead."

For a moment, I thought Luke was going to disagree, but he stared ahead, his lips set in a thin line. The faintest hint of a tear in the corner of his eye was the only giveaway he was listening.

"When you are ready, and when all of this is over and we have our Alice back with us, Tom might open up about what happened," Darren promised, giving Luke's shoulders a reassuring squeeze. "History may or may not be relevant to the mess we find ourselves in, but we won't know until we get your sister back. She will be able to tell us more than anyone."

"Dad should have known Damien had something to do with her disappearance," Luke muttered, unsurprisingly losing his ability to bite his tongue.

I swallowed, but Darren remained calm, walking back to take his seat opposite us and meeting Luke's steady gaze. "You think it never crossed our minds? That we didn't look?"

"No, I—"

Darren raised his hand to cut Luke off, his tone darkening. "She wasn't there back when she was taken. I don't know where she was, but Alice wasn't on pack territory. We scoured the place, so your father could only assume someone else had taken her, the witches, or worse. Who knows?"

I reached out to take Luke's hand in mine, lacing our fingers. Heat radiated from his skin as he traced uneven circles on the back of my hand.

"Your dad had to assume she was dead," Darren said firmly, planting his palms on the table. "He got used to holding it all in, keeping his head, but there's only so much one man can take. Let the man hug his daughter again, and then you can demand an explanation."

Luke gently released my hand, pushing his chair out and heading straight for the door. "I'll speak to him."

"Good lad," Darren said, his tone softening as he nodded in approval. "Your father needs you."

CHAPTER 43

I woke to screaming downstairs, shooting up in the bed so hard I sent the burner phone Luke had given me flying across the room. The hairs on my arms stood on end. The scream came again, loud, shrill, and childlike. Once I realised it was just Max, my racing heart gradually slowed, and my shoulders slumped. I glanced at the clock beside the bed; it wasn't even ten yet, but it was the weekend and apparently, kids don't like lie ins. Who knew?

More yelling joined Max, and I realised that the pack must already be here. I jumped out of bed and yanked on a pair of tracksuit bottoms I had borrowed from Luke. They swamped my waist but did the job. As I pulled the curtains, the morning sun illuminated the room. The sky was cloudless. We had been hoping for some cloud cover that night, but it wasn't a good enough reason to postpone. The full moon wouldn't cause too many problems in the forest. If Josh kept the cameras down and everyone stuck to the shadows of the buildings, we should still be able to reach her without raising any suspicions.

I sighed and rubbed my arms, my fingers brushing across goose bumps. Today would be a long day, whether it went according to plan or not.

Crouching down, I reached into the small rucksack I'd prepped, rummaging around until I found a small patch in the lining. My fingers closed around the cool metal, and I pulled my hand out, the delicate silver bracelet Ryan had given to me for my birthday lying in my palm. A wave of unease swept over me as I turned the silver chain over in my hand. It used to hold some meaning, now it was my secret weapon to tug on Ryan's warped little heartstrings.

A familiar knock came from the door, and I quickly slipped the bracelet into my bag. I turned to see Luke in the doorway, holding a steaming cup of coffee out to me.

"I thought you might need a bit of a kick this morning," he said, offering a shaky smile.

I laughed and stepped out onto the landing with him. "As opposed to the usual type of kicks you give? The ones that leave me on my ass?"

"You can have one of those too if you want."

I shook my head, gratefully taking the coffee from Luke. As I followed him down the stairs, I noted the stiffness in his shoulders and the way he wrung his hands. He seemed beyond jittery.

Luke paused at the bottom step and turned to me. For once, I was at eye level with him.

"Are you sure about this?" he asked, giving my shoulder a squeeze.

His touch was light but sent too many emotions to count rushing through me. I pushed them aside and tried to stop my cheeks from burning. It was nice to have someone care, but now wasn't the time. Things were confusing enough as it was.

I nodded, forcing a smile I hoped was more reassuring than it felt. "As sure as I'll ever be."

Luke stepped to the side to block my attempt to squeeze past. "I'm serious, Eve." He stared into my eyes, his voice a low rumble. "This is dangerous. I want Alice back, but I won't trade her life for yours."

Nervous butterflies somersaulted in my stomach. "I have to do this."

"No, you don't."

"Let me rephrase, I want to do this," I whispered, placing my free hand over his and taking a sip of the coffee to settle my nerves. It didn't help. "You need to let me do this. Ryan killed my best friend. I can't have her dying for nothing."

My throat constricted at the mention of Kate, my eyes burning. Luke noticed and brushed his thumb across my cheek.

"I understand revenge. Believe me, I do," he said, that haunted look I had seen before lingering in his gaze. "But you are to stick to the plan, got it? Do not lose yourself to the anger."

I nodded, remaining tight-lipped. I wanted to rip Ryan limb from limb, something I never imagined I would be capable of thinking, let alone act on. In all my life, I had never felt hatred like this. I wished I could blame my wolf side, the protective instinct, but this was all me.

Luke's gaze lingered on mine, the intensity between us sparking, and for a moment I thought he might lean in, but a loud squeal interrupted us. A stampede of kids ran past us in the hallway, chasing one another until one of them fell and erupted into tears. Darren rushed out into the hall, scooping the little girl up into his arms and kissing her forehead.

"Morning you two." He grinned, rubbing dark circles under his eyes. His daughter clung to him, crying into his chest.

Darren had two kids under the age of four and enough positivity to carry the entire pack. I had quickly learned that he was the living embodiment of the Crescent pack.

I waved and Luke sidestepped, turning and leading us towards the kitchen with a grumble of acknowledgement to Darren.

"Niamh, you're fine. You are a big, strong wolf. A bump on the head isn't going to stop you, is it?" Darren cooed, holding his child up and placing a kiss on her nose that made the girl giggle. "Good. Now, go play."

He set her down and followed us into the kitchen. I looked back to see the little girl on all fours, pretending to be a wolf with the others. They growled as they assumed a play fight. My heart stung knowing the danger their parents were about to walk into.

By the time night fell, I was jittery from too much caffeine and a bundle of nerves. The sun had set, and the navy blue of dusk hung above us, the full moon casting a dim glow across the sky. All sense of bravado had well and truly gone out the window, so I focused on trying to keep my breathing steady. The headlights of the alpha's car flashed in the wing mirror as Luke hugged another corner. When I looked over, he was gripping the steering wheel so tightly his fingers had dented the plastic. He didn't notice me, his gaze firmly fixed on the winding road ahead. We sat in strained silence.

I took the time to study his face, the light stubble lining his jaw, the way it tensed now and then at whatever was going through his mind. We wore matching black t-shirts, his stretching across the rippling muscles of his broad shoulders. I'd chosen to borrow one of his instead of Alice's. It smelled just like him, a mix of burnt orange and pine. Everyone had a change of clothes stored in their boot for if—when—we made it back. His lips were pursed in a thin line, and his brow wrinkled in a permanent frown. Despite all this, his presence still had a calming effect on me.

"What will happen after?" I asked.

The question hung in the air for a moment before Luke answered. "After what?"

"Tonight," I said, twisting my hands in my lap. The question had weighed on my mind for days.

"It depends on how tonight goes." Luke tore his eyes off the road to cast a quick glance my way. "If it all goes well, Alice comes home, and we celebrate."

I swallowed, chewing nervously on my lip. "And if it doesn't?"

"Then we cross that bridge when we come to it."

The burner phone made a soft click each time I flipped it open and closed it. In the corner of my eye, I noticed Luke's jaw twitch. I stopped playing with the phone and placed it back in my lap.

"What about me?"

With so much happening over the past week, this was the question I had spent little time dwelling on. I had been so caught up in the action and planning, I never thought about the aftermath. If there was one.

"What about you?" Luke repeated my question, raising an eyebrow.

I shuffled in the seat. He made me feel like a teenage girl, and I hated it. "I don't know what I will do once we have rescued Alice."

Luke shrugged. "I presume Mam will put on a bit of a welcome home party, and the pack will have a lot to talk about. I'm sure it will take her some time to settle back in."

Part of me wondered if he was making this intentionally awkward, or if he really was clueless.

"I meant what am I going to do. Kate's gone and Ryan... Well, that's just not happening." Each time I said her name, it tasted like ash on my tongue.

Luke's frown deepened. "Why would Ryan even matter?"

"I'm technically homeless," I said flatly, trying my best to get the point across without sounding like I was begging, but I would need somewhere to stay until I found my feet.

Luke shot me a bewildered look. "What do you mean you're homeless?"

I opened my mouth to explain, but a glimpse of realisation dawned on Luke's face, and he cut me off.

"You idiot," Luke said with a low rumbling laugh.

"What?"

He slowed the car down as the mountains came into view ahead. "You're a Crescent, Eve."

"How?" I blurted, not bothering to hide my astonishment.

"We don't have crazy induction ceremonies. If you run with us, if you fight with us, you are a Crescent," Luke said softly, an emotion I couldn't quite place shining in his eye. Was he proud?

"Only if you want to be one though, but we can talk about this after."

Luke glanced away from the road, his eyes locking on mine. A gentle smile played on his lips as he watched my reaction, the corners quirking up in amusement.

I bit my lip, fighting back the unexpected surge of emotion and tears that threatened to spill. "Thank you," I whispered, sinking into the passenger seat. My heart was racing, and it wasn't about to slow down anytime soon.

Luke stopped the car on the far side of the mountain, just outside the Faolchúnna pack territory, parking beside his father's silver hatchback. I caught sight of a child booster seat in the back of the car. My stomach flipped as the reality of what we were about to do came crashing down on me like a tonne of bricks, burying any small piece of happiness I had been feeling. Others pulled up around us, and pack members climbed out of their cars, talking in hushed whispers.

They had chosen the perfect spot, concealed and downwind of the hunt. We gathered around the alpha as he ran through the instructions one last time. The plan was to enter through the forest, and for most groups to intercept the hunt and isolate the pack into small groups. Josh and Dylan would stay with the cars and work on keeping the cameras down. Meanwhile, I would slip away along with Luke and a few others who would find Alice. It was a simple plan that could go wrong in so many ways, but it was all we had.

A light drizzle had settled in for the night. The ground was damp under my paws as I ran, nails digging into the dirt with each step. Luke stayed close to my side, paws light as we tore through the forest with the rest of the Crescent wolves. Tall trees stretched up towards the night sky, casting shadows across the forest floor. Luke's father led the pack, running a few feet in front. He was a head taller than me, with a broad chest, and an ivory coat that shone almost silver in the moonlight. The alpha kept his nose to the ground, moving with the defiant confidence of a natural born leader.

The pack followed, snaking through the trees like ghosts in the night. Sluggish butterflies stirred in my stomach, but at the same time, an exhilarated thrill tingled my spine. It felt incredible running freely like this, with a proper pack. Whenever I ran with Ryan's pack, I was an outcast, and I could feel the disconnect in every bone in my body. With the Crescents, we ran as one.

As we approached the creek, the alpha slowed, and the rest of the pack pulled up behind him. Those attacking the Faolchúnna hunt tore off into their group while Darren, Luke, and his father stayed with me.

Luke stepped towards me and nuzzled my neck as I dropped the bag I had been gripping in my jaw. We were both covered in a light coating of rain, and it made Luke more dog like in a way. I licked his nose before head-butting his muzzle affectionately. We stood for a moment, staring wordlessly into each other's eyes. So much was left unsaid.

The alpha barked and Luke nudged my shoulder before reluctantly joining his father's side. I looked up to see the alpha's silver eyes focused on me. Taking my cue, I inclined my head before snatching the bag off the ground and racing off towards the main house. My stomach lurched with each step, and I tried to resist the urge to look back. When I did, the forest clearing was empty.

Chapter 44

I stopped to get changed at the edge of the forest, my numb fingers fumbling with the buttons of my jeans. I tugged them on and rushed to finish getting dressed, dumping the empty bag back under the trees. My skin was still damp, and despite a hoody, the cold bite of the night began creeping into my bones. Without my shaggy coat, I had to rely solely on adrenaline to stay warm. I grit my teeth and started towards the main house.

One thing I hadn't anticipated was the weather. My hair was still wet after shifting back to my human form, but maybe Ryan would buy the cover story that I had waited for him like a lost little puppy in the pouring rain. *I'm sure he'd love how pathetic that sounds.*

As I sneaked through the flower garden, I noticed the lights in the manor were off and breathed a sigh of relief. The guys delaying Ryan at work must have pulled it off. They had planned to slash his tyres, but I had warned them it could backfire. In the end, we settled on a fake meeting with a witch who would never show, because Ryan's ego would make him wait around for as long as it took to please his father. Plus, I didn't want him too angry by the time he ran into me.

I smiled smugly to myself and edged around the side of the house. The driveway was empty, so I traipsed across the gravel and sat on the steps, making sure that I had a full view of any incoming cars. Tactically, I kept my back to the front door and cast my senses out. In the far distance, I could hear a muffled howl. My breath hitched, but I kept listening until another wolf answered the call. Howls of excitement echoed through the night.

The house was empty.

Good.

Forcing my shoulders back, I stared down the dark driveway while trying to ignore the knot in my stomach.

Not long after I arrived, the sound of tyres squeaking on the tarmac, followed by the crunch of gravel, reached my ears. My heart thundered in my chest. Adrenaline coursed through my body, urging me to shift—to flee. It felt wrong though, like when I was only coming into my abilities. I couldn't push the burning urge down or wrangle it under control.

It's just nerves.

I took a slow, deliberate breath and focused on reciting the speech I had rehearsed over and over in my head.

Headlights swung around the corner as Ryan's Mercedes came into view. I blinked, squinting as I held up a hand to shield my eyes. His expression changed as he caught sight of me, a mixture of emotions crossing his face— surprise first, followed by hurt, and then of course, rage.

I stood and slowly picked my way down the front steps, my trainers squelching with each step. My hands wouldn't stop twitching, so I laced my fingers and kept my hands twined in front of me, painting my best apologetic downcast look on my face.

Ryan stepped out of the car, slamming the door shut behind him. The sound was jarring, and I noticed a shadow shifting in the passenger seat. I wasn't looking forward to facing the alpha again. The headlights still beaming in my direction stung my eyes, making white patches dance in my vision.

A pair of cars pulled up on either side of Ryan's. Two men I half recognised from his workplace jumped out, poised and ready to rush at me. I tensed and felt a defensive growl build in my throat.

Ryan watched me eagerly, his face twisted into a disgruntled scowl. At the last minute, he held up his hand. "Stop."

At his command, his goons fell back and retreated to their cars where they hovered, ready to pounce.

My shoulders slumped, and I schooled my expression, silently reminding myself that I was meant to look weak, even if I hated the thought of it.

"What are you doing here, Eve?" Ryan asked, demanded rather, his lips curled back in a twisted snarl. "I know you went running off to that outcast."

I licked my lips, struggling to fight against the urge to throw myself at him, but not in the way he wanted. The days of me being shy of killing a deer were long gone. Holding my best friend's cold dead body in my arms had changed me. He would pay.

"I came to talk to you," I said quietly, worrying a stone with my foot and lowering my eyes to the ground. I needed to play this right.

"You're assuming that I even want to look at you," he sneered, hovering a few feet away from me.

Ryan's scent filled my nostrils, and I shuddered at the memories that came with them. Kate's face flashed through my mind, followed by Alice's cries for help, making my hackles rise further. I caught another scent and my eyes narrowed.

He took a step towards me, raising his voice. Always one for dramatics, Ryan made sure to put on a show. "Well?"

"If you didn't want to see me, you would have let them gut me already," I said, struggling to stop the venom from seeping into my voice as I gestured to his cronies watching our exchange with interest.

He snorted. "Who says I won't?"

I closed the distance between us and heard Ryan's breath catch in his throat. His entire body tensed, the unsteady beat of his heart betrayed him. A sick sense of satisfaction ran through me, knowing I still had this effect on him—this power over him, but I squashed that feeling as quickly as it came. This was no time to let my ego run wild.

"You still love me, Ryan," I whispered softly, holding my hand out. "Don't you remember what you said on my birthday?"

His gaze followed my movement, eyes widening as he caught sight of the bracelet clasped around my wrist—the one he had given me for my birthday. It was meant to be a sweet representation of the moon that bonded us. I stopped wearing it the day I stumbled across Alice, a day that would forever mark the proverbial nail in the coffin of our relationship.

I looked up at him from under my lashes, a small smile playing on my lips.

His heart rate quickened. Ryan reached up tentatively to push a stray strand of hair behind my ear, his expression torn.

"I've had enough of this." A voice I hadn't expected interrupted the moment, followed by the slam of a car door.

We looked up to see Nadine stalking toward us, her smooth curls matching the fire burning in those coal eyes of hers.

I swallowed, panic rising as I peered into the car and realised no one else was present. The alpha wasn't with Ryan and I had no way to warn Luke and his pack.

Nadine's jaw twitched as she approached. A stiletto heel caught in the gravel and she would have fallen had it not been for one of Ryan's friends catching her under the arms. Once they had righted her, they escorted her to the steps where she could pace back and forth with ease.

"What are you standing there for?" she snapped, her eyes narrowed at Ryan. "Why are you even entertaining this bitch?"

I bit my cheek, knowing she meant that insult in every sense of the word.

"What's she doing here?" I asked, feigning innocence. "Were you not at work?"

Ryan shook his head, running a hand through his dark mop of curls. "I was."

Nadine smirked, but I continued pushing. My script may have changed, but I needed to keep Ryan as distracted as possible. "I thought the pack kept girls out of the business?"

Behind me, I heard a growl rip from Nadine at the slight.

"Since when do you care? You left me," Ryan snapped, shooting Nadine a warning look, which she completely ignored.

I side-stepped so I was no longer between Ryan and his mistress. We were in an ironic little triangle, except now there was no love lost between us. Nadine glowered, towering above me in her heels. I was supposed to play the broken-hearted lover, a pathetic mess, but I decided to change tact.

"Like when she used to visit you in your bedroom? Your office?"

Ryan's upper lip stiffened. "That was after we had our differences."

"No, it wasn't. Don't lie, I saw you."

Ryan faltered but Nadine smirked, her cat-like eyes narrowed at me. "What's the point in lying, darling?" She asked Ryan, haughty as ever. "She deserves know the truth."

"Nadine's right. You said she was nothing, remember?" I ignored the hiss that followed my words. "That you loved me, and that she was a big mistake."

Ryan looked between the two of us, caught in his web of lies. He had business smarts, but he was terrible at reading people, even worse when it came to women. The only way he knew how to keep a woman happy was to gaslight her.

Nadine's face contorted in a thunderous mask of fury but still she directed all of her rage at me.

"Really? You blame me?" I asked, shaking my head. "How desperate are you for status?"

"No mongrel would have ever led with an alpha, anyway," she spat, venom dripping from her words. "You were always just a means to an end."

"Oh, so you knew about the hybrid breeding programme they were planning then?"

She paled at my revelation, and then it was Ryan growling.

"You would have been happy with him fucking me, would you?" I pressed, a vicious grin curving my lips. "Since I can give him stronger offspring. I'm probably a better lay, too." I had no idea where the last part came from. My mouth was on autopilot. All the pent-up anger from when he had cheated, the shit that Nadine had put me through, it all came out now.

"You're nothing but a lab rat."

"Nadine, I think you should go inside." Ryan finally broke his silence, pinching the bridge of his nose.

Her expression darkened. "No, I'm not leaving you out here with that mutt."

"Why did you kill her?" I asked, the words spewing out so fast my voice had no time to waver.

Ryan spun to face me, raking a hand through his ebony curls. "I didn't mean to, Eve."

"How the fuck do you accidentally kill someone?" I spat, my temper ramping up.

"You don't," Nadine chimed, snaking an arm around Ryan's waist, looking every inch the queen bee as she sneered over his shoulder.

The thought of Nadine being involved sent my mind reeling, and the anger boiling in my veins soared. I was so angry. I had caught Ryan's scent and, in my anguish, had never searched for anything more. What kind of friend was I, that I got her killer wrong? It might not have been Ryan who delivered the blow, but it was him who had caused all of this.

Nadine took a step forward, placing herself between me and Ryan. "I thought it would've gotten the message across," she sneered, looking down her nose at me. "You're no longer welcome here."

"Then why was Ryan still searching for me?"

She frowned, all traces of her smirk vanishing as she looked to Ryan for an answer. I took my opportunity and lunged.

We tumbled to the ground in a mass of limbs, Nadine slamming against the granite steps. Her back cracked, and a howl pierced the night sky. Claws extended from my fingertips, power pulsing in my veins. I pushed the urge to change away. Nadine writhed on the steps, snapping at my throat. Her teeth grazed my skin as I twisted out of reach, taking a swipe at her shoulder and ripping through her fancy blouse. Blood seeped into the fabric, and she hissed. I crouched, ready to lunge again when something grabbed my arm and tossed me aside.

I skid across the gravel, stones ripping the palm of my hands as I broke my fall. Ignoring the pain, I leapt to my feet and saw Ryan's hit men helping Nadine up. Ryan stood in front of me, his hands balled into tight fists.

"Don't make this difficult, Eve."

"I just wanted to talk," I murmured, stepping towards him and wincing as I wiped gravel off my palms and onto my thighs.

He shook his head slowly, gritting his teeth. "You left me."

"You killed my best friend."

Nadine hollered as the men carried her inside, dragging her through the doors kicking and screaming. Ryan cast a quick glance towards her, genuine worry in his eyes. The fact that he did care for her in some deep, dark recess of his stone heart made my stomach churn.

"Why did you ever bother with me, if you liked her?" I asked, cursing inwardly at the weakness in my voice.

"I loved you," Ryan said, his gaze lingering on the bracelet that glistened in the moonlight.

"Then why kill Kate?" I cried, kicking the gravel. "If you were going to let me go?"

"You know too much, Eve. If you had just kept your nose out of things, we could have been happy," he growled, no remorse in his eyes. This was all about the pack for him. there was no grey area so long as it pleased his father. "You ruined things."

"None of this is my fault. You kidnapped a girl!"

He shrugged, not bothering to deny it. "She wasn't part of the plan back then, we just needed hybrid blood for research."

"She's a person, not a test subject."

Ryan rolled his eyes, clearly growing impatient. I stared at him, struggling to fathom how I got it so wrong. I could still hear Nadine inside of the house, baying to be let at me like a rabid dog. He just stood there, fists balled by his sides, as if this was some kind of business exchange. Hell, this probably was how they went. Kidnapping was a small step away from human trafficking.

"You don't understand, we need to ensure the pack's survival."

I threw my hands in the air, my stomach lurching at the thought of ever having allowed him touch me. "You're fucking crazy."

"She's a hybrid," he said, this time showing his true distaste for the word.

"I'm a hybrid!"

His eyes flashed silver, and I could tell by the tension in his shoulders, the rippling muscles in his arms, and the tell-tale tick in his jaw that he was fighting the change too. The conversation had not gone the way I had expected, but as much as I wanted to rip his jugular out, I was outnumbered.

Ryan started towards me when a loud shriek pierced the silence. He paused, and my head snapped up. The howl came again, louder this time. My stomach flipped. It wasn't a howl of excitement—it was one of pain.

Without a second thought, I turned on my heel and bolted around the back of the house. I tried to shift but something was stopping me. The urge to change was there, but I had no control over it.

Tears of frustration pricked the corners of my eyes. I was so much slower in human form. I could hear Ryan on my heels, his paws thumping the gravel as I sprinted into the gardens and through the meadow, making a beeline towards the cottage. He'd already shifted, streaking past me with ease.

I raced past the corner of the old man's sheds to find four wolves fighting in the clearing and one body on the ground.

Luke.

CHAPTER 45

Growls and snapping echoed in the night. My stomach flipped at the sight of what was unfolding before me. In the centre of the clearing, the two alphas squared off while Darren fought with a black wolf I didn't recognise. Luke lay deathly still a few feet from the cottage, but he wasn't alone. A small girl with freckles that stood out starkly against her pale skin cradled him in her lap, her strawberry blonde hair skimming his chest. *Alice*. I could hear other factions of the pack fighting in the distance beyond the edge of the forest, but my attention snapped back just in time to see Ryan jumping in to join the fight. At the last moment, he changed direction, his body twisting towards Luke.

A surge of anger and fear rushed through me, the world seeming to slow as Ryan lunged towards Luke and his sister. The magic within me pulsed, surging to the point every nerve ending was on fire. Pain seared through me as the urge to change swept through me. The natural call to shift swelled, burning me from the inside out as it fought and clawed to be set free, the pain forcing me to my knees. I let out a blood curdling scream that left my throat raw, stars dancing in my vision. Something snapped and all of a sudden a second wave of magic swept through me, enveloping me in a soothing warmth as the change finally took over. I fell forward, landing on all fours with a deft thud.

I opened my eyes to find the bracelet on the ground beneath one of my front paws, steam rising from the charred and blackened remains. My screams had drawn enough attention to make Ryan pause, giving me a chance.

A snarl ripped from my chest as I rushed towards them, throwing myself in front of Luke just as Ryan lunged. He missed Luke but caught my foreleg, his teeth tearing through the flesh. I kicked him off him off and screamed in pain. Alice scampered back into the cover of the cottage doorway and I couldn't help but notice how frail she looked gripping the wooden remains of the door Luke must have kicked in.

Ryan backed up shock contorting his wolven features and blood dripping from his canines. My blood.

Our eyes locked for a long moment before another shriek of pain sounded and Ryan's head whipped towards his father. He hesitated before bounding away into the fight.

Tom was panting heavily, his pale coat matted with blood. The alpha had a deep laceration across his eye. Darren and the other wolf were both covered in cuts. Tom jerked his head towards the cottage before the two alphas leapt at one another, clashing in the air and falling to the ground in a mass of writhing limbs. Every howl of pain pulled my attention back to the fight as I tried to reassure myself it wasn't a Crescent.

I tore my gaze away from the clash of fur and teeth. Luke lay a few feet away, unmoving. The sight of his chest rising and falling with a shallow breath forced a sob from my throat. I limped over to him, cursing as pain shot through my leg with each step.

He was naked, clearly having been attacked while in his wolf form, lying on his side with one hand reaching out as if he had fallen while protecting his sister. I wasn't sure what it took to knock a wolf out, but he was covered in streaks of blood. It stained his stubble and matted his blonde hair in patches of sticky red. But he was breathing, and that was all that mattered. A deep gash sliced from his left shoulder across his back in an arc. Every wound pointed to being attacked from behind.

Cowards.

"Is he alive?"

Alice had crept out of her hiding place, wringing her hands as her gaze flicked between the fight unfolding and her brother's unconscious body.

I nodded, nudging Luke's chest with my muzzle gently at first and then harder. She didn't recognise me, but the fact that I was guarding her father was enough to gain her trust. Her clothes, a white t-shirt and faded jeans, were covered in blood and hung loosely on her slight frame. Where Luke had power and strength, her gaunt cheekbones and ghostly complexion told a different story.

A loud howl of agony pulled my attention back to the fight and my heart plummeted as I watched Darren go down, Nick tearing a strip of flesh off his flank. An excited howl sounded from the direction of the manor and I noticed a handful of wolves tearing towards the meadow. Reinforcements were on the way and we were outnumbered.

Luke! We need you, please wake up.

I pounced on his chest with my two front paws, my wounded hind leg screeching in protest. He didn't stir, his even breaths at odds with the panic taking hold of me. I stood over him, licking his face, nudging and nipping at his shoulders and chest.

Another cry rang out and tears pricked my eyes.

Please, Luke. I need you. I can't win this fight alone and I don't want to lose my pack when I've only just found them.

"You're not losing anyone."

I'd never been happier to hear that familiar husky voice.

Relief washed through me as Luke's eyes flickered opening, lingering on me before looking to his sister. His shoulders sagged at the sight of Alice unharmed.

He sat up slowly, leaning on me to steady himself as his gaze locked on the fight just as the new wolves joined up. A low growl ripped from Luke's throat at the sight and he clambered to his feet too quickly, bracing one had on the wall as he swayed.

I stood guard while he gathered his bearings and waited for his legs to stop shaking. My heart was in my mouth, each blow landing on Darren or Tom making me flinch.

Luke cursed under his breath, his hands shaking as he grabbed Alice by the shoulders. "You need to run, the cars are parked at Manon's peak. The guys will keep you safe," he said, his mouth set in a grim line as he reached out to pet the back of my head. "Both of you."

Unable to scream in frustration like I wanted, I nipped Luke's arm, but he shrugged me off. He crouched down, ready to shift.

Over my dead body.

Luke reached out, his touch feather-light as he cupped my jaw and tipped my chin up to meet his gaze. "That's what I'm afraid of."

Shock rippled through me as I realised he could hear my thoughts. I'd never been able to hear Ryan's. He'd once told me that it wasn't possible.

Snarling, I moved to stand in front of Luke and backed him up against the cottage door. He kept holding his head and I didn't need to be a doctor to know he had a concussion. He was stubborn, but it was obvious that he was in no fit state to protect anyone. Luke looked at me, pleading, but I turned away and set my shoulders. There was no way I was leaving.

Alice shook her head, reaching out with a shaky hand to grasp Luke's forearm and pull him into tight hug. "Promise you'll come back."

Luke's throat bobbed as he pulled his little sister close, nuzzling the top of her head. "I promise. Now go."

I knew he was still speaking to me too, but I kept my gaze firmly fixed on the battle in front of me. Alice's scent faded as she retreated under the cover of the forest and I felt the air shimmer beside me as Luke shifted and landed by my side. His shaggy cream coat was matted and covered in blood, but a fiery determination shone in in his eyes as they met mine. He radiated power and a thirst for revenge, his hulking frame dwarfing mine.

I fight with you, or you don't fight at all.
He nodded in agreement. *For Alice.*

CHAPTER 46

S parring in the boxing ring hadn't prepared me for a real fight and I was all too aware how out of depth I was as sprinted into the centre of the action. We split up, Luke diving in to defend his father from the Faolchúnna alpha. The three wolves that joined in as back up seemed to be targeting Tom who was desperately trying to defend a wounded Darren.

I took over, cutting across into Ryan and Nick's path as they zeroed in on Darren who was backing up towards the forest. He gave me small nod and shrunk back, his legs trembling as he fought to stay upright. Torn flesh hung from the gaping wound on his flank, leaving a bloody trail in his wake. I knew he couldn't hold on much longer.

Ryan's head snapped towards me, the air fogging in front of him as he panted and blood dripped from his tongue. Nick lurked beside him, his shiny black coat sticky with Darren's blood.

I willed Darren to keep retreating, to drop back with the rest of the pack. But I wasn't sure how the mind-talking worked and I didn't dare take my eyes off the wolves in front of me. I could only hope Darren heard me.

Ryan wasted no time, his eyes flashing with anger as he raced towards me.

I gulped and braced my shoulders, sick of waiting like bait. Kicking off my haunches, I began sprinting towards him. I pulled my lips back and reared up on my back legs as we collided, claws extended, my jaw aimed for his throat. He twisted and instead my teeth sunk into the flesh of his shoulder. A metallic taste flooded my mouth, but this time the urge to heave never came. Ryan clawed my stomach, his claws digging into the exposed flesh until I released hm.

Ryan cried out and stumbled back, his muzzle spattered with blood. I went to dive on him again, but he ducked and caught my back leg in his jaw as I overshot my jump. I lurched forward, kicking and twisting in his grasp. My free foot caught his mouth, nails slicing as I kept pumping my legs until he lost his grip.

I raced towards the cover of the cottage, adrenaline coursing through my veins.

Before I could get there, my belly hit the floor with a thud, closely followed by my jaw bouncing off the ground with a clunk. Fire ripped through my shoulder as Nick landed on top of me, the brunt force of the impact driving his claws into my shoulder blades. I hissed in pain and pushed my haunches up, keeping my nose low. The movement threw Nick off balance and over my head, cutting his growl of victory short.

I swear a look of satisfaction crossed Ryan's face as he watched Nick land with a thud. It was quickly replaced by an icy hatred as he began circling me.

From the corner of my eye, I could see the alphas fighting. They were both exhausted, and Tom had a deep gash across his shoulder which was slowing him down. Luke fought alongside his father, taking out the backup wolves with ease, but the Faolchúnna alpha fought with the strength of several.

Ryan closed in and I knew I was no match one to one. He might have been bigger, but I was faster, so I took off again. My plan was in tatters anyway. All I could do was keep Ryan and Nick distracted. The new plan was to survive.

I dodged a blow from Ryan, but my triumph was short lived as Nick pounced and slammed me into a tree. Something cracked and I yelped, pain searing through my chest. I grit my teeth and forced myself to my feet, my injured hind leg protesting as I wove between the edge of the treeline.

Out of the corner of my eye, I saw Luke's father slumped on the ground. The Faolchúnna alpha stood over him, fangs bared.

Ryan shot past my left, but I whipped my head around, a guttural snarl I didn't think myself capable of ripping from my throat. I caught him just below the neck and clamped my jaw down. Instead of stopping in his tracks, he kept running, and my teeth ripped through the muscle. I came away with a chunk of his flesh in my mouth.

He howled and clattered to the ground. The alpha looked up, distracted by Ryan who lay there shrieking in agony. I retched, shuddering as I watched him writhe. Damien's eyes met mine, hard and cold, his stare unwavering as he threw his head back with a feral howl. He went for the rival alpha's throat.

I wanted to scream, but only a pathetic whine came out as I raced forward. I knew I was too late.

Barely a blur, Luke came from behind and barrelled into Ryan's father, slamming the alpha into the dirt in one swift movement. The two tore into one another, their growls echoing throughout the forest. I dashed over to Tom, nudging his shoulder, but he was perfectly still. Ryan was still howling where he lay. A whimper escaped my lips as I looked at the fight. Blood specked Luke's shaggy coat already as he warred with Ryan's father, his large jaw snapping. Damien was strong and experienced, but Luke was fast and smart. For each blow Ryan's father landed, Luke doubled it. I watched them, growling and panting as I stood guard over Tom.

"Dad!" A cry came from my left, and I spun to see Alice lingering in the cottage doorway, gripping the frame as if it were the only thing holding her up. I could smell her fear as she caught sight of Ryan in the distance. What scared us both more was when Luke fell to the ground.

Damien clamped his jaw around Luke's throat, just as Luke buried his teeth in the alpha's neck. They rolled and kicked, drawing yelps from one another. I flinched each time the alpha caught Luke. An agonising snarl ripped from Luke's throat as Damien's claws sank into the open wound behind Luke's shoulder blades and sliced down. With every attack the other one came out on top. Every inch of my body begged to join Luke in the fight but I held back, knowing I would only distract him. Despite all my training, no one but him stood a chance in this fight.

Another wolf emerged from the shadows, their fiery coat glowing under the full moon. I snapped at them and circled the doorway, placing myself in front of Alice.

Nadine.

She stepped into the clearing and stalked towards me with a vicious look I knew all too well, her teeth flashing in the moonlight.

I dropped my head and snarled. Ryan took a shaky step forward, and every muscle fibre in my body tensed.

Nadine stopped short and looked over my shoulder. I followed her gaze to see a battered Darren limping from behind the cottage, followed by the rest of the Crescent pack. Even Dylan and Josh had joined the fight. My heart swelled. I turned back to Nadine and squared my shoulders, standing tall. Darren and the pack took their place by my side, forming a protective circle around Alice and the Crescent alpha.

Luke had the alpha on the floor now, his claws pinning the alpha's shoulder to the ground. His jaw was poised Damien's jugular, just like the alpha had his father only minutes before, ready to land the killing blow.

A scream lodged in my throat as Nick leapt out of the undergrowth to tackle Luke, but his blow never landed. Luke released the alpha, twisting in time to sink his fangs into Nick's throat. Momentum drove Nick's body into the ground with a sickening thud and a loud snap echoed in the clearing. His body slumped, lifeless and severed at the neck.

Luke retracted his fangs, releasing Nick's neck, and retreated. The severed head landed with a sickening clunk and rolled to a stop at the Faolchúnna alpha's feet.

Covered in blood, the alpha's stomach rose and fell with shallow, ragged breaths. Wheezing, he made no effort to move or retaliate.

Ryan roared and hobbled over to his father's side. A steely look flashed in Luke's eyes, but he continued towards his pack. Ryan hovered near his father, whining, but paying no attention to his fallen uncle. The alpha shoved him away, staring unblinking at his brother's head.

Wolves emerged from the forest slowly and cautiously, some wounded but most stunned. My heart quickened. Even now they outnumbered us, but at the sight of their injured alpha and Nick's limp body, the wolves dropped back with Nadine.

As Luke approached us, the air shimmered, and Luke shifted back into his human form. The pack bowed their head in respect. He was favouring one ankle and deep gashes crisscrossed his back, but strode forward with confidence. He stopped by my side, his body stained red and speckled with bruises. He crouched beside his father, and I barked as I caught sight of the rise and fall of Tom's chest.

I wasn't the only one who had noticed.

Nadine snarled and Ryan's head shot up. He moved to join her side and I knew what they were thinking. An eye for an eye. I inclined my head and watched the rival pack nervously, but all eyes were on Nick's mangled corpse.

Luke's shoulders relaxed a fraction, barely noticeable to anyone but me. He stood tall, not showing any embarrassment over his state of undress.

"We don't want another fight," he said, his voice booming across the empty space. He looked every inch the alpha. "Let us go in peace. No one else needs to die. Unlike your leader, killing gives me no pleasure."

A string of snarls and baying ripped from the front line, led by Nadine. I tensed, but Ryan stepped forward, a loud growl rumbling from his chest. He glanced at the pack and then at Nadine, his shoulders wider and a head taller. She was no match for him, and she knew it, dropping her head and slinking back into line.

Alice moved from the doorway and walked over to us, her movements stiff. She stopped by my side, her hands clasping my fur like a nervous child.

Ryan began to stand. I held my breath.

"Go. Go now, or I will kill all of you," Ryan said, his fists balled tightly by his side. "Now."

Alice latched onto Luke's arm, and with a sombre smile, he hugged her tightly to his chest before gently nudging her back over to my side. Kneeling on one leg, he gathered his father's weary body in his arms. Tom was still in his wolf form, all legs and fur, but Luke held him effortlessly. Tom's eyes remained closed, but his stomach rose and fell with each breath.

"Leave now," Luke ordered, rising to his feet.

He turned his back on the Faolchúnna pack, walking towards the forest area behind the cottage in the direction we had come from while cradling our alpha in his arms.

Alice lingered, her fingers gripping my coat so tightly it stung. She kept her gaze locked firmly on Ryan, her jaw working as she watched him. I noticed her glance at the cottage and plant her feet, ready to run. I caught her shirt between my teeth with a firm growl.

"You don't understand," she said, tears glistening in the corner of her eyes.

I gave her a sympathetic look and nudged her side gently. The rest of the pack had retreated, it wasn't safe to hang around.

She refused to move, so I dragged her towards the forest after Luke. Alice watched the cottage disappear, tears rolling down her cheeks. A small pang of guilt hit me. The poor girl was in shock. I could smell the nightshade on her. This would be a long walk.

My last image of the Faolchúnna pack was Ryan standing beside his father, his face an expressionless mask as the alpha crouched over his brother's body, head bowed. Now they knew how it felt.

CHAPTER 47

I tried to focus on the moment, but the past week's events were looping on repeat through my mind. So much had happened—too much. The scene unfolding in front of me still felt like a dream, distant and surreal. My head swam, and I couldn't tell if I was going to faint, or if it was the black dress I had borrowed squeezing the air out of my lungs. I'd almost forgotten funerals were a thing, but when we arrived back with Alice in the early hours of the morning, Luke had pulled me aside and shown me the details online. I knew I had to go, Kate deserved a goodbye.

Thunder rumbled in the distance, the grey sky brooding. Beside me, Luke stood tall with one arm clamped firmly around my waist.

He looked dapper in a suit, but the thought tasted sour in my mouth. I didn't have the emotional spoons to even begin to wonder what *this* was.

"Are you all right?" Luke asked, his husky voice breaking through and dragging me back to our skewed reality.

"Not really," I mumbled. "Am I meant to be?"

He shook his head with a sombre smile. "No."

I stiffened as the coffin appeared in front of us. I recognised Kate's brother and father, but another familiar face was among the pallbearers. Craig's hair was dyed electric blue, Kate's signature colour, standing out in stark contrast to his black suit. He had dark bags under his eyes, which were raw and red. A wave of guilt smashed into me.

With everything going on, I had completely dropped off the radar. I'd had no chance to visit Kate's family or comfort Craig. A few nights ago I had been fighting werewolves on some crazy mission, and now I stood watching my best friend being buried from a distance. Skipping the church service had been my call. I wasn't able to sit there and lie to their faces, but Luke had insisted on coming to the burial. He said it would help bring closure. I couldn't imagine ever getting over the last few days.

"Do you want to move closer?" he whispered, his breath tickling my ear and sending an involuntary shudder down my spine.

"Not much. I can't be seen."

Luke sighed. "We can make up a story."

"No," I said firmly, my teeth set on edge. "That's what Ryan did after I attacked her. I'm sick of lying and I never want my friends to forget against their will again."

I still had no idea how he did that, and I didn't want to know. It was wrong, and I should never have gone along with it. Kate died without knowing the full truth. Maybe if she had known, she would never have let Ryan and Nadine in that night, maybe the truth would have saved her life. The memory of her screaming, the terror in Kate's eyes as I attacked her that night months ago, still surfaced loud and clear. One of my last memories of my best friend. I swallowed the lump in my throat and stepped closer to Luke.

"You can go back to this, the life you had before." Luke said, keeping his voice low. "You don't have to give it all up."

I frowned. I wanted to go back, to laugh with my friends and whine about exams again, but something had changed, I wasn't the same girl I was before I found out I was a hybrid. Everything that had once seemed normal felt so small now.

"Kate is dead," I said, as if saying the words aloud would make it feel like a horrible nightmare that I could still wake up from, but there was no escaping this. "Even if I went back, things would never be the same."

He nodded. "I know, but you can rebuild things step by step."

I exhaled slowly, clenching my jaw as I tried to bite back tears.

"You can still have friends—Craig, the others, you don't have to give it all up." Luke slouched slightly and inclined his head to nuzzle the top of mine. "You can be a part of the pack and build a new life, a different one."

My lip was raw from all my chewing.

"You don't have to turn your back on the past, Eve."

The dam broke at his words and tears rolled down my cheeks unbidden. I tried my best to keep my breathing calm, but I hiccoughed with each sob. Luke wrapped his arm around my shoulders and pulled me against his chest. I let my head rest there, listening to the steady beat of his heart thrumming in my ear.

Tears blurred my vision as the priest closed the mass, and they slowly lowered the coffin into the ground. It's not smooth like in the movies, and more than once I thought the coffin would fall. This was the first funeral I could remember. I never wanted to see another one.

Kate's parents stepped up to the grave first, throwing a single rose each on top of the coffin. Craig followed suit, collapsing into a fit of tears. A friend I didn't recognise picked him up and led him away from the grave. Watching him suffer without me twisted my heart.

The crowd lined up and paid their respects one by one. Mascara stained my cheeks, and my chest wouldn't stop heaving. The tears were endless. Eventually, the sea of black dispersed and the only person left by the grave was Kate's mother saying her final goodbyes. Even at a distance, I could see the anguish on her face. After some time, her husband led her away, and they walked arm in arm towards the last remaining car, supporting one another. I wished I could go to them, tell them how fantastic their daughter was, how she had held me all those nights when I cried, how fiercely protective she was of her friends, but my words meant nothing now. Their daughter was dead, and they would never know why.

"It's time."

Luke pried me from him and placed a gentle hand between my shoulder blades, coaxing me toward the fresh plot. I dragged my feet, the heels of the black patent shoes Luke's mother had loaned me sinking in the damp grass. Autumn leaves littered the graveyard, a colourful mix of yellows and reds. We stopped in front of the grave, and I felt all the blood drain from my face as reality set in.

Kate's coffin lay in the dirt, surrounded by the purple ribbons used to lower it into the ground and the mountain of roses that had been scattered on top. At the head of the grave, a large headstone was inscribed with her name and 'beloved daughter'.

"I'm so sorry," I cried, tears obscuring my vision as I stared at the coffin. I couldn't fathom that my best friend was in there and she was never coming back. "I should have told you everything. I was selfish for trying to keep you in my life."

Luke stayed silent, but his arm hooked in mine was the only thing keeping me standing.

"I'm sorry for all the times I hogged the bathroom, for not giving you the last can in the fridge, for the redhead guy I kissed first." I had a long list of things I wanted to apologise for and would never get a chance to. "Most of all, I'm sorry for not listening to the best advice you ever gave me. I'm sorry I didn't listen when you said Ryan was a prick."

I felt Luke's grip on me tense slightly, but other than that, there was no sound or movement from him apart from his thumb tracing circles my arm.

"I should have listened. You were always right." I knelt down to pick up a stray rose resting at the side of the grave. "I promise to always listen to my instincts from now on. I will do my best to make things right."

The rose drifted in the wind as I released it, slowly coming to rest above Kate's name on the coffin. I glanced up to see the final inscription on Kate's grave 'Only the good die young'. A strangled laugh escaped my lips, closely followed by a fresh wave of tears building.

"I will make this right," I whispered, choking back a sob. "I love you."

With that, I gave in to the grief and fell into Luke's arms. He held me against his chest and kissed the top of my head. A lone raindrop hit my shoulder before the heavens opened. We said nothing, he just held me in the rain while I cried for the friend I had once called a sister.

EPILOGUE

The car ride was long, cold, and silent. Autumn leaves clung to bare branches as we sped past the countryside, a stark reminder that everything comes to an end. A chill had set in my bones, and the tears had run dry. There were no words. When we arrived at Luke's house, a string of cars blocked the small driveway. I frowned as we pulled up.

It had been the early hours of the morning when Tom had discharged himself from the hospital. Even having Alice at his bedside wasn't enough to keep him resting. With a broken rib, leg, and a punctured lung that had healed too fast, the alpha had demanded he be let home. The doctors were too baffled to argue, and because Tom was a doctor, we had plenty of strings to pull. We made sure to leave before the Gardaí could question him about a suspected mugging that never took place. Luke reassured me that the cover story didn't matter, someone paranormal in the police force would squash the case.

Luke eyed the number of cars, his puzzled expression mirroring mine. "What is everyone doing here?"

I shrugged. "They were all gone when I woke up."

"I don't like this," he muttered, snatching the keys out of the ignition.

I shook my head and followed him towards the house. His shoulders were tense, and he scuffed the ground with his foot. I was sure he hadn't slept a wink in the last few days, and it wasn't because he had downgraded himself to the couch after offering me his bedroom. With Alice home, he insisted on sleeping on her bedroom floor most nights anyway. Even though she was back, he was still on high alert.

The second the door opened, Max slid down the hall and catapulted himself into Luke's arms. The car keys clattered on the floor as Luke dropped them and caught his brother at the last moment, propping an unfazed Max on his hip.

"Alice is home!" he cried, always parroting what the adults were saying.

Luke's expression softened, the corners of his lips quirking. "She is indeed. Where's Dad?"

Max twisted in his arms and pointed giddily down the hallway towards the kitchen door. He kicked Luke in the side like you would a horse. He caught sight of me, and a bright grin lit up his round little face. "Eve!"

"Hello Max." I attempted a weary smile.

Luke winced at the kick and rubbed his sides, setting his little brother down on the floor and shooing him in the opposite direction. "Go play with the girls."

"Ew, not the girls!" Max giggled, but tore off in that direction regardless.

We picked our way towards the kitchen, dodging Lego pieces and toy cars along the way. As we neared, I picked up muffled voices arguing in hushed tones. As Luke pushed the door open, we stepped into the room to find all the main pack representatives present. Those in seats were hunched over the table, other standing huddled around the dining table. They were all staring at something.

Alice.

She sat at the head of the table, her hair a tousled mess and her cheeks slick with tears. Luke's parents sat on either side of Alice, Tom's bad leg propped up on a footstool. He was arguing with Darren, his mouth set in a grim line. At the same time,

Helena was in the middle of an icy exchange with a Liz, whose eyes bordered on silver, but Helena didn't seem the least bit perturbed.

Their heads snapped up the moment we entered the room. The discussion stopped immediately, an undeniable tension in the air.

Alice stared at the table, shaking hands clasped and her eyes downcast.

"What the hell is going on here?" Luke demanded, the house rattling as he slammed the kitchen door shut behind us.

"Oh, look who finally decided to show up," Liz piped up, her bright eyes blazing.

Helena shot a wicked glare her way. "Shut up, Liz."

"She's just upset, Helena," Darren said coldly, casting a pointed look towards Alice. "We all are."

"This is ridiculous."

More bickering broke out, and the volume in the room escalated as pack members jumped at each other's throats. Adrenaline levels soared, and I felt the tension spark. Eyes were flashing silver, and tempers were on fire.

"Stop it!" The alpha's voice rang out, cutting through the noise.

The commotion subsided, and Luke spoke again, looking to his father for answers. "Someone tell me what's going on."

Tom pinched his nose and exhaled slowly. He opened his mouth to respond but burst into a coughing fit. Helena rushed to his side, stroking his back and murmuring something in his ear about taking it easy.

Luke's jaw twitched. "Well?"

He looked at the others, but each pack member averted their eyes and shuffled, uncomfortable under the heat of Luke's gaze. Even Josh and Dylan shrank back from him.

I chewed my lip and hovered nervously by Luke's side. Alice snivelled, but no one moved to console her.

"What's wrong?" I asked, my question directed at Alice.

She shook her head and gulped, wringing her hands.

Luke strode forward, his face like thunder. The pack members backed away from the table, chair legs grating on the tiled floor as they distanced themselves, keeping their mouths firmly shut. Tom was wheezing and trying to catch his breath.

"Stop it, Tom, you need to rest and this isn't helping," Helena fussed, dabbing a small speck of blood off her husband's chin with a napkin.

I held my breath and watched as Luke moved to his little sister's side. He crouched down beside Alice, his knees cracking at the sudden movement. She was trembling all over now.

"There's more," she croaked.

Tom shared a poignant look with his son, their gaze travelling to me. Although, I couldn't read the look in Luke's eyes, a multitude of emotions flickered across his face.

"What?" I asked, my mind still struggling to connect the puzzle pieces.

Alice pushed her chair back, the wooden legs groaning. She swayed and Luke reached out to help, but she slapped his hand away, placing her palms flat on the table to steady herself. It was clearer in daylight just how pale she had become, but when she looked at me, there was no weakness her eyes. Only fire.

"I'm not the only hybrid they've taken."

Killer Instinct

The Hybrid Wolf Series: Prequel

GET YOUR FREE COPY:
www.ciaradelahunt.com

The alpha was murdered and it was an inside job. Can Tom step up and save the future of his pack before it's too late?

Getting the call to say his alpha had been killed in an accident was the last nudge Tom needed to come home. The move would be a fresh start. Or so he thought.

Tom's homecoming quickly becomes a nightmare when he discovers the alpha's death wasn't an accident. He teams up with old friends to find out who is responsible.

He finds himself playing undercover detective while juggling a toddler and family tensions. Helping his best friend's brother ends up bringing up emotions and a connection that Tom never thought he'd feel again.

When the truth comes to light and Tom realises just how far the culprit is willing to go in their hunt for power, he has to choose between family and his pack's future. Can Tom find a way to salvage his pack before it's too late?

AUTHOR'S NOTE

Thank you so much for reading Wolf Bait. This book will always hold a special place in my heart as my first, I fell in love with the characters and I hope you did too.

While this story is fictional and werewolves (unfortunately) don't exist, I hope you enjoy watching Eve find herself throughout this series. Being a woman in your early twenties is hard, so many of us hand our hearts to the wrong boy, forget to trust our instincts, and experience betrayal. You don't have to be fighting fantastical evils to find your voice and self-belief again.

I'm an indie author, I have a full time job and sacrifice a lot to get these books out there. So, if you could spare two minutes to post a review it would mean the world to me. You can also follow me on Amazon to get notified about upcoming releases.

To be the first to get updates, bonus content, and special sneak peeks, sign up to my newsletter. Newsletter subscribers also get exclusive access to an ebook copy of Killer Instinct, *The Hybrid Wolf Series: Prequel*. This is a full length novel set twenty years in the past that details what caused the packs to split. Baby Luke makes an appearance and there might be some easter eggs for the series in there too if you keep an eye out!

If email isn't your thing, come hang out in our Facebook reader group ***Ciara Delahunt's Reader Den***:
www.facebook.com/groups/ciaradelahuntsreaderden

Alternatively, you can find me on Tiktok (@ciaradelahuntbooks) and Instagram (@ciaradelahunt). I update my social media channels regularly and love to hear from readers.

Love,

Ciara x

Acknowledgements

It's both amazing and terrifying to finally let Wolf Bait out into the world. I wrote this book before the pandemic when I reignited my love of writing. The first scene where Eve wakes up in the park popped into my head, inspiration hit me like a bus, and Eve's story refused to leave me. I always wanted to be an author growing up. Everyone told me that it wasn't a real job and that it would never happen. It's crazy to think that I have finally fulfilled that dream.

Writing isn't easy and I would have never made it this far without a small army of wonderful people behind me, cheering me on every step of the way.

To my editor, whose advice and encouragement has made me a better writer, thank you for working your magic on my books. Huge thanks to Natalie for designing such a beautiful cover and bringing the Hybrid Wolf Series world to life. You always surpass my expectations.

I also need to thank some fellow authors who helped keep me in line and kicked my ass when I let imposter syndrome or my magpie tendencies get in the way. Lasairiona, Brian, Erika – thank you for listening to my meltdowns and keeping me in check. Your advice and guidance have helped me get this book over the line without tearing my hair out.

To everyone who has followed me on this journey, especially those who beta read my books, thank you for helping me make this dream a reality. Special thanks to Jodi and Fran for being amazing, inspirational women who believed in this series from the start. This book may have never seen the light if it weren't for your enthusiasm and reassurance.

I'm so lucky to have friends and family who have supported me in this journey. Thank you, mam, for passing on your love of books. It's been a bit of a rollercoaster, but what good adventure isn't? Please don't read the series, you promised you wouldn't! To Aoife, I love that despite everything we both ended up with the same reading taste. You will always have dibs on a signed copy.

Finally, thank you to my partner for putting up with my craziness. From listening to my ideas and rambling, the plot twists that I blurt out when drunk or in the shower, to reminding me to find balance and look after myself. You make me feel like I can take on the world and have given me the space to follow my dreams. You're my person and I will always be grateful for your unrelenting support.

To you, the reader, thank you for taking a chance on me and picking up Wolf Bait. I promise Eve's journey isn't over, the games have just begun. There is plenty of drama, action, sarcasm, and more of the Crescents to come.

About the Author

Ciara is an Irish urban fantasy writer who works in Dublin and lives in the countryside, the perfect balance in her eyes. A bookdragon from birth, her love of reading bled into writing when she was a teenager. After getting a 'real job' and reigniting her passion for writing in her late twenties, Ciara set her sights on realising her childhood dream of being an author.

When she doesn't have her head stuck in a book, you will find Ciara walking in the parklands nearby, smashing a combat class, passed out on her yoga mat, or screaming at a rugby match. She is a massive animal lover and her fluffy writing buddies are plastered over her social media. Ciara can't write without music and loves nothing more to be curled up with her laptop and a mocha in her favourite Starbucks, writing to her hearts content.

Contact info:
www.ciaradelahunt.com

tiktok.com/@ciaradelahuntbooks

instagram.com/ciaradelahunt/

facebook.com/authorciaradelahunt

amazon.com/author/ciaradelahunt

goodreads.com/ciaradelahunt

bookbub.com/authors/ciara-delahunt

Printed in Great Britain
by Amazon

10387090R00201